ALSO BY CARRIE FISHER

Delusions of Grandma
Surrender the Pink
Postcards from the Edge

THE

BEST
AWFUL

A Novel

CARRIE FISHER

Simon & Schuster
New York   London   Toronto   Sydney

SIMON & SCHUSTER
Rockefeller Center
1230 Avenue of the Americas
New York, NY 10020

SIMON & SCHUSTER and colophon are registered trademarks
of Simon & Schuster, Inc.

For information regarding special discounts for bulk purchases,
please contact Simon & Schuster Special Sales:
1-800-456-6798 or business@simonandschuster.com.

Manufactured in the United States of America

1   3   5   7   9   10   8   6   4   2

Library of Congress Cataloging-in-Publication Data
Fisher, Carrie.
The best awful / Carrie Fisher.
p. cm.
I. Title.
PS3556.I8115 B4 2003
813'.54—dc21   2002042705
ISBN 0-684-80913-3

PERMISSIONS

The author and publisher gratefully acknowledge permission from the following publishers, writers, and artists:

For my daughter, Billie,
and her father, Bryan

In a field
I am the absence
of field.
This is
always the case.
Wherever I am
I am what is missing.

When I walk
I part the air
and always
the air moves in
to fill the spaces
where my body's been.

We all have reasons
for moving.
I move
to keep things whole.
　　—Mark Strand,
　　　"Keeping Things Whole"

You cannot put a Fire out—
A Thing that can ignite
Can go, itself, without a Fan—
Open the slowest night—

You cannot fold a Flood—
And put it in a Drawer—
Because the Winds would find it out—
And tell your Cedar Floor.
　　—Emily Dickinson,
　　　Part One: Life, CXXXIII

Remember when you ran away and
I got on my knees and begged you
Not to leave because I'd go berserk? Well,
You left me anyhow and then the
Days got worse and worse and now you
See I've gone completely out of my mind. And,

They're coming to take me away, ha-haaa.
They're coming to take me away, ho-ho, hee-hee, ha-haaa,
To the funny farm, where life is beautiful all the time . . .
      —Dr. Demento

ACKNOWLEDGMENTS

For Clancy Imislund—for the structure, the funny, a sane life, and everything ending in 'ing'—and everything but the blue pants . . . those, I bought myself.

For my mother—who not only had me but had me at "Hello dear . . ." Without you, my DNA would be in shambles and the neighborhood in disarray. What would I have done without you? And where? And could we meet there later and go shopping?

For my brother, Todd—we'll always have lockup. Remember that time Debbie got pregnant with us and our whole lives happened? Good times . . .

For Suzanne Gluck—the real bona fide Suzanne with an actual Doris mother to match—the literary agent who negotiated me out of the newfangled fix I was in and into a better world.

I'm not worthy (my name is Lisa).

For Betsy Rapoport—my bottom of the 99.9th editor . . . you had me at hell. Thank you for not only saving the day but a lot of the book along with it.

For Kim Painter—for the translation, transcribing, train spotting, and lap dancing.

For Mrs. Gummer, my higher, better, celluloid self.

ACKNOWLEDGMENTS

For Craig Bierko, my higher self, but only in terms of height.

For Helen—for the notes, tea, and mother racing.

For Tracey and Johnny—thank you both *so*—bullocks—much for your continued—tits tits tits—support. Without the two of you—cockring—these lingering coughs would be more difficult to—wanker—bear.

And lastly, for David Rosenthal—my newfangled fix, whom I almost forgive when I'm sleeping. You had me at . . .

Hello?

THE
BEST
AWFUL

THE MAN THAT GOT THE
MAN THAT GOT AWAY

Suzanne Vale had a problem, and it was the one she least liked thinking about: She'd had a child with someone who forgot to tell her he was gay.

He forgot to tell her, and she forgot to notice.

He might've forgotten to mention it because he'd hoped she would save him. Making him into a normal "family man" with a wife and a child and a job running a studio. And hadn't she wanted to be saved from certain things also? From life alone? From being childless? From a life that might've looked a little sad from the outside?

So, merging their secret hopes for rescue, they'd had a baby with their unwritten pact of androgyny, an androgyny that informed the life they lived out loud.

Suzanne had never seen herself as what she called a squeezy tilty girl. She was a breadwinner with a very yang personality. A person who wore a lot of severely tailored little black suits. And Leland Franklin would never be called up for the butch patrol. Not that he was effeminate in any way—far from it.

Suzanne's pregnancy had betrayed their pact, however, transforming her into a girl—a vulnerable woman even—leaving Leland to be what he couldn't: a straight and certain man . . . certain of his sexuality anyway.

Looking back, perhaps Suzanne should've guessed based on his affection for Biedermeier furniture or even his fastidiousness with his grooming . . . she should've known when, toward the end, he'd begun rigorously attending a gym, perfecting a body she knew wasn't being perfected for her.

Their alliance had broken under the strain of their attempt at normalcy gone wrong. When their daughter Honey was three, Leland had left her for a man, though initially this was not what he'd said. He'd said he was leaving because Suzanne was crazy. Kept him up all night. Refused to take her bipolar medication, and she would talk talk talk . . . *talk* all the time. Maybe she'd talked him out of staying with her. Won the argument for why to leave her without meaning to.

After Leland had left—right after, when feelings were still high, with winds of hurt and blame storming out of her Cape Fear—he'd mentioned to Suzanne late one evening in a particularly blistering phone call that she might've helped turn him gay, "By taking all that codeine again!" to which Suzanne replied tearfully, "Oh, I'm sorry—I hadn't read that part of the warning on the label! I thought it said *heavy machinery,* not *homosexuality!* Here I could have been driving those big farmyard tractors all along!" and she'd slammed the phone down, red-faced and weeping.

After the dust from his departure had settled, she'd found herself with a child, a grudge, and a bright phosphorus gnaw of pain glowing in the hot spot of her chest.

It turned out he'd left her with this tender wound of love for him, a warm ache informing her she'd accidently grown to care. He'd outlasted her disinclination to ever love deeply, winning the race to the end of her arm's-length way of figuring everything out until it couldn't hurt her again.

Unbeknownst to her, she'd come to look at him with lively eyes tenderized pink with vulnerability. She longed for the return of

Leland's subtle way of patrolling her murky borders, guarding her from her own less than commendable instincts. Protecting her when he could from all that stood between her and her far-flung best self, drawing her to the center of his uncrackable safekeeping.

While she'd spent every last hard-earned dollar of her energy charming those she met so that they would like her, be amused by her, think her smart, or all three, Leland would do some other neat trick all but invisible to her trained seal eye. He would manage the room, make its occupants comfortable, well taken care of, at ease. He would find out a little about each person, an ambassador of good will trying to make certain everyone aboard his ship was seaworthy. His was a miracle of care, concern, and control. And for the life of her, Suzanne could never figure out how it was done—it took her years to realize that it *was* done—but she admired it with a kind of awe before she knew and ever after. This was Leland's gift: a way with people, a way of making their burdens lighter and their days a little less dark. Suzanne would tickle you and make you laugh and like her; Leland would tuck you in bed for the night—and wake you up with juice and coffee the next morning.

Suzanne wanted you to have a good experience of her—*"Did you hear that hilarious thing she said about her father? 'What you see is what you* don't *get'!"* Leland wanted you to have a good experience of yourself, courtesy of him. Sure, you'd come away with a good memory or two of Suzanne, but spend a single afternoon with Leland and you'd want to float down through all time with him, parented by him, partnering with him, and throwing all your business his way.

Leland had cared for her and she'd somehow not seen it working its subtle charm on her. She didn't realize she needed tending like some exotic fragile flower. She had always been self-contained, no? Making her all but impervious to most of the care he'd painstakingly shown to her. Smoothing her brow, picking up her pieces each time she broke down and cried. Hospital Man, so careful with her, watching over her while she slept and making sure she was safe and warm. Who knew she'd come to count on the net he'd always put beneath her not so infrequent falls? No one had ever attended to her needs in quite this way. How could she have missed it happening? What had made him tick, and why couldn't her tock ever quite manage that beat?

While he'd busied himself with breaking her falls, Suzanne had blundered on, chatting gaily, never slowing enough to notice the charm he was working on her life, her frantic ways. Still and all, she'd paused sufficiently to have a child with him, paying tribute to the thing in their union that smacked of mutual concern and trust—a trust accompanied by what she understood later as the closest thing she might have come to love.

For the next three years, she'd taken advantage of him and giddily run with it straight through center, careless of his ministrations, not noticing his restless dissatisfaction. Or taking it for something else, something annoyingly in her way. She'd given him little choice but to move on to the thing in his nature that would inevitably capture his attention's bright flag. Assuming she'd loved him offhandedly, even cavalierly, how could she know that down deep, her once-tended flower was turning more and more toward the warm comfort of his too-distant sun, growing this subtle devotion to him, strung to his tuning, guided by his star. Leland had provided her with something vital, something she'd come to depend on as utterly as oxygen. Which she only realized, of course, once it turned up missing.

Oh, horrible!

Having subtly outsmarted her sensors, Leland had now passed into the dark world of "Someone She'd Inadvertently Come to Need." First he'd slipped the mickey of their daughter Honey into her, and now, leaving her drunk with a love she'd misrepresented both to herself and anyone who'd listen, he'd tiptoed out the door in search of something saner and more sensible for himself.

Need. Ugly need with its scowling face, its features twisted with regret and love gone awry, now leered at her from the darkness when she'd wake into this place she couldn't imagine was any longer really her life.

Ugh! Disfigured by loss, she grieved for Honey's father. "Come back!" she wanted to implore him. "Give me myself back—the *me* I was with you—and I'll be good this time, I promise! You can even date men! I'll look the other way, like they do in Europe! I'll do anything you say! Just stay . . . please . . . just *stay* with me . . . help me *breathe*!"

But it was too late.

Once escaped, she knew he'd never return. It had been difficult enough for him to pull himself away in the first place, away from his only child and greatest joy.

No, once away, he would stay there, leaving her with this outsized love now grown larger and unwieldy as a goiter, magnified by rejection, humiliation, and desperate aging-girl despair.

She'd just have to wait to outlast this worst aspect of being human, for the wound of rejection and self-incrimination to heal.

Her mother Doris had been wonderful after Leland had gone. She'd come over and fluffed up Suzanne's pillows and made her cold toast.

"You're just like me, dear. We can't pick men," Doris said matter-of-factly, sitting on the edge of Suzanne's bed and brushing her daughter's hair back from her frowning forehead. Doris Mann was a famous fifties movie icon whose three failed marriage had left her publicly humiliated, bankrupted, and bankrupted again. "Anyway, think of it this way; we've had every kind of man in this family. We've had horse thieves and alcoholics and one-man bands and singers—but this is our first homosexual!" She punctuated her congratulatory speech with raised eyebrows and trademark grin and outflung arms.

At least the whole situation was great for Suzanne's weight, this "Diet of the Disappearing Dad." Remember how fat she'd gotten when she was pregnant with Honey? And how it had hung around afterward, no matter what she did? Layers of fat clinging to her like frightened tenants in dark houses when the ghosts come out.

Well, after Leland left, about twenty pounds or so of her must have missed him, too, because little by little, it took leave of her as well. Perhaps leaving her for a man also. Perhaps there was some newly fat guy roaming around with her former pounds encircling him lovingly. Suzanne had a Teflon quality that summer. Things would come unstuck from her surface and jump free, leaving her even more alone. Items began to show up missing around her home, and not just the usual things like glasses, pens, and cameras. Now it was books, a disc player, and finally even a dog. Just couldn't be found. Boom! Disappeared one day.

Was it something she'd said? Or maybe a bad hairstyle or an overabundance of makeup? How had she become this jumping-off point, so easy to leave? And how did Leland's boyfriend Nick become the man that got this lovely man that got away from her?

Honey turned four, then five, then six. And still Suzanne kept on with the endless hashing and rehashing, going over what had happened, as if that was going to solve anything. As if that served any purpose other than getting her friends' eyes to glaze.

"You've totally taken all the charm and romance out of self-pity for me, I'll tell you that for nothing," Suzanne's best friend Lucy told her one day.

"Fuck off," she'd countered miserably, without moving her unseeing eyes from the television screen at the foot of her bed.

"Hey, show me where off is, and I'll fuck there," Lucy had replied.

Lucy wasn't the only one who was fed up listening to Suzanne—she was just the most vocal about it. Everyone wanted the funny, untroubled version of their friend back. And finally so did Suzanne, she really and truly did.

Surely the solution was to find something or someone to distract her. A Situation. Something or someone leading her to other things: tasks tacked neatly on a bulletin board. Plans. Completing one errand and onto the next, running like the wind toward something new. Stations of life, bridges to cross, stages to go through. Surely there were dragons to slay and fresh matters to tend to, until one day when she would escape from what had formerly been the matter with her, and would now be able to see it as simply her own jumping-off point.

Insult to injury
and back again

"Three-picture deal for your thoughts." That was the first thing Leland had ever said to her the first time she met him, at one of those Hollywood Hills ratfucks Lucy had dragged her to. She'd turned to look at him. "How did we get to that from a penny?"

He shrugged. "A combination of inflation, my job description, and what I'm guessing might be the caliber of your thinking."

That was how she'd found out he was a studio executive. She'd sometimes had fantasies of having a job like that. A job that would hold her between its stern regimen of required hours and obligations like a long-lost friend. An office built to keep her from getting too far afield from herself and who she was expected and encouraged to remain being, who she would under no circumstances be allowed to become. Four walls of "Stay right where you are," employment laid out like tomorrow's school clothes. No guesswork, precise as the military, rules set in stone. You knew where to go, how to act, and who to be. And she would come to like drinking coffee, and look forward to breaks, and go to office parties and complain about the hours or Xerox her ass. She'd be a worker among workers whose life revolved around a job well done.

Instead, she'd always had what she knew were considered "glamorous" jobs, when all she'd ever really done was go helplessly into the family business, predestined to join the ranks of their fabulous cult. When she was very young, she'd visited her mother on a film set and stood round-eyed to one side with her nanny and younger brother Thomas while Doris danced and sang or ran around dressed up in wigs and fine clothing, yelling at handsome men, surrounded by something called a "crew": a throng of men, their eyes trained on her beautiful mother's every gesture. And to Suzanne, it looked like playtime—between the singing and the old-age makeup and stuntmen falling out of buildings and western towns and New York skylines and her perfectly groomed mother falling facedown in the mud and everyone laughing themselves silly after someone yelled the word *"Cut!"* and it started all over again. And all that attention—miles of it stretched in all directions around the activities being played out under the cameras, haloed in lights.

This was a job?

No, it couldn't be . . . it looked more like a weird sort of recess—something you did on a playdate or way far behind the handball court with classmates from some distant, lighthearted country.

By the time she was a teenager, her mother's film career was for all intents and purposes over, and Doris moved almost imperceptibly to nightclubs, singing on the road in the East and in gambling towns from Las Vegas to Lake Tahoe. She took her kids with her. To add insult to injury (Suzanne was injury, her brother was insult), they were put in the act. Her guitar-playing brother Thomas backed Suzanne while she sang, trembling with (of all things) stage fright. Since then, it was one glorious, glamorous foray into some facet of being a public figure after the next. Film actress by accident (a friend got her an audition for a small part in a big film), then television actress because why not? And then becoming a talk show hostess on some off-radar cable show that no one paid too much attention to, so she could pretty much ask guests whatever she wanted and behave whatever way she wished.

Suzanne had fallen into doing the cable talk show "thing" like she'd fallen into acting and then just as easily fallen out of it—though it felt to her as though the tumble was a little slower going out than it had been crashing in. And it wasn't as though she didn't still visit— only now it was more as a tourist than a resident. Which was hilarious when she considered it—which wasn't often—for how could she ever be a tourist to the fictitious kingdom of Hollywood? The daughter of two people whose job basically was to depict people—whether acting like themselves in nightclubs or acting like others in movies. Suzanne had heard once—and believed it—that if you pretend something long enough, it comes true. So Suzanne was a product of people pretending to be pretending; so now there was every chance she was the child of two people who were not only really unreal but who acted as though they were no different from just regular people— though when they actually had to make something of an effort, the regularness was absurd.

Suzanne thought a law ought to be passed forbidding two celebrities from actually breeding. She believed a case could be made proving that children born of a double celebrity union run an extremely high risk of delayed "crib death"—sometimes occurring as late as their mid-thirties—caused by alcohol addiction and self-obsession (without actually having any real sense of self).

The problem with being born into show business was that if you got in that early, you rarely got out. The closest she could come to an actual exit was behaving as though she was a celebrity bystander. A rubbernecker to this eternally entertaining happy accident it appeared everyone wanted to see. It was why she accepted this off-center-to-the-center job of interviewing those she had been one of for much of her life.

Being off-center to the center was a theme of Suzanne's life. The salad to the main meal, a shadow behind more spectacular events, like being her mother's daughter or the girl in that movie or the friend of that famous person. So it wasn't such a big jump to interviewing people. Even the cable part was in keeping with her salad ways, her salad days next to the network feast. And out there in Snackland she could chat with luminaries not as some starstruck journalist but more like a proper not-quite-has-been. Hamburger Helper next to the juicy porterhouse of "currently starring in."

How the show ended up filming at her house, she really couldn't remember. The thing that was good about it was that she didn't have to get up so early. The thing that was bad about it was what Honey felt about it. Honey didn't like all the lights in the living room and the crew stomping through the front door and pouring back out onto the patio where they ate pizza and drank sodas and talked loudly. She didn't like the sound guys setting up their headphones and speaker things in the kitchen and the producers and directors with their monitors to check the lighting and the angles and the sound level. And cables—cables everywhere. And she really didn't like that she had to be quiet and stay out of the way and that there was not only a generator but a wardrobe truck in the driveway so she couldn't ride her bike.

Suzanne tried to schedule the interviews for when Honey was at her father's, but sometimes that just couldn't be done. So whenever possible, Suzanne would have Honey's Irish nanny, Kathleen, schedule her a playdate and take her to the 99-cent store or Chuck E. Cheese's, with the 99-cent store being the hands-down favorite. There was nothing Honey so dearly loved as a good bargain.

Certainly she wasn't interested in anyone Suzanne had on her talk show, what Honey called her mom's "never shut up" show. Honey had been around celebrities for much of her life, and though she liked the art—or in many cases, the thing—that had made them famous, she was far less interested in the humans offscreen. For her, meeting them rendered the extraordinary ordinary, commonplace. The real stars for her were the Game Boys, the X Boxes, and DVDs she would save up for, doing chores, tucking away her allowance, and assessing nearby adults penalties for swear words. She demanded a firm price of one dollar for every "fuck," "shit," and "asshole," and fifty cents per "damn" and "God damn it" and words beginning with *"c"* that she sensed were dirty but hadn't made her definitive list. Thanks to the abundance of obscenities from Suzanne and the crew, Honey had almost saved up enough for a new Game Boy complete with the magnifier screen.

Suzanne liked to think of her talk show as the anti–talk show; she'd originally wanted the set to be either her bath or bed. But she finally settled on the living room so she could reassure audiences that they were in the presence of professional show business folk. She was, wasn't she? The show was filmed on an allegedly well-lit, two-chair setup—she couldn't vouch for that because she'd never seen it, couldn't bring herself to look at herself at this point, or ever for that matter. She would lead the guest inside, apologizing all the way—"I completely don't know why they have us enter this way. Is the thinking that we look somehow more natural? Look! It's *me,* being trailed by a big celebrity into my own *living room*!" And then Suzanne would slide into her chair, fold her legs and bare feet under her, and face a familiar face—either because she'd seen them in a film or knew them or both—and proceed to grin at them inanely, saying, "Helloooooo" until a producerish person called *"Cut!"* from behind a camera somewhere. Then all manner of crew types would scramble to Suzanne and her celebrity guest, fixing their hair or powdering them or adjusting their body mikes until everybody was thrilled with the results— and all the while Suzanne and the celebrity would chatter with publicists or each other or smoke or sip a drink until the show began and Suzanne would ask them how they learned about the birds and the bees. "Is anyone crazy in your family? Alcoholic? How did you explain sex to your children? Would you please explain it to me? Thank you for being a guest on my show."

She was a worker bee to a wacky hive; she'd even interviewed her Queen Bee mom on her show. Doris was better lit than Suzanne, of course, having insisted on a beauty light and a certain kind of shadowing achieved by having a man of a certain height and weight hold a shiny board under her chin, undetectable on camera, until the man's arms went into spasms, "But not before achieving that elusive glow shining from the light—a trick I learned from Garbo's stand-in . . . shhhhhh!"

And all of it worked out basically okay because Suzanne got free clothes and didn't have to do it that often and it kept her busy, distracted her. Besides that, the crew was nice, the money so-so, so between that and the speeches she gave and the occasional day's work on a big film, she covered her overhead, which included the nanny, Honey's lessons, and the cost of all those swear words.

But Suzanne hated missing out on the excursions to Target or Ross with Honey; it was horrible to have to delegate all the fun stuff to Kathleen. She hated the necessary evil of having a nanny in the first place. Oh, she knew it was a luxury, even a necessity for the working mom. And it wasn't that there was anything wrong with Kathleen— she was a perfectly nice person—it was just Suzanne's experience of nannies in general from when she was a child. She'd always had nannies, a long, white row of them, white from their crisp collars to their squeaky shoes. Sometimes they even had the hair and the teeth to go with it.

Not much had changed since Suzanne was a child, except the uniforms were gone. The nannies were still the arrangers of things, the organizers of all the activities that make up a child of Hollywood's life. The time parceled out to lessons—the dreaded lessons—piano, ice skating, tennis, art, swimming, French, computer. The squiring of armies of overqualified, pampered children of the privileged through their paces. The parents missing—for what parents these days aren't?

Suzanne was never actually sure what she was preparing Honey for with all those lessons. Miss America? *American Idol?* A very athletic, musical, French ambassadorship? And all that shit about thanking her later—when had she ever thanked Doris later? Unless later turned out to be later than she thought it was.

Her sweet Honey hambone. Who did she look like? Well, she was fair-haired like her father, that was certain. She was even fair of face. But she didn't have Leland's pale eyes the color of the bluest of Easter eggs. No, Honey's eyes were a dramatic shade of golden brown, well suited to steady gazing, for figuring things out. It was only in direct sunlight that these dark orbs revealed a cast of green, streaking them hazel. She came by this subtle greening courtesy of Doris, who was thrilled to have this evidence of what she claimed to have known all along: "I told you—she's just like me—she has my flair for athletics among other things. Have you seen her play tetherball? The other day she practically *beat* me and *don't* get me started on her badminton—" As if there was a concern about getting Suzanne started about that odd sport. "And she has your body *exactly,*" Doris continued, generously handing Suzanne a slice of Honey's genetic pie. And it was true—Honey did have her mother's shape—when her mother was young, of course. A petite, sturdy shape, perfectly proportioned, with long willowy legs and feet that turned in when she ran really fast, giving her the appearance of wild abandon, perhaps the wild abandon of a computer geek.

Honey loved all outdoor activities, from swimming to bike riding to playing those weird sports with her colorful grandmother from the silver screen. She was a busy little girl of six, chasing her fun at full tilt. And she was a girl who worried about her friends. "Mommy, I think Hannah has a self-esteem problem."

Suzanne managed to keep a straight face. "And what do you think that means?" she asked.

Honey frowned and thought for a minute. "She says she doesn't like herself because she's fat. She one time wouldn't believe I liked her on account of it." Honey's expression was grave. "I think she needs to see a therapist." She gazed steadily at her mother, awaiting her verdict.

Suzanne smiled the smallest of smiles, not certain if Honey knew precisely what a therapist was. Still, she must have known that they were there to guide you, to help you put yourself together when you threatened to come apart. Honey had met Norma, Suzanne's psychiatrist for lo these many years now, and spent time in her office, first drinking her baba or crawling on the floor, later spinning in her chair or doodling on scratchpads. Oh, Suzanne hadn't brought her there often—just now and then to show Norma how solidly and surely her daughter was growing. Is this where she'd learned about that thing called therapy? Suzanne stroked her daughter's serious face. "Therapy is really expensive, baby. I don't think Hannah's family could afford to send her right now."

Honey blinked into the space before her and then back up at her mom. "I would give some money to it," she said earnestly. "To help her go, I mean. I have almost two hundred dollars, remember? From Christmas?"

Helpful Honey. Watching, always watching, wanting everything to be in its place, to work out right. Nurse Honey, daughter of Hospital Man. And then there was impatient Honey, wanting things to be in their place and all right but right now and her way. Not so different, surely, from a lot of children—but with an extra wrinkle. She needed things to be absolutely okay with her mom, and if they couldn't be, then they *had* to be with everyone and everything else. They just had to be and that's all there was to it—anything else was unfair.

Maybe in this way, too, her dad became her hero, her sure thing in a sea of uncertainty. Leland could say, "Everything's gonna be all right," and she could believe it. If Suzanne said it, it was because she wanted it to be true or because she was sorry about something. But not her dad. He provided her a safe harbor, something she could rely on and flourish in. Maybe her dad made her mother possible.

When Honey started wanting to be things—things other than veterinarians " 'cause some animals die and I would never be able to get used to that"—she astonished everyone by announcing that she'd like to be "a neurologist with a specialty in schizophrenia." They'd laughed; they'd been unable to stop themselves. "Those are awfully big words for such a little girl," said her nanny, Kathleen. Sadly, Suzanne felt she understood where all the big words came from.

"Buddy, what do you think schizophrenia *is*? I mean, just so I know."

Honey looked at her mother like she was an idiot. "It's when you hear things that aren't there and think people are mad at you. I saw a show about it. It was really good."

The irony of her very young daughter's career choice was not lost on Suzanne, but soon enough Honey had her sights set on a new one: She wanted to be a comic. Suzanne wanted to say, "Maybe all a comic really *is* is a neurologist with a specialty in schizophrenia," but what she'd actually said was, "Well, great, but if you want to be a comic, you have to be a writer." Honey frowned and chewed her lip thoughtfully.

"But don't you worry about a thing," Suzanne assured her. "You've got enough material to last you for years of monologues." She stood in front of her solemn, saucer-eyed daughter and ticked off the possibilities: "Your father is gay, your mother is a drug addict/manic-depressive, your grandmother tap dances for a living, and your grandfather shot speed."

Honey regarded her mother with a degree of hesitation, then laughed her funny, throaty laugh—the one that made her big eyes small and showed off her tiny baby teeth. Suzanne watched her daughter laughing for the briefest of moments before gathering her into her arms and kissing the top of her head. "And the fact that you think that's funny, Bitsy, is gonna save your whole life."

ONCE IN A BLUE PRODUCER

Jack Burroughs's funeral promised to be an elaborate affair. Everybody in Hollywood would be there. Everyone that Jack had known or worked with, anyway—and was still on speaking terms with when he died.

Although it seemed somehow sudden when it happened, people had been forecasting Jack's death for years. No one could do drugs like that and get away with it other than Hunter Thompson and Dean Bradbury, but Dean was a movie star—an icon—so the ordinary rules didn't seem to apply to him. And Hunter was just "doing research" for his books. Everyone knew that.

Suzanne remembered Jack once telling her that he'd discovered the meaning of life one night on twelve tabs of mescaline, ". . . but it melted before I had a chance to write it down." He'd told her this while inhaling another lungful of opium from the aluminum foil he'd held under his mouth and nostrils. Then he'd sunk back into the pillows of his red suede couch and, gazing with glazed eyes into the space before him as though lost, he hadn't spoken again for upward of an hour. But then that was the point, wasn't it? At least that had been one of the reasons Suzanne did it, preferring to be anywhere but here . . . even if that anywhere was nowhere in particular.

"Man," he whispered to her decades later, finally exhaling a cloud of exotically scented breath, "I'm lunched."

And as the perfumed smoke swirled around him, Jack smiled, his pupils pinned and his lids at half-mast, and settled into a sleepy, comfortable haze. Its willing captive, once again having given reality the slip—the oh-so-crafty escape artist painting his dreamy escape, inhaling each color until, heavy with this mad rainbow and oblivious to the gray world around him, he'd finally been suffocated by his own sunset.

But that was years ago. The last time Suzanne had seen Jack had been a little over seven months ago at the Los Angeles screening of his movie and the latest Jack Burroughs production, *Remembering Tomorrow,* as he moved through the invited audience with Helen Kestler, white powder faintly dusting the end of his nose. She'd considered saying something to him about the telltale powder, then thought better of it. Who was she, the drug janitor? The substance chaperone? Besides, she couldn't bear Helen Kestler, who not only wanted you to find her intelligent, no, that wasn't enough—the broad wanted you to think she was *profound.* It was exhausting. Suzanne remembered thinking how perfect she was for Jack and how they probably stayed up till dawn deconstructing Hollywood in the nude. But did she want to be a fly on the wall for any part of that conversation?

The lights had dimmed and *Remembering Tomorrow* started, an action movie centered around a black hole about to collapse, taking the Milky Way galaxy with it, and the five scientists who have to save the world from blah blah blah.

Since then, *Remembering* had accumulated a domestic gross of over $200 million (despite the fact that it had been condemned by Stephen Hawking as simplistic, fraudulent, and misleading) and it was about to open overseas, where there was no reason to believe it wouldn't do just as well . . . perhaps even better. But a week and a half ago, Jack's assistant, Marge, had gone to his home to ready him for his flight to Japan for the big opening and found him dead, clad in lacy women's underwear in a fetal position beside his toilet, surrounded by feces, vomit, and fishing magazines. Of course, the newspapers and trade magazines reported her finding him "in bed," but the "Smoking Gun" website had cheerfully carried the more repellent account.

"At least he went out with dignity," Lucy had deadpanned on the phone to Suzanne. "I don't think he would have had it any other way."

Now a breathless Lucy in the flesh—very much in the flesh, since she was in her seventh month with twins—brushed past Suzanne, who stood holding the door open for her pretty friend, panting with effort from her climb, the morning dew of third-trimester effort shimmering on her face. She'd come to babysit Honey, her goddaughter, while Suzanne went to Jack's funeral service.

"I'm about to have a heart attack from how steep your ridiculous hill is." Lucy managed each word only when oxygen permitted, making her laborious way to Suzanne's bedroom and easing herself onto her friend's bed.

Deeply pregnant and well over forty, Lucy was understandably irritable. Yet even with all the weight—both water, amniotic fluid, and other—somehow her quite beautiful face remained untouched; the pounds instead settling uncomfortably in her chest and everywhere south, while her high cheek-boned, porcelain-skinned face looked out serenely independent of the business boiling beneath, an infant factory overseen by its elegant queen.

Suzanne sat on the edge of the bed beside her, putting her hand on Lucy's massive swell of belly, searching for signs of life percolating beneath the fashionable maternity clothes. Lucy's stomach tightened slightly and then, from somewhere deep within her, Suzanne felt the ordinary magic of an infant move.

Suzanne readied herself for the memorial while Lucy sat on the edge of the bed, playing with the TiVo remote gravely, her blue overalert eyes fixed on the ever-changing images on the television screen.

"How did we live without TiVo, could you tell me, please?" Lucy pushed her hair away from her face to get a better look at the upcoming Direct TV movie selections listed on the screen. "Man, it's too bad Jack died before seeing what they came up with next." Suzanne suspended her eye makeup application and looked at Lucy levelly, hand on hip, regarding her with what she hoped would be a self-explanatory withering look.

"Shit, I've seen all of these," Lucy complained at the TV, then glanced over at Suzanne. "Oh, please, if it was good enough for Elvis and Lenny Bruce, then it's got to be good enough for Jack Burroughs. I mean, give me a—"

Suzanne interrupted, shaking her head in exasperation. "They died *on* the toilet—Jack died 'around it.' There's a difference."

"Oh, good! Let's argue about something like this. Seriously. It'd be something we could tell our grandkids—not that we'll live to see them, but still—"

"Shut up and help me pick out something to wear."

"Really, Suzanne—*everything* in your closet is ready-made for a funeral." Lucy waved her hand dismissively. "Wear anything you have. It's all grim and respectful."

Lucy was right. All Suzanne had to do was wear what she'd always been wearing: a black skirt and jacket, some shirt or other, no stockings, and sensible little nonspindly heels she couldn't fall off of. The only difference now to her overall ensemble was her eyeglasses; one of many snappy little bifocals she'd spent a mint on in shops all over town, wearing for a while before promptly losing.

"Oh, shit, what am I thinking?" Suzanne moaned. "It's insane for me to go to this thing. Leland will probably be there. With the hideously affable Nick, the man with an agenda for a disposition. Look how we're all so *okay*! All 'Hi—oh, look—the pathetic one's here! The one who couldn't identify a homosexual! C'mon, let's be nice to the creature—*smile!*' Oh, holy high mother of shit. Forget it."

Lucy stared at her friend contemptuously. "Oh, right, that's good. Yeah, stay in the house like a frightened old maid. Let him win. Jesus, Suze, it's been over three fuckin' years already."

"Whoa, wait a minute! A: I didn't realize there was a time limit on upset. Also, I forget what the contest is but he won, and B: I can't be an old maid because old maids don't have kids. So C: blow me!"

Lucy rolled her eyes and crossed her arms, glaring impatiently at Suzanne. "You *have* to go! For fag widows everywhere! You have to show those turncoats what you're made of!"

Suzanne looked at Lucy cautiously. *"Fag widow*? I don't think I want to be called—"

"Would you please just shut the fuck up and get dressed! If for no other reason than so you can come back and entertain me. Face it, you haven't done anything interesting in *ages."*

"Oh, I see . . . it's for *you*. I thought it was some stupid self-esteem thing, but if it's for *your* amusement, I'm on my way."

Honey had been in her room, her eyes affixed to the television, watching the cartoon *KimPossible,* a show Suzanne grudgingly approved of not because of the strong female multi-culti role model playing the lead, but because of the cleverness of the show's name. When she heard her godmother's voice, however, Honey tumbled back into Suzanne's bedroom, frankly more to check on the progress of the pregnancy than on Lucy herself. Lucy had promised Honey that she could be the babies' godmother. "I mean, let's face it. You're the only one who's going to still be walking when it comes time for their high school graduation."

Honey paused in the doorway, surveying her godmother's precious swell. "There she is!" crooned Lucy from her prone position on the bed. "Come give your fat old godmountain a hug." Honey padded obediently over to Lucy and submitted to her awkward embrace. "And if you have some pull with these godchildren of yours, would you mind asking them to hurry up already and get out of there?"

Honey regarded Lucy for the briefest of moments. "Could they hear us?" she wondered.

Suzanne pulled Honey onto her lap, near Lucy's swollen feet. "I didn't think you could understand things, or I would've taught you French and gotten it out of the way." Honey despised the French lessons her mother sent her to.

"I wish you had taught me French when I was in your stomach, too," said Honey sulkily. "Then I could have playdates on Wednesday instead of some stinky lessons."

"You tell her, Honey Bun!" Lucy cheered.

Suzanne shot Lucy a look. "Hey, thanks for backing me up. When you finally do spit out these kids, don't expect me to back *you* up when they pierce their asses to their foreheads."

Honey stuck out her hand victoriously. "You said the *A* word. You owe me a dollar."

Suzanne sighed and retrieved her purse from the chair, rummaging for her red wallet. She extracted a five-dollar bill and handed it to Honey.

"That's for the *A* word. And here's for the other four: shit shit shit shit!"

Later, as they parted in Suzanne's driveway, Lucy stopped suddenly and gasped, regarding Suzanne with alarmed eyes.

"Oh, my God!— Now you've slept with a dead person!" she exclaimed with a mixture of exaggerated horror and compassion.

Lucy was referring to the sad fact that Suzanne had indeed had something like an affair with Jack. Not a love affair, more a love of drugs, words, and mutual self-obsession. Perhaps that did qualify as Hollywood love. Hollywood together.

"I'm *so* sorry—is there anything I can do?" Lucy asked. "Is there anything TiVo can do? Like, record these guys while they're young and living for you to turn them on whenever you want them—and I mean that in two ways—one of the ways is so they don't need all that fucking Viagra and the other—"

"You know the only good thing about TiVo?" Suzanne slid behind the wheel of her car and put the keys in the ignition. "Now that I'm experiencing total memory loss, I can watch things again and again to boost my sagging memory. I mean, given that the other day, I actually forgot the term *senior moment.*"

Lucy pushed the car door shut. "Go forth, and for God's sake, don't multiply. That's *my* job."

Suzanne turned up the radio and, gunning the engine, backed out

of her drive, heading off into the ubiquitous sunshine and traffic—
two things Los Angeles had TiVo'd long ago and were now stored,
playing endlessly all around them.

As she drove along Sunset in the waning light, she found herself
unable to let go of what Lucy had said. Had she really not done anything interesting in ages? Had she become cowardly and hesitant,
with no misadventures to recount to some stunned and captive audience? No all-too-interesting life to recount and recover from?

It was true that she hadn't dated in a while. The air around her
had once been thin, but now it had thickened. And this heavier air had
settled around her like fog, warding off men. In droves. The latest in a
long line of good ideas. First there were cigarettes, then Post-Its, then
the Internet. The latest innovation was not dating her. All over the
world, guys were not dating her daily.

But that was best, wasn't it? Best for Honey, since surely the less
interesting life was the more mature one. The predictable, dependable
outcome was the only one to arrive at, once children arrived, right? A
big bland blob of a life with no sharp edges and surprises? A little fun
here and there, but nothing too vivid or alarming.

Suzanne nodded to herself absently, her fingers drumming the
wheel to the rhythm of the song on the radio:

> *It's getting hot in herre—*
> *So take off all your clothes. . . .*

Absolutely, no question. Predictable and dependable were required
when assembling a safe world for Honey to thrive in.

And yet . . .

If she didn't have an interesting life, what could she contribute to
Honey? What would her legacy be? What would Honey write her
book about—her soulful Pulitzer Award–winning account of living
with an empathetic psycho? How could Honey write *that* if
Suzanne's inner riches and eccentricities were kept hidden under the
watchful round eyes of the little pills she took to medicate the colorful version of herself back to a drabber, whiter shade of pale? Who

would Honey think she was but the offspring of some once-sprung someone, now simply a shadow cast by the giant of her former self?

Suzanne waved the troubling thoughts away as she cruised east along Wilshire and made a smooth turn to the right, just across from the Academy of Motion Picture Arts & Sciences. (What sciences, by the way? Where were those bubbling beakers? That chart of the elements? Do the microscopes and dissections have something to do with the new special effects cameras? Was that it?) She saw the flash of cameras through the darkened windows lining the front of the imposing steel-and-glass building.

Media at a memorial, what was that about? Press at the opening of a film she vaguely understood. That was promotion. It sold the film by selling pictures of the celebrities starring in it and those attending its opening. But what did this sell? Death? "Coming Soon! Sooner than you'd care to think!"

Promoting closings. End of subject. End of life.

Well, actually, maybe it made a funny sort of sense: It *was* a memorial after all, wasn't it? And how better to remember things than to have a little photo to refer to later on? One where you say: "Aww, remember that day? That was when we went not to bury Caesar, but to praise Jack Burroughs." And you would have your photo in place of a memory, a Kodak moment from Hollywood . . . the Kodak capital of a Kodak world.

She should've known. The death of a powerful Hollywood producer was not going to be a simple memorial so much as an event—a somber premiere to celebrate Jack's ascension to a better place. Where dead agents could convince him he'd achieved the elusive nirvana: a place full of deceased hookers and dealers, maybe even a triplicate pad or two with a bevy of understanding pharmacists. At the very least a stalled Porsche and a grounded G-IV.

Suzanne stepped out of the growing twilight and through the door, attempting to slip past the organizers of this surreal memorial photo shoot, this preparty to bemoan the end of Jack's earthly partying, mull the passage of yet another privileged life gone horribly wrong.

She held her breath and, keeping her eyes down in an effort to escape contact with any photo wrangler, she slunk around the back of the lobby and away from the flashing lights toward what was normally the screening room but was now being used as a kind of launch pad to the hereafter party. Then, just as she thought she was home free, with one foot on the first stair leading up and away from her fellow mourners and paparazzi, a hand gripped her arm firmly, arresting her flight.

"Suzanne—it's Marge. Jack's assistant," an almost urgent voice said from behind her.

Marge: the finder of Jack in the bathroom, now grasping her arm with perhaps the same hand that had dialed the paramedics that fateful night, after no doubt trying to rid Jack's house of what illegal substances she was able to unearth, reburying them where they'd never be found. The hands that had seen to Jack's needs in life as she no doubt had in death, tidying his body, planning a suitable final resting place—as far as possible from the squalor of his restroom.

Suzanne froze, caught in the crosshairs of this woman's fierce agenda.

Sheepishly, she turned to Marge. "Hey. I was just going up to . . ." she paused, searching her mind for an excuse, then, giving up, she shrugged helplessly.

"Too bad about Jack," she finally offered, studying the floor guiltily.

Marge looked philosophical, almost as if listening to beautiful, faraway music, a pleasant peaceful melody Suzanne was sadly not privy to.

"Yes, well . . . I wish I could say I was shocked," then, giving Suzanne a sad, sympathetic look for a moment, Marge abruptly switched back to the business at hand: show business. In this case, showing Jack the door in a memorably efficient way. "We're asking everyone to be photographed with the family as they enter. . . ." And with her hands clasped in front of her, her face expectant and alert, she tilted her head to one side, indicating the bereaved family's location.

Marge was a stocky middle-aged woman who had a wide, smooth, expressionless face with nervous blue eyes and short blond hair. She seemed to have had something unfortunate done surgically to her face, giving it its unnatural shine—but the most noticable thing was the size of her lips. Or what had once been her lips, and had now been augmented to the point of explosion. Suzanne could never fully understand why so many women were "getting their lips blown up," as she called it. Were they meant to look younger? Sexier by virtue of this pouty, bee-stung mouth? More often than not, it looked as if their mouths had nothing to do with the rest of their faces. Their lips had, in effect, gone on without them—continuing to grow, while the rest of their features slunk back, looking on in dismay. Most of these augmentations were done with either collagen or the more permanent silicone, but there was a new lip-increasing substance available, an infusion of fat abducted from their own asses. Yes, women were having fat harvested from their posteriors and surgically inserted into their lips, so that when and if you kissed them, you were getting a little more than you bargained for. Two mints in one.

Suzanne wondered if Marge had had her ass put in her mouth or used the more conventional collagen or silicone and then realized her expression might have betrayed her thoughts because she caught herself gazing at Marge's lower face with just a hint of revulsion—as though she had picked up the scent of Marge's buttocks faintly wafting from her highly glossed mouth.

Forcing her eyes upward, she saw that Marge's usually shiny cheeks now shone bright pink, the color also traveling to her forehead and pooling just over her eyes.

". . . So if you could follow me, I think they're just finishing up with Dean."

Marge began walking briskly, holding her arm out as she did in an effort to usher Suzanne in front of her, moving past small constellations of the sympathetic—a throng of agents, managers, studio executives, producers, directors, and actors alike, all of them gathered here to pay their last respects to the clearly dearly departed Jack Burroughs; a man few respected as a human but whom everyone respected as a canny, consistently successful producer with unimaginable wealth.

For a somber occasion, it was swinging. A happening for someone who'd happened for as long as he could stomach before coming to an abrupt stop while everyone around him continued jauntily along.

Obediently following Marge and her engorged lips toward what seemed to be the holding area, Suzanne noticed with some excitement the ever-electrifying Dean Bradbury standing next to a woman Suzanne assumed was some sort of relative of Jack's, perhaps a sister—something where blood was involved—maybe even a third cousin twice removed, either by force, by marriage, or both.

The flashbulbs blinked bright and glaring as Dean begged off, finally backing away from the firing line of the photographers, squinting and shielding his eyes with one hand while giving a courteous wave of dismissal with the other. As he walked past her, he cut Suzanne a sharp look with his gleaming, sly eyes.

"Just puttin' the 'fun' in funeral," he muttered out of the side of his mouth, the motor of his growling voice idling as he passed her, his public respects paid in full with his famous top-dollar smile.

Then Dean disappeared into the safe haven of the show business crowd as it closed around its oldest and arguably favorite delinquent son, heading up the stairs to safety, away from the prying eyes that had pried their pictures from him with their crowbar cameras for years and years.

Marge then steered Suzanne toward the woman recently abandoned by Dean, now waiting for the next mourner to stand, soldier straight, at her side. Together, they would solemnly smile for tomorrow's back page of the industry trade papers.

Suzanne recognized some of the photographers from a lifetime of walking down red carpets and ducking through doors on the way to or from somewhere, and it dismayed her to realize this. First as a young girl with her mother, then youngish during her decade of acting in movies, and then stoned, then married, then sober, then single—every phase of her life captured in the lens of a camera—in a flash. Captured and released. A record of a girl turned woman turned middle-aged lady. A daughter, a wife, a mother, a mess. Actress, fag widow, talk show hostess—the cameras were always there to a greater or lesser extent, recording her battle to accept a life so often seeming so inexplicably unacceptable.

She was in the business of seeming—she had done time as a celebrity, and it had stayed with her like a vague, exotic smell: a scent that was kicked up at events such as this. The thing about famous was that it was a little like opiates to Suzanne. It always felt like too much or too little—she never got out of it quite what she'd originally been looking for.

The only part of fame she understood was the thing that had purchased it—talent. She figured the acting or writing or singing or talk show hosting you did, in essence, for free because you at least at one point had liked doing them. All the by-products—being reviewed or scrutinized, signing autographs, and posing for pictures—*those* were the things you got paid for. The photo ops and sound bites you delivered as requested, those were actually the things that paid the rent.

Suzanne sometimes thought people saw her as many of those things she had done to arrive at her current incarnation; they couldn't possibly see who she felt herself to be. But then she reckoned that probably very few felt appreciated for who they "really" were. For some, it might be a long walk from innermost self to public person, for others, it was no distance at all. The latter being people who could more easily communicate their authentic self to journalists or talk show hosts without feeling when they got home the cupboard was bare. Others found intimacy all but impossible with some special person, having already given at the office, where in the name of publicity, they'd allowed access to what they could once call a soul.

Suzanne had given herself up without a struggle, relinquishing anything in her no-longer-private life to be explored over entertainment airwaves or in print. She'd been spent down to her last dollar; now all that remained was to photograph the bank. Suzanne, the girl who had over time signed over all existing rights to herself to any takers still wanting a piece.

This thought depressed her, so she looked appropriately crestfallen when greeting Karen, Jack Burroughs's sister, who immediately took her arm, turning once more toward the flashing lights and men with cameras like a forlorn Santa who had forgotten to ask the kid of the moment what she wanted for Christmas.

"Karen, look here!"

"Miss Burroughs, to your left!"

"Straight ahead, Suzanne!"

"Smile!"

"Aw, c'mon, one more!"

"See, it's not so bad—over here, Ms. Vale!"

"Karen, Suze, over here, one last one!!"

"I'm so sorry about Jack," Suzanne said with a tight smile through clenched teeth. "He was such a . . ." she drifted off in search of some positive thing Jack had given to the world other than action films to offer up to the sister in solace, but was unable to come up with anything. Just as Suzanne was about to invent some charm, Karen interrupted her, rendering it obsolete.

"Thanks. Oh, by the way, did Marge give you a call sheet?" She smelled powerfully of perfume and alcohol, and losing her balance a little, she clutched Suzanne closer to her to prevent her fall.

Suzanne grabbed Karen's elbow until she returned to some semblance of order.

"Are you okay?" She noticed the sheen of perspiration around Karen's dark hair and around her two dark glazed eyes.

"Yes," she mumbled softly. Looking into this woman's face, Suzanne realized she'd never heard Jack mention he even had a sister. In all the times she'd been to his house, she could never recall seeing anything resembling a family picture—a souvenir from his life before he made a name for himself, before he became a self-made man. All she'd ever seen were pictures of Jack fastened to the side of some celebrity or other—Jack affixed to a Golden Globe or sitting astride an Arabian stallion or in one of those sports cars people get killed in or proudly wielding the carcass of a magnificent fish. But nowhere was there a faded picture of a cherished mother or a blurred couple of kids climbing a tree, dressed in clothes from another time. No, this sister was the first evidence that Jack had had a life before his bigger-than-life out here in Hollywood, living the high life, high on everything but life and now dead. His former life had finally arrived—a little worse for wear, but not so unlike him—running from whatever life he'd left behind. Here by Suzanne's side, his sole heir had arrived to cash in the chips he'd hoarded working in his soulless corner of the entertainment profession.

Come to think of it, Suzanne didn't feel so bad for Karen after all, though she couldn't exactly say she felt good either.

She read the pages Marge had handed her. *Don't that beat all,* she thought. *A memorial with a call sheet, as my late grandma would say.* Marge pointed her toward the large screening room one floor up—the same screening room where she'd seen *Remembering Tomorrow*—the one with the claret-colored velvet curtains and upholstered seats, presided over by the large gold statue of Oscar in the right-hand corner, with its blank burnished face, tightly gripped sword, and military stance.

Then, as if by some black ooze of magic, the crowd of movie-making mourners parted, offering up the sight of Leland's familiar face engaged in animated conversation, surrounded by a semicircle of somber designer-suited coworkers, or so Suzanne assumed. Suzanne assumed a lot of things. It was a lot easier than collecting the facts. Coworkers from his studio or agents or lawyers or other operator-type types, either working the A-list memorial, or just working him. But whoever it was didn't matter to Suzanne, because after seeing Leland, she only had eyes for her insides and the fine-looking man standing beside him . . . the man Leland had replaced her with, if something like that was even possible. Here they all were, just as she'd feared they'd be. Complete with a captive audience to watch the measured civilities that would pass between them—as they must given the flag of appearances they had to hoist ever after, with Honey between them.

Besides which, who could sustain all the intense nonsense and high-burning flame of bitterness and rage? Well, a lot of people, in point of fact, but lately Suzanne was not one of them. She finally found grudges to be unwieldy things—hold those, and pretty soon you have to drop amusements to maintain your grudge grip; blow your energy on that and you may have none left for mischief. Up to you. She'd worked so hard to turn her boiling grudge against Leland down to a low-simmering ache. It was best put by what she'd heard someone in AA say a few years back: "Resentment is like drinking a poison and then waiting for the other person to die."

Well, Suzanne drank far too much Diet Coke to take on the acid of "fuck you!" and she'd promised herself she didn't have to ever give *that* up. After everything else fell or faded away—men, drugs, a world without physical exercise—all that remained for Suzanne was diet soda: loyal, steadfast, light, cool, and apparently able to eat through tables and disintegrate teeth overnight in a single bound.

That was good enough for her. No one could say she didn't still have one foot in the fabulous, exhilarating world of unapologetic self-destruction.

The fuck of it was, whenever she saw him, she still found Leland attractive. Something in her responded to him without her permission. She called it "the Bossy Phenomenon," when your body wants what it wants despite what you tell it—it goes lumbering on without you, greedy with need, because that was the other thing she couldn't forget—their sex life had been great. Figure that one.

Leland's eyebrows rose to welcoming heights when he saw her, and he passed his hand over the shine and fuzz of his always neatly shaved head.

"Hi, Bun!" he exclaimed, closing the distance between them to kiss the cool of her offered cheek. "Bun" being short for the taller "bunny." Suzanne briefly took him in with alert, wary eyes.

"Well, if it isn't Honey's father." She ducked her head back from his warm, familiar sweet-corn scent and stinging ping of a kiss. "And Honey's stepmother, too." She nodded to the easy, grinning Nick standing beside him with his bespectacled, boyishly handsome face. "Why, it's old home week."

"Hey, Suzanne," offered Nick, revealing his bright, perfectly even teeth. "Good to see you. You're looking great. Did you lose some more weight or something?"

"You mean counting Leland? Or not counting him?"

Those assembled laughed a little uneasily. Leland again passed a hand over his smooth head and, seeming to hold his breath, he briefly glanced at his boyfriend, and then at her again. "Bun . . . ," he began uneasily, and Suzanne knew that he would now do whatever he could to dispel the tension that seemed to be gathering around them. She'd always liked this about him—his need to put people at ease and she had grown accustomed to being one of them. One of the easy people around Leland . . . ah, to be placed at ease and stay put. What bliss that would be!

This would be yet another one of the last times she listened to Lucy. How was this a good idea—all this was managing to do was make her feel faintly ill and very uncomfortable. Besides which, she just *hated* it when Nick complimented her. Was that supposed to make everything all right between all of them? This smooth manager trained to sign people. He'd finally signed Leland and now what? Was it her turn? Well, fuck that. And anyway, she lacked the pen. It was going to take a lot more than smiling and compliments about her weight to get her to forget who he was in all this. Anyway, she was still busy trying to forget who *she* was in it and once she'd done that, why she was that person and *that* person still couldn't move on.

"You're looking marvelous, too, Nick, as usual. I guess these solemn occasions bring out the best in all of us in some weird way, don't they?" She wrung the straps of her purse further up her arm, and glanced furtively ahead, planning her escape.

"You know Jim Rogers and Owen Birnbaum, don't you?" Leland was saying as Suzanne quickly attempted to gauge some seamless way to take her leave of the assembled gentlemen without appearing too much of a coward—just a tourist passing through this picturesque funeralscape. Finding no one or nothing immediate to relieve her, she returned to the task at hand, this test of sorts.

"Oh, yes, hello, Owen . . . Jim."

Unseeing, she smiled through both of them, realizing for the umpteenth time that here was Leland with someone, all paired up and set for life, while she remained alone. A sad solitary figure—someone Nick magnanimously complimented and others pitied, if they even noticed her at all. Nick, the man who now shared the bed of the last man Suzanne had slept with while Suzanne had slept alone. For four years. Four . . . *years?*

"Oh, my God," she inadvertently moaned aloud, her eyes widening with this sad realization.

"What's the matter?" asked Leland, reaching out to touch her arm in concern, always ready to help her, even when the problem was ever so indirectly him.

Her eyes refocused, and finding him again, she shook her head, dispelling the bleak vision she'd so recently summoned.

"Oh, nothing, I just remembered I'm supposed to meet someone, and I'm already pretty late." Then, looking again at Nick and the rest of them with a sort of smile, she returned to Leland. "I'll see you early Saturday then—under the clock. Don't forget to wear the carnation." And leaning in conspiratorially to him, she concluded, "There are spies everywhere—trust no one." And turning, she took what was left of her leave. "Bye boys. Nick," she called over her shoulder.

And that was when she decided. She would not continue this way one more day. Leland could not be the last person she slept with, simple as that. She wasn't *his* last person, why should he be hers? It was unseemly. As soon as she could find a man whose heterosexuality she could be absolutely certain of, she would correct this oversight. The last man she had been intimate with couldn't be someone that was able to jump free of her that easily, that completely. Couldn't be someone who now preferred men. Now, and probably always had. Perhaps all the time he seemed to have been looking at her with longing there had been scantily clad men leaning in doorframes with arms crossed over taut, lean bodies lurking behind his eyes. Muscular men who'd set up housekeeping in his head, doing sit-ups with smoldering looks, their washboard abdomens glistening with a subtle sheen of perspiration.

She needed someone to place between Leland and the rest of her life. She needed someone who'd definitely pledge allegiance to the female flag. A signal that something new had begun. She was surrendering her badge for the Border Patrol. She would no longer be a Customs Agent stationed at the outskirts of heterosexual land's end, waiting to stamp men's asses as they crossed the line into the colorful Kingdom of Queens. No!

She would find someone that night. At the memorial. No time like the present for proving to yourself your past is indeed behind you. And today was the first day of the rest of the guys she would date who wouldn't be gay. She carefully surveyed the sexual landscape in search of the straightest, highest tree. Through the smoke and the chatter, the crowd slowly parted and Suzanne smiled, having seen the glazed, knowing eyes of Dean Bradbury. And sure, she'd known him, known of him as well as about him, for ages. And wasn't he notorious? Anybody who'd been around the sexual Hollywood block had made a stop at Dean's place—or, as her friend Craig had so elegantly put it, Dean had "fucked the fuck out of everyone." A hedonistic ingestor and collector of all things pleasurable. An appreciator of the opposite sex—which meant he fit Suzanne's criteria perfectly. She followed him discreetly down the aisle like a bad bride and slipped into the seat beside him, brushing up against him as she did.

Dean smelled like high salaries and first-dollar gross laced with fairly strong marijuana. A heady mix. Suzanne inhaled the sweat and drug scent of him and smiled. Dean was Hollywood's original bad boy—who more than likely hadn't drawn a sober breath since somewhere around 1968. Suzanne slid down in her seat and leaned into him, doing her best impression of being forward, suggestive, available—whatever the word was for "let's have sex now." Behavior she would never, could never as a rule, be able to manage while properly medicated. But desperate times called for desperate measures, and Suzanne would have to muddle through. She let Dean know that, oddly enough, she was doing her best version of coming on to him when he looked over to her with eyebrows raised. She looked back at him meaningfully, and, to the extent that these things could be, it was done. The rest was just detail, the thing God was ordinarily in when there was room for Him and Dean wasn't hogging all available air space.

"Hey," she whispered to him, keeping her eyes on the Oscar, the oversized prize in front of them. "You come here often?"

Without looking, he muttered, "Just once in a blue producer."

Suzanne suppressed a laugh as the lights began to dim and she settled into her seat in anticipation of the "Farewell to Jack" show. It felt good sitting next to a big celebrity. She could relax and let Dean's reputation do the driving. Steer by proxy to his stardom. Chosen by a chosen. They're great, therefore I am.

Dean had been a star since audiences had first clapped eyes on him in *Two in the Bush*—a low-budget thriller about a happy detective who goes undercover when a lot of flower children begin getting murdered in Haight-Ashbury in the height of the 60s: "Where love-ins become death vigils," was the film's ad, and the movie wasn't much better than that particular advertisement's promise, but what was good about it was great, and that was Dean.

Especially when he turned out to be the killer in the end, and somehow you *still* liked him. He had that much charm, that intangible irresistibleness that you couldn't get enough of, the thing that made him a star. And, like the character he played in that first film, Dean was irresistible to the ladies—a lady-killer—though the real Dean didn't actually have to wrest pulses from his victims once he was finished feasting; finished getting his fill, if that was possible (which, with the actual Dean, it really wasn't).

"I see you made it into the lineup," she whispered again, leaning farther into him, looking at the call sheet, which listed each speaker and clip and the exact amount of time their tribute was expected to take, down to the second. Dean was introducing a clip from one of Jack's films toward the end of the evening. Right after Meg Ryan read a letter from Salman Rushdie and before Candice Bergen introduced the clip from *These Hands*.

"I could only talk about him behind his back while he was living— this is so refreshing," he said low, his lips barely moving, his eyes fixed on the lectern in front of the claret-colored velvet curtains that had just been hit with a spotlight. Suzanne thought, *Yeah, now you're talking behind his whole body.*

Ed Begley, Jr., appeared from behind the curtains and moved into the light, urging the microphone upward toward his tall blond head. Leaning down, he cleared his throat. "Good evening, everybody. I have the dubious distinction of being your host for this evening."

Pausing, he regarded the sea of faces gazing expectantly at him, a field of flowers trained toward his sun.

"Dubious for you because I don't know what I'm doing, but it's an honor for me to have anything to do with an event honoring such a great man." He moved his yellow hair off of his forehead and licked his lips. "But then I never know what I'm doing, so why should tonight be any different? But seriously, folks . . ."

People laughed around them. Dean raised his eyebrows but said nothing, and then Ed continued, his face appearing even paler than usual against the rich, dark backdrop.

"And now I'd like to start off this evening by introducing a very dear friend and colleague of Jack's—a giant in the industry, not only because he's tall but this man's accomplishments are even more towering than he is, throwing shadows on everything except his wife, whose taste runs toward direct lighting. One of the few women who are enhanced by it. Not that you need it, Renata. Renata Engelson. Could she be more beautiful, ladies and gentlemen? But why throw yourself away on Carl? I mean, the man can't possibly have enough time for you between writing and directing. Now, I don't mean to brag, but I'm out of work a lot, which means I could devote a lot more time to you than Carl could. I mean, c'mon! Why waste your time with a mere Oscar-winning writer and director when you can have an elderly albino actor with an electric car and a bone to pick? The tragedy is, I even hear the guy is *acting* in his latest epic! What's the matter, Carl? You couldn't get ahold of my agent?"

The assembly laughed appreciatively as a frowning Suzanne leaned again into Dean.

"I'm sorry—are people getting introduced along with their credits at a *memorial?*"

Dean eased his elbows onto the armrests and folded his hands in front of him. When he spoke, it was from under his fingers now clasped in front of his mouth.

"I don't know, I find people's credits very comforting at a time like this."

Suzanne shook her head and sat back, determined to try to pay attention, but the level of surreal absurdity frequently overwhelmed her. Carl Weber was now telling an amazingly long story about Jack and fly-fishing. Suzanne squirmed in her seat, longing for a Diet Coke. It was difficult for her to imagine Jack having the patience to fly-fish. Standing very still in a river seemed at odds with his excessive drug use. Unless they'd come up with a drug that enhanced your effectiveness as an outdoorsman while she'd slept on Percodan. She liked this idea. "Specifically designed for fly-fishermen" the label on the designer drug bottle would declare. It was this thought that sustained her through Carl's fifteen-minute bait-and-cast soliloquy.

"He's stealing all my best material," Dean muttered, after ten thousand lifetimes had been extinguished in her. Suzanne slid farther down in her seat and clapped her hand over her mouth to keep from laughing out loud.

Not that what he said was so particularly funny—what was funny was Suzanne acting like this coy, giggly teenage girl, doing everything but squeal and bat her eyelashes, and that was only because she hadn't had much batting practice. "You were doing the fly-fishing stuff, too?"

Dean nodded gravely, a grin partially visible under his clasped hands.

"This is great shit, man . . . listen to it."

From the stage, Carl droned on monotonously.

". . . And the great river spread out all around us, and as most of you know, Jack loved that river. The way the water played on it in different lights, hours passing like a procession of gurgling ants, carrying us to a place of pure

nature—*where he was just a man catching fish. A fisherman among fisher-men. A man among men."*

"See, I was gonna do a riff on the gurgling ants—the man's now leaving me with *nothing."* Dean cut her a sly look.

". . . So there we were, and Jack's catching fish after fish while I'm get-ting bupkes, *when suddenly I notice he's doing that thing with his chin . . ."*

Suzanne had to cover her mouth again. She felt like she was back with her eighth-grade friends, trying not to laugh during assembly in the school auditorium.

"Is it just me, or do you find memorials a little bit of an aphro-disiac?" Dean learned over to her and winked.

"Not *aphro*disiac, *anglo*disiac," she corrected him sharply. "We're white, remember?" Now she had him truly, had him for sure. He flashed her his biggest grin and nodded his head. That's when she knew for certain. She hadn't forgotten how to flirt with and attract men. And Dean was the certified, unadulterated, tried-and-true arti-cle—no one could deny her that. He had received her signals; her transmitter wasn't as rusty as she feared.

A well-dressed woman looked back at them sternly and was about to shush them when she recognized Dean, and her face relaxed, registering a surprise that bordered on glee. Facing forward and lean-ing into her girlfriend, she whispered in her ear, no doubt sounding the discreet alarm that a very big star was seated behind them.

"Now you like me, don't you?" Suzanne said, happily flushing. Dean nodded.

"Oh, yeah . . . anglodisiac . . . that's good."

". . . And he's wearing one of those little cloth hats which somehow looks great on him, but on me, it's suddenly 'Mr. Magoo'—anyway, Jack baits up and with a flick of his wrist, he casts over and out . . ."

Suzanne didn't know how she would survive not leaving with Dean that very moment and getting inoculated against her celibacy. But if she had lasted almost four years, she could last through a lot of clips and insincere tributes to a man most people hated save a few drug dealers and as many hookers. Sex had never been a big part of her day anyway. Finally it was Dean's turn up at the podium: "Adios to my fellow compatriot and bad boy, Jack—one of the few men who had the decency to occasionally make even me look like a Boy Scout." Here he paused for laughter. "All right, maybe not a scout, how about a boy? You know, in one of those goofy uniforms with a flashlight?"

Suzanne watched the audience fall apart with laughter from the back of the screening room where she waited, exhilarated by pre-arrangement, as Dean eulogized a man he could barely stand.

"All right, look, I'll make you a deal—I'll let you think what you want if you let me get out of here, how's that? But before I go, I'd like to introduce a clip from a film produced by this truly energetic, unique, visionary man—even if that vision was sometimes blurred and bloodshot like mine. Hey, man, all the real greats have needed their downtime—know what I mean?" Dean grinned his naughty grin and raised those famous eyebrows, indicating the screen. "And now without further ado—'cause I snorted most of that ado earlier— here's a clip from a movie I did with Jack in 1910 called *Down the Dark Path Go Easy.*"

The lights dimmed as the audience applauded wildly.

"You wanna get out of here?" Suzanne murmured as Dean joined her in the back of the room.

"Sure thing, Suzy Q. You wanna follow me to my place?"

She shrugged, feeling almost giddy, almost squeezy and tilty. "Why not?"

So in front of God, Leland, Nick, and everyone else, Suzanne left with this infamous Pinocchio—the original straight bad boy.

Not that it was simple to pick up Dean Bradbury, but a few things were working in her favor that particular night. For one thing, Suzanne looked pretty good, and two, she had gotten to him early and made her agenda known. Last but perhaps most important, she knew—and Dean knew she knew—where to get some of the drugs that he liked. She used the word *some* advisedly, for no one on earth could have enough of the right assortment of chemicals for Dean.

"Let's stop at my friend Michael's first. I want to pick up that little surprise for you," Suzanne said teasingly. She had no intention of partaking, but she could hardly go empty-handed to Dean's house, could she?

Dean cocked an eyebrow at her. "Like I said, should you be picking up surprises, Suzy? I mean, aren't you—?"

Suzanne scowled. "I'm not going to do them, sadly, I'm just gonna offer you a sampling of these riches, and then stand by and live vicariously, sobbing."

Dean reached over and touched her face. "How could I not recognize this as the selfless act of a true friend?"

Michael was only too happy to contribute to Dean's deliquency. Michael had HIV, which is why he had Dean's favorite drug du jour, Marinol. Prescription medical marijuana in a pill. Suzanne was confident that this would please Dean, which was important because Suzanne was a people-pleasing person and Dean so much more than just people.

She followed Dean back to his house and placed a furtive call to Lucy from the bathroom phone.

"Would you mind staying over with Honey?"

"Why? Who is it? You have to tell me! I'm holding your daughter hostage! Between my knees!" Lucy could barely contain her excitement.

"Details to come," Suzanne whispered. "Gotta go."

"But I'm your best friend!" Lucy wailed as the phone line went dead.

There ensued a night of raucous sexual escapades. A long night under stars both celestial and cinematic—a night filled with Dean's leering naughty sex talk—something as a rule Suzanne didn't enjoy, but made a magnanimous exception to in this case because, after all, wasn't this one of the things that ensured Dean's fixed and certain sexuality? Wasn't this something totally for damn sure straight guys did? Things to offend, like talking dirty, belching loudly, and leaving the toilet seat up?

"Oh, yeah, baby, you like that, don't you? Tell me just how much you like it . . ."

Looking back on all this later with bloodshot eyes, she thought that the dating gods must have taken pity on her and thrown her this well-known bone, which she accepted gratefully. Suzanne was with this bigger-than-life good old boy—getting onto *very* old, but that hardly mattered. The important thing was this liaison with Dean could be a sign of people and things to come. Regular things: show business regular. No more exotic upsets or surprises. She could go back to those halcyon days of being left for other women or because she was self-centered or any one of a dozen expected exits. What she experienced as her overall talent to disappoint. Perhaps now a new chapter in her life had begun and she could turn the page on any lingering pains from her past and face an unknown future with the sun on her face, hope in her heart, and a condom in her wallet.

Suzanne would have gladly had more of a relationship with Dean. It would've made her whole life simpler . . . her fantasy life, that is. She'd be "Mrs. Dean Bradbury": Mrs. "I'm with him, that's who."

The only problem with that was, Dean wasn't capable of more. Logically, you would think that given he was bigger than life, his little would be quite a lot, wouldn't it? It would have to be, right? But Dean didn't really have "relationships." He had sex with people for various lengths of time and then moved on. He liked them new and liked to keep them coming, one after another, fresh off the truck, step lively now, quick, quick, before the old love begins to get rancid and starts to smell. He'd leave the newly replaced loves with a nickname, an anecdote, and the strange sad status of belonging to a classification of subspecies related to Dean Bradbury by fertilization. A kind of plant: female genus—*deangenuspenus celebritoriumus.*

"Aren't you glad we waited?" she asked the next morning as Dean headed off to the golf course.

Pausing, he looked over his shoulder and grinned mischievously. "Not at the time, no." And with that he was gone, leaving Suzanne lying there in the large, anointed aftermath of him.

As she lay there between sheets of impossibly high thread count, Suzanne started putting together the casual way she would inform the disbelieving Lucy. She couldn't wait to go home and share the wealth, bestow the bright coin of joyful feeling bubbling behind her smile. Cut her now and she would bleed music and the song would sing only of wonderful things to be. So she hadn't done anything interesting in ages, had she? She wanted to see Lucy's face when she told her how she'd ended her nearly four-year-old sex draught with a really big box-office bang.

WATERS OF WORRY

Honey had gotten used to living with her mother most of the time and with her father for the rest of it. And little by little she seemed to have forgotten the three of them had ever shared a home, never demonstrating any sign she missed living any other way than the way she lived now.

Strung between their lives like a line of twinkling lights, she lit the way between Leland's life and Suzanne's—the last of the fading umbilical cord that connected them. And they hung on to this lovable lifeline, waiting to be rescued by better times.

Better for the three of them—for Honey and her parents. Standing poised between them, her pale, little hands held out to each—beckoning them to meet in the middle of the world where she waited, where she always was. Their world: the one Leland and Suzanne had made together when they created her. For wasn't Honey all the world to each of them?

"Am I at your house tonight or Daddy's?" she would ask Suzanne. And how Suzanne hated to see her go to his. To take her chubby legs and funny throaty laugh with her and bundle up her other riches, her Frisbee and her blankie and her chapter book—for at six she was already an avid reader—into her blue backpack, spreading them at Leland's feet. Watching *Rugrats* round-eyed with wonder with Leland and his just-so boyfriend—giggling on the floor of his well-designed house on his soft, white shag carpet in front of his big plasma-screen TV.

Of course Leland and Nick would have to have the latest, largest, flattest TV, and of course Honey would have to love it. So Suzanne had been delighted when the cable station she worked for presented her with her own plasma TV, for the secret sick reason that it fed into that Beverly Hills one-upmanship where you kept up with the Joneses—once they married into the Rockefeller family.

And also because no matter how many times Suzanne reminded herself it wasn't about "things," deep down she didn't really believe it, having been raised by the bribe and comfort of things given—especially when the love had been detained indefinitely on the road. As a child, she'd learned an important life lesson. When love fails, hey, don't sweat it! Here come the gifts! At times these offerings were an almost totally acceptable alternative to love and warmth and time spent; even if they weren't, what could you do about it? Best to be the greatest sort of good sport—there're far greater tragedies than this, so move on. Maybe the gifts weren't meant as a substitute, but Suzanne knew in emergencies they could act as a sort of marker. Something to tide you over till the groovy human stuff showed up. Just because they might not be what you needed, didn't mean they weren't worth *something.* So if Leland could give Honey a plasma TV—then Suzanne felt really good that she could provide one for Honey as well.

Then she discovered that the TV was the gift that kept on taking. It cost her twelve hundred dollars for the special cables and hookup. Five thousand dollars for the necessary hydraulics that made it rise out of its moorings like Esther Williams from her shimmering pool. Somehow she found the strength to nix the $3500 for special speakers. And then she found out about the super deluxe remote.

"I'm sorry—what?"

She'd been told there were these amazing, over-the-top-of-the-line remote controls to end all remotes—and sure, she'd seen one of them in Leland's living room and in the living rooms of other wealthy folk. And they were nice, as far as remotes go, but never having been much of a clicker girl, she didn't give it much thought. That is, until she heard the clicker cost $1300.

"Jesus . . . for what?" she'd asked the man installing her plasma TV. "Does it do dishes? Can it guess your weight?—Not that I'd pay extra for a clicker that did *that* but still, for thirteen hundred bucks, it better have the power to heal."

She'd stood in her living room with Stan, the plasma TV–installing man to the rich and famous. The same man who'd installed Leland's system; along with just about everybody else's. Dean Bradbury's, Jack Burroughs's, Carl Weber's, everyone's.

Stan looked embarrassed, or perhaps it was uncomfortable—it hardly mattered to Suzanne. Who was he but the evil overpriced clicker pusher? A large blond man built like a linebacker, wearing a tool belt and trailing an assistant, he now stood red-faced and sweating before her and cleared his throat.

"Actually, the remote that's in Mr. Franklin's living room is a different one entirely. The one I'm talking about—the one that costs thirteen hundred dollars plus installation, which is . . ." Stan paused and looked to the skies to receive another incoming obscene dollar amount, ". . . say, four hundred dollars. So that makes it . . ." he wiped the back of his wide neck with a dirty, money-grubbing hand.

"Around seventeen hundred bucks," Suzanne snapped at him angrily. "You're basically telling me that Leland has a two-thousand-dollar clicker to go with his plasma TV."

Stan looked at her like she'd made the most basic of human mistakes. And being a compassionate man of technology, he pitied her.

"Actually . . . Leland got the two-thousand-dollar remotes for all the rooms in the house. His bedroom, the kitchen, Honey's room, the guest house, his office . . ."

Suzanne looked at him with incomprehension.

"Wait a minute! Honey has one of those big clickers that Allah and Buddha and everyone else can be summoned from? The Mecca Clicker?"

The dawn of comprehension lit Stan's red face from within and his large shoulders sagged in relief.

"Oh, you're thinking of the *big* clicker in his living room!" he laughed at her gently as one would a halfwit or an autistic child. "Oh, that's a different thing entirely. Those are five thousand dollars. They're like the Rolls-Royce of TV toys."

Suzanne went silent everywhere, inside and out. When she spoke, it was from a faraway place, where money wasn't used and material things didn't matter.

"Leland has a five-thousand-dollar clicker—and there *is* such a thing."

Stan smiled, relieved he'd discovered the source of their simple misunderstanding.

"But I'm not talking about those. This is the other one. You know, one of those more affordable remotes."

Suzanne nodded. "You mean the bargain two-thousand-dollar gizmos. I understand."

"So should I order you one?"

Finally, it was the clicker that released her from her mad frenzy of trying to keep up with Leland materially as a means of securing Honey's love. The crazy mortgage she'd thought she had needed to pay for the choice real estate of her daughter's heart. She could finally banish the thought that she could aim the five-thousand-dollar remote control at whoever she wanted to love her and presto!— They'd come alive with that affectionate programming. The clicker that had made her bipolar. The clicker that had turned Leland gay. That found stations no other remote could get to, stealing over time zones and pouncing on the show that was just what she needed right then. That found Suzanne on TV the moment she appeared there and changed the channel when she'd turned up gone.

But while Honey was at Leland's maddeningly understated palatial home in Bel-Air—the one with the pool that didn't have chlorine because it was cleaned by silent holistic devices invisible to the eye and gentle on the skin—Suzanne all but stood in the doorway staring out at the horizon, wringing her hands in despair at what she imagined was going on there right now that she was powerless to stop—or duplicate.

They might be barbecuing right about now—rustling up some burgers and ribs and corn, someone maybe even wearing one of those big chef's hats. And, oh, there might be Leland's normal, homestyle relatives—and they had children and dogs and charming accents and played with squirt guns and ran around laughing, playing touch football in the tall, cool, perfectly manicured grass—the 2.5-million-dollar landscaped backyard groomed for such tomfoolery. So much fun.

At Leland's house, Honey got normal grandparents; at Suzanne's, she got Doris (Tony was eternally missing in action). Doris with her tearful tales of beach houses lost to second husbands ("he was a gambler"). This was Doris's idea of a bedtime story, as Suzanne learned when she'd asked Honey what she and Bubbe had talked about at bedtime. *Bubbe* is the Yiddish word for grandmother—not that Doris was Jewish, but she had married several Jewish men which Doris more than felt gave her the right to utilize some of their culture in a crunch. And let's face it, the word "grandma" was, for Doris, the most crushing sort of crunch. So Bubbe she became and Bubbe she stayed. And Honey would answer Suzanne with "She said she didn't mind about the Palm Springs house, but the beach house had special tiles or something. Then she cried."

But could Suzanne give Honey any of the things Leland gave so freely and easily? Oh, woe is her—blub blub blub she couldn't console herself any which way. She hated playing the never-ending games of Monopoly with Honey—oh, *God* not again. If I see that little tin hat and dog again, I will go directly to jail. Do not pass go, do not collect $200. And swimming—look at me in a swimsuit at this age after having a kid and three hundred thousand desserts. Are you kidding? But with Leland and his friends—all the hiking and yoga-going guys so eager to throw Honey squealing into the deep end—how could her daughter ever want to return to the House on Bitch Mountain? To Kennecuntport?

Is it any wonder Suzanne felt threatened? Or was it perhaps her tendency to feel envious and competitive to begin with? Oh, fuck it.

But what good did it do her, strangling herself with these scenes constructed so carefully with the mean part of her mind. Reinflaming her bitterness over the whole bad business with Leland. No. Though she could resent the man that had left her for Nick, she could never resent Honey's dad. Never resent anyone who gave Honey so much pleasure. Sure, she still had moments she lamented marrying a fine familial person like Leland. No! She should have married someone who was a worse parent to Honey—making Suzanne the popular one, the one Honey relied on and ran to when life's little difficulties snapped at her heels, scaring her straight into the safe harbor of Suzanne's warm, secure arms instead of Leland's.

It wasn't fair. Suzanne hadn't enjoyed her own childhood the way she thought you were supposed to—and now it seemed that Honey wouldn't let her enjoy *her* childhood the same way she allowed her father to.

So when Suzanne's emotional weather clouded over and her self-pity began to threaten to storm, she was always hardest hit when it came to Honey. Did Honey really love her? Well, yes, she couldn't deny that her daughter was fond of her and even seemed to find her amusing sometimes, frequently asking Suzanne to stay until she fell asleep—sometimes even wanting her mother to sing to her or read to her, and always, *always* telling Suzanne she loved her when she said goodnight or good-bye to her on the phone.

But when the waters of worry rose in Suzanne, she began to look at these things in a different light. And from this self-pitying slant, it seemed she was the third wheel in the family unit, the parent to pass over en route to finer fatherly scenes. The clumsy one, all thumbs when it came to the delicate handiwork entailed in holding someone dear. And from her contaminated perch, Suzanne viewed Honey's declaration of love at the end of the phone call as a convenient way to exit the ever-awkward conversation with her mother. Sometimes Honey would plea-to-flee bargain: "Do you want to talk to Daddy?" If that didn't work, her pronunciation of affection was her ticket to freedom, signaling the always-brief phone chat was officially at an end. Honey's offering of love was the sweet ammunition she needed to blast an exit out of this place of required, ritual interaction with her mother, whose questions Honey answered briefly, tolerating them as long as she felt she had to. "Okay, Mommy, I love you, bye!" And with that reverse incantation, she'd be gone, taking her magic spell with her.

"Why do they call it gay?" Honey asked in her best-perplexed voice one night, lying next to her mother in the shadowy dim of her darkened room. Suzanne lay very still in the waiting place on the outskirts of her daughter's question, both of them wondering what Suzanne's reply would be.

"Well, I don't really know," she replied carefully, stroking her daughter's fine hair fanned out on the pillow behind her and then scratching her back over her little pink nightgown edged in lace. "Another word for it, though, is *homosexual,*" Suzanne offered tentatively. "And the word *homo* means 'same'—you know, like when two men love each other or even two women. They love each other just like when men and women do. People of the opposite sex—and the word for opposite is *hetero*—so when a man and woman love one another, they're called heterosexuals. That's why—"

"Mom?" Honey said, interrupting Suzanne's halting tour of love in the new millennium. Suzanne breathed for the first time since the start of her explanation all those interminable moments ago.

"Yes, baby?" she wondered if she'd made enough of a hash of it to fuck up her child for life and made a mental note to charge Leland big money for putting her in the position of delivering this information. If she had, she would've worked out a method. "Homo means same. And domo means thanks and Dumbo's a cute little elephant and dodos are birds which go *wee wee wee* all the way home!" She hadn't signed up for this, had she? No! This was extra. This one was thrown in with the whole-man-that-got-the-man-that-got-away business. A bonus prize. Free with this one-time-only low-ball offer.

"Yes, baby?" she repeated, thoroughly chastened, fully knowing she'd ruined the rest of the best part of her daughter's life.

"I don't think I want to hear about this until I'm seven." Suzanne smiled at the impossible sweetness of this response.

"Maybe we should both wait," Suzanne said.

Honey wriggled away from her mother a little and rearranged herself in the covers to a new position of presleep.

"Will you sing me something?" she asked.

Suzanne smiled. "Sure, dirndl, which song do you want first?"

Honey thought for a minute, "The blackbird one."

Kissing the back of her daughter's head, Suzanne lingered there to inhale the particular night scent of her—an amalgam of shampoo and pert whispery completeness. Honey was wholly herself, animated with inquiry, poised, wry and suspicious, utterly unto herself, thoughtful, capable, and fun. And after everything else, a good soldier careful in her command—careful not to hurt or trust too quickly. Little Honey, animal lover, boss of her peers, able student and basketball player. Honey, who knew all the lyrics to the songs in the Top 40, who watched *Will & Grace* and *Fear Factor* for reasons she might not even have recognized. Attila the Honey—the best girl on any block Suzanne bladed on.

"Pack up all your cares and woe, here I go, singin' low, bye, bye, blackbird. Where somebody waits for me, sugar sweet, so is she . . ."

How best to bury the beast of her hurt and disappointment over Leland? How *not* to think about losing Honey to her father's affections after losing the father first? It seemed to her that the only way to not think about something so interesting and awful, and so in her mind all about her, was to find something new to think about. Something or someone. Or both. Whatever it took.

She'd started with Dean and his name-above-the-title dirty talking; now it was time to follow that up. She had to take advantage of the momentum initiated by that episode, making sure the rest of her life as a razor-straight person able to identify other razor-straight people had truly begun.

So Suzanne began to search her available world for bigger and better things to think on. A new North Star by which to steer her treacherous course.

WODEN'S WIFE, FRIGG

Some days Suzanne liked words more than people, but she found that all too frequently they came as a mismatched team. She liked where words hailed from, their individual histories, their expansive uses, their meanings molting over time. Unlike people, words went on forever, or as long as there were books or mouths to invoke them, while people eventually slowed and came reluctantly to a stop.

One day, while Suzanne was waiting for her daughter to finish her piano lesson, she'd chanced upon a line in a book: "Drawing is taking a line for a walk." She imagined herself holding the hand of the last letter of the last word of a particularly pithy sentence and, pulling gently on that hand, walking that last letter of that word of that line halfway across the world, always (as she might be) on the end of some sentence or other—ready to hurl herself off the end of it into that cool pool of no words at all.

The history of the names of days of the week fascinated her most of all; discovering they were named for Norse gods, ones once deemed Pagan by those finicky priests. Monday was of course Moon Day, and Tuesday was a god with the unfortunate handle of Tiu. Ah, but Wednesday, Wednesday was one part of her favorite weekday couple—Woden. And Woden's devoted wife, Frigg, for Friday. Between them stood Thursday, named for Thor, and who hadn't heard of him? Thor the Storm-bringer, ruler of Olympus? (Or whatever the Norse equivalent was—ruler of somewhere on high and made for scaling. The god pretty much ruled whatever he rained on.) All in all, a pretty popular guy up there, and the only god bold enough to stand between Woden and his blushing bride, Frigg.

Woden and Frigg: happy, happy.

Or at least once or twice a week.

A short time after Jack's ashes had been scattered on a nude beach somewhere in the Caribbean, and Suzanne's one-night stand with Dean Bradbury had either sat or walked resolutely away, she met a boy, a tall boy. Beautiful and blond. His Serbian mother had named him Michael but Suzanne never called him that. No. He looked too much like Woden and Frigg's eternal third wheel, the god who weekly came between them. So she nicknamed him Thor. Thor the magnificent, the Wonder God, the younger-than-she-by-a-lot-of-years.

He'd been brought to Suzanne by her infatuated trainer, Kip, who'd found him at the gym in the cool shade of a weight machine. Captured between reps, Kip brought his hoped-for prize to Suzanne's house. Not so much an offering as a trophy; perhaps by introducing him to his quasi-famous clients, Kip would impress him and once impressed Thor would even love him. So Thor was presented to Suzanne, and songwriter Megan Campbell, even to Roger Nelson, the infomercial king. Not an amazing array, but perhaps enough to do the trick, overcome any inconvenient obstacles in the way of Kip and Thor sharing a life together—one of these obstacles being Thor's insistence he wasn't gay. Kip considered that point negotiable, in part because people weren't always what they claimed to be. Besides, even if he was straight, perhaps Kip could convert him with some gentle coaxing—trade his heterosexual travelers' checks for new gay funds. Currency Kip could then spend lavishly on himself. In any event, this was Kip's secret fantasy, but a fantasy it remained because Thor wanted coddling and not converting

Thor had been brought up in the old country by his grandparents, older people who taught him good manners, to say his prayers and to sit up straight. Both gentle and good and raised with values from a by-gone era, one day Thor was old enough to set out on his own. After kissing the dry, upturned face of his grandmother and grasping the firm grip of his grandfather's hand, Thor sailed for America in search of someone who'd love him and keep him near her in the manner to which he hoped to become accustomed. This sweet, smooth, sculpted god was determined to find his fortune, to fashion himself into something infinitely collectable, something no woman could resist.

At first, Suzanne couldn't imagine being that fortune, being with anyone so young, so well put together and handsome—and so tall. Thor even needed to duck when going through several of her doorways. What would she do with such a person? Where would she put him and what would she talk to him about? And perhaps most important, what would her friends think when they saw her with him and how stupid would she look on a scale of one to pushing forty?

Besides, what was he doing hanging out with Kip? A funny little gay man so obviously infatuated with him; what was that about? Suzanne thought it decidedly suspicious in light of Leland. It was more than suspicious—it was frigging terrifying. All she needed at this or any other point was another guy with questionable sexuality. How, and why, did they find her? And where oh where would it end?

No. It was unseemly—would never do. Best to leave him as she found him.

And yet . . . look at him—so smooth and pretty, delicious. How could you not bite into him just for the sweet untroubled taste—a newly baked, cream-filled, nougat-centered human? It was just too tempting.

But no. It wasn't right.

Here was this youthful physical creature who looked out at the new world with newer eyes, while she lived entirely in her unaerobi-cized brain—in every way his opposite. He'd never be able to appreciate her for who she was—not that she could pin that down at any given moment. He would only be able to admire her as other than he was—a quick-thinking creature who didn't drink enough water or exercise as often as she should. Would that really be so bad?

It was her friend Marcus who helped decide for her. Having seen a picture of Thor in a magazine when he'd first arrived from Serbia, Marcus called the photographer to find out if the model was as gorgeous in person. Satisfied with the report, he'd sent for Thor to see for himself. Marcus could do things like that—it being one of the privileges of the Forbes list of wealthy and powerful—summon anyone to his exclusive estate by a simple call from a well-spoken assistant.

Thor arrived, wearing jeans, a T-shirt, and cowboy boots, making him even taller than he was. He sat at Marcus's table and had pizza with him. Or perhaps a less pielike pasta. "Anyway, it had many carbohydrates in it, that is a sure thing," Thor told Suzanne later when describing the evening he'd spent with her influential friend. "So I told him what this food would do to him and that to eat a salad would be so filling, delicious, and yes, healthier."

Afterward they'd gone to Marcus's screening room and watched a movie that had yet to be released. Then Thor politely thanked Marcus for his hospitality and bade him goodnight, clomp, clomp, clomping his boots down the path, through the hush of the manicured garden gate, supervised by hidden cameras, to the real-world street.

"You have to sleep with him, sweetheart," Marcus informed her firmly afterward. "He's perfect-looking. Don't be insane. Why wouldn't you? He wasn't interested in men or God knows I would have slept with him, no question. I'm telling you, he's straight. He's this well-brought-up boy from wherever the hell he's from—Bosnia or some awful place like that."

"Serbia," Suzanne picked at the the palm of her left hand with great absorption, as if the answer to whether or not she should get involved with Thor lay somewhere beneath the top layer of her skin.

"Who cares? Anyway, you're silly to not do this. It's absurd to worry about him being a fag. I'm telling you he's not, and I would know. So just fuck him. Not to would be such a waste."

"Oh, *please.*" Suzanne sighed, closing her eyes. Maybe Marcus was right. He sounded right. More than right, he sounded fiercely certain. And there was something infectious about his oh-so-strong convictions.

"Let's stop talking about it. I want you to call him, invite him over, and fuck him. And don't call me until you do. The next time I hear from you, I just want you to tell me how it was and if his hands are any indication of the rest of him."

But how on earth to override her understandable inhibitions concerning a possible liaison with this overstyled kid? The solution was simple, though ultimately fraught with complications and potential chaos.

Have Lucrezia do it. Have her go fetch him while Suzanne waited behind.

Lucrezia was named of course for Lucrezia Borgia, who lived in late fifteenth-century Florence and was an unprincipled aristocratic woman, rumored to have coupled with her father and brother, perhaps even to have borne a child by one of them, and more than likely even poisoned someone. Oh, she got up to all sorts of hijinks, that Lucrezia did.

Unleashing Lucrezia was for emergencies only. Though Lucrezia would apply herself to any and all existing emergencies, they were ones she'd usually put into motion herself, and once released from her medicated cage, Lucrezia was famous for going on to cause all sorts of additional mischief, inaugurating fresh emergencies all over Suzanne's free-fall world.

And what Suzanne couldn't and wouldn't do, her Lucrezia did for her, functioning virtually and entirely without morals, qualms, or compunctions, rather with an unbridled glee. One could never predict quite what would happen once Lucrezia was unleashed on an unsuspecting world. Especially when it came to men, shopping, traveling, outbursts of sudden generosity, and taking drugs.

Lucrezia wanted what she wanted and would flatten whatever obstacle had the audacity to appear in her way. She was a queen and men were her subjects—and not very interesting ones at that.

"Come, come, speak up . . . what's that you say? Oh, no matter—off with his head—it's empty enough to float away as it is anyway."

So where Suzanne was hesitant and insecure, Lucrezia was effervescent, easily amused (by herself), and onto the next. Eventually, nothing or no one could hold her and she . . . well . . . as to what happened next, Suzanne was reluctant to say. But the truth was, once Lucrezia burned her bridges, the pills were sent for—relief was needed and lots of it—keep it coming 'til you don't see anyone at all. The cavalry came and went, leaving her body and that was all she—no, make that somebody else—would have to write.

So was it worth it to summon Lucrezia just to do away with all this heterosexual hesitancy? This was one of those times Suzanne forgot the real answer and pondered risking the answer that she preferred.

All she had to do was just push a few pills to the side when taking her morning dose of medication—and then overlook one or two of the five she was supposed to take at night. A simple enough slip-up of a solution. Any fool could make it. And that way, she wouldn't be going for a full-throttle light-up-the-skies Lucrezia visit, just some benefits and characteristics that came with this higher, sluttier self— a self unrestrained by the annoying restraints imposed by modern psychiatric medicine. And in case it wasn't Lucrezia that came but her dark other—the creature that could not be named and was decidedly uninterested in her sex life, if not actually life itself—why, then she could just resume her regular dose as though nothing had happened— and nothing would have, right? Suzanne would be oh so very wary and careful and not like before.

It was decided. She'd unleash Lucrezia, would turn down the sound, turn up the drowned-out song that could sing her into situations usually screaming for second thought. And once Lucrezia had fetched Thor, she'd return to her usual dose of meds, Honey having continued along in the merry meantime obliviously happy. Mission accomplished, with no one noticing there'd been anything amiss.

Yes, it was a perfect, foolproof plan.

So Suzanne palmed a few pills and let Thor take her to the movies, and when they got back to her house, she invited him in. She put on some music, served him the water he requested—"It is very important to always be hydrated," he informed her solemnly—and made the necessary small talk to someone so tall on everything but talking.

Before long, she found herself sprawled underneath him, as though an enormous warm sequoia had toppled onto her and, wrapping her in his strong branches, he kissed her. Thor's body pressed against hers and slowly and almost without warning, her black and white parts began their warm slow melt to Technicolor.

Suzanne burrowed deeper into the wonderful warm of his neck where, if things continued to go well, she might winter.

Ohhhhh. . . .

It was as though a rhythm had begun in some distant place and was now urging them toward its dreamy planet, and on it, his larger hand found her smaller one, and everything after that began drifting further and further away from kosher—everything began happening that in some wonderful way was wrong.

After a while, she moved her mouth away from his for some much needed breathing and regarded this big, brawny boy. Sir Lancelot the true. A knight with the sweetest look in his eye, a little boy trapped in a body exercised to within an inch of everybody's life. Especially, right now, hers.

"I'm going to propose to you seven times," he said, grabbing her shoulders suddenly and holding her a little away from him in order to see her reaction.

Suzanne frowned, confused. "Excuse me? What are you talking about?"

A hank of hair fell down over the forehead of this boy who looked like someone who read comic books, rode bicycles, and skinned his knees.

"I'm going to ask you to marry me seven times," he repeated firmly, with traces of his Eastern European accent. "But that is all. You either are saying yes by then or—that is the last time. I wouldn't ask you again."

Suzanne narrowed her eyes and studied him, brushing his hair from his green Round Table eyes, his fresh-from-the-joust-forehead, his noble brow.

"And I'm going to get you long pants and help you with your homework. We'll have cookies and milk when we're finished and . . ."

Suzanne's index finger gently traced the length of his razor-straight nose.

"If this is our age being different, then you should not speak of this further," he pushed her off of him, frowning moodily. "Age doesn't matter. It is a number, and what are they but only small things that are mattering in math, to some people."

But, oh, Suzanne thought, the numbers did matter. They advanced you closer to the end of your existence, wilted you, simultaneously diminished you as they rose insistently. She opened her mouth to speak, but Thor gave her no chance.

"Anyway, this is silliness, you know?" he went on. "You look better than many women my age. And this age you have makes you very interesting. You have so very much life experience and that is something interesting to me. The ones who have lived longer have the wisdom—this is what is taught where I come from, and what I am telling you is true. You understand me?"

Suzanne found herself beaming happily at him as his grasp of English loosened with every endearingly fractured phrase.

"In my country, the ones who have lived longer have the *wrinkles,*" she said, touching his cheek, and continuing to smile at him with affection. "This is what I tell *you.*"

He scowled and pulled away from her, looking frustrated and sullen.

"Now you are making some kind of fun of me."

"No, I'm not," she leaned toward him to indicate assurance. "Really! I'm completely not. I really *do* think it's nice. I like the idea of you on the farm with your grandparents. I like it so much it's *pathetic.*"

She pictured them all padding through stiff hay, warm from the Eastern European sunshine. Grandparents caring for their beloved Thor in the years remaining them, their little growing god frolicking politely on the farm.

Once he had determined that she wasn't, in fact, mocking him, Thor breathed easy again, returning to his role as the youthful suitor, courting Suzanne in broken English—the unofficial language of new-millennium love.

So Suzanne settled uneasily into something with Thor. Even moving him in with her a little, always careful that Honey would think he was a guest that slept in the spare room. But guest or no, Honey seemed to love Thor the moment she laid eyes on him, having never seen anything like him in her short life.

"He's like Superman," she told her mother in hushed tones of awe. "But bigger than him. He's a Super Superman, isn't he, Mommy?"

And Thor would lift Honey up onto his mountainous shoulders, high, high up in the sky above his head. And swinging her around, he'd throw her on the bed, laughing and squealing.

"More!" She'd beg him after each sail through the air, arms and legs flailing until she landed, tangled hair crisscrossing her delighted face. "Again Thor! Pleeeease!? Do it again! Mommy, make him!"

Now finally Suzanne could join in that unhealthy competition taking place in her crowded head—for there was Honey in the pool high above Thor's head, giggling with unbridled glee, the sun blazing down on them as though bestowing the long-awaited blessing. "Watch, Mommy! Thor taught me to do this!" And Honey would dive away from the side of the pool, her hands in a praying position over her head, and emerge delighted from the depths of the blue, untroubled water.

"Did you see me, Mommy?" Honey would plead with delight and without waiting for Suzanne's response her eyes would sweep around to find her gentle giant playmate. "Did you see me, Thor?" she'd ask, pushing her hair back with one hand. "That was right, wasn't it?" And Thor would sit silently looking at her for a moment—to tease her, knowing what an audience he had in this lovely little girl—and then he'd rise up with a growl and dive toward her with a splash and grab hold of her with his huge hands and hold her high above his head for just long enough for her to kick her little legs in joyful protest a few times before tossing her in a high arc toward the deep end where she would land with a slap and a splash and reemerge coughing and spitting and laughing and feigning anger. Suzanne watched it all thinking, *I brought her this. I can bring her happiness after all, see?*

On weekends they'd go to the pier down at the beach and get too many quarters and the three of them would play Skeeball—yes, even Suzanne!—and they'd save up tickets and Honey would pick out prizes: stuffed blue snakes or big ugly long yellow dogs with black tongues and rolling eyes. And Thor would win those games with his feats of strength, knocking over bottles or sinking basketballs or wielding the mallet that made the ball rise to the top of the column— and don't you know Thor hit that thing with all his might and rang the bell at the very top. And after he presented Honey with the biggest prize bear that could be won in the kingdom, this prince of the pier hoisted her and her hard-won booty up onto his shoulders and she rode her hero back out to the car, trailed by her mother in a cloud of cotton candy.

These were Suzanne's children: Thor and Honey. Big, bouncing Thor and precocious Honey with her swooped-up nose and lone freckle on her left eyelid. Honey, who slept with her mouth open ever so slightly, her breath warm and sweet as a clear summer day.

And then there was the other baby in Suzanne's bed. Her son Thor, the perfect specimen, more sculpted with each passing day. But beneath his physique, Suzanne couldn't believe the untrammeled pastures in his head; she had never spent so much time before with someone so apparently lacking in education. Not that Suzanne was a scholar—far from it—but she'd always felt some urgency to learn. Whereas Thor, perhaps worn out from his exertions perfecting his body, seemed to have no innate curiosity or appetite for wisdom or information. Oh, he tried. He really did—he wanting so much to please her. And Suzanne did her best to pretend she didn't care when the books she pressed on him remained unopened, their lure lost on him completely.

He looked at her one night with large, hurt eyes. "You think I'm stupid, don't you?"

"No!" she said in a voice higher than her own—an octave reserved for emphasis. "How can you say that? You're not stupid at all!"

But though her tone was the urgent tone of someone sincere, ultimately they both knew she wasn't. Not really.

"Okay, maybe you're not as smart as I am," she added, apologetically, "but why should you be or why would you want to be? A lot of the time, I'm just smart enough to be unhappy. Also, Jesus . . . I'm not as extraordinary-looking or as young as you are, so we're beyond even."

And though it might have sounded reasonable from a certain angle, who could access this angle without undue exertion? Still, they coasted along anyway. Suzanne and Thor. Thor and Honey. Honey and Suzanne.

Woden's wife, Frigg.

What finally made it unbearable was mixing Thor in with her friends. Or trying to. And just as she had feared, it was a horror. Though they were very nice about him—being genuinely thrilled to see her with anyone at all—even this boy—in the end, she couldn't live with what she assumed they were thinking. As Lucy told her, "I know there's a dumb blond joke that covers this and I can't wait for you to live it so I can see what it is."

Planting her fears of how she looked with Thor in her friends' eyes and then watering them with her embarrassment, she'd watch them grow. She just knew she looked ridiculous. A middle-aged woman with a far-too-young man from the old country. Norma Desmond and William Holden. "If the lady is buying sir, I'd get the vicuña." Because oh, Lord, yes, that, too. She had bought him clothes as well as books. Something to wear while not reading.

The last straw came at a party. She was talking to Dani Campbell, Hollywood's first lesbian of cinema, while her pretty girlfriend stood to one side chatting up Thor.

"What does he do for you?" Dani asked her with some interest, indicating Thor with a slight incline of her blond head. Suzanne flushed in embarrassment, and for the smallest of seconds, was at a loss for something to say. Then, with eyebrows raised and an expression every inch the picture of nonchalance, she sailed herself onto a yacht in a Noël Coward play and replied, "Probably a lot of the same things your girlfriend does for you."

Dani looked surprised, then impressed. She raised her glass to Suzanne. "Good for you," she said. "I didn't know you went for the gay pinup type."

Suzanne groaned and hung her head, believing and fearing the worst: This was what everyone had been thinking about her. Thinking and laughing behind her old, foolish, cradle-robbing back.

"Oh, God, don't say that . . . you make me sound like . . . I don't know . . ."

"Cher?" Dani offered brightly.

Suzanne closed her eyes, shutting out that grim possibility, wishing she were far, far away where people's opinions couldn't reach her—a choice piece of real estate.

And that was it. Suzanne could barely look at Thor again without thinking of Peter Allen or Barry Manilow. No, it wouldn't do. She couldn't keep him. She had to send him back to the boy pool. Exchange him for someone more appropriate, more sedate and mature, with a paunch and a prescription for Viagra. And though Honey would miss her Super Superman—Suzanne elided over this understatement quickly—and Suzanne would no longer be able to indirectly irritate Leland with Honey's tales of Thor the Magnificent, it had to be done, and soon. But as to when . . . well, not just yet, and when it came to how, oh, God, she hadn't the vaguest notion.

Suzanne had always been loath to deliver blows. Oh, Thor would get over it; there was no question about that. He was young, and older women everywhere would like nothing better than to be rescued from the jaws of unwanted chastity by this gallant Galahad. Take this knight home and keep him for their own. It was unfair to keep his services off the market for much longer.

So, after long and fraught consideration, and waiting daily for Lucrezia's delayed arrival and assistance, Suzanne drew herself up decisively and marched into the next room, where Thor and Honey were watching the Disney Channel, her little legs tangled up with his bigger ones, her left hand gripping the sleeve of his tight white T-shirt. Neither seemed to notice her there in the doorway, gazing in despair as they cheered the TV screen.

"*Get him,* you big stupid head butt!" shouted Thor in his emphatic, funny English, his clear eyes fixed on the colorful characters in the cartoon.

"Yeah, you weenie! Hurry!" Honey added, grabbing as much of his upper arm as she could with her little hand. "Go, go, *go!*" she yelled at the screen, bouncing up and down as the little blue dog ran, his tongue hanging out and dragging on the ground underneath him. Perilously close to being scooped up by the snarling, red-faced dogcatcher following closely at his frisky puppy heels.

Putting her hands over her face, Suzanne turned and walked back into the hallway unnoticed. "Oh, God, what have I done?" she moaned to herself weakly.

And, walking briskly past the guest bathroom, she found herself in her small red den. Sitting in an overstuffed chair, she dialed her friend Craig Westerly. Craig was smart; Suzanne knew that if anyone could craft her an exit from this situation, it was him.

Suzanne and Craig had been friends for a long time. He was tall—very tall—frequently prompting him to remind Suzanne that he had "thoughts bigger than her." With high cheekbones, dark alert eyes, and a smile one could easily refer to as dashing, he was an undeniable DNA jackpot.

But the odd thing about Craig's 1000-watt appearance was that he somehow made all of it beside the point. Moments after you were working on dismissing him as just another pretty face, you found yourself being dragged off to a far more unusual conclusion. This was a funny guy whose looks were lost on him. How do you lose a thing like that so finally and so long ago? How did Craig end up the geeky psychic soul mate of Woody Allen or Philip Seymour Hoffman, with the personality of someone accustomed to inventing software or winning science fairs, not getting the girl?

Years before, Suzanne had dimly realized that Craig undermined a lot of his appearance by his unending snarky asides, seeing eventually that his relentless jesting had the quality of entreaty—imploring you to forgive his appearance—or forgo it anyway; leap over the decorative wall to the silly meat of him, the kooky creamy center of his invention hiding behind the happy accident of his genetic windfall.

Suzanne knew something about this proclivity herself, since she housed—or at least rented space to—the spirit of "Betty the Fat Girl," the gum-snapping, wisecracking, always-single sidekick to the blond likes of Renée Zellweger or Gwyneth Paltrow.

Suzanne and Craig: the unattractive good-looking pretty people, determined to make people like them, whether they wanted to or not. God, how she hoped he was home and had a spare month to fix her whole life. She exhaled with relief when he answered on the third ring. Speaking low into the phone and always looking over her shoulder, lest Disney's magic should cease working its goofy charm and one of her innocents should enter, Suzanne pleaded, "I have a giant favor to ask of you. Really big."

"Yeah, what is it? How may I be of service in some way that doesn't involve effort? Hmm? Tell your Auntie Craigie."

She put her hand over her eyes in shame and desperation. "Is there any way I could get you to break up with Thor for me?"

She waited impatiently for Craig to stop laughing. "I'm serious! I can't do it; I can't! I don't know how. But more than that . . . I really don't want to, okay?"

"Okay . . . calm down, honey . . . we'll think of something. This doesn't have to be that big of a deal. You will simply have to do as I tell you for the rest of your life. Even if it requires dangerous nudity."

Suzanne closed her eyes and hazarded a sigh of hopeful relief. "I swear I'll do anything you want, okay? Any favor *ever*. I'll set fire to your ego; I'll burn down the memories of your prom and Lisa Fine who didn't blow you that time when it was really important—I'll even fly you back from New York . . ."

"Okay, buddy, I get it. Just . . . stop talking in that pathetic tone and don't worry about it. I'll get it done." Suzanne sat up very straight now, alerted to every possibility, trying to anticipate anything that could happen in this situation now perhaps able to spin the wheel and turn out right.

"But be nice, okay?"

He laughed.

"Anything else? You want fries with that?"

She smiled ruefully, looking down wearily at the hands that rested in her lap like beached fish.

"Just the check."

Craig was used to getting his friend out of jams. She was his little jelly's last jam except they were never last jams: they were just one more in a long line of bad judgment calls—more drugs, more bad relationships—and Craig was always there because, well, a lot of times it was hard to remember. It wasn't as if they'd grown up together. From what he could glean (he loved gleaning and did it often), she hadn't grown up with much of anyone. They hadn't shared cafeterias, camps, proms, pimples, playgrounds, playdates, recess, or preschool. But he was her someone when she had no one. And she needed her someone now. Craig sighed, thought for a moment, and picked up the phone.

Of course Suzanne could never bring herself to ask Craig how he did it; she couldn't bear to. Making her cowardice complete. Not only making Craig get rid of Thor for her, but worse: explaining his disappearance to Honey. In this, she was perhaps most cowardly and as a result, most ashamed.

"He had to go back to Serbia, Baby," she held Honey on her lap, carefully sweeping her golden hair from her shoulders and onto her back.

"But why didn't he say good-bye to me?" a bewildered Honey asked in a high, hurt voice, a voice signaling to Suzanne that she was going to Mother Hell.

No, it was for absolute certain she was eternally damned now; damned for toying with the hearts of these two pure, trusting children. Redemption was completely out of the question, though that more than likely had been assured long ago. But now not only did she deserve whatever evil befell her in the future, she looked forward to it as her lunatic karmic penance necessary to settle black scores of this size.

She held Honey tightly to her, whispering.

"He tried to, baby, but you were sleeping. And he had to go back suddenly 'cause his grandpa was sick, so he told me to tell you he'd see you really soon and he'd miss you and . . ."

Honey struggled in her mother's arms, at the same time trying to hold back the rush of coming tears. It never occurred to Honey that she would lose this large, fun-loving boy-man. Honey wasn't in the habit of losing anyone and now, the first time in her life, someone was falling out of her orbit.

"Mommy, I can't breathe," she asserted in a thin voice, pulling a little away from her, increasing Suzanne's growing assurance she'd done her child irreparable harm. She vowed to set aside a fund for Honey's therapy, therapy she'd need from all the traumatic experiences while in her mother's care. Hell, she should probably have started that fund long ago—started saving while Honey was in utero, so when she was up shit creek, Suzanne would have a paddle fund already accruing—enough to afford three of the fucking things.

Suzanne took Honey by her shoulders and looked directly into her daughter's sweet, distressed face.

"But guess what! He got you a good-bye present!" Suzanne smiled hopefully. Was there no end to her evil? Apparently not. "You wait here while I go get it!"

"Is it alive?" Honey asked hopefully, still sniffling slightly as Suzanne trotted down the hall.

"Baby, you have four dogs, two birds, a guinea pig, and a fat fish you barely pay attention to," Suzanne shouted back to Honey over her shoulder, straightening the bow on the package she'd retrieved from under her bed. "So no, it's not living. Do you still want it or should I give it to the kids at the homeless shelter?"

Suzanne hesitated briefly for her daughter's expected reply.

"I want it! I want it!" shrieked the little girl excitedly.

Suzanne handed Honey a long, wrapped box and watched with

anxious anticipation as her excited child tore the wrapping from the treasure concealed beneath.

"What is it?" Honey's soft brown eyes were fixed on her prize and glowing.

"What does it look like, baby?" Suzanne reached out, caressing the smooth curve of Honey's freshly happy face.

And helping her daughter put the batteries in her new robot—the one that shot darts that were supposed to stick to things—Suzanne promised herself that she would never again lie to her daughter. From here on out she would be the best mother possible. She would rise early and fix her breakfast and drive her to school and buy an alarm clock she could master and learn how to sit on the floor and play games with Honey like she liked. A whole new Suzanne. Mother Earthlink. Yes, starting tomorrow she'd throw herself into this like . . . like . . . someone hurling herself over the side of a cliff and hoping to hit the ground as someone else. Someone dependable and domestic, and yes, even normal. And depending on who you looked at, someone who felt like others seemed. Tomorrow.

THE NEW REASONABLE

Suzanne suddenly realized that what she should be doing and actually *could* be doing very well was cooking for Honey. Sure, on the surface it seemed like an unlikely combination—her and anything practical or potentially flammable, a pastime where she might burn herself, poison others, or even create explosions on a grand scale. Still, she recalled that the director Charlotte Migler, a notoriously good cook, had once said to her, "Oh, please, if you can read, you can cook." Suzanne hadn't thought much of the remark at the time, only that she wanted to tell Charlotte, "Well, my mother reads the *National Enquirer*—what kind of cook do you think that makes her?"

But Suzanne could read—and not just the *Enquirer*, which she devoured in a darkened room like a thief, away from prying eyes, and would deny with a sniff of contempt to anyone with the nerve to ask—she could read almost anything. She'd always been a most marvelous reader! Ask anyone! Why, books were her first drug! So why not read cookbooks? And while she was about it, why not try some of those recipes? The best thing about her new hobby was that no one would expect her to do it. It would be completely out of character and therefore inclined to shock as she came barreling out at people from left field crying, "Soup's on, everyone! Dinner!" Why hadn't she thought of it before? She'd whip up the unexpected, make a feast fit for a king for her little princess. And wasn't the quickest way to a man's heart through his stomach?

She would show them all. She would make things not even the most advanced chefs would hazard. Move over, Betty Crocker! Nigella Lawson, step aside! She'd soon have tables crammed with delicious, intricate dishes of every description, and everyone would wonder, how did she make that sweet potato casserole, that delectable risotto, and have you ever tasted such a scrumptious apple-pecan pie?

The first problem was that the food never seemed to be ready until well past Honey's bedtime.

"But Mommy, I'm tiiiiiired," she'd lament, her woeful eyes blinking toward sleep as the clock ticked closer to midnight.

"But it's almost ready, nickelback!" Suzanne promised, squeezing her arm. "And it's your favorite . . . banana bread—no nuts!"

Honey would yawn an enormous yawn. "Please, Mommy, can't I have it for breakfast?"

Suzanne, wielding a wooden spoon and covered in powdered sugar, laughed in spite of herself.

"Yes, sea biscuit, I'll put it in your lunch."

The bigger problem was that it turned out that Honey didn't *like* sweet potato casserole or apple-pecan pie or quiche Lorraine or spinach soufflé. She wanted the plain, ordinary things that didn't show off Suzanne's immense new talent.

"Why can't you just make macaroni and cheese" Honey would wonder. "Or pizza? Pizza's better than that yucky soufflé."

Suzanne sighed. "But, buttons, you had pizza at Emily's for lunch. I'll tell you what! Why don't I make you some potato pancakes! How'd that be! With homemade applesauce and—" But Honey's nose wrinkled and she burst out, "I don't *like* those things, Mommy. I'm sorry. Couldn't I have a PB&J instead?"

Suzanne stood dejected, wooden spoon in hand, an overbred terrier headed for the Westminster dog show only to find herself at the pound instead.

• • •

The evening was mild and a breeze stirred the trees in Suzanne's yard A bright patch of cacti bloomed in unabashed orange, and the scent of night-blooming jasmine filled the walkway from its vines. Doris was in the living room with Honey, trying to teach her reluctant granddaughter how to jitterbug.

". . . Now that's when the man would take hold of your other hand and spin it out with your hand out like this. But you'd be wearing a wonderful dress with a puffy skirt that would twirl up like that. See! Ta da!!"

The front gate sounded and, picking up her phone, Suzanne dialed the magic code numbers that admitted Lucy into her private world, her banishment not so near the sea. A minute later, the screen door squeaked, then slammed open and a red-faced Lucy waddled in, breathing hard and heavy. Doris was clearly displeased about the interruption Lucy posed to herself and her granddaughter's time. But, not being someone prone to confrontation or impoliteness of any kind—especially to a fellow blond actress—she simply smiled at Lucy mildly and stood, her hand outstretched.

"Hello, dear, I don't know if you remember me? I'm Doris Mann—Suzanne's mother?"

Lucy gazed at Doris, leaning against the door frame, with an expression that was difficult to read. Finally, she said, "Yes, we've only met about three thousand times, but how've you been?"

The two women's eyes lit up with fires both amused and territorial.

Doris pursed her lips before stretching them into a smile. "Well, you never know, sometimes pregnant people . . . ," but Honey had gone to Lucy, who bent down as best she could to swoop her into her strong, water-retentive arms.

"And how's the most beautiful little goddaughter in the world tonight? Hmmm?" Honey squirmed and laughed, tangled in Lucy's coiffed blond hairstyle.

"When do the babies come?" Honey asked.

"Soon," Lucy shook her head, "but not soon enough, Baby. Not soon enough." She looked around. "Now, where's your crazy momma?"

Doris, now seated on a leather couch, cleared her throat delicately and shifted to one side. "Suzanne is in the kitchen . . . *cooking*," but it came out sounding more like "Suzanne's in the kitchen . . . *shaving her head.*" Doris always acted as if, in cooking, Suzanne had betrayed everything the family stood for and believed in.

Lucy let Honey go, feigning alarm. "Oh, my *God,* why didn't you tell me? Well. I better get in there and do something. Jesus. I hope it's not—I mean, don't tell me it's—we're not talking *gourmet* cooking, are we? 'Cause then, well . . . that's pretty serious. Honey, get me a phone—we're gonna have to call dine-one-one."

Suzanne's mouth tightened in annoyance as she eavesdropped from the kitchen. Had Doris ever given Suzanne jitterbug lessons? Not on your life. Had she wanted them or in any way missed them? Absolutely not. But that wasn't the point. The point was—the point was—what was it? Well, it was something to do with the fact that Suzanne would've at least liked the *option* of having the jitterbug lessons, but did her mother have *time* then? No! And the only reason she got to have time now was because Suzanne was doing all this fucking cooking! Oh sure, don't mind me, I'm just Hazel the maid back here cooking while all of you are out there enjoying yourselves. If she heard one more condescending word from Doris about her cooking, she was going to shove her whisk right up Doris's—

Okay, so maybe her new reasonable wasn't going so great—but at least she'd tried. She'd given the intangible and inexplicable a run for their money. Maybe everyone was right. Maybe she should just stick to her strengths, which really came down to talking a lot about a weird assortment of things including old movies, composers' lives, and eighteenth-century jewelry. If she'd stuck to those instead of branching out into domesticity, maybe she'd never have gotten into this mess.

She also knew a lot about early Norway.

Suzanne wiped her hands on a dishcloth and sighed. "Come on,

Honey, time to get ready for bed." Honey kissed Doris and Lucy good-night and headed down the hall.

Suzanne parked her Diet Coke on Lucy's swollen belly. "I'm just going to put Honey down for the night." Rubbing her daughter's back, she sang her some of her favorites: selections from *Porgy and Bess, West Side Story,* and *The Sound of Music.*

"I loves you, Porgy, don't let him take me, don't let him handle me with his hot hands."

"What a weird thing to say," she said to Lucy after she'd turned on Honey's nightlight, kissed the top of her head one last time, and tip-toed out. "Putting your kid down. Like I'm insulting her: 'You idiot! Can't you even go to sleep?' "

"How about how weird that you're singing her that song," Lucy suggested dryly, taking a sip of her iced tea.

But putting Honey down was just what she did: a child's last hu-miliation of the day. Honey was leaving in the morning with Leland for two weeks to visit her grandparents, great-grandparents, favorite cousin, and others in Jackson, Mississippi—where Leland's family hailed from. Honey loved visiting this homey, slowed-down world of her extended family. Loved this place composed of sounds and hues all its own: a place of unlocked doors and potluck dinners and drive-ins. The reassuring feel of the relative reclined in the La-Z-Boy chair, doz-ing or watching TV till the early call of "Supper's on!"

Suzanne's grandparents had come from such a place, too, a similar world boasting flags and America. LOVE IT OR LEAVE IT! signs just a few hours' drive from Leland's jumping-off place. But show business had blunted her mother's accent away, even some of her mother's mother's. It had taken the small town out of both women—or buried it anyway under a flashy blaze of Hollywood tinsel. Hollywood had taken all that remained of Suzanne's extended family, leaving only her parents and brother and a father who generally went missing under the covers of some woman. Oh, she had cousins and even a few scattered aunts and uncles, but most lived in far-flung states and Suzanne had never really known or met them—perhaps they were intimidated by the Hollywood "thing" or felt uninvited and snubbed. Perhaps all three. The end result was that Leland supplied the mother lode of family, while Suzanne contributed the celebrity and glitz. It wasn't surprising which Honey drew more nourishment from, regardless of how many impressions Doris could perform or how many tap dancing lessons she could provide her only grandchild.

That night, Suzanne dreamt that she'd been skiing with Honey and was looking forward to speeding with her daughter down the slopes that one final time. But Honey didn't want to ski anymore. Instead, she'd preferred to take the chair lift or tram. "Please, baby," Suzanne pleaded to her daughter on the snowy mountaintop. "Just one last run," she'd begged. *"Please . . . I promise! That'll be the end of it."* But her little girl was adamant, so in the end, Suzanne had reluctantly taken the chair lift down, down, down, slowly, slowly, slowly, longingly looking back up at all the smooth perfect runs she would now be denied.

Oh, she thought when she remembered the dream the next morning.

Duh. That's it.

One last run.

A drug run. And her daughter adamant in wanting her mother not to go.

Maybe this explained why Suzanne hadn't gone back on all her medications now that Lucrezia was no longer required for the Thor situation. Why not push her back into her cage with a few well-placed pills taken each day as prescribed? Well, for one thing, because Suzanne had forgotten how good it felt to feel she could do almost anything. She knew that wasn't precisely true—who gave a shit—but it felt true and that was the main thing. And yeah, feelings weren't facts, but how fun were facts when the facts didn't proclaim you king? And what an ingenious party trick: *don't* take drugs and get high.

And besides, she'd never taken her bipolar diagnosis that seriously. She really just considered it some quirky tendency she had—no more true or of more consequence than being a Virgo or a baby boomer or a certain nationality. It was never an overriding issue she needed to address with undue urgency. It was No Big Deal. She couldn't touch it or see it, and even when she felt it, it always went away eventually. Why dwell on it? Better to laugh it off and make a joke of it. Manic depression—what did it mean but "moody"? And other than when it came in handy as an excuse for drug use or an amusing anecdote at dinner, it was just one of the many things about her—no more, no less.

And one thing it definitely *wasn't* was a mental illness. No fucking way. Nothing so threatening or dire as that, so forget it. Mentally ill people couldn't hold jobs—and they certainly weren't successful at anything. Those afflicted with mental illness were institutionalized or lived in group homes, overly medicated and under supervision, while Suzanne lived behind gates in a house outfitted with a pool and a two-bedroom guesthouse. She had accomplished friends and a good job. Did *that* sound like the life of a mentally ill person? Don't be hilarious. If it was, then *vive la maladie de votre tête,* or however they'd say it.

The first psychiatrist she'd finally gone to told her she might be something called "hypomanic," which he said was a more moderate type of manic depression—breezy bipolar two instead of the more challenging bipolar one. It sounded like a mood you'd shoot in your arm—or nothing. It sounded like nothing. Suzanne had thought the man ridiculous and regarded him with scorn. All doctors want to do is diagnose you, she thought; place you in a category with a label or a handy tag. Suzanne knew if she allowed herself to fall into that category, there was a chance that she'd never get up again, sentenced to live out her life as some psycho specimen. You put things into categories when none of the finer, more respectable places will have them. She decided ultimately to let him think what he wanted, she would do her best to forget about it.

Of course, after her inadvertent overdose a few years later, the subject returned with a vengeance or two. But Suzanne knew the more urgent thing at that point was treating her alcoholism. And to the extent that she had taken painkillers or hallucinogens alcoholically, she fit that definition completely. *That's* what was the matter. Why complicate it with other issues? She had more than enough on her plate dealing with her substance abuse issues; she didn't need any other distractions threatening to keep her from getting this runaway habit under control.

But after a year of being sober, Suzanne began to notice she was frequently the source of annoying outbursts—outbursts that seemed only to increase over time, plaguing her at unpredictable intervals, doing their unlevel best to burn her down to the ground. Whether it was tears that never seemed to subside, or a kind of wild extreme frustration, she felt herself too small a vessel to harbor these storms. After experiencing a level of impatience outsizing any appropriate relationship to the alleged inciting incident, she'd blunder away bewildered, unable to explain herself away. Occasionally, she was even overcome by a rage she didn't recognize being the author of. These things troubled her enough that she considered a return to the doctors who'd given her those annoying labels in the past. Maybe now she'd have to listen a little differently to what it was they said.

Maybe.

But in addition to these unmanageable upsets that overcame her, she'd been having those glorious times as well—times too wonderful to stop for sustenance or sleep, too glorious to blaspheme with ordinary tangibles like words. Put things into words and there's no telling when you'll get them out again. Give a feeling a name? How? You don't have feelings, they have you. Too enormous to deny or fail to be swept up into, these feelings fueled her to people, places, and things filling to spilling with an effervescence too thrilling to contain. Unable to stay in one place, to one topic, or on any person for very long. If this was what it was to be bipolar, then the bank error was in her favor. Let the festivities begin! Far from experiencing it as a handicap, it felt like an advantage: giving her the edge. Mental illness? Why, she couldn't remember feeling so well. If this was sick, then it was from suffering a series of lesser-evolved ordinary bores trooping through her otherwise spectacular day.

But when Lucrezia inevitably abandoned her, leaving the beast that could not be named in its wake—*this* she recognized as a kind of sickness, an evil infecting her every cell. *This* dark beast covered her in misery and drained the light from her universe. The dark creeping evil—the mood that could not be named, for to her that would be an act of summoning—a calling forth of the creature from its hellish lair.

When not stuck in this landscape, she barely remembered having been there. Why should she ponder something so morbid and grim? When she somehow awakened one awful anxious day to find herself within its dark and guarded borders, she knew it . . . it was as though she'd never left. How could she have forgotten, and more important, would she ever . . . no, she'd never be able to escape its fierce determined grasp again.

And it was this she took back to the doctor, dragging with her the dead weight of the corpse of all the joy that had died inside her. And pointing at this demon now residing in her, she implored the doctor to wave his curing hand and banish it, posthaste. Restore her to her pleasure pole.

First she'd gone to Dr. Mulligan, who'd put her on the lithium that had made her fat and caused her skin to break out of its blemish-free jail, so even if she felt better, she looked like shit and where was the improvement there? So after a few ridiculous months of enduring that, she'd discontinued it, making sure she was far away from these prying medical eyes, so far she'd seen fit to leave the country. She'd taken a dumb job in Australia, and while there stopped the pesky salt entirely, ultimately sending her higher than she'd ever been, which culminated in a chaotic trip through China—it seemed so close on the globe, just inches away—trailed by her ever-patient brother recording on video her giddy ascent and ultimate descent in Shanghai. After that, she'd seen a Dr. Waterstone, who treated her with assorted anti-depressants and a new mood stabilizer. When that didn't work, she was referred to Dr. Wexler, followed by Dr. Korshack, Dr. Lim, and Dr. Goldstein, each one armed with a different regime of medicines designed to bring her highs and lows to a well-managed, level playing field.

Suzanne thought it hilarious that there was an illness whose symptoms were spending sprees, substance abuse, and sexual promiscuity. These didn't sound like symptoms at all—just a typical weekend in Vegas. Symptoms were things like runny noses, sore throats, and fever. Overconfidence and quick thinking weren't symptoms— they were goals. The personality traits of someone who was fun to be with and successful in her chosen profession—never things to medicate away, reducing one to an ordinary member of the human egg-in-spoon race.

The traits the doctors diagnosed and sought to medicate were some of her favorite aspects of herself. She relied on them to do her not so dirty work. This heady stuff was what made her special and set her apart from the rest. An assurance of finer times, romantic interludes, lickety-split wit and out-of-this-world-class adventures. Medicate it? Better to get in league with it, in line for it, in bed with it, send it a thank-you note and enjoy it while it lasts; save your medicine for someone who has something bad—like pneumonia. The only thing to give this was the benefit of the doubt and wide berth.

Once she'd invited Lucrezia to the ball, nothing could keep that evil aristocrat from dancing now that her pulse had quickened. So had everything else and she wanted more and more and the way to that was less and less meds. Suzanne had given regularity and calmness a fair run. The incumbent Republicans had had their share of no fun— now it was time to give the low-med Democrats a shot at running the great, let's-mate Suzanne nation.

TWENTY-FIRST-CENTURY
COINCIDENCE

Suzanne had been out all day shopping for two reasons. The main one being that Craig was coming to town for a few weeks to oversee the production of *Never You Mind,* an action adventure film about sleep—or at least that's how Craig described it. The other reason was because stores existed with things in them to buy and Lucrezia wanted to buy them. She needed something to wear for the dinner party she was going to tonight, and little gag gifts to hide all over Craig's room for him to find—it would take him *days* if she was lucky—mints under his pillow, a laxative called Perdiem next to his bed, Spanish fly in the refrigerator, maximum-size condoms everywhere, porno magazines under his sheets (preferably ones starring horses and lactating women and rubber), an inflatable female dwarf with fully functional orifices. Everything to make her houseguest feel welcome.

The dinner party outfit was a little more challenging. Not that she didn't have plenty of nice black outfits, but Lucrezia wanted something new—something that made a statement, preferably a monologue stretching into two-thousand two two two. Clothing that opened its mouth and didn't close it till everyone unzipped you with their bedroom eyes. So Suzanne bought something she could ill afford and with several songs in her swelling heart, she sped home to prepare for the marvelous day ahead.

She could never get over that Craig had a studio job with a title. Not a title like "Duke" or "Czar," but "Vice President in Charge of Production." His title sounded as though he'd been elected to office: "Vice President Westerly." Did this mean that he would become president of the great land of production if the reigning president died? Well, in a way, yes. Only death in this case meant being buried somewhere in one of the vast cemeteries of "Independent Production" or "Overall Deal." And then the king and queen of the studio would survey the waiting retinue and put the best available candidate on the throne. It was a hearty mix of business and autocracy Suzanne had once heard described as "Reel Royalty." Her fantasy was that someone would shout: "Off with their studio heads!" and these disloyal subjects, having fallen out of favor, would be exiled to distant lands populated with bad agents, wrong numbers, and insufficient financing.

Suzanne had met Craig during that annoying period in her life when people began being younger than she in droves—whatever droves were—and right before she could no longer wear anything sleeveless, as it would risk exposing unmentionable upper-arm cellulite.

She'd been invited to join a sort of elite website where people from all over the overposting planet gathered to exhange amusing commentary. A comedy Vatican where a clutch of clownish cardinals would frantically e-compete daily to see who would emerge as the reigning pope.

Suzanne was skeptical. *The Round Table* sounded like an electronic ratfuck, another life-wasting opportunity to her, and she already had enough of those. What with all the tributes she participated in and *LIFETIME/A&E Biographies* she had to do when they were covering the life of one of her old to just aging friends, coupled with lunches with agents or lawyers or producers she either wanted to or was working with, she barely had time to waste her life in the ways she actually preferred to: i.e., watching hours of *Court TV, Forensic Files,* and *American Justice.* She adored the grim solace of Bill Kurtis recounting the tale of some gruesome crime and how investigators had gotten to the bottom of it, everything neat and final, with liberty and justice for all, even if it took a really long time and lots of footage to prove it.

But ultimately, she'd decided to check out *The Round Table,* if only in the name of her ongoing search for all members of the tribe of smart and funny. But soon enough she'd found herself planted in front of her computer for hours, struggling to compose witty, people-pleasing responses for people that she, for the most part, didn't even know. She'd finally slithered away, but not before having her electronic eye caught by someone who went by the name "Big Head," or "Lars St. Fuck You"—a member she knew she'd love forever the day he'd posted: "Yes, I have a good head on my shoulders, which, by the way, means I have no neck."

One day Suzanne had posted on *The Round Table* that her mother (who regularly dreamt in financial advice for her two children) had been having a series of dreams relating to different ways her daughter could get tax breaks by changing business managers. Suzanne had speculated that instead of these dreams being prophetic in nature as her mother had always assumed, she had begun to suspect that they in fact might be more sexual in nature, "Stemming from my mother's long-standing fantasy of blowing all my money." Craig had Instant Messaged her to meet him behind the buddies' list, "To share a grope and a smoke," where it turned out that "The Mother Westerly" also had elaborate nightly visions concerning both his personal and professional life and had likewise long been urging him to follow the guidance contained in these nocturnal reveries. He told her that recently he'd even gone into couples therapy with her.

Ever after that, they were friends, comrades with their respective crazy parents who also worked their own corners in "The Business of Show," Craig behind the scenes and Suzanne both in that weird world but somehow not of it, each still finding time to try to one-up the other on whose life was the more insane. More often than not, she won, but he would hilariously light up the sky trying.

When she'd found out he was a studio executive, she couldn't believe it. That was what Leland did—but Leland seemed more suited to that job, whereas Craig, well . . . Craig seemed like someone suited to anything but regular hours, end-of-year bonuses, an assistant, a desk, and his own parking space. He had her insatiable appetite for the absurd and tendency toward gallows humor, though his had been honed in New Rochelle and hers in West Los Angeles. Still, they seemed to have arrived at the same destination of one-liners and bad relationships almost simultaneously, without breaking a sweat and barely out of breath.

The only major problem with her friendship with Craig was that though most studio executives lived in Los Angeles, Craig obstinately resided in New York, overseeing Miramax's East Coast offices.

"How could you do this to me?" she constantly complained. "Why can't you be a normal lame suit and live here next to me?"

"You take my breath away, you know that?" he'd responded on one of their endless phone calls. "And now I want it back."

"That's *my* line," Suzanne shot back, "which I'll happily give to you if you'll behave yourself and move here."

And now he'd done just that, for a few weeks anyway. Suzanne moved Craig into the far room of her guesthouse, happily anticipating his discovery of each of the treasures she'd buried there.

That night she drove out to a dinner party at the immense home of Ted DeBecker, the president of one of the networks. Ted always invited someone or other who worked on his network, a writer or producer or even an actor. Along with the dates or spouses and assorted others, he had the occasional surprise entertainer—one time he'd had a psychic, another time the Cirque du Soleil performed in his backyard, another time Rufus Wainwright played and sang. He and his wife Emily always served good food and, when not providing live entertainment, screened a movie, so Suzanne could rarely resist an invitation.

The DeBecker house sat atop rolling lawns, amidst gardens with views of the smoggy city spread beneath the large bay windows of the immense living room. A grand Mediterranean home, decorated discreetly with overstuffed furniture and French country antiques. The house always looked freshly buffed to Suzanne, as though scrubbed and polished in preparation for an imminent presidential visit or photo shoot for *Architectural Digest*.

A young houseman greeted Suzanne at the door. She didn't know what his title was; what do you call a fresh-faced Ivy League import dressed in khaki pants and a work shirt who opens doors and offers to take your coat? The first time Suzanne came to dinner, she'd mistaken him for another guest or family friend—hardly for hired help. But when he offered to get her a drink as he ushered her in to the living room, she adjusted her initial impression. Now she realized it was the new version of young mogul help—the "unhelp" as Suzanne preferred to think of them—"Help-Lite: Employees with Just One Calorie" and no added subservience. We were all equal now, no formalities. Powerful people could hire others to help them stay as equal as they wanted to be, helping them to keep their equilibrium and show people to their seats.

Early in the evening, she'd held the party hostage by dominating the conversation with stories and information she felt utterly unable to keep to herself.

"The other day, someone told me one of those things you could only hear in L.A. though I may have actually been somewhere else at the time—anyway, this chick said, 'If you want to know how you think of your life'—something like that—anyway, she said 'Look at the pictures on your bedroom wall.' This wasn't great news for me 'cause on my bedroom wall, all I have are paintings of dwarf-throwing contests, freakish-looking toddlers—little boys dressed as girls—and a few cats wearing dresses. So if that's what I think of my life—what does that *mean*?" Without waiting for an answer from the circle of faces turning toward her, she continued. "Of course, I was also told that having a red wallet insures that you make a lot of money. Now even *I* know how stupid that sounded but I go ahead and buy a red wallet just in case. Anyway, could someone please *not* explain what's the matter with me? 'Cause if you told me I might have to do something about it." She stopped and took a much-needed breath. "Anyway, it's someone else's turn. Your witness."

She was seated to Ted's left at the head of the table while Emily commandeered the opposite end. On her other side was a young man who produced an extremely successful reality show.

"Like *Animal House,* which was really my initial inspiration. I love Tim Matheson in that . . . I think he's a god," the young producer said expressively, leaning into Suzanne confidentially. "Anyway, we meant for it to be like a frat house or a crazy dorm or something—you know—which was how my partner and I pitched it to Ted," he finished with a flourish and gazed at her triumphantly. "And *voilà!* History was made!" He took a sip of his wine, then placed the glass back on the linen coaster in front of him. "Actually, ratings were made, is more like it. Advertisers were happy, so . . . well, anyway . . ." Putting his hand out he said, "By the way, I'm Harvey Metzker."

She shook his hand. "Suzanne Vale."

He tilted his head to one side. "I know. I'm a big fan of your talk show. Especially your interview with your mother, who I'm obsessed with. When I was a teenager, I wanted to be her, which was a little tough on my father. My mother understood perfectly."

Not particularly enthused by this topic, Suzanne leaned in close to Harvey, presenting a diversion.

"Not to change the subject, but I have to tell you a secret. If I don't I'll just burst and then you'll have to send your suit to the cleaners and your hair will be matted and in need of—"

"Please!" Harvey insisted, "Fire away! It just so happens I love secrets and *detest* bursting . . ." Harvey's eyes were twinkling. He leaned in even closer to her. "Proceed."

"Well, the thing is . . . I have a superpower," she whispered conspiratorially.

Harvey feigned amazement.

"No!" he gasped. "How exciting!" He folded his hands, gazing at her expectantly. "I'm all ears," he said, then added proudly, "Even my ass is an ear."

Suzanne leaned even further forward and continued in her stage whisper, "I turn people gay."

Harvey sat back in his chair as though shocked.

"No . . . ," he breathed; his eyes wide with wonder as he held one hand to his chest waiting for her to continue. She nodded gravely.

"Now, mind you, this is not a superpower that's called for a lot. But when it is . . ." she snapped her fingers above her head, "I'm there like a shot. Sometimes I just drive around when I'm bored, doing practice drive-by gay-turnings."

Harvey reached for his wine again, bringing it to his lips and sipping thoughtfully.

"You know, I believe I might've seen some of your work."

"Really?" Suzanne was now perhaps just a little concerned that she was in danger of losing control of her joke. "Ah, well then, I have a hunch I know which of my efforts you've seen." She looked at the table, moving a coaster round and round with her index finger, unable to take her dark eyes away.

"And seeing is actually what we did," Harvey said, chewing his salad. "I mean, we saw each other for a while. Plus, what with the hearing and the rest of it—I'd say it was a pretty well-rounded, square meal if you know what I mean."

"What a small, modern world it is, then," she remarked, now looking at him without really seeing him anymore. "Where else but in the tiny enclave of Hollywood, at the other side of the turn of the century, could a woman randomly sit next to a man who had dated her ex-husband?" And without waiting for a reply, she turned to the unsuspecting table, proclaiming in a loud voice, "Did you hear that, everybody? Harvey here went out with my ex-husband, Leland. Is that a coincidence or what?"

People regarded her with strained looks of varying intensity. At least that's how she perceived it.

"A twenty-first-century coincidence, that is," she added. "Swimming pools, movie stars."

There was the briefest of pauses, then Ted said, "I didn't know that. When did you and Leland get together?" but before Harvey could answer, Suzanne barreled in.

"Which one of us are you asking?"

A few people laughed.

"We were set up on a blind date," began Harvey. "So I thought I'd be adorable and take him to the Braille Institute on Ventura." He rolled his eyes. "Unfortunately, he didn't think it was very funny, and it went downhill from there."

Suzanne hit him on the shoulder.

"I've gone downhill with Leland also!" she said brightly. "Another coincidence! Which hill did you go down? One of the Beverly ones?"

"How long did you guys see each other?" interjected a minor TV star from the other end of the table with his mouth full.

"Jesus, I didn't expect this to be a group discussion," Harvey moaned, his head in his hands.

"But how long, anyway?" echoed Suzanne, looking at him with as cheerful an expression as she could muster.

Harvey frowned in concentration, drumming his fingers. "Hmmmm. I don't know . . . a few months, I guess. Anyway, at least until Christmas, when he went away on his yacht and I—" he suddenly stopped talking and looked around him. "And that's it. That's all I'm gonna tell you." He brushed his dark bangs back off his boyish face. "This is getting too much like one of those daytime talk shows."

Suzanne laughed, but her eyes remained unsmiling. "I'm sorry. We're going to have to break away for station identification."

"Aaaaaand, we're back," added Harvey.

"Uh-oh—I'm afraid we're going to have to break away again." Suzanne turned back to Ted on her right, desperately hoping he'd bail her out.

Mark Vogel, the writer/producer of the hit show that took place at a newspaper in Washington, arrived at the party just in time to pick at his dessert.

"Sorry, sorry, sorry, sorry—the dreaded last-minute changes to to-

morrow's shooting script." He shrugged helplessly. It was complicated to be him, but he would muddle through—just like a prima bal-
lerina might muddle through *Giselle*.

His handsome actor looks tucked behind thick glasses, highlight-
ing his oh-so-much-smarter-than-actor intellect, Mark gradually and
effortlessly wrested the party from Suzanne's semi-able custody and
into his own capable ink-stained hands.

"What have I missed?" he asked as he grabbed some biscotti and
took a seat beside the hostess on whose pleased proffered cheek he
planted a kiss. "Anything at all? Or can the party really begin now?"
Then, biting into a cookie, he looked around him, vaguely curious as
to who would have the nerve and talent to reply.

Suzanne eagerly leapt into the fray, as who could stop her? And
what was a fray? "As you no doubt guessed, we'd been talking about
you nonstop right up until you entered. Our host had just finished
taking us through your early days of not being nurtured enough, but
showing clear signs of true genius, and I think we were about to get
into your education when you came in." Suzanne watched him carefully as she said all this, in part eager that he saw how bright she was
but also hoping he wouldn't see that she wanted him to see that.
"There were a few toasts, one song, and several cried," she added
lightly, using her fork to move her salad around to further demon-
strate her cavalier attitude about almost everything, whether it be
food or men.

The writer regarded her with mild interest. "Excellent," he offered
with a slight incline of his head, nodding and chewing, "or as the
Knights of the Round Table were reputed to have said, 'Well met.'"
He then looked down the table to his host.

"Where have you been keeping this one, DeBecker—holding out
on me, are you?"

"You two don't know each other?" Ted marveled, eyebrows up as
far as they could rise. "I'm stunned." He gestured first at one, then the
other, "Mark Vogel, meet Suzanne Vale."

It was now Mark's turn to raise his eyebrows. "Ahhh, the actress
from the long-ago silly movies."

Suzanne scowled. "Retired, I'm afraid. Now I do yard work and a sometime talk show on the outskirts of cable—"

"All of cable is an outskirt," Mark reminded her dismissively with a wave of the hand, still chewing.

"That, of course, receives a hard *'duh'* classification," said Suzanne. "However, I must continue to make ends meet, since I can't seem to make them poultry."

Mark studied her silently, narrowing his eyes ever so slightly.

"Funny," he concluded finally, then indicated some French doors with a slight incline of his Phi Beta Kappa cute head. "Cigarette?"

Suzanne nodded and they both rose to retire to the outside veranda to indulge in their no-longer-PC-inside vice.

"Well, I guess that's the end of the rest of us, ladies and gentlemen," laughed Ted. "I don't think I've felt quite this superfluous since . . . well, really, my wedding."

"Not 'superfluous,' DeBecker," assured Mark, "super-to-*us*—right, everybody?"

The other guests murmured in agreement, or so Suzanne preferred to assume so she could concentrate more fully at the task at hand: making Mark love her with a love that was lasting, fixing her life forever by being the man she was certain didn't exist—the one who could step into her life and not be thrown by it, *and* magically make her both feel and seem respectable and witty. Also thin.

"I'm assuming that joke was beneath you," Suzanne said out of the side of her mouth as Mark lit her cigarette. "I mean, I found myself stepping over something resembling a half-assed remark, which I believe was yours."

Mark nodded silently as he lit his own cigarette. "Look, we got out of there, didn't we? Think of it as a through-line . . . as in, through the fucking door." Smoke issued from his mouth in a great, grateful cloud, fugitive late of his greedy dark lungs.

Perhaps it was because she was fairly fresh from her success with Dean Bradbury that she made to be so bold with Mark that night—or maybe it was due to the reduction in her hesitation-inducing meds.

She'd not only make Leland sorry he left her, she'd make him rue the day. He would rue it over and over, a rue awakening, taking up new residence at rue St. Regret.

Imagine Suzanne's shock and awe when, despite his legendary status as the new up-and-coming coke addict Bradbury-style woman-izer, Mark ever-so-not-politely rebuffed her not so subtle seduction.

The humiliation rang through her pulsing halls like cold hell.

So it was true then. She'd been neutralized by modern medicine. They'd taken the best of her away. At one time long ago, premedicine, she'd have been able to attract someone like Mark Vogel, no question. But they'd leached the color from her once-bright plumes—calmed the "Wa-hoo!!!" raging water that was once her and reduced her to anyone at all. Just another 'Once upon a time' pretty face. Now her scotch was turned to milk, or worse, soymilk. Her silk was cotton, her diamonds were cubic zirconias. All the magic was gone. The white rabbit was on the run. Now when she said, "Nothing up my sleeve," she really meant *nothing*.

C'mon, what was the harm of one last run? Really . . . what? Es-pecially if she promised to keep it a good distance from Honey. She just couldn't let herself get blown off, man after man. One more dance in the light, in the center ring where it's all happening. Fuck Mark Vogel—or not fuck—she'd show him and soon. Show them all and herself. She'd take this one last big ride on the Lucrezia high-roller run and then return a better woman for it, ready to all but sleep through the rest of her noble lump-of-dough-dull life.

BAD MATH

The next morning was the first day Suzanne completely stopped taking her medication. The medicine that fixed it so she could contain herself before starting to spill. But that day became two days, then three, and before she knew it, a week had passed—or, to be more precise, she had passed a week, sprinting quickly by it, through it, and never looking back.

Things refused to happen in order after that. Monday came after Thursday, night no longer followed day—or so it seemed to her. In this place, good times could get hopelessly jumbled up with bad times until they were just times—places she went where she happened to events. After a while only she happened, doing so at the quickest of clips. Events ran together like spilt colors down a steep hill, and she ran after them and was run over by them and everything was wonderful. Causing her to wonder, when these events came to a close, could she come, too? If she promised to be good-looking, promised to be good to go wherever one went to reclaim a sense that all was orderly and well?

Suzanne believed you could do anything you set your mind to—that even a lost mind or a mind on the loose could be found if you knew the right places to go looking. And once you'd found it you could set it free—perhaps even on the right track—why shouldn't you be able to? You would do things you couldn't do until you could do them again. This is what she figured. Figuring anything less, to this way of thinking, would be really bad math.

She began talking for eight hours a day on the phone.

"I'm a complex cell," she would virtually shout at people, the phone cord wrapped around her legs and one arm. "I'm a complex cell who needs other complex cells on which to feed. Once I've dined like that I'm able to cope with that simpler fare of less compelling creatures." She was arranging words again, words in rows with rhythms all her own, words where everything worked out right.

"Race you to the end of my personality!" she challenged her brother Thomas loudly on one of those marathon calls. "You won!" And then she was laughing, laughing like a person pregnant with happy, giggling for two.

"I hate to change the subject, but—," Thomas began.

"I'm way ahead of you," announced Suzanne emphatically. "In fact, I'm waiting for you over at the end of the sentence you're about to start and I don't want to be the one to have to break it to you, but it ends badly. You might wanna borrow a comma or an exclamation point. On account. Besides, you're practically family. I know you're good for it."

That night when Craig came home from work, Suzanne and Honey lay in wait for him in the bushes by the garage and when he turned off the motor on his rental Mustang and opened the door, Suzanne yelled "Now!" and he was hit full blast with water from the hose that Honey gleefully wielded. Suzanne stood behind her daughter at the faucet, doubled over with silent, breathless laughter, her eyes wet with tears. Craig looked at Honey and Suzanne with great dignity, then said calmly, "You missed a spot behind my ear." Honey looked at her mother for permission, then aimed the hose as best she could up at Craig's head. He made a mad grab for her and she dropped the hose and tried to scramble away, but Craig threw her over his shoulder. Then he retrieved the hose and turning it first on the little child, then on the bigger one, shouted "There! You like this? Huh? Isn't this fun? Oh, boy, we're having some fun now, aren't we?"

Honey struggled, drenched and delighted in Craig's enormous arms. "Nooooo! Put me dooown! Mommy, help!"

Suzanne ran over and grabbed Craig's leg. "Citizen's arrest! Citizen's arrest!" Anyone coming on the scene would have seen a large man—well over six feet—clad in an elegant suit and soaked to the skin, carrying a very wet, squealing six-year-old and fending off an also-drenched, fully-grown woman sinking her teeth into his calf.

Later that night, Craig had had to put the overstimulated little girl to bed himself and sing her to a much-needed slumber. Suzanne was unable to, as she couldn't very well inspire in others something that she couldn't currently experience herself—anything like calmness or rest and certainly not sleep. She was far too afraid of missing something, for things were happening everywhere! All over the civilized world and even those worlds oriented otherwise, things were cropping up with a regularity that boggled Suzanne's busy to sizzling mind.

When Craig crept out of Honey's darkened room, he found Suzanne on the kitchen floor dyeing Easter eggs for Honey's school lunch.

"Hi! Is she sleeping?" she asked cheerfully, looking up from a bowl of blue.

Craig studied her seriously for a moment. "Okay, I think now is the moment we talk about your medication."

Suzanne scowled. "I *knew* you were going to say something like that. Why can't you just be happy that Honey is finally having fun with me, huh? I mean, what's with the half-empty, half-full-of-shit thing?"

"I think it's great you're having fun with your kid, but let's just for one sec get back to the medication thing."

Suzanne was rummaging through the box of Easter egg dye. "Do you see a little wire thingy anywhere—you know, to dip the eggs with?"

Craig sighed. "I guess it doesn't bother you at all that it's nowhere *near* Easter."

Suzanne got on her haunches and leaned forward to pick something off the floor. "There it is!" She held the copper egg holder aloft, then looked at her frowning friend. "And for your information, *yes,* it does bother me that it's not nearer to Easter, because for one thing, I really wanted to get started on my Christmas shopping."

Suzanne slid to the floor, leaning her head back with her eyes closed, indescribably happy. Hugging her knees to her chest, she hummed with good feeling. The good that grew legs, running to better, until better gets . . . well, it couldn't get better than this, could it? Feeling as though any moment now, she would be pulled over by the cops of calm-down, regardless of whether she happened to be in the car or not. Either way, she was driving herself crazy, but the kind of crazy she couldn't wait to get to. Bliss beat at the back of her eyelids with both of its beautiful fists.

HIGH-FREQUENCY
FLOWER OF FEELING

Craig struggled to the surface of deep, sound sleep, opening his eyes, groggy and not yet fully awake. His room was still shrouded in darkness as he lifted his head and peered in the direction of the bedside table where his digital clock read 2:37 AM. Plumping his pillow until it was in a perfect position, he laid his head back down, preparing to resubmerge himself into the deep-sea slumber carrying him downstream to the morning of a new day.

That's when he heard it again.

A loud whack—something hitting something else with a thud, followed by an odd clatter. Opening his eyes, Craig sat bolt upright, alarmed. He swung his legs off the bed, grabbed his robe from the chair, and started for the door. Then he stopped, briefly considering his next move. Though a large man, he was not violent by nature and now, with heart pounding, he looked around his dark room for a suitable weapon. Deciding on an acoustic guitar he'd found in the closet plus an extension cord, lest he should have occasion to restrain the intruder while waiting for the authorities, Craig crept away from his guesthouse quarters toward the main house and source of the ominous sound.

Nearing the house, he slowed, his breathing heavy, the noise sounding stranger and louder to him than before. *Thud,* then a low grunt and the clatter of something sounding fairly heavy. Taking a deep breath and getting a stronger, renewed grip on his menacing guitar, Craig whipped around the corner, his muscles taut, ready to rescue his hostess and friend from certain death.

"Okay, stop whatever you're doing and put your hands out where I can . . ." his loud voice trailed off, as he registered the vision before him in Suzanne's backyard patio.

Suzanne stood in her white cotton nightgown and Nixon slippers, her face slick with perspiration, hammer in her hand. All around her lay the large square clay bricks that had once been her serene California Spanish patio. But now in place of the large tiled area surrounding the fountain lay a jumble of dirt, debris, and shattered tiles, and in the center of this work site stood a triumphant Suzanne, wielding her hammer with one hand and waving excitedly at Craig with the other.

"Oh, I'm so glad you're up!" she exclaimed breathlessly in greeting. "Now you can help me! Though I'm pretty much almost completely—"

"What in the high holy fuck are you doing, you midget psycho?" He was shouting at her, truly angry. "Do you think this is cute or something?" He carefully picked his way toward her through the pile of rubble.

"It's fucking three o'clock in the morning, you do know that, don't you? Does that even matter to you? I mean, I thought that . . . some murderer-type person was hurting you or something and . . . *ow!"* Craig stopped in midsentence, dropping the guitar and grabbing the toe he'd just stubbed on a low pile of broken tiles.

"Oh no! C'mon, I was just doing this 'cause I couldn't sleep and I'd always wanted to take out all this tile, you know? I mean, it looks so *forbidding,* right? Who would want to come out here and hang out on hot concrete? *You* never have, right? I mean, in the whole time you've been—"

"Shut *up!*" roared Craig, squatting in the dirt, red-faced, still clutching his sore toe. "Something is really wrong with you now, okay? You don't redo your patio in the middle of the night on some stupid whim." His face was stern and severe. "Stupid *loud* whim," he amended, returning to his examination of his angry, swollen foot.

"It's not a whim," sulked Suzanne, wiping her wet face with the sleeve of her nightgown. "I've been wanting to do this for a long time now, and I just—"

Craig stood, holding out his hand. "Give me the hammer," he commanded. *"Now!"*

Frowning, Suzanne tilted her head down, away from the force of him. "But—"

"Just *give* it to me!" So she handed over the hammer sullenly, without looking up into his furiously boiling eyes. "Now, go to your room." He pointed toward Suzanne's bedroom with the claw end of the hammer.

As she padded by him obediently, her frowning mouth small and tight, Craig added, "I never thought I'd say this, but I'm turning into my mother. That's what you've done to me, you know that? You've turned me into a shrieking, bloated, menopausal woman with all your nutty shenanigans!"

Suzanne glared at him darkly before disappearing into the house, away from him forever.

"I'm even saying 'shenanigans,' which is a word she would use, not me. The one good thing about that is I can go to couples therapy with myself. Something you might consider doing."

But Suzanne was already inside the door, shutting it noisily behind her. Sighing, Craig looked once more at his injured foot and the offending jumble of tile around him. Then, picking up the discarded guitar, he gingerly limped back through the obstacle course and followed Suzanne back to her bedroom.

He stalked into her bathroom, rifled drawers and cabinets, then marched back into the bedroom, holding his open palm out to her. It was littered with a pastel constellation of Suzanne's medication.

"Jesus Christ, what a nag you are," she said with exasperation, standing and scooping up the pills, haughty with the indignation of the oppressed as she flounced back into the bathroom.

"Where are you going!" he shouted after her.

"To take this lame-ass medicine so you'll leave me alone!" she shouted back, flinging the door shut behind her.

"I want you to do it in front of me where I can see you," he called.

Suzanne, with heart racing, fumbled through her cabinets, dumping the contents of a few bottles into her hand and replacing the pills that Craig had given her with aspirin and vitamins. She'd barely finished stuffing her real medication behind a chair cushion when Craig appeared in the doorway, just missing her deception.

"What are you doing?" he asked suspiciously, leaning against the doorframe and looking at her through narrowed lids.

Suzanne assumed an expression of benign amusement in an attempt to conceal the fact that she was flushed and breathing hard.

"I'm getting a glass of water to take my pills with. Is that okay with you, Dad?"

She strode to the sink and filled her dirty toothbrush glass with a quick rush of water, splashing herself and the sink in the process.

"Forgive me for not wanting anything bad to happen to you." Craig crossed his arms as she swallowed the replacement pills in quick succession.

"Mania is not *bad,* you know," she said with the odd impediment of having a pill in her mouth.

"Oh, sure, it's great for you, but what about those of us you leave mangled in your wake?" He sighed. "Listen, I want you to promise me you'll see Mishkin in the morning. I mean it, I'm really worried about you."

"All right, all right, I promise. You killed me at hello. I'll go tomorrow," Suzanne said, more to get this lumbering giant out of her sight than anything else.

"Good, and while you're doing the promising, I want one more thing."

Suzanne glared at him as though to burn a hole in the middle of all these practical wants, rendering them impotent, insignificant, obsolete. "Okay, what?"

"I want you to promise me to take these fuckin' meds of yours properly."

Suzanne was suddenly overcome with the withering and endless boredom of it all. "Okay. So may I go now? Or do I need to sign a notarized document of some kind?"

Craig shrugged in exasperation. "Okay, fine, make me the bad guy and you're like some big misunderstood—oh, who gives a shit—I'm going back to bed now. Have a grand and glorious good evening." He shook his head one last time and limped back to the guesthouse.

She had a perfectly good reason for not wanting to take her medication. Perfect to her, anyway. She realized on some level that her logic would more than likely fail to impress most people, but it impressed her, so nothing else mattered in the end. All the while inside her, she was nurturing the seed of her other über-self, listening for the high-frequency flower of feeling to burst into bloom; the giddy, glittering high-octane thrill to surge through her system, carbonating her blood as it swept through her veins.

Who could blame her for courting this infallible feeling? This sensation that once she arrived anywhere all would be well?

Having arrived at the top of her lungs, she'd planted her brightly colored flag there, plotting the rest of her trajectory where she would be indomitable, indisputable king. Her magic mood would make certain of it. Servicing her needs and the needs of others without breaking a sweat or pausing to breathe.

So, she tiptoed around in army boots waiting for the rest of her, the last, the best of her, to awaken, and when it did, when she opened every iota of herself on that irrepressible morning, she would be more than ready to greet the glorious dawning of each lucky day.

MOODWEATHER

With a bullying Craig practically flinging her bodily into her car the next morning, Suzanne found herself in the outer office of her psychopharmacologist in Century City.

Maybe Dr. Mishkin wouldn't notice her ecstatic state too much, somehow not notice that everywhere she went, all light was absorbed directly into her, with no chance to escape. She was barely able to sit still, squirming with sunshine, this chaos of pleasure bubbling up in her, rendering her barely able to see. So intent was she on these inner workings that she wouldn't be surprised if her eyes glowed, if every word she uttered pulsed with a knowing, phosphorous glow. Everything outside her looked electric, friendly, and coated with silvery zinc.

So it was true, then. She was everywhere now, heading for the far hills at the high speed of delight . . . falling out of the blue and a place she knew only too well once she got there.

The door to Dr. Mishkin's tiny waiting room opened and a distinguished-looking older man with mournful blue eyes shuffled inside, crossing the short distance to the only sofa in the room. Slowly turning, he took a seat. The man appeared to be weighed down by insupportable burdens—smothered in a life-sapping sadness, both his skin and hair gray with grief.

She knew it was rude to stare, but she found herself unable to pull her eyes away from him because in the almost two years she had been seeing Mishkin, the impossible had happened—she had finally run into someone in his waiting room. This was no doubt in part because she had until today deliberately come so late to her appointments, hoping to spend less time in this shameful office with the good doctor waving his synthetic monkey wrench inside the heads of all his factory rejects. But whatever the reason, she was fascinated by this sad shadow of a man and wondered what his diagnosis was. You show me your diagnosis, I'll show you mine.

Suzanne smiled for no real reason then looked away, not wanting this apparently wounded man to think she was laughing at him. All he needed, she thought, on top of whatever else that had brought him here, was to have his nose rubbed in how unbelievably happy she was. No. It was pretty clear that this man was in the fierce grips of a depression. But was he just a depressive, or manic-depressive? Suzanne found herself needing to know. And maybe more than that . . . needing to talk.

"What time was your appointment?" the man with the crushed voice asked her, a voice which probably hadn't lately seen much of the light of day.

"Twelve fifteen," she responded cheerfully, but also attempting not to make him too jealous that he wasn't her. "But don't go by me. I think I was late anyway. But anyway, he's late a lot, don't you think?" she continued. "Off somewhere fitting someone for a straitjacket or coaxing them in from a ledge. Something like that."

The man looked at her with his stricken eyes. "Yup, guess that must be so," and then he looked away and down at the carpeted floor.

Suzanne suddenly realized maybe she shouldn't have alluded to asylums or suicide, that these might be sensitive topics for this man, given his sorry shape. Shit! How insensitive of her! She'd better fix this and be quick about it—which couldn't be that difficult since quick was her current claim to fame. She couldn't let this guy blow his brains out on her watch.

"So what are you in for?" she put her hand gently on his arm, made an effort to shift gears, and heal him into her way of being. But he continued staring at the floor before him, and for an awful moment Suzanne didn't think he was going to favor her with a reply. His feet seemed gripped flat to the floor, hands clinging desperately to knees. She now noticed his shirt was rumpled and half untucked, and he appeared not to have shaved for a few days, giving his crestfallen face a grizzled, abandoned quality: Smokey the Unbearably Sad Guy.

"My medication stopped working," he all but whispered to her, as though to say it any louder would only cause it to continue on its dark and final path.

"What was the medicine?" she leaned her head very far down so she could see up into his face, as his eyes were still intent on the floor.

"Serzone," he replied harshly, as if the taste of the word itself was bitter and he needed to expel it quickly from his mouth.

"Oooooh, I took that once. It's great in the beginning, though, right? Then it just wears off, like World War Two for the Germans. You know, I find that certain antidepressants have the effect of something like cocaine on me—at least initially. Then that just blends off into nothing after a while—not that I tell *them* that. Shit, half the time, I feel like these guys don't even know what they're doing—you know, turn a dial here, stick a pill in there and BOOM! Nothing changes." Something in his alarmed face told her to modify this point to suit his current crisis. "Of course, I'm sure it's different with you. Anyway, they're probably doing a great job with me only I can't see it 'cause it *is* me, you know what I mean?" She beamed her sunny disposition bright on him, trying to shine him back to life.

He was looking at her, his despairing eyes wide. "Is that a fact," he managed.

"Yup," Suzanne nodded. "That's absolutely a fact. I'd know one anywhere." She smiled and leaned into him eagerly. "You know what I used to say about being bipolar? That it was weather, that's all it was—mood weather." She pursed her lips thoughtfully, frowning and looking off. "How did I get onto that?"

He watched her, mouth slightly open, transfixed now, while Suzanne brightened and turned her sparkling eyes to him again.

"Oh, yeah! I would say the facts of my life stayed the same, just the fiction I made up about it differed, the fiction being the weather, see? 'Cause we were talking about facts. Or I was. Am I talking too much? Just tell me and I'll shut up. Actually, I probably won't, but I'll try, which is at least something, right?" She grinned at him inanely, hoping he was well enough to like her just a little bit. Then they would have something in common!

He nodded, listening to her from all the way down in his dark where he cowered, waiting for rescue. A ghost haunting his bombed-out ruin of a life.

"Now, you say something," she said, nudging him gently. "Say something or I'll feel like I'm talking too much."

He blinked quickly a few times and licked his lips, thinking. "What kind of thing should I say?"

"I don't know—say what your diagnosis is—you know, like I'm a manic-depressive, or bipolar, or whatever. So, then, what are you?"

Rubbing his hands on his pant legs, he looked away bashfully. "Oh, you know. I'm a depressive." He fell silent, then rose again. "Yup. That's all she wrote. A big ol' depressive to the core."

Suzanne finally noticed now that he had a Southern accent that put a lilt in a voice that might otherwise be lifeless and monotone, lying flat as old wax on a forgotten floor.

"But my daddy was manic-depressive," he offered up, glancing at her. "Yup. That he was." He continued nodding, looking off and into his black-and-white mind in an effort to summon a few colorful memories from long ago. Suzanne leaned into him once more, her eyes again shining with excitement. "Oh, man, I'm sorry. What a bummer for you, getting the short end of the shit bag mood disorder stick!"

"That I did," affirmed the gray man. "I did at that."

"What was he like, your father? When was he manic? Was it great?"

The faintest smile threatened the corners of the man's mouth as he summoned this pleasant vision. "Oh, yeah, it was fun. *He* was fun. We had us some good times, me and my daddy, when he was like that.

Everybody liked Daddy, cept'n Mama a'course, when he was hell bent
on what he called—"

She interrupted. "Tell me what he did. Please. I love this stuff; my
name's Suzanne by the way."

"Pleased to meet you, Suzanne. My name is Hoyt. Hoyt Jackson,
from Memphis, Tennessee." He extended a pallid, bony hand and
Suzanne grasped it, giving it a quick shake.

"Okay, Hoyt, so now tell me."

"About Daddy?"

Suzanne nodded eagerly, turning to face him more completely in
her seat.

"Well, he would buy me all sorts of things. One time he even
bought me a car with a trailer hitched to the back. I thought Mama
was gonna take a switch to him, but instead she just locked him in the
basement overnight."

"Wow, that's impressive. Could he afford all that?"

"Oh, well, yeah. He could."

"Really? What'd he do?"

"Our family was in the construction business."

"I only ask 'cause I had this friend when I first moved to New York
who bought his elevator man thirty thousand dollars' worth of furniture this one time he got manic and he *really* couldn't afford it. Besides
which—I mean, even if he liked his elevator man—who I'm sure was
a great guy and whatever—that would still be considered a really inappropriate gift to anyone, don't you think?"

"Well, I'll be. Thirty thousand dollars? That right there's a whole
bunch of money."

"I know. And it was because of him—the guy that bought the furniture—that I didn't think I was bipolar when they first told me I
was. Because, I mean, get real—I knew I wasn't like Joey. I mean, this
guy would get on his roof and drink perfume while he wore these Ha-
sidic beards that he'd buy in a magic store. After that, he'd try to
crawl into the TV, but of course, only if he really liked the movie.
Then he'd say things like 'When you see the darkness come toward
you, throw out the light.' Well, I mean, come on! *Hello?! That* was

crazy, or bipolar, or whatever you call it. I just had these up-and-down things. In fact, that's what I'd say when I wound up in bed after being on a tear, or whatever. 'What goes up must come down.' Not very original, but you know, I was moody. Maybe more than most, but shit, I certainly didn't thirst for perfume or get fresh with the TV." Suzanne sat back, satisfied she'd told a very good story. Jiggling her leg, she checked the red light she'd switched on when she'd entered, which told Mishkin back in the treatment room that a patient was waiting to see him. "Hey, do you think Mishkin's forgotten about us? We've been out here for ages."

Hoyt looked ashen.

"Lord, I hope not. I'm in a fix, I gotta tell you. I need some kind of help in the worst way." He shifted uncomfortably in his seat, his eyes pulsing with terror as though hunted by unseen creatures, his forehead shiny with sweat.

"Yeah, I could tell you were having a tough time when you walked in," she said sympathetically. "Of course, being in this office in the first place is a dead giveaway that something's up. Or *not* up, depending."

"That's for gosh-darn sure, and I got somethin' real dead I wanna give away, real soon, that's for damn sure, too."

Suzanne laughed and laughed at this. A depressive making a joke was a very big deal. Everyone in the "mood disorder know" knew that. Whenever she'd been depressed—and there'd been a few times which she did her not-so-level best not to think about—humor was the first thing to go, taking with it the energy or inclination to wash one's hair or brush one's teeth, or ever leave the house again. Everything got weighed down, was so hopeless and heavy—but Hoyt had come up with a joke and a joke was hope, wasn't it? It had to be.

A flushed Hoyt looked at his lap, maybe now just a little pleased with himself. After Suzanne's laughter had died down, her bright eyes widened eagerly, the lightbulb almost noticeable over her head.

"Hey, I've got an idea," she declared, suffused with her miraculous inspiration. And, smiling conspiratorially, she checked behind her to make certain no one untrustworthy was listening. Touching his arm one last time, she proceeded to lay out her manic little plan.

EMERGENCY CENTRAL

"No, you *can't* keep him," Craig said sternly, looking down at Suzanne like the ever-increasing madwoman she'd been behaving like as of late.

Suzanne had brought the forlorn Hoyt home with her from Mishkin's office and installed him over his mildest of polite protests in the little room next to Craig's.

Not that she could take care of Hoyt in the usual food and cleaning way. Well, okay, she could handle the cleaning, yes, because she didn't do it—someone really nice came in. But she could take care of him in the fun, "Let's go see a movie!" kind of way. She could take care of him by providing him community and comfort and friendship and DSL lines.

At least that was her argument in the best of times. She couldn't remember quite what had finally persuaded him, but was amazingly glad that whatever it was did.

But for some odd reason, Craig wasn't buying her logic. "He's not a Chia Pet, for Christ's sake, he's a very depressed Southern out-of-work actor with a home somewhere to go back to. Anyway, *you* wouldn't end up living with him, *I* would, seeing as how he'd get the room next to mine in your adorable guesthouse by the sea—where

I'm only staying, as it turns out, to keep you from doing further mischief to yourself. I mean, I'm very sorry he's having a bad time, but things aren't exactly smooth sailing around here with you doing whatever you're doing with your medicine besides taking it, and obviously very tied up with your twenty-four-hour responsibilities as Prime Minister of Holy Mother of Fuck Lunatic Land. I'd say we're busy as it is. And by 'we,' I mean me and my two balls."

Suzanne looked up at him with her biggest, saddest, most pleading pair of wild eyes.

"But—"

"*No!* What're you, crazy?" Then, clearly remembering who he was talking to, Craig waved what he'd just said away. "Okay, scratch that. But even crazy people do the occasional sane thing, even if only to supply contrast."

When Suzanne uncharacteristically failed to respond, Craig continued in exasperation. "Look, getting off of this subject for a moment—but we're obviously not done with it—did you actually see Mishkin or just raid his waiting room?"

"Of *course* I saw him," she lied emphatically. "Where do you think I got Hoyt from? The Sad Café? Mishkin came in really late after some emergency with a schizophrenic or something." Which was plausible, she told herself. Schizophrenics must have emergencies all the time, don't they? What with all those voices and delusions, it must be Emergency Central.

Suzanne stopped to watch a hummingbird dart in and out of the orange blossoms, temporarily absorbed in its activities and subsequent flight. Finally, sighing in exasperation, Craig tapped her roughly on the shoulder.

"Earth to Anna Nicole Smith?"

Suzanne looked back at him, startled. What were they talking about again? It couldn't have been all that interesting if she'd already forgotten it. No, this interaction had worn out its welcome. Craig was trying to put her on the spot of impossible scrutiny, when all she wanted to do was wade back into the waiting world, where she would ultimately wash up on the shore of a more appreciative beach.

"I'm sorry," she mused. "I was just thinking—will you remind me that I have to get rid of the rest of those azaleas on the hill? You know how I fucking hate azaleas. I mean, they bloom like, once a—"

Craig cut her off. "As riveting as any conversation about azaleas is, can we please go back to what Mishkin said? I mean, what's he doing about you fucking with your medication?"

"Well, you know," she frowned and looked off, wishing he would drop this line of questioning. Suzanne hated lying, having little talent for it and preferring to do things that showed her off in a more flattering light, like driving the car with the music turned up and honking and waving to bewildered strangers she passed in the street.

"No, I don't know. That's why I'm asking."

"Let me finish, okay?" She ran her hand through her hair, badly in need of washing, but Suzanne had no time for mundane tasks like personal hygiene. She no longer identified with her body—she existed largely in her mind, the carrier of the bright flame burning within her. Tasks relating to maintenance of her flesh broke her forward motion, delaying her arrival at the next opportune place.

"Obviously he's not thrilled that I seem a little manic," she offered, hoping this would appease Craig, so she could return to her happy place in a breathless whirl.

Instead, he rolled his eyes, his face alive with disbelief. "A *little*?" He glared down at her from his great height, arms crossed as if to keep from spilling over with exasperation.

"Can I finish?"

Craig just looked at her without replying, so she went on lying.

"So he upped my Seriquel and put me on a bigger morning dose of Depakote and Neurontin." She hadn't been on Neurontin for years, but Craig had no way of knowing that. Besides, her lying seemed to be going all right so far, so who knew? This time she just might get away with it. She also figured that if she threw a lot of names of medications at him it would temporarily confuse him, subsequently removing him from her crowded back. "Happy now, Mr. Stern-Taskmaster Rain-on-My-Parade Man?"

He narrowed his eyes suspiciously in an effort to better read her, or glare at her, or both. She couldn't really tell. "And you're going to do this, right? I mean, I don't have to worry that—"

"For the last time, *yes,* you nagging son of a sea cat!" she shouted at him, backing out of the room, having tired of this confrontation long ago and longing to run through the hills with the wind at her back, free! "Can I go now? I mean, is class dismissed, or do you have more instructions for me?" She turned to walk out of the room and his life forever—at least for the upcoming forever in her near future, shining ever bright.

"Hey, where are you going? I hope you're going to tell that Mr. Sad Sack Stray Chucklehead you brought home that he can't stay here!"

But Suzanne had disappeared, fleeing the dreadful glare of his disapproval. If Craig were really her friend, he'd be happy she was so happy. Not only was she helping someone, she'd made a new friend. And putting all that to the side, what she did was none of his fucking business.

"I'm off to Switzerland for a rest," she called over her shoulder en route to the guesthouse, the cabin in her sky, new home to sweet, suicidal Hoyt, her current one true friend and unabashed supporter. He alone appreciated her for the undeniably special creature she was. She would go to him now, finding what was best about herself in his eyes and leaving behind any misunderstanding naysayers and other sticks in her magical mud. She would rise in both his and her esteem and, born aloft on both these moonbeams, she'd streak her streaming radiance across the starry night sky.

Craig now realized he'd made a total mistake coming out here. Mistake for him, anyway. But who else would take care of Suzanne? Not Doris; Suzanne knew too well how to fool or get around her. Partly because Suzanne was crafty, but mostly because Doris couldn't conceive of the magnitude of this thing that could sometimes take hold of her all-too-willing daughter. And certainly neither her parents nor MGM nor the Girl Scouts of America had prepared Doris for this kind of reckoning. So, finally, it was up to Craig to take care of the kook. But who was going to take care of the Craigster?

They would cross that bridge when Suzanne burned it.

Hoyt would've been thrilled to help if he'd have been able to experience anything close to joyful. As it was, he was something like grateful to be in the company of anyone who didn't try to heal him or worry over him. His friends had finally given up on him after he had oh so quietly and carefully avoided them for months and months, lying at first in bed in his perfectly nice apartment, and then under it, not eating his meals or cleaning himself, just watching the light changing on the wall.

After a while, he figured he had to pull himself up by the bootstraps and get out of this thing or nothing was gonna happen besides something just awful. So when this chatty lady offered to bring him home from Dr. Mishkin's office, it was like getting a second chance at the second half of his life: life like other people live it. So without looking this gift horse in her all-too-busy mouth, he told himself this was as close as he needed to be to good fortune, something close to glad.

No little piece of jewelry

Leland and Honey weren't due to return for . . . when was it again? Suzanne tried to make a mental note to work out exactly when they were returning and exactly when it was now, but found no blank spot in her head to leave herself a note on. She shrugged it off, having a sense that all would be well, or better than well . . . as well as things could possibly be. Better times beat their steady beat all around her in perfect sync with her happy heart, and man was it was good to be her.

Smiling, she sang, strolling down the path from her house. *"Could be, who knows? There's something due any day, I will know right away, soon as it showwwws!"*

"Send for the Sherpas!" she cried to Hoyt hours later from her car phone en route to the next big intrigue. "I'm high on Everest, with the wind in my hair!"

She was speeding down Laurel Canyon, windows open, music blaring, giddy and incandescent, eager for anything.

"I wondered where you went," Hoyt managed from the other end. "I was lookin' all over for you. How you doin'?"

Suzanne laughed, turning onto Sunset. Trees and houses swam by, other cars might've hindered her car's quick progress, but nothing at all could hinder her. "You know when they tell you when you stop looking for a relationship, that's when you find one?" She didn't wait for an answer. "That's not true—a lot of people stop looking for a relationship and you know what happens then? Nothing! Hey! You want me to come and get you? I mean, are you doing anything right now? Is your St. Vitus's dance card full?"

"Nope," Hoyt answered. "I'm pretty much free as a—"

"Have no help, fear is on the way!" and, pressing down on her accelerator, Suzanne sped ahead of the cars in front of her, trying to keep pace with the guitar solo playing somewhere in the front of her head.

Ten minutes later, Hoyt was in the car next to her, studying her from the passenger side as she tapped the wheel, talking.

"Here's how brilliant I am, you wanna hear?" and again without waiting for an answer, she went on, "I mean, sure, there are a lot of gorgeous women and some of them are even smart, but have *they* had an enormous amount of unneccesary dental work just for the morphine? I don't think so!" Suzanne slapped the wheel, grinning. "Beat that, big top!"

Music leaked out at her from the radio and she closed her eyes, inhaling it.

"Is there some place particular we're goin'?" Hoyt asked finally.

"Sorry, that's a state secret. State of mind." She bobbed her head to the song's sturdy beat now surging through all her pores.

"Uh-huh. Well, no offense or nothin', but would you mind slowin' down a little, 'cause, you know, even though I'm in the middle of this awful—*Look out!*" Hoyt braced his hands on the dashboard emphatically to break his fall.

"I *saw* him," Suzanne said, as though Hoyt was the only crazy one, overreacting like always, when it was just business as usual—Suzanne's idea of business—which had everything to do with play.

"*Saw* him?" Hoyt exclaimed, both hands still clutching the dashboard. "It looked like you was aimin' fer him, I mean, if you don't mind me sayin'!"

Suzanne rolled her eyes, smiling patiently at him. Slowing, she turned the car into a parking lot and pulled into a spot. She turned off the ignition and sighed as Hoyt looked around him blankly, and then at Suzanne for clues.

"Are we somewhere that we were headed?"

And, smiling her most enigmatic smile, she opened her car door. "We sure are," she said meaningfully. "C'mon."

The Flying Pig Tattoo Parlor was in the 9000 block of Sunset Boulevard next to Ted's Smoke Shop and the Spinning Vinyl Record Store, which bought and sold everything from 78s to 45s to 33⅓s. It even boasted having an eight-track cassette section and hard-to-get recordings of live performances from long ago. Ted's Smoke Shop specialized in cigars and exotic cigarettes—from foreign to herb to limited editions. And between them nestled the Flying Pig, one of five local tattoo parlors and body piercing establishments.

Suzanne sat in the back of the Flying Pig with her right foot in the bald tattoo artist's hand, his head gleaming as he hunched over the creation coming to life under his able hand. His large muscular body was covered with colorful inky pictures of every description, each inch filled in with the exception of his ruddy, sunburnt face. Hoyt sat over to one side, holding a *Rolling Stone* magazine in front of him without reading it, surrounded by a cloud of cigarette smoke and heavy metal music, seemingly mesmerized by the low, persistent buzz of the needle drilling its ink into Suzanne's lower leg, but otherwise a little out of place with his surroundings—a carnation lost in a sea of blue roses.

While her other foot kept time to the music, Suzanne swatted away some flies that were flying lazily through the warm, close air throughout the shop via the open doorway. A nearby fan moved its blank white face back and forth, an upper-class appliance haughtily surveying the scene, infusing it with its insufficient hush of recycled air. The walls and even the ceiling were crammed with samples of all manner of ink creations one could have buzzed into them: skeletons or devils on horseback, four-leaf clovers, maps of Ireland, sailing ships on rough seas, Chinese symbols, naked women holding four aces, broken hearts dripping blood, or hearts taking to the skies with angel wings.

Suzanne had settled on no less than a small solar system on her ankle, only forgoing a portrait of Honey since she lacked a recent and really good photo worthy of having doodled permanently onto the sketch pad of her skin. Besides, the man who drew the best likenesses was in rehab with his wife until next week, so a small solar system would have to do.

To render her creation, she chose Tony, an ex-con—though it wasn't as if she'd had a wide variety of choices in ink artists at her disposal when initially making her selection. Part of the problem was that not only did Suzanne want a fabulous tattoo, she wanted one now. *Now* was probably the more vital part of it. There had been only two "artists" working when they'd walked in: Tony, her ex-con, and Big Bird—and really, Big Bird was more of an expert when it came to piercings or brandings and most especially shaving heads; because, you see, he didn't just shave them, he shaved them into designs and patterns such as Jerry Garcia ascending to heaven on a winged motorcycle, Saddam Hussein descending into hell, and pigs flying through the eye of a needle.

"Is that how you got the name of the store?" wondered Hoyt politely from his perch after Tony had finished this fairly lengthy explanation. Rather than reply, Tony just looked at him blankly for a moment before once again dipping his needle in red ink and continuing to fill in Saturn.

Suzanne found the tattoo parlor to be a peaceful place. She felt soothed by the droning buzz of Tony's needle and the new selection of music Big Bird had just put on the CD player. This time it was the Black Crowes and Black Sabbath and Megadeth, and finally, the Grateful Dead.

"Any band with black or death in its name," Big Bird explained unnecessarily while returning change to a young man settling accounts for his nose piercing.

"What about Cilla Black?" asked Hoyt meekly from his perch by the doorway. "Or Shirley Temple Black?"

"Are those bands?" Tony dipped his needle into the tiny plastic cylinder of red ink and returned it to Suzanne's ankle, where he began filling in a star.

Hoyt and Suzanne looked at one another and smiled. Didn't these tattoo artists know anything?

"Cilla Black is a British singer and Shirley Temple—"

"I've heard of her!" Big Bird interrupted victoriously. "She's a drink!"

Suzanne squirmed uncomfortably, biting her lower lip.

"Ow." She uttered the syllable sadly, as though reluctant to give it up, perhaps having bigger plans for it at a later date.

"Am I hurting you?" Tony sounded surprised, as if pain was an unusual outcome in his line of work.

"A little," she admitted sheepishly. "Could we take a teeny break?"

Tony sat back, the designs on the front of his bulging arms suddenly visible: pyramids at sunset, a herd of buffalo with a stealth bomber flying above them, addressed to a name Suzanne didn't recognize (not that *that* was much of a surprise), and Count Chocula spreading his ominous batwing sleeves. Then he stood, stretching his arms, briefly distorting all these pictures, and yawned.

"Sure, go ahead. I was getting a crick in my neck anyway."

Suzanne leaned forward, to better scrutinize Tony's handiwork on her ankle. As far as she could make out, he'd outlined the whole area with an odd sort of uneven blue—perhaps to give it the effect of atmosphere or of outer space, she couldn't be sure—she was also uncertain if Tony recognized any difference—and inside that blue, there appeared to be the beginnings of two stars, Saturn and something very like, if she wasn't mistaken . . . the Turkish flag. All in all, it somehow had the overall effect of a patriotic solar bruise, but patriotic to a country in the Middle East, as if customs wasn't complicated enough as it was.

"How's it comin'?" Hoyt asked, crossing to her, looking a little less sad than when she found him. That was the Girl Scout credo, wasn't it? Leave things less sad than when you found them, and when possible, tattoo them with the Turkish flag.

"Good," she chirped. "See?"

She lifted her leg with the drawing on it and leaned forward.

"Uh-huh," he said. "Yes sir, it's a tattoo all right. My mama would bust my butt if I got one of them things. You better believe it." Suzanne smiled ironically at him. Sometimes he sounded to her like one of those characters on a long-ago sitcom like the *Andy Griffith Show*.

"Well then, it's a good thing you're not getting one!" She began rummaging through her purse for her cigarettes with great absorption, which was when the girl with short maroon hair and pierced chin must have entered the front door. With her wide, pale face and heavily made-up blue eyes matching the bright blue stud on her chin, she looked like a less-than-savory Cabbage Patch Doll or yet another close personal friend of the Addams Family. Or Family Osbourne.

"How much to get my tongue pierced?" the girl asked in a high nasal voice, her hands resting on the counter. She had silver rings on all her fingers and both thumbs, with black nail polish and black clothes to match: a short black skirt, bare midriff, ripped black shirt, black socks, and high-topped black sneakers.

Suzanne groaned at the mention of tongue piercing and, crossing to the girl, she took hold of her upper arm. "Don't get your tongue pierced. *Please*. Why the fuck would you do that?"

The girl opened her mouth to reply but Suzanne cut her off. "And don't tell me it's because your boyfriend wants you to do it, 'cause then I'll kill not only just you, but I'll also kill him mainly . . . not that *that* makes sense."

The girl drew back, attempting to move to safety, but Suzanne held on, committed to the task at hand.

" 'Cause if it's for what I think it's for, and you're not good at that thing to begin with, then no little piece of jewelry is going to save the day."

The girl looked around her for assistance, but none of the three men present seemed quite certain of what to do.

"Anyway, what if you break up with this guy? Who's going to get the stud . . . him or you? 'Cause my advice would be to give it to him, cause who wants a stinky piece of jewelry that smells like the penis of a guy you're no longer seeing?"

Hoyt now approached, touching Suzanne's shoulder in an attempt to distract her from this boisterous crusade, but she'd warmed to her subject sentences ago and now was coming to a boil.

"If you're insecure about the effectiveness of your blow jobs, then a little gold ball twisted into your tongue isn't going to improve things. I mean, either you're good at fellating a guy or you're not; why not get some tips on how to give head before you go poking holes in yourself like a human dartboard?"

"*Suzanne!*" Hoyt grabbed her arm, pulling her to him, attempting to silence her. "Maybe the young lady likes wearing jewelry in her mouth."

Suzanne scowled at him darkly.

"Don't be insane." Then she turned back to the pale girl, now grown paler. "Do you?" she challenged her, speaking to her in a tone generally reserved for idiots. "Well? Do you or do you not like wearing earrings in your mouth that will one day smell like your ex-boyfriend's dick?"

The girl blinked at her briefly, caught in Suzanne's fierce tractor beam. Confused, her jaw seemed to be working invisibly and her eyes grew wider. She suddenly found her opening and dashed out of the tattoo parlor back into the warm shelter of the uninquisitive day, free again.

"Well, aren't you great for business," Big Bird marveled. "What the fuck was all that?"

"Don't worry," Hoyt reassured him anxiously, "we'll pay you for the tongue piercing she woulda gotten. How much was it?" He reached into his back pocket for his wallet, opened it, and began leafing through bills.

"Hell, I'll pay for ten tongue piercings you *don't* give," Suzanne said, "and while you're not poking more holes into these airheads, why don't you just give these girls manuals on how to give good head?"

Hoyt removed a fifty-dollar bill from his wallet and handed it to Big Bird, who pocketed it with a terse nod.

"Thanks," said Big Bird. "So where could I get a hold of some of these manuals you're talking about, 'cause I'd like to give one to my girlfriend for starters. And then, who knows? They would be like a great stocking stuffer, wouldn't they, buddy?" Big Bird looked over at Tony for a reaction, but Tony was watching Suzanne.

"No one can have a pamphlet if she has the tongue piercing. If you don't have it—" But before she could finish, Hoyt began dragging a resistant Suzanne toward the door. She slapped at his hand.

"Hey, at least let me get my shoes!" she whined, pulling away from him. "And my tattoo's not really done and I still have to pay Tony and anyway, why—" But Hoyt had already separated one world from another. Removed Suzanne from the world of tattoos and pierced tongues and ex-cons, and rescued Tony and Big Bird from Suzanne's world of actions taken at speeds too quick to concern themselves with consequences.

Speeding west down Sunset, away from the Flying Pig and all who toiled there, Hoyt was hunched over the wheel while Suzanne sat in the passenger seat, reluctantly listening to the voice of reason as she had so many times before. Why did everyone end up talking to her like this? Like she was a water baby head? She stared out the window, looking forward to the end of his meager attempt to talk sense to her. The bland leading the berserk.

"Are you okay? I mean—," Hoyt began, his face ashen with worry, his eyes leaving the street thick with cars just long enough to look at her in dismay. This was the person that was supposed to save *him*— how could she do that if she now went so far awry?

"Oh, don't be such an old woman," she said dismissively. "C'mon, admit it, it was funny."

Suzanne slumped down in the seat with her arms crossed in front of her, as if to shield herself from any and all incoming oppressive logic, and closed her eyes, feeling the sun on her face. How could someone be critical of her on such a day as this?

"Besides, we paid for the pierced tongue thing," she whined petulantly. "We *overpaid* for it, if you ask me."

She picked nonexistent lint from her sleeve, frowning, as the light changed and Hoyt steered her toward the safer world of her hillside home to prepare for further adventures.

"Okay, but really, are you okay?"

"What do you mean?" she asked, sitting back, angelic and innocent, her eyes on the road ahead. "I'm completely and totally fine, and the reason you can't see it is because your perception's all fucked up by depression. If you weren't so sad, you'd be having a great time here." She beamed at him while he continued to look at her doubtfully, perhaps hoping her shine would overwhelm the doubt and rule the day.

Of course, she knew her argument was flawed, but so what? His point of view only ensured you of more worry and concern and what was the good of that?

She smiled at Hoyt enigmatically, sending him waves of good will and affection and when she was certain he had received at least a portion of her energizing personality, she leaned forward and turned up the radio's volume in an effort to drown out the sound of more of this less-than-pleasant exchange.

GROOMING AMBUSH

After dropping Hoyt off, with no specific plans for when they would meet next, Suzanne headed back out into the happy planet she hailed from. She was somewhat relieved to be quit of him, though she wished he'd been more interested in staying with her today and every day; she couldn't understand how he could resist her. How anyone could, for that matter. But it wasn't important anymore. Her ankle had begun to throb a little where the incomplete tattoo had been inscribed, and she fought the impulse to rub it by turning up the radio and drowning out the itch with the rallying sound of rock 'n' roll.

Suzanne was off to get her hair cut. She really hadn't planned to—it had just happened. A kind of grooming ambush.

Keeping in mind she hadn't been bathing so much lately—a bath was so pedestrian, so everyman, so je ne sais Kuala Lumpur. And Suzanne had more important things to do. Things of national insignificance! Now was the time for all good men to come to the aid of the party! And, oh, what a party it would be! They would do things. Oh, not anything really specific, just things where it was necessary to be in motion, and you would want to be on hand when it happened, because what happened was you. An event such as yourself would be as far-reaching as Timbuktu and Madagascar. Your ripple effect would be felt on the moon. She was all ideas and talk and motion now that the medicine curtain had been drawn back, revealing what Suzanne knew to be the best in her. A best that was fast becoming better and better with each passing day, requiring less and less sleep, as she could now fuel off sunlight and color and fun.

She now thought she understood what her father was going for ingesting all that speed. Trying to live twice the life in half the time—like a fire blazing out of control, burning a path wherever you went, eyes bright, your brain a raging inferno of insights, ideas, and plain old big bad busy plans.

She could hardly be expected to tend to her hygiene, given as there was nothing high about it anyway. It was menial, regular woman's work. And she had graduated from regular to high octane to super-cool. Far better to just remove her offending brunette locks anyway, make way for her burgeoning, very-far-from-lame brain. So, driving over to West Hollywood and cruising Melrose, she'd search for a handy place for someone to hack off her hair at a moment's ago notice—like now. Waving to people, motoring along and chatting with her friendly radio, finally settling on a place called the Hair-Brained Hair Salon, choosing it more for the name than the look of it. In point of fact, it looked rather run-down, nestled between an adult bookstore and a doughnut joint. Suzanne, finding a parking spot she was certain had been selected for her by the auto placement gods, found herself leaning up against the reception desk moments later.

"Is there someone who could cut my hair right now?" she asked, her head tilted coyly toward her shoulder, a bashful, shy girl in want of grooming.

"Do you have an appointment?" the girl behind the desk said lazily, chewing gum and playing absently with her pen, doodling on paper.

"No, but the sign in the window says 'Walk-ins Welcome,' and . . . well . . . that's me! My family name is actually 'Walkin' . . . isn't that weird? Of course, you've heard of Christopher Walken, right? Well, he's my—"

"Reuben!" the girl called toward the back of the shop, interrupting Suzanne's tour of the netherworld of her crowded head.

A small dark man emerged from the back of the salon, passing through a beaded curtain. Wearing a yarmulke and a plastic colored smock, he walked toward Suzanne deliberately, a thoughtful, almost solemn expression on his bearded face.

"Yes, Anika?" He wiped his hands on a small towel, waiting.

"This lady wants a haircut. Do you think you have enough time to do her before your next client?"

Reuben nodded gravely, looking at Suzanne with his black eyes.

"I think so. I have Mrs. Finkleman at two o'clock but she is usually late," he said. "Follow me, please."

Suzanne thanked the receptionist, trailing Reuben down the center of the small shop, passing other stylists on their way to the shampoo sink. Taking a blue smock from a shelf, he handed it to Suzanne silently, almost as though it was an ancient prayer shawl or some other holy garment readying her for the ritual they were about to engage in.

"Put this on and Masha will shampoo you. Then you will follow her to my station where I will be waiting for you."

When Masha was finished, she brought Suzanne up to Reuben's chair at the front, where, as promised, he stood at the ready.

"Now, what can I do for you?" He held his comb aloft, watching Suzanne's reflection in the mirror and awaiting her orders, an assassin of locks ready to execute her orders.

"I want my hair cut off," she explained. "It's hot."

Reuben waited for her to continue and when she didn't, he asked: "Yes, but in what style?"

Suzanne shrugged.

"Just something I can wash and do nothing to." She shrugged. "Or better yet, not wash and do more nothing again." She smiled her best smile.

Reuben frowned, pursing his lips. "But you have such lovely long—"

"I don't care. I'm sick of it. I don't want it anymore."

Reuben sighed deeply.

"Well, all right, it shall be as you wish." He said this sadly, almost as though admitting something shameful from his past.

Lifting a long strand of her wet hair between his fingers until it was level with his solemn, dark eyes, he began snipping.

Soon Suzanne's hair lay in strips all over the floor around her.

And as with Tony and the tattoo, she no longer watched what he was doing or how she was being altered; instead, she listened intently to Reuben speaking of his faith.

"I could not live in Los Angeles without being Orthodox." He was bent over, concentrating on cutting the hair over Suzanne's ear evenly, as she listened spellbound, barely registering the metallic slashing of his scissors and the touch of his small, careful hands.

"I find that the teachings of the Torah and attending Temple, observing the Sabbath—all these things bring order and meaning in my life, and teach my children about their heritage, as well as giving them gratitude and respect they can carry with them throughout this frequently chaotic life."

Suzanne listened to him speechlessly. It was important she hear every word for the simple reason that she had been brought by God to Reuben in order to receive his divine message. No other explanation would serve. Surely God himself had insinuated this insistent grooming itch into her head—an itch that required immediate scratching. And that scratch had led her to this spiritual lock-shearing. The key to living her hair-brained life the right way was the religion of her long-lost father! The message was so clear! And it was then that she decided to convert to Judaism.

Reuben's voice was mesmerizing to her, filling areas in her mind where earlier only she could be found. His was a world of peace and prayers and lit candles, a world following the word of God—all of this sounded so wonderful to Suzanne. So . . . so defined by ritual and law. Perhaps this could calm the wild thing in her. A thing that yes, she had courted and nurtured into bloom, she'd done all that and more but . . .

but something small and still at the back of her sensed there was danger at the end of all this frantic happiness . . . and maybe there really was no way of knowing what it might lead to, which was part of what was so thrilling about it, but then again . . . if she remembered rightly, it was also what could get quite scary, bringing her to a place where there was no governing sensibility. Just a blur of forward motion, damn the torpedoes, take no prisoners, but ultimately, little else. So, perhaps if she converted to Judaism, she would be taken care of; God would watch over her, and as one of God's chosen folk she could walk upright in a world of other like-minded people, living a life laid out—everything considered in advance. A sensible, studious person who frowned when she thought thoughts stretching back thousands of years to her lost tribe's beginning—well, that burden of considering could crush even the noblest of brows. Why, she might even rub her chin as a newly profound ponderer! And she was already enraged at those people who blew themselves up in Israel, killing innocent Israelis, plus she just didn't like them; that was a start, no?

Listening to Reuben speaking of the teachings of the Torah in that calm voice, punctuated by the *snip snip snip* of his skilled scissors, Suzanne felt herself getting smaller with each sentence, her body made miniature by the meter of his words, though her soul was somehow magnified with exhilaration. To be in the presence of this man's faith, intoxicated by the peace she heard in this hairdresser's soothing voice, she would follow this voice to the end of everything he had to say about this most awesome of subjects, camp out until he continued. Yes, she had decided she would now start down the path of righteousness toward a safe and holy destination. Closing her eyes, she felt a warm breeze blow in through the open doorway. And all at once she understood the breeze to be the breath of God, sent to this hair salon to sigh her in the right direction. Fate had brought her to Reuben to hear the word of God spoken through him and, having listened, she was stirred—stirred, blown, and cut, in preparation for her entrance into Reuben's peaceful heaven on earth.

Yes.

She would become Jewish and everything would be fine.

Twenty minutes later Suzanne walked out of the Hair-Brained Hair Salon with Reuben's number and his rabbi's name and number written in his neat hand on a slip of paper along with the time she was to meet him and his family at temple on Friday night and an invitation to the break-fast after the High Holy Days at his home. Armed with this and her new, very short haircut, she strode down the street feeling determined, resolute, coiffed, and spiritual. Then, just as she was about the cross the street to her car, she glimpsed the beauty supply shop with the boxes of fluorescent haircolor prominently displayed in the window.

A short time later, Suzanne stood at the cash register with seven cans of glitter hair spray set out in front of her on the counter, three silver and four gold. She was about to pay for her bounty when her cell phone rang from deep inside her purse. Quickly shoving her hand into its depths, she frantically rummaged for it.

"I'll get it!" she sang out in a loud voice, continuing to sort through the contents of her bag. "If it's for you, is there anyone you'd rather not talk to?" she asked the man behind the counter cheerfully.

"Pardon?" he had a heavy accent and a puzzled expression on his wide, dark face. "I do not understand."

"Never mind!" Grasping the phone, Suzanne brought it to her ear. "Ron's Beauty Supply," she shouted into the receiver. "If you're beautiful, we've got the supplies for you!"

Then, realizing there was no one on earth she wanted to talk to, she quickly clicked the phone off and tossed it back into her purse.

THE ROAD OUT
OF EARSHOT

Craig was planning to spend a romantic weekend with Angelica Mellon (Angel to her friends). Angelica was originally a friend of Leland's that Craig had met one day when she helped ferry Honey from Leland's house to Suzanne's. Suzanne wasn't sure what branch of the bona fide Mellon family Angelica hailed from, but that she came from it at all was, for most people, more than enough. Initially, Suzanne found herself quite annoyed with the Angelica/Craig equation, regarding Angelica as a pretender to the throne Suzanne had so recently been thrown from. In Suzanne's eyes, this made Angelica Honey's other stepmother when that position wasn't being occupied by Leland's boyfriend, Nick.

Here was yet another contest of her own devising, a contest she could only lose: viewing Angelica as next in line to top dog in Honey's or Leland's imagined kennel. How could she compete with this smiling heiress, this alpha bitch complete with pedigree, East Coast class, and connections? Clearly, her crown was threatened: Leland simply wasn't allowed to have a close girlfriend; that violated every unspoken agreement she had with him, each unarticulated vow, especially the one where she remained the one and only woman in his life, having been simply replaced by a man. This notion had always been such a comfort to her.

But now, this classy upstart was everywhere only Suzanne had formerly been, her prints visible not only on Leland and Honey but now on Craig as well; Suzanne feared that soon she would be all over everything! The melting, sticky heiress! Gangway! Oh, it was too awful. Too horrible for anything but the worst of worlds. How could everyone treat her with such disregard? How could Craig particularly? To cast his own lot in with Leland! The traitor!

"You bastard! You ass-grabbing class fucker!" Suzanne shrieked upon discovering his treachery. "How could you betray me like this!"

Craig's arms were crossed and he regarded Suzanne quizzically. "What time are you going to stop making no sense? 'Cause I want to make sure I'm here for that. Maybe by then you'll have grown out some of your new army crewcut. Hey, as long as he was hacking away up there going for that Squeaky Fromme member of the wedding thing, why didn't he cut out some of that nonsense flubbered all over your brains making you think me dating Angelica had anything to do with that homo ex of yours?"

"Really?" she began sarcastically. "You don't see how I might think it was weird that you were dating a friend of Leland's? And not just *any* friend, but his date when his boyfriend has more pressing nationally important plans? Him being the Prime Minister of Su Casa Mi Casa Hairstyle, he has a lot of duties to perform. Howdy Duties, that is."

Craig shook his head wearily. Suzanne looked out the window and watched as the gardener blew the leaves in her yard into tidy, submissive piles with the loudest machine ever invented, scaring the leaves into corners, roaring her yard slowly into neat.

"Between you and that gardening device of torture, I'm getting a raging headache," he said. "The funniest thing is that I was going to say that I didn't know which was worse, but I've decided you definitely have the edge. At least at the end of this god-awful racket, the yard is neat, but after your idiotic bullshit, there's pretty much nothing."

"Well, not nothing, just me feeling like whenever I'm around you, it's as if you have name above the title in the movie of my life and I'm a bit player or background atmosphere. Somehow you became Lucy and I'm Ethel. I mean, look at me! I'm one step away from wearing a turban and housecoat and calling you 'girlfriend'—" Craig started toward the front door, hesitating on the threshhold of the awful din of the high-decibel leaf blower, then pivoting dramatically. "And *no,* for the last time, you can't be in Ricky's show!"

And turning once more with a flourish, he strode from the house.

"Where are you going?" Suzanne hadn't anticipated his irritation, and his disapproval worked on her like a corrosive poison, eating away at her good opinion of herself like a glutton.

"I'm going to my cosy hut to get ready for my weekend. Does that meet with your approval?" he shouted over his shoulder, stalking away from her down the brick path to the guesthouse. Suzanne was shocked to discover she'd not only crossed a line but might in fact be completely in the wrong. And even if she wasn't wrong, it didn't matter. Nothing mattered except that she recover the lost ground of amity that had so recently existed between them. Amity that had carried her to the high ground of no longer alone.

"Okay, look, I'm sorry I've been acting like such a brat," she called after him.

Craig froze, his hand gripping the doorknob, one foot slightly raised, arrested in midstep. "Could you repeat that? I could barely hear you with the shrieking leaf blower and—"

Suzanne interjected, childlike. "Okay. I'm sorry I've been acting like such an asshole."

Craig nodded, listening with his eyes closed. After a brief moment, he opened them, smiling.

"Fantastic, thank you. I recommend saying those exact words to me twice a day until the end of time." He pulled the door open. "Angelica and I should be back Sunday afternoon. Sunday night at the

latest. I'll have my cell phone with me in case you have the ill-advised
need to call me. But I'd prefer to only hear from you in the event of an
emergency on the order of one or both of your heads bursting into
flame. Also, while I'm gone, could you please rescue me from this
Hoyt guy? He's not only depressing me but on top of everything else,
he smokes cigars and this morning he asked me if I'd give him a hug.
It's driving me nuts. I keep expecting to find him stinking up the
whole kitchen with his big dead head in the oven."

Suzanne smiled. "Okay, Charlie the Tuna-breath. I'll take care of it
tomorrow," she called after him emphatically. But Craig had disappeared into his room, slamming the screen door behind him. Suzanne
waited for a moment in case of an encore, but when none appeared,
she turned and walked out to the car.

What was ordinary in her was being overwhelmed by the extraordinary. Her nerves had lost their endings. They just kept on going and
going, oozing out into the future, performing odd jobs and intuiting
how best to manage a given situation, or even a situation that wasn't
given so much as a happy product of give and take.

It seemed to Suzanne she was an avalanche ever gathering force,
growing more undeniable in her effect, everything around her adding
to her effluence and efficiency. It felt as though the entire world eagerly fought for her attention, fought and won, infusing her with
pleasure, refusing her nothing. In short, she was so very pleased to be
here.

Yes, the experiment of her without her medication was very rap-
idly becoming a great success. She slowly strode to where her car
awaited; it too sensed an imminent ovation.

"Good evening, ladies and gentleman and welcome to the Ver-
sailles Room. Let's give a warm round of applause for Doris Mann!
Let's give a square meal to Tony Miller! Put your hands together—let
other things fall apart—your marriage! Your house of cards! Your cool
customer veneer, let it crack to kingdom come, 'cause, baby, I'm cleaning my oven! You're soaking in it! A sail! A sale! What ho, the prince!
Good night, you've been a great audience! Thank you, Detroit!"

Then Suzanne realized if she was going to talk to herself, she should wait until she was out of earshot. Earshot, like Dodge, was a town that was dangerous to her. A chatty girl could get in trouble there. And, slamming her car door, she inserted her keys into the ignition, gunned her motor, and backed down the drive. Turning her radio up full blast, she made her way toward . . . well, it hardly mattered. She was recently sprung and ready for anything, momentum once again gathering her in its strong arms and holding her close, the prodigal daughter, home for the harvest. Home and hungry for it all.

OxyCOFFIN

Stopping at a liquor store to buy some cigarettes, Suzanne found herself at the counter standing right next to Tony, the tattoo artist from the Flying Pig. He was handing the clerk a twenty-dollar bill for a bottle of grappa and waiting for his change. "There you go, sir." Tony tucked the bottle under his arm, then turning to exit, almost knocked Suzanne over. "Oh, sorry." He stopped, then peered at her through narrowed eyes. "Say, aren't you the crazy chick from the parlor?" He frowned. "The one who scared the chick who . . ." Then nodding, he answered his own question. "Yeah, you are. Your hair's different, that's what it is, right?" That's when he smiled at her and Suzanne noticed for the first time just how heterosexual he was. This guy wasn't just not gay like Leland, and not a boy-toy like Thor—no, he was an honest-to-not-so-goodness felon with tattoos, a fondness for weapons, and a probation officer. To Suzanne's way of thinking, even if Tony was an ex-con, well, let's just say he'd never been anyone's bitch back there in the pen. Making him even more straight than the womanizing Dean Bradbury.

"Hey, I'm sorry about losing that client or whatever. It was just that—"

"Hey, why be sorry? It was funny." Tony pocketed his change and shook his head laughing. Outside, several motorcyclists gunned their way down the boulevard. " 'No little piece of jewelry is going to save the day.' Funny stuff, man." He nodded appreciatively, "You're a wild chick." Suzanne blushed, paying the man behind the counter for two packs of cigarettes. Then turning once more to Tony, she smiled sheepishly.

"So you guys weren't mad or anything?" Tony dismissed this absurd notion with a wave of his big hand.

"Get real," he scoffed. "Most of our business is tattoos anyway. I mean, Big Bird wants us to get more into piercings, but I could give a fuck."

As they started out of the liquor store together, Suzanne took note of Tony's pale blue eyes and of how the tattoos on his head seemed to complement them. As they passed from the brightly lit store to the dusky night, a bell sounded, tripped by their stepping over the mat, alerting the liquor store employee to the shop's ebb and flow of customers. But Suzanne chose to interpret the bell in her own way, bending it to her profound purposes, as a sign for her to remain with Tony. To marry their two fates together, however briefly, and see what came of it.

Stopping onto the sidewalk in front of the store, Tony gazed up the street thoughtfully.

"Hey, you know, if you're not busy, we should finish that tat of yours." He looked at her matter-of-factly, moving the bag of grappa from under one arm to the other. "I like to finish everything I start, you know what I mean?"

Suzanne nodded. She understood perfectly.

Hadn't she tried to finish things with Leland? And hadn't he prevented her from doing so? Well, here was someone who was as conscientious as she was. A tattoo artist who liked to see things through.

"You mean now?" Opening her cigarettes, she hit the pack, extracting one. As she was about to light it, Tony took the matches from her hand and struck one, holding it to her cigarette like a scribbled-on Paul Heinreid.

"Now." He threw the match to the ground and looked at her expectantly. "What do ya say?" She shrugged.

"Where should we do it? The shop?"

He scratched the bristles on his chin thoughtfully. "We could go anywhere, really. My place or yours. Or the shop. Whatever." He shrugged.

Suzanne started toward the curb. "So let's go to your place." He nodded, following her curbside. They stood together in silence as a helicopter flew low over their heads. "My van's just over there."

Sitting in the high, torn leather seat of Tony's orange van, Suzanne smiled, content; she was finally with a real, regular human. Just a simple, unassuming ex-con tattoo artist out for a good time, like she was. Her worries were over. Tony started the engine, turning to her.

"You don't mind if we stopped at my dealer's first, do you? He was getting me some OxyContin and . . ."

"No problem."

Tony revved the engine before putting it into gear. "To Oz?" He glanced at her, his eyebrow arched ironically.

"To Oz," she echoed, smiling. Tony sped noisily down the dark street.

Howard wasn't anything like any dealer Suzanne had ever known before. But then she hadn't had occasion to frequent dealers during her last round in the drug ring. Instead, she'd simply had a lot of unnecessary dental surgery, raided medicine chests, or got friends to buy her some of the preferred pastel pills from the oh-so-black market. For a while after Leland left, she'd drifted back into drug use, thinking that no one could really blame her for wanting to dial her bright sparkle of pain down to a twinkling. Surely they would understand that this interval of ingesting evil again in the hopes of feeling good was a necessary one, under the circumstances. She was simply doing what any reasonable abandoned person would do, wasn't she?

But in fact, they did blame her. But more to the point, she blamed herself. Blamed herself mercilessly because of Honey. With Honey in her care, everything had changed. There was no question but that it was wrong to expose a child to a subdued and sometimes even slurred mother. No. She should have just taken it like the man Leland had left her for. So, after yet another struggle with herself, Suzanne had given up, turning herself into the AA police, getting sober yet one more time, getting yet one more sponsor, and sitting through what sometimes felt to her to be millions more meetings week after week, snuggling down again between the safety of those two tall capital letters and pulling them toward herself fearfully. This time she wouldn't leave again. No more go-rounds, round and round the proverbial drain; sobriety's harsh bright sunlight burning into her. Where was the holy healing of chemical rain to pour on life's stinky endless parade? It cooled the hot sober march to nowhere good, shaded the glare of the sunny, not-so-funny drug-free day.

But now she couldn't wait to dart through her escape hatch marked "Bipolar Emergency Exit"—and of course, the way to this exit was to stop your meds, go to Howard's, and continue straight on till morning. And once you throw out that bath water, you can bring on board all sorts of other babies—like the little tykes at Howard's. So in a way, you could say she had maternal instincts, just of a higher order.

"I've never tried OxyContin," she shouted to Tony over the din of the radio, her arm dangling out the window, keeping beat to the music on the side of the van. The wind was cool on her face; it felt wonderful. She was free . . . her latest, greatest adventure had finally begun, the one she obviously had been preparing for for weeks and weeks without really knowing it.

"Really? Oh, you're gonna love it. I mean, if you like opiates."

They sped west down Olympic Boulevard toward Santa Monica, passing several cars sporting yellow-and-purple Lakers flags fluttering proudly from their windows.

"If I like opiates?" Suzanne asked rhetorically, for all of the world knew the answer.

"I love opiates!" she cheered as they continued down the boulevard past all the car dealerships and fast food outlets. "Go Lakers!" she shouted gaily as they pulled up next to a truck at the stoplight. The truck driver looked at her strangely, then stared straight in front of him. "What's the matter with him?" Suzanne asked Tony, who shrugged, making an illegal U-turn once the light had changed.

"Some people are just assholes." He cranked the radio up as far as it would go. "Fuck 'em!" he shouted, turning down Fourteenth Street, but he could barely be heard under the mocking voice of Eminem.

They pulled up in front of a run-down one-story house set back behind tall bushes at the end of a dry, brown lawn. The curtains were drawn over the large picture window, and a pale man sat on a chair on the front porch, smoking peacefully.

"He doesn't look like a dealer. He looks like a . . ." Suzanne managed somehow not to say nerd or geek, ". . . a math genius or something." Tony laughed, rubbing the dark stubble on his chin again, mounting the front steps to the porch where Howard waited.

"You hear that, buddy? My friend here thinks you look like a math geek." Suzanne flushed, punching Tony's muscular arm under his black leather jacket.

"I didn't say geek. I said genius." God forbid she insult this circumspect, trim little drug dealer who now gave her a polite grin as he pushed his rimless glasses farther up on his large nose before standing, opening his screen door, and entering his sparsely decorated living room. Suzanne and Tony followed him wordlessly as if by prearrangement, moving to the brown leather couch he indicated.

"Well, I am pretty good with numbers," Howard offered, pulling marijuana and rolling papers from a smooth wooden box with the words AND THEN SOME emblazoned on the lid. He rolled a joint with meticulous care on the coffee table in front of him as Tony cackled with laughter, slapping Suzanne hard on the small of her back.

"Get it? He's good with *numbers!*" Tony pulled her down onto the rug beside him where they watched Howard finish rolling the perfect joint. Suzanne smiled weakly, dimly recalling that joints were called numbers in some universe she'd visited back there somewhere. She felt she should try to join in the spirit of the evening, whatever the effort, for the sake of camaraderie and the promise of experiencing a new drug not too far ahead.

Firing up his so-called number, Howard dragged on it deeply and then, every inch the consummate host, he offered the sharp-smelling cigarette to his assembled guests. Suzanne was reminded of a T-shirt she'd just seen on a recent shopping spree while picking up some Afro Sheen and adult diapers for the guesthouse: TAKE ME TO YOUR DEALER.

She shook her head. "It makes me think about death," she explained apologetically, shrugging. "You know, the inevitability of it. I used to love it, but it turned on me. Not pot, death. Thanks anyway, though." Tony delicately took the joint from between Howard's fingers and carefully brought it to his lips.

"Bummer." Howard released the word with the smoke, coughing slightly. Then rising, he crossed to a desk at the side of the room and opened a drawer, withdrawing an envelope and spilling its contents onto the table.

Tony leaned forward, exhaling his smoke and examining the treasure now lying before them. "Ahhhh," he exclaimed admiringly, his blue eyes shining. "Just what the doctor ordered."

"Literally, at one point," Suzanne added, as one of the yellow pills began rolling toward the edge of the table. Howard leaned forward and slapped the wayward pill with the flat of his bony, hash-scented hand. "Get back here, you fucker," he urged the pill tenderly, picking it up almost daintily with his thumb and forefinger and holding it aloft for his guests to see.

"What've you got to crush them with?" Tony asked in a businesslike manner. Howard absently picked up a round crystal paperweight with red letters spelling out the word MOTHER and brought it down with a loud smack on the first of the little golden pills lined up, waiting for obliteration. Suzanne looked away from the paperweight guiltily, as if further exposure to the word would implicate her somehow. Of what she didn't know, but whatever it was, she wanted no part of it. But deep down she knew it was something she was in her other life—a title she'd earned by having Honey. Still a little girl with soft hair and softer skin. Wasn't she the one who pronounced "hamburger" as "hangburger" and "magazine" as "magnazine?" Who walked late because she had Suzanne's funny triple-jointed hips but

133

talked early because she had her triple-jointed way of talking? Or was that another child? Or was that perhaps her? She didn't want to think about it. She was on a break from that part of her life. Just now she wasn't a mother. She let those thoughts slip away from her before they could find purchase.

Anyway, that wasn't the main and only thing. It couldn't be, could it? She was all things to all people. She was nothing to no one. She was a work in progress that required very little effort. She couldn't be someone to other people, she needed to be free to become who she was going to be: a mercurial creature able to burrow into music, slide onto chords and ride them, hold onto their wiry sound like she belonged; ride their warm, bouncing rock 'n' roll ride.

She was taken, no longer a person, but a citizen of wherever she was, whatever she could gather hands on, whoever ambled through her sights—a, "What's that? Can I come have some?" Have some more, more, more everything and everyone was strawberry ice cream to her—a child of "Now what?" as opposed to "Now." All upward and forward motion—all, "Look at that!" Let's be here and there simultaneously—make the soon the new now (and be quick about it).

So the drive down to Tijuana was pleasant for a variety of reasons, the first and foremost being that probably anything would be pleasant experienced on three OxyContins. As she understood it, when ingested as prescribed, it killed your extreme pain all day. But when crushed and snorted through a dollar bill for no good reason save pleasure, it was morphine, pure and simple. And as such produced a feeling of such blissful well-being that it couldn't but enhance any road trip, or anything at all really. Sure she'd read reports of entire towns getting addicted to it and knew it had been nicknamed OxyCoffin by those who'd seen its tragic effects. But those were other people, careless people, guided by different stars, subject to different rules, marked for sadder destinies. And anyway, information like this quickly lost its hard-won space in Suzanne's head, as her mind was now crowded with faster, happier things.

The second reason the trip was pleasant was the delightful ab-

sence of other cars inhibiting their trajectory. For not too many travelers tended to make their trip at two in the morning, making their
passage virtually clear straight through to the border with Tony navigating his van over the gray snaking freeway, taking them even farther down the river where it would ultimately empty into the
bustling cove where the treasure of more OxyContin ostensibly lay
buried. And it was this irresistibly tempting treasure that Tony and
Suzanne were presently en route to dig up.

The radio blasted a mix of Tony's favorite bands: Grateful Dead,
Aerosmith, and Butthole Surfers, and with her head resting halfway
in and out of the window and her eyes closed and with one bare foot
resting against his leg, keeping beat with the rhythm of the songs and
her other foot in Tony's right hand, Suzanne felt as though her life finally had purpose and meaning. Tony drove and chain-smoked with
his remaining hand as Suzanne breathed in the breezes from the
nearby ocean, whose rolling waves could occasionally be seen beyond
the freeway or between a few newly constructed beach houses in the
complexes being built there.

She had talked almost the entire way out of Los Angeles proper,
east through Pomona, continuing south through Long Beach, Westminster, Irvine, and San Juan Capistrano with Tony at the wheel,
smoking silently with his heavily lidded eyes on the open road.

"The thing about getting collagen is that it's so temporary, you
know? I mean it's great, but it's so expensive. I mean, one day it occurred to me I was virtually paying rent on my face, you know? Well,
so maybe I should buy, right? I mean you add up all that rent and I've
probably spent more than a face-lift at this point, you know? But
only old ladies get face-lifts, right? Or my weird father. He gets face-
lifts. Can you believe that? He's had so many, he looks Chinese.
Which is handy 'cause he likes to go out with Asian women. Go out
with or marry, depending. And totally great women, like always. But
I'm not kidding; I mean he's had so many face-lifts that he's lost his
sideburns. They're probably the hair at the back of his head now,
right? I'm not joking, it's like he looks polished, you know, as if he
buffs his face after he brushes his teeth, which if you knew my father,

isn't entirely out of the question. Do you know what he did the last time I saw him? Well, he hasn't been able to hear that well for years, right? Talking to him, you always felt like you had one of those bad connections on a ship-to-shore radio—or maybe that's redundant—anyway he's been saying "Hello? Suzanne? What?" for years. So finally it's official: he can't hear, so he gets hearing aids, right? You know, those really expensive ones that are super-tiny and fit inside your ears? Whatever. Anyway, one night he takes them out and puts them in his pillbox by his bed so he'll remember where he put them. And, of course, he's pretty much a pill addict, so in the morning, yup, you got it. He eats them. All eight thousand dollars of them right down the hatch in one gulp. I mean, with that same money you could buy one and a half Mecca clickers or pay the equivalent of four months' rent on your face. Anyway, the last time we saw him—Honey and I—which was the next day, well, after he told us what had happened, we started shouting into his stomach or his ass whenever he couldn't hear us. Which was most of the time. Honey totally loved that. She barely has any idea who he is, of course, 'cause he's such a bad grandfather. Bad meaning absent. You know—never there. Same like he was as a dad. That's why I always wanted to make sure Honey had a good father, and, you know . . . a real relationship with him. 'Cause I never had that and I missed it a lot. I mean, I pretended I didn't as a kid, I think, but I did. It's not that he's a bad person, I've decided. He just has emotional A.D.D., meaning like when you're with him, he's nuts about you, you're literally the greatest person in his life and you believe it 'cause right then so absolutely does he. But if he walks into the hallway the next minute and sees a jacket he likes, BOOM! You're not even a memory. It's a wipeout. You never happened. It's all about the jacket. Anyway, Honey doesn't have that; she has this great relationship with Leland—that's my ex's name. Leland. He turned out to be gay, I told you that, right?"

The sudden silence from Suzanne's side of the van startled Tony. Had she asked him something, or was her interminable chatter finally at an end? He looked at her, rounding what he could of his chemically clouded eyes.

"Huh?" he managed, blinking.

Suzanne smiled, leaning in from the window. "You weren't listening to me, were you, nugget? *Nugget?*"

Tony went to flick his ash out the window too late, and the wind knocked the lit ash into his lap. "Shit," he muttered, sweeping the mess off himself irritably and then flinging what remained of his cigarette out onto the road. "Hell, yeah, I was listening. I just missed the question, 'cause I was looking at the ugly oil distillery thing over there." He pointed toward the coastline and Suzanne peered through the darkness at what appeared to be a factory in the shape of two side-by-side domes topped by cylindrical towers. "It looks like two tits," Suzanne pronounced, then saw a sign at the off ramp. "Look! It's the San Onofre nuclear power plant. Or a little thing I like to call 'Nuclear Nipples by the Sea.' This must be Mother Earth's breast-feeding outlet—her ample rack filled with lethal glowing milk to breast-feed a naughty nation." Since there was no specified rejoinder indicated by her comments, Tony nodded gravely, lighting another cigarette with his Zippo lighter and closing it with a clack.

"Fuck, it sure does look like tits." He inhaled deeply and began kneading Suzanne's foot again, having given all he could conversationally give for the moment.

"What was I saying?" Then she remembered, "Oh, yeah, fathers. Honey has a good gay one and I have one that's straight and pretty bad. Did I tell you about the time I called him when I was on acid? When would I have told you that? Last year when I didn't know you, or the year before? Anyway, first I called my stepfather, who I hadn't spoken to in, like, four thousand years 'cause—well never mind why—mostly 'cause he stole my mother's money and fucked hookers who we were told were manicurists, and who were brought to the house by his barber. Sure, they were manicurists if cuticle is another way of saying dick. My brother, Thomas, tried to film him in action by putting a camera under a doll's skirt in my stepfather Sydney's room—hopefully not for the same reason he got the manicures. Anyway, this isn't about Sydney, I only mention my stepfather at all 'cause I called him first on the acid and said I was sorry I hadn't spoken to him in, like, forever because he's never really done anything to me. Which was true, by the way, but probably only because he was too busy doing such a good job on my mother. But I'm glad I called him in a way, 'cause he died a little while later in this freakish way from some guy punching him in the arm which made a clot go to his heart or something. Anyway, I called my real father next 'cause I guess I was on a real 'call your dads on acid' roll and blah blah blah. I musta said this one thing out of twelve hundred thousand blathering acid things, 'You should come stay with me here in New York'—I was living in this little apartment in New York at the time—I was, you know, like twenty-one or something. Anyway, boom! Like, sixteen hours later, I'm just waking up from, like, two minutes' sleep after a night of a thousand calls to a thousand fathers and the doorbell rings and *voilà!* There he is! The original, one-and-only, instant belated dad, complete with suitcase and no sideburns, ready to finally have a relationship with his long-lost-on-purpose daughter, all set to move in with me. After that I made up a saying regarding my family. Ready?" Without waiting for an answer or taking a breath, Suzanne continued. " 'The apple doesn't fall apart far from the tree.' First it was 'The apple doesn't fall down far from the tree,' but my friend Lucy said it sounded too much like the original. Hers, by the way, was 'The apple doesn't fuck far from the tree.' "

Suzanne paused for a moment, looking around her, as if in search of a lost thing, though she was unable to recall what exactly it was she was missing. "Is the sun coming up? Look over there behind the mountain . . . the sky's lighter. I always think that's funny—the sun on one side and the moon on the other. Some people say that's a sign of fertility. Oh yeah, look! There's a sign, see? San Diego, sixty-two miles. That's good, 'cause I probably should go to the bathroom. Plus, maybe eat something—not that I'm hungry—it's just . . . Have you ever been to Escondido?"

Tony took a drag of his cigarette, shaking his head. "Uh-uh."

"Me either. So now we still haven't been there! Your witness." Suzanne suddenly pointed to another sign that was whizzing by outside the window. "Oh look! The Zoo! I forgot about that! And Sea-

World! They have all that shit down here; I totally forgot about all that! My dad took me to the zoo once as an adult—or maybe I took him. Yeah, that's it. I took him when I was taking Honey, and I wanted her to have the whole grandfather experience thing. You know—in case he—whatever—he's older now, and she should meet this grandfather she has out there somewhere, right? I wanted to give her an installation for her family museum. Oh, by the way, this is why I wanted to have a child with Leland, 'cause I knew he would be a really good father and I wasn't totally positive about my abilities as a mom. You know, the funny thing is, is that while I knew Leland would be a great dad, it really bothers me sometimes. You know, so that he can give her all the nice normal stuff that I can't. Plus, I never had it, the whole nurturing father thing. Never mind nurturing, try there at all. So sometimes I'm almost . . . not jealous, because I want her to have the best of everything, even if I can't give it all to her—but I feel like, why couldn't I have had all that, too? It looks so great. You know. I finally see what I always suspected I was missing and it turns out it *is* actually all it's cracked up to be. I mean, I mostly had TV dads to go on, but still I see Leland with her and it's like, shit! I never had that! But I hate when I catch myself doing that 'cause it's so selfish and self-pitying. Blub blub blub! Me! Me! Me! Ugh—it's so gross. Anyway, the funny thing is, I always knew I'd be the substandard parent, even when she was little. Plus, the other funny thing is that even the nanny treats me that way sometimes. Like she's the mother or Leland's wife or something and I'm the weird aunt who they tolerate visits from 'cause I only have six months to live." Suzanne paused, frowning. "Ew! That's a morbid thought. Where did that come from? No more like that, please!" She shouted the latter, as though pleading with her inner ventriloquist responsible for the lion's share of her roar of chatter.

The sky was brightening all around them, seagulls squawking in the sky, flying in over the housing developments that clogged the hillside like dividing cells, one after another, overtaking everything.

The air rushing through her open window was gradually warming as it blew by her and Suzanne smiled up at the new sun. A sun promising to see to her needs, watching over her and guiding her. She leaned back, closing her eyes with a kind of energized contentment, a serenity experienced at high speeds. Bliss breaking the sound barrier and picking up speed along with a few other goodies at Mach 1.

Tony lit yet another cigarette as they drove past downtown San Diego.

"Hey, have you got a pen and paper? Sometimes when I feel like this, I write something. And think of it this way, if I write, you don't have to listen to me! At least until we get to the border. Then maybe I send it as an urgent telegram to my congressman and all my friends. Good deal, huh?"

Tony didn't have any paper and the only pen he had was out of ink, so they pulled off the freeway, stopping at a gas station to refuel the van and for Tony to "water the porcelain lawn" as he put it. In the market, Suzanne bought six Diet Cokes, three packs of Marlboro Ultra Lights, a legal pad, and two blue Roller Ball pens, while Tony purchased Visine, a Red Bull, and four 100,000 Grand bars.

Back in the van, Suzanne tore the clear wrapping off the pad, throwing it into the backseat. "This will be my last will and testament. Well, my second-to-last anyway. And not so much a will, but a will she or won't she, a will 'o the wisp coupled with a willingness to say what's on my mind. To get what's on my mind off my chest, if you will—or even if you won't—other than that, cover me; I'm going in. Dive! Dive!" And with that, she bent over the pad and began to scribble furiously.

Get up, you big trout-loving sea creature
He emerged from the deep sea, emerged from that deep
    thinking sea how you are.
The EmergenSea.
To look in the mirror.
Go look in the mirror,
See what Jesus did to your head.
See it up there glowing softly,
See it say the things it's said.

How does your head howl without your say-so?
Why does it play so round the clock,
Between a rock and a hard place.
Your heart's the hard place.
Your head's the rock.
Your soft rock head just swells with the info,
All sick from the facts it's fed.
Way way up there.
See it shining.
Watch the eyes watch . . . just see them see.
Think, except for square teeth,
I'm sweet soft roundness—
I'm round say,
Therefore I'm me.
Awwww, look now, see a smile start,
Little hard teeth,
In a big soft head.
Where's that smile now?
Now that we need it.
What's this look you leaked instead?
Then there's my head;
See, look . . . it's chewy.
It waits for word,
Word from the wise.
My head watches.
Shhh, now it's sleeping.
It gives what's taken by big surprise.
My head's surrounded by air that's hostile;
Air seeps through nostrils.
It knows no bounds.
My head knows your head is out there.
It combs the night air to brush out clowns.

Suzanne looked up from her writing pad as Tony turned off the freeway toward a large sign reading MEXICOACH.

"Where are we?" She put the pen down and leaned out the window, blinking, examining her new surroundings.

"Without actually being there, we're here," and turning into the Mexicoach parking lot, Tony took a ticket at the gate.

"But this isn't the border guard place, is it?"

They drove slowly through the congested parking lot, hunting for a free space.

"We leave the car here and take the bus into TJ proper. Otherwise some fuck could rip off the van." Tony pulled into a space and turned off the ignition. "If we need wheels, we can always take a cab."

This was the most Suzanne had heard Tony say since she'd met him. "Okay!" She smiled. "You don't need to scream at me. I mean, I'm right here."

Tony looked baffled. "I didn't—"

"I was *kidding!*" Suzanne was eager to get on with the next part of her life. And the next and the next and the next. "Come on! Look, there's the bus! Let's go!" Flinging her door open, she jumped into the midmorning sunshine and bounded toward the departing bus that would take her into Mexico, the Oxycontinent and beyond.

THE STEEP HILL OF LONGING

Craig's friend Charlie had suggested he take Angelica to Two Bunch Palms for the weekend, telling him it was, "A wonderful and enchanting spot to take someone for whom you have deep feelings . . . where you can fuck her till her ears bleed. Till her tits shit. Till her tits beg you to stop but her ass says, for God's sake, Go!" Charlie frowned, "Or is it her butt says . . . No, I'm pretty sure it's ass . . ."

Craig had shaken his head at Charlie, smiling sadly. "You have a way with words, my friend," he sighed. "Plus you weigh a lot, making you heavy, but thankfully not my brother, which is unfortunate in this particular instance 'cause if you were, I'd make you lend me your car. Remind me though to have you do the toast at my wedding." But in the end, he'd opted for Charlie's suggestion, figuring that, what with Charlie being a wealthy television star and all, he would know his way around romantic getaways. Besides which, he might even be able to help him secure the Bugsy Siegel Hideaway Suite, complete with its own outdoor Jacuzzi and bullet hole in the bathroom wall.

Craig and Angelica had driven out midmorning so as to avoid as much weekend traffic and heat as possible—as much as one could avoid in the California desert in summertime. Also, they'd wanted to get in early to soak in the hot springs they'd heard about. Float around together in warm water, wearing the smallest of swimsuits, perhaps even have an outdoor couples massage. "Not as kinky as it sounds," Charlie told Craig apologetically. "But somehow kinky all the same, if you play it the right way."

So, with high hopes for a wild weekend, Angelica and Craig set out in his convertible, their overnight bags stowed safely in the trunk of the car. Angelica's long brown hair blew every which way from underneath her orange Hermès scarf secured Audrey Hepburn–style over her head; large Gucci glasses shielded her light blue eyes.

Laughing and talking all the way along the San Bernardino freeway, Craig's compilation tape underscoring their mutual gestalt, any opportunity to express tactile emphasis was taken. He might touch her shoulder or hand to make a point, or she, doubling up in laughter, would touch his arm, his leg, even his hair, so that by the time they reached Desert Hot Springs, a warm undercurrent of desire coursed though them both. As they checked in, she leaned against him, her hand stealing around his broad back as he bent to sign their registration form.

"I don't know . . . do we want to dine in the dining room tonight?" Craig echoed the check-in clerk's question to them. His eyes were both mild and corrupted with meaning as his hand swept over Angelica's shoulder to the small of her back.

Leaning in, Angelica whispered, "Unless that's a euphemism, no." Her forehead snuggled into his neck and he smiled, his face warm.

They followed Walter the bellboy to the room, wound around one another like creeping, caressing anacondas, giggling and whispering like delighted teenagers, oblivious to their surroundings, to the heat, to everything but one another and their urgent, ophidian plans. These teenage water snakes.

Walter did his best showing them the appointments of the room, indicating the bathroom, the closet, the minibar, and the television, while Craig presented him with his most earnest, engaged expressions, as though following each word with rapt fascination, nodding. "Really? I would have never guessed! Well, it doesn't look mini to me, my friend." Angelica suppressed her laughter as best she could, giddy with wanting, breathless and tumbling down the steep hill of longing toward the inevitable intimacies of love. And while Walter pointed out how to use the Jacuzzi, Craig continued making his fascinated listening faces as he slipped his hand down the back of Angelica's pants, under the elastic of her underwear . . . and where all would very soon be lost.

FALSE IDOLS AND TRUE

Suzanne couldn't believe how Third World Tijuana was, given how close it was to the First World. "If this is the Third World," she stared around her as they emerged onto the main drag from the Mexicoach terminal, "Then where is the Second World? Not that I want to go there, but I feel somehow we skipped something, which could be viewed by some as sloppy traveling." They'd already found a pharmacy and purchased not only OxyContin but even a few little purple morphine pills for good to great measure.

Steering her by the elbow past souvenir shops displaying garish blankets, T-shirts, and statues of Spiderman, Bart Simpson, and Jesus—false idols and true—Tony told her, "The Second World is the one we enter through the drug door, which is on our right. Two blocks down from the looking glass." He rubbed his nose as lowriders rolled by them down the boulevard, growling and gunning their motors.

Suzanne nodded gravely. "Not to be confused with second star on the left and straight on toward morning. Which, of course, is the way madness lies. Flat on its back and sunning in the dark and moonless night high up there inside our heads."

Strolling past more bars, and more shops, and more and more pharmacies, it seemed to Suzanne that that's all there was, a rotation of these three types of places: you had your bars with their strippers and every sort of alcohol, with the occasional offering of food; and then you'd come to the stores selling Day of the Dead statues, or maracas, embroidered blouses, colorful skirts, and Hello Kitty children's desks; and then came the pharmacies. The pharmacies were everywhere, selling every sort of antibiotic, Viagra, Rogaine, and most important, all manner of codeine-based painkillers, over-the-counter and in strengths ranging from mild to deadly.

These controlled substances reined the out-of-control in her right in. She could use them to dial down the up in her. Water down the 120-proof of her and sprinkle it with winner-take-all spice. Jack's beans, thirty genies in a bottle, the hedonist's cocktail: they were all this to her and more. But to be able to just saunter in and order them up, well it was wrong, just shouldn't be, it tampered with the rules of what was required to unearth the buried treasure, steal the golden goose, find the elusive Holy Grail. The unwritten rules stated that a price had to be paid to find the pot of gold at rainbow's end—a pound of flesh, your soul, or first-born son. Everybody that was anybody longing to feel a little like someone else knew the truth of that. It was basic junkie law. One of the things you held to be true and took to heart or to your early grave, depending.

This easy Tijuana access flew in the face of all she'd ever known about achieving an entrance to the altered state. If the entrance wasn't a secret passage, where was the illicit thrill, the quest, the urgency?

Suzanne shook her head with wonder. "I don't believe it," her eyes wide and ever so gradually glazing, her pupils shrinking down to the size of a pin, until they were hardly pupils at all—uneducated dots at best. "If I'd known about this years ago, I'd be dead by now. I mean, it just seems so unbelievably wrong to just make it so easy to buy this shit. If it's this easy, well, it's as wrong as . . . as world war whatever—I don't know, you pick a number."

"Seven?"

Tony peered into the dark doorway of a seedy bar they were just passing. Suzanne looked inside, but couldn't see anything that caught her bloodshot eye with its double-fisted view.

"What?" she asked him without real interest. He shrugged.

"Nothin'. Just thought I'd see a guy I'd met there once." He extracted a cigarette and lit it with his Zippo. "No big." Suzanne nodded slowly, partially in agreement, partially in time with her slowed south-of-the-border-born-again-born-morphine-free-from-the-world's-cares-close-your-eyes-to-the-world-around-you troubles, *it makes you no never mind you are sure-footed and fancy-free to be or not to be you or me myself and I had a dream—I dreamed it for you baby—it wasn't for me and if it wasn't for me then where would you be, miss. . . .*

They'd come down a side street where the pharmacies were even more flexible—or anyway, where Tony knew a guy who knew a guy who had a friend.

Suzanne loved all this. She was so inside—felt so related—so hip—so taken care of and discarded at the same time. She was not only tattooed, she was a tattoo artist's sidekick drug-addicted friend. Sure, she knew something was wrong with this and that fact tickled at the back of her swollen, slowed-down consciousness. Tickled—a little girl. A little girl that said things like, "You like daddy more than me!" Well, of course she did—look at her—what choice did she have?

"No!" Suzanne cried out loud suddenly. Tony slowed and swung his bald head in her direction.

"What's up, little bit?" he wondered without interest. Suzanne smiled sheepishly and shook her head.

"Nothing—that's just my thought-dispersal-technique bowling ball bowling down some bad think pins. Never you mind, felon of mine. No biggie." She smiled her best smile. "As you were."

She drew her energy from down through the soles of her feet deep deep down through earth sand shale pay dirt, down lower still to the depths to the core: the great wild burning magma, that storeroom of passion, prehistoric and otherwise. The otherwise Wise Men and all the great soprano, bass, alto, tenor voices, this was where they sprang from; arias were unleashed from these great ovens and slipped into silences all over an unsuspecting operatic world.

It occurred to her that at some point she'd closed her eyes and another border had been crossed: a rough kiss, bringing a taste of beer and ten thousand cigarettes. A kiss she knew was coming once it arrived, but not how it had gotten there. It was both too late and too early—and only in that sense was it right on time. She stood like a good soldier receiving this unwelcome army—tried to alchemize it into the holy communion of OxyContin this unorthodox priest had only too recently blessed her with, ascending her into the heaven of its out-of-this-worldliness. How could she not embrace the man who had done so much for her by making so little of her? If she didn't embrace him in passion, then in gratitude?

But a kiss only. He couldn't expect much more, could he? Not after they'd numbed themselves to all feeling. And weren't they, after all, in the street somewhere in the middle of the day? Not exactly aphrodisiac material.

Then she recalled what she'd said to Dean Bradbury, *"Anglodesiac. We're white, remember?"* and she laughed . . . certain death to most sexual activity.

He broke away gruffly. "What's so funny?" Suzanne tried to get her giggling under control, she really did.

"Nothing. I mean, it totally had nothing to do with you. I was just remembering this thing I said to this guy. It was Dean Bradbury actually. Anyway, we were at this funeral and he said something about something not being an 'aphrodisiac,' and I go 'Anglodisiac. We're white, remember?' "

She waited for Tony's response, and when none came, when he in fact looked angry of all things—was that what it was? Angry? She wasn't used to making people angry—or . . . shit, maybe everyone *had* gotten mad and she hadn't seen it. Maybe she'd ruined everything and didn't know it and was only now catching up.

Man, she had to fix this and quick. *Pronto,* as her fellow Mexicans would say. Wasn't that it? Fuck the pronto—on with the fixing, starting with the stinky felon and working up.

"Look, I'm sorry, I was just—," and then something happened that was unthinkable. So unthinkable, really, that at first she couldn't conceive of it having happened to her: Tony hit her. Hit her hard right across the face.

No, she couldn't have imagined it. She didn't have an imagination like that. Besides . . . well, she couldn't think of anything else after. He'd knocked the sense right out of her head. More to the point, she was something like frightened right under the drugs she'd taken not to feel or care about anything at all.

"Jesus fucking Christ, I didn't figure there was no other way to get you to shut the fuck up. Girls like you . . ." Tony paused, unable to finish his thought for the moment. He lit a cigarette then noticed her eyes were wet with something. "Oh, for fuck's sake, don't go get all weepy on me, will ya? I barely tapped ya anyway. Anyway, if I hadn't done it, you'da probably gone on yammering again—telling me all that shit you say." He paused at this, taking a drag of his Marlboro. His lidded bloodshot eyes were hard and cruel.

Now his voice jumped an octave or so in an attempt to mimic the stunned Suzanne. "Oh, look how sad and human I am even though I'm a big celebrity with lots of money. Watch me pretend I don't think I'm better than you." He threw his just-lit cigarette down in disgust.

His voice returned to its normal range. "Like I'm some dumb fuck who can't recognize a con. Baby, get one thing straight, okay?—I *am* a con, so—"

Suzanne's heart had begun steadily pounding harder and faster through most of Tony's outrage; now she watched his raging face in terror. How could she escape him? Where could she go and *who* could she go to? Her cell phone didn't work here, and she'd spent all her money on drugs, having given it to this man who seemed to suddenly and inexplicably hate her.

She had to get away from this unpredictable twice-imprisoned man *now*—no time for anything but go go *go!* Get away from drugs and this sinister southerly OxyContinent, scene of Lucrezia's last stand and Suzanne's Waterloo—get away, stay away, and hide hide *hide*!!!

"Are you listening to me, you dizzy brat?"

Suzanne blinked. She was making him even more mad and she had to stop it. She nodded eagerly. "I'm listening, I am."

He looked at her suspiciously. "What did I say then?"

Suzanne froze. "You, well . . . see, you can't do that, you're making me nervous . . . ," and that was when he grabbed her by the shoulders and started shaking her, so she pulled away from him and just blindly began to run—down the street in whatever direction that was away from him.

The spell of the potion she'd ingested was broken. The fog had burned off and things had returned to being the way they were, but worse, ten times worse. So she kept running, blindly, in any direction that presented itself. She couldn't bring herself to look back. If she did, she might summon him with her terrified glance. And that wouldn't do, no. Better to just run run run.

Back onto the main drag now, more people shuffling up and down the sidewalks and cars revving their motors as they made their way down the street. Crosswalks and motorcycles and street vendors and heat; the sun was high in the sky and beating down, glaring down on the goings-on beneath it. It too was angry with her—on Tony's side, everyone against her. She ran, daring a backward glance—because she finally had to, didn't she?—and stumbled into an old woman who cried out in agony. "I'm sorry, I didn't see you and—"

The woman began to shout at her in Spanish. Suzanne looked up and there was Tony coming toward her, and with eyes streaming and sweat pouring off her, Suzanne took off yet again, into the street this time, zigzagging through the cars and—oh! barely jumping out of the way of a motorcycle! She sprinted down one street, turned a corner, and ran up another. She ran until she could barely breathe and was covered in sweat. She turned down another side street and dodged out of the way of a man feeding his donkey and fell right over some kind of cement block, tearing her knee open.

"Fuck it," she wheezed, her chest rising and falling with the effort of breathing. "Fuck . . . me . . ." Dots of blood were beginning to well up on her knee, and then the dots swelled to circles and then the circles just ran to tears. And once her knee began to weep, Suzanne wept with it—wept great crocodile tears of self-recrimination, self-pity, exhaustion, and . . . something else. Something unrelated to the skinned knee and the weeping and the heat. What was it then? Oh, no, not . . . her mouth was weeping, too, now, a thing that could only mean—*oh right, the drugs: the whole opiate thing where your mouth fills with saliva and then you have to . . .*

Suzanne began to look for anywhere that might have a bathroom, a rabbit hole to jump down, where Tony couldn't find her and where . . .

. . . Shit. Now she'd broken out in a cold sweat. At the end of the street there was a place that looked like some kind of bar. With her hand over her mouth and a glance over her shoulder, Suzanne limped as quickly as she could toward this oasis where she could hide, vomit her gutless guts out, and decide what, in a world of slim choices, to do next.

Running through the darkened doorway, she frantically scanned the establishment for a ladies' room. Spying a man seated behind the bar, she shouted, *"La chamber de la toiletta?"* Looking at her with a level of indifference, he pointed to a few doors at the back of the bar, which Suzanne made a mad dash toward, praying all the way, her hand over her mouth.

Just as she crossed the threshold of the low-lit, yellow-tiled room, she felt codeine force up everything she'd eaten that morning in a volcanic rush all over the floor and two of the walls. But that was not the end of it, no. Sinking to her knees with a groan, the remainder of what felt like everything she'd ever eaten gushed out of her and all over the filthy toilet. Her face now slick with sweat, she rested her forehead on the rim of the toilet bowl, eyes closed, sicker than she'd ever been in her life. What if she died in Tijuana, her head in a toilet, knee-deep in every meal she'd ever ingested, organs strewn every which way around the room? It felt as if she'd thrown up something she needed, like a liver or a kidney or a lung. What was the thing Lucy called vomiting? Barking at ants? No, that was something else. Lucy called it "laughing at the ground." This sure didn't feel like laughing. There she was, trapped in the aftermath of an ill-considered judgment call, a hated, hunted thing paying the price till tapped out and deeply in debt. How could she have thought this was a good idea? What had she been thinking? Oh, sure, she'd been in and out of this hell before—in different bathrooms, having done a different version of the same drug, with a version of the same companion, rendering similar results. How could it possibly have seemed like any type of good idea at any time?

"Because I'm an asshole," she groaned into the vomit-filled toilet bowl. "It looked a lot better going in, I'll say that," and wiping her mouth and face with some questionable toilet paper, she sighed an enormous sigh and surveyed her war-torn surroundings. "Great," she commented to the audience she carried around within her—the one that wasn't applauding right about now, either. "I'm some class act, that's for sure." She began cleaning up the bathroom and herself, tile by tile, hand by hand, shoe by shoe. "I can never do this again, okay? It's ridiculous. I'm ridiculous. If I was with me, I'd slap me, too."

Shaking her head sadly, she wet paper towels and wiped the floor clean. Running water in the sink, she splashed it on her face. At least now she didn't have to go to hell; she was already there and had been for some time now. Inhaling deeply with her eyes closed, she gripped the sides of the sink, realizing that what she couldn't throw up was having been stupid enough to take OxyContin. And not just take it, but travel all the way down to Tijuana with a virtual stranger whose only positive characteristics were . . . well, that he was absolutely for certain heterosexual. And this, in and itself, was not enough to base an entire relationship on. Only a few hours before it had all seemed so amusing. What a lark! Driving down to Mexico on the spur of the manic moment with a tattoo artist who'd spent half his life in prison, twice for attempted murder. Maybe heterosexuality wasn't all it was cracked up to be.

Tears of self-pity filled her glazed eyes as she threw another filthy rag into the trash, now piled high with her efforts. "The best thing I ever had in me was Honey and even she escaped. And a good thing, too . . . imagine . . ." Suzanne stopped midsentence, stock-still and stunned.

Honey! She had forgotten about Honey. She'd barely even thought of her once since she'd left with Leland for Mississippi all those days ago. Whenever that was. Had she called her once? No. And that could only be good because if Leland had heard how she sounded, he'd think all sorts of things, maybe he'd even—Oh, God.

If Leland should ever discover what she'd done, what she was still in effect doing, he'd take Honey away. And he *should* take her. Suzanne knew that, she was an unfit mother. "I'm unfit as almost everything," she said miserably. And with that, she folded back onto the floor sobbing like the child she no longer was or should be.

She couldn't wait to get away from this unasked-for abundance of magic beans, feeling at any moment it might swallow her. The beans would eat Jack, the pills would take her, this time taking her far, far, away to a place from which she could never return. And what was to prevent her from ingesting enough beans to secure herself a permanent exit? The answer was—nothing. With all her using, she had always counted on her contraband to do what it always did, which was run out, fail to rematerialize, and finally to dry up.

That was it, then. If her supply wouldn't run out on her, she would have to run out on it. So, once her stomach had quieted and she'd crossed acres of time to get to where she was finally upright, she brushed back her hair and found the nearest pay phone, checking to make sure Tony was nowhere in sight, then sounded the alarm in the general direction of Craig.

The instant Walter had left Craig and Angelica alone together, they'd fallen into one another; starved for a feast of flesh, a banquet of bite-size bounty. The spoils of warm, squirming, holding tighter, tighter, tighter—like falling down a hill on a warm day to the only music you want to hear: the music of the person next to you, under you, on top of you, breathing, moaning, agreeing with everything that's ongoing and about to happen. Hastening it ever forward. Are we there yet? Are we there yet? When will we . . . when will we . . . and then, yes . . . oh, God, yes, oh, my God, Jesus, don't! Stop! Oh, don't stop! Oh . . .

And then Craig's cell phone rang, from the back of his very recently discarded jeans, just as he was moving his mouth, eyes closed, up the inside of Angelica's thigh toward the place where it ended and the true business began.

With one hand in his hair, the other over her head, her face turned into the inside of her upper arm, her neck taut, Angelica bit her lip breathless, and it was in this position that the ring caught them, rendering them motionless. Suspended in midair, over the next moment, wondering what the ring could possibly do to their ongoing goings-on. Could it, would it, weave itself into the impending up and coming arousal, disappearing into the ongoing action altogether? Couldn't it, oh, please, God, wouldn't it just wait till . . . Craig rose up onto one elbow and sighed.

"That isn't by any chance a sound of enjoyment that you or your body is making, is it?" Angelica expelled her held breath in unrealized anticipation.

She shook her head. "No, but it sure could be."

The phone, having rung four or five times, finally fell silent, returning them tenderly into the ensuing hush. And hesitating there for the briefest of moments, Craig said, "Man, I am starving. You wouldn't happen to know of anything around here that I could possibly tuck into, would you? I mean it doesn't have to be—oh wait! Here's something right here! How amazing! Excuse me for a moment, will you?" As he moved his face forward toward this not-so-sinful snack, hovering precariously over her heartland, the phone once again began its meddlesome ringing.

He pounded the bed with his fist. "Oh, come on!" raging in the direction of the intrusion, subtracting his foreplay three, two, and none. "What the fuck!" Disengaging himself from Angelica's legs, he swung his feet over the side of the bed. "I'm going to fucking kill her . . . *kill* her! Unless she's already killed herself, in which case, I won't go to her funeral." Grabbing his jeans, Craig angrily extracted his cell phone and snapped it open, "What!" he shouted. "This better be fucking brilliant!"

The sun was coming down slowly, reluctantly, leaving its calling card of pink bloom spread over the border town skies. Buses crawled to points north and south. Turning his silver Mustang into the Mexi-coach parking lot, Craig peered around to better ascertain just where Suzanne might be lurking.

"Is that her?" Angelica squinted through her tinted sunglasses, looking in the direction of a bench beneath a tree.

And sure enough, there she was, her head resting on her arms, curled up as though asleep. As if something that disruptive ever rested.

"Yes, that's her," he muttered, turning the car toward her, and for the briefest of moments, he imagined running Suzanne down. Unable to realize this fantasy, he did the next best thing, which was to bring his car as close to her as he could without hitting her and pointedly sound his horn. Suzanne jolted upright with a moan of pain and shuffled, bent over, toward his car.

Angelica frowned at him, "That wasn't very nice." Craig looked at her, round-eyed with amazement.

"Honking? In many countries honking is considered a tribute of joy from the Goddess of Pain and Singing." Then he continued tensely, "After interrupting my weekend and driving hundreds of miles to wrench her from a cesspool that she more than likely belongs in . . . ?" Suzanne tapped on the window.

"Craig?" Suzanne began miserably, "I—"

"Hang on!" he blazed a brief fierce look at her, then turned back to Angelica, ". . . I save her from a fate that she not only deserves but actually brings on herself—"

"It was my weekend too, you know," Angelica interjected. "I mean, in case you've forgotten, I was there, too!" Angelica's mouth tightened as she spoke, her eyes narrowing, as if drawing herself into herself, and further away from him. She glared at him for the briefest of moments, and then without a word, she turned her head sharply away, the groomed ends of her long hair flicking the side of his face. She opened the car door, swung her long legs out, stood, and slammed the door behind her. Suzanne looked on in bemused silence, scratching the remaining opiate itch from her nose and chin. Craig hit his hand hard against the wheel.

"Now do you see what else you did?" he implored Suzanne, looking up at her through the window of the car in the gathering dusk. But before she could reply, Angelica was by her side, grabbing her arm and leading her away from him.

"Come on, let's go to the bathroom," she half-urged, half-instructed. "I need to pee before we start back," and drawing Suzanne toward the bathroom, she added meaningfully, "and I need a break from *him.*"

Craig was mad, but how else was Suzanne supposed to get home from Tijuana? Hadn't he said to call him in case of emergency? And what was more of an emergency than being abandoned at the border without any way to get home (not that she'd actually been abandoned, but it had felt like abandonment, and in the long run would perhaps make a more sympathetic, cleaner story). Anyway, having spent all her money on OxyContin and vomiting her guts out, what was she supposed to do? Call her mother? Her agent? A limo? Let Craig be mad; he would get over it. Eventually. She would see to it by doing thoughtful things for him until then.

She didn't remember much about the drive back up to Los Angeles, having snorted, in one final act of cowardice, her remaining three OxyContin while in the bathroom with Angelica. She'd wanted to be as far away from her feelings as the pills could possibly take her.

But no amount of OxyContin could sufficiently blur the sharp feelings she had inside when it came to Honey—the internal knife she'd drawn in that dingy bathroom and plunged farther and farther into herself.

How would she let herself off the hook this time? Perhaps she belonged permanently pinned on the hook's sharp informative point? Maybe she should just let Leland have Honey—raise her the right weird way with him, instead of the wrong weird way with her. Then, if her maternal instinct should happen to flare up, she could get a plant or a pet or adopt a child from some starving place—a kid who'd be grateful just to be alive, who would barely notice what a bad parent she was. They'd be too busy eating.

Maybe she'd been selfish to have had a child anyway. She remembered that one time she went to see about having another baby. Leland had left for Nick already, but Suzanne wanted to see if she could have another child. Maybe they could take care of each other. Hell, maybe the kids could take care of *her.* And the doctor—why had he said this?—his specialty was manic depression and reproduction—the doctor had said to her with obvious distaste, "You *have* a child already, why would you want to have another one and risk loading *it* up with a bunch of affective disorder?" Like a gun to shoot into the future. Honey didn't appear to have any of these wild bullets in her so let's roll the dice and try to arm us another little one! And head on down to Texas!

Anyway, sitting in the backseat of Craig's silver Mustang, heading north along the coast to Los Angeles, Suzanne bubbled, toiled, and troubled with her affective disorder, up from Alamo way, Peck's bad girl, naughty Marietta, everybody's fool but maybe shouldn't be no baby's mother.

This time she'd done it for sure . . . done it again and one too many times. If she got away with it, she promised to never do it again. Nope. She'd never cut her hair and get a tattoo and buy glitter spray and convert to Judaism. From now on, she'd do all manner of regular things just as soon as she could remember what they were; she'd be as organically boring as everyone older was to everyone younger in half a minute.

And with all these thoughts—thoughts ranging from self-loathing to confusion to searing guilt and back again, Suzanne lay in the backseat all the way to Los Angeles, the Entertainment Capital of the World, a place of almost year-round sun. Then, closing her eyes and half listening to the sound of Craig and Angelica bickering, Suzanne curled up around the rhythm of their interaction, covered by a blanket of exchanged words, and with the feel of the road rumbling beneath her, slept her way out of what she'd just done, and who'd just slapped her, into what she'd do next.

It was close to midnight by the time they arrived back at Suzanne's. That night, she dreamt she was looking into the night sky when suddenly it began raining shooting stars. "Please let Honey be healthy and happy," she wished on one of the stars. "And let my talk show be a hit." And the stars fell—glowing streaks of electricity, a meteor shower to hope upon. Bits of celestial bodies broke free and made their way briefly across the dark sky as the dreaming Suzanne gazed up in wonder.

She woke in the backseat of the car. Craig and Angelica must have left her there, unable to rouse her and unwilling to carry her up the steep path to her bed. As she unfolded herself stiffly from her awkward sleeping position, she reflected on the dream she'd had, baffled she'd found so little to wish for. So many stars in the back of her mind to pin her hopes on and so few hopes to actually pin.

When she'd been younger, she'd wished for so much—babies, men, success, weight loss—and not necessarily in that order. And now none of these seemed to be particularly pressing. Suzanne liked to live in the land of likelihood, and in that place there was little chance of her being paired off anytime soon. And the later soon got the less chance there'd be, until there was no chance at all. Maybe she was at an age where hopes were meant to mature into gratitude and acceptance. If that was so, why hadn't she been notified? She was glad that in her dream the lion's share of her wishes and longings had gone to Honey. But a wish for her talk show to be a success? How pathetic. She could only hope that in Jungian terms it meant something sexual—maybe even represented her fear of death. For wasn't the talk show a little death in a way? I mean when you really got down to it without climbing too far?

As far as having more children, well, she was getting a little long in the tubes for that. She should be grateful that she had one child— and what a one she was. She should content herself with her lot and let it go at that. There were women in China starving to have more than their allotted one child. And wasn't this just another version of thinking that all that was keeping her from perfect happiness was one fewer pimple or five fewer pounds or lighter eyes? Would one more child do the trick, enabling her to finally experience contentment? Having lived her whole life beaten down by some unseen unachievable ideal, would she finally figure out that if only she could appreciate all that she had, she had a shot at being something like happy? Would some future Suzanne—Suzanne, say at sixty—look wistfully back and think how dumb she'd been to waste her time wishing for youth and toned arms and smaller breasts and more even-textured skin, seeing from her senior distance that middle age had been a cakewalk compared to the life of this stooped, arthritic, mottled, symptomatic old lady she'd more than likely become? She'd probably end up a poor man's Norma Desmond, watching reruns of herself on late-night TV, but with no butler, no younger man caged above her garage writing *Salome* for her. Where was her William Holden? Thor. She probably should have married him. Now who would feed her and push her wheelchair, visiting her at the Motion Picture Relief Home when Honey was sick of her? Who would remind her of her friends' names when she forgot them and dole out her medicine and talk loud when she couldn't hear and arrange for new hearing aids after she swallowed them?

WAKING ON THE WRONG
SIDE OF HER HEAD

Suzanne had been sleeping off and on for the next few days, and during the off times, trying to make any and every important decision concerning her life as best she could in order that she might be a better mother—no, scratch that—a wonderful mother to Honey from now on. She'd frightened herself to a degree she didn't think possible and she had to do something drastic now before something drastic was done. Wasn't that right? It was difficult for her to think clearly; that much was certain. But she had to try, had to stop while the stopping was good.

Honey deserved better. Everyone did. Everyone but her. And threaded through all this feverish self-recrimination in her hot head was a distant ringing above all the other sounds, an almost continuous jingling until she found the phone with one of her hands and put it to her ears and in that phone was the suspicious voice of Leland.

She said she'd been pretty sick, and in a way wasn't that true? Was sick and always would be—she just wasn't sick in the way she told him now. No, it was a lie told to protect her relationship with Honey. A lie to enable everything to go on just as though nothing had happened. Over time perhaps they could all go back to believing it to be. All but the crabby Craig—but maybe even he, too, would forget eventually.

At least, this was Suzanne's desperate postmanic plan as she stood waiting for Leland to drop off Honey for her first visit since her trip to Mississippi and her mother's "flu." Suzanne patted her haircut nervously as she watched Honey slide down from her father's big black sport utility vehicle and start up the brick path. Suzanne met her and Leland halfway, scooping Honey up into her arms.

"Where's your hair?" Honey asked her mother, who hung her head, smiling sheepishly.

"I lost my hair in a fight," Suzanne told her. "You should see the other guy!"

"I don't like it. How long will it take to grow?" Honey touched her mother's hair gingerly, several strands at a time.

"I think it looks good," offered the ever-gracious Leland. "Besides, I bet it's easy to fix and feels really good in this hot weather, right?" Honey scrambled down from her mother's arms and started into the house.

"I want to see the dogs—"

"What, I don't get a kiss or anything?" Leland arrested his daughter in midflight. Honey turned her face up to her dad and kissed him and then darted through the front door.

"Are you okay?" Leland asked Suzanne after a moment, with some concern.

Suzanne looked confused and felt alarm. "What do you mean? Yeah, I'm fine." She forcibly changed her expression to that of utter innocence.

"The haircut, the tattoo . . ."

Suzanne's heart jumped. She didn't think he'd seen it—so he suspected! He knew! What would happen now?

The dogs barked with joy from inside the house at the apparent sight of Honey. Leland sighed. "Well, you'll let me know if there's anything . . ." He shrugged as he backed away. "Just make sure that you're okay."

Suzanne nodded eagerly. "I will," she said. "Don't worry about anything."

But her little trip to Tijuana had pulled crazy closer to her as though it had grown two strong powerful hands; hands that could grip and grab had gotten their mitts on madness and very slowly and carefully pulled it her way—pulled its long length toward her to wrap around her neck in a noose in readiness for the hanging that was to take place in one, two, three, four, five . . . no one knew how many days, just that they were coming and she was being dragged along to meet them and that was all, that was all, there was no stopping this thing that was already under way, that was already going to happen. All she could really do is go down and meet crazy when it finally came, or hide from it (like that would stop it) like a big sane baby underneath the bed.

Suzanne had just put Honey to bed, sung her to sleep with her long list of songs beginning with "I Loves You, Porgy," and continuing with "Amazing Grace," "The Way You Look Tonight," and "Better Luck Next Time" till the blackbird song when she saw Honey was sleeping soundly, holding Suzanne's first finger, curled on her side, a question mark in her answer of sleep.

Suzanne ever so quietly rose up on one elbow, slipping her finger from out of her daughter's loose fist and then, as if underwater, she stood in one impossibly smooth slow motion and and tiptoed from Honey's darkened room.

"Where are you going?" came Honey's fluffy, sleepy voice, a voice wrenched from her last dregs of consciousness. Suzanne froze, halfway out the doorway.

"I'm just going to the bathroom, baby," she assured Honey in a whisper, who then put her head back down on her pillow and snuggled under the covers.

"Okay," her daughter murmured, satisfied. "Are you coming back?"

"Of course, buzzard. In a minute." This was what Suzanne always said, though she rarely returned and was fairly certain Honey knew this. Still, it comforted Honey to think of their presleep connection as unbroken and for that reason, she believed.

"Okay," pronounced the little voice, "I love you, Mommy." Honey was decidedly imperturbable. This resilient quality had already contributed mightily to her ability to sail smoothly through whatever rough seas she'd encountered in her short life thus far, serving her during her parents' separation and their subsequent estrangement, and navigating her through the white water of her mother's mood swings.

Yet Honey could hardly have failed to notice the danger hanging in the air around her mother now. Children just seem to have an instinct for things like that. The way certain animals sense earthquakes well before they occur, like dogs barking in the stillness just before the shaking starts.

Honey must surely have sensed that her mother's behavior had caused something delicate and fine to stir deep inside her, like a strange scent brought in by a strong wind, a thing causing her to watch her mother more closely, with more searching, wary eyes. Suzanne knew that Honey needed to be reassured of something Suzanne could no longer reassure her of. For despite all her last-ditch attempts, she'd done that thing with her hands—lost her grip. Maybe she could get her grip back if she could only think just where to look . . . But in the meantime, she watched her little girl looking at her and hoped things didn't look as bad from the outside as they were starting to cringe in from within. Honey blinked in the near-darkness, watching her mother do what she couldn't. Situating herself in such a way so as not to burn her small fingers, Honey lay back against her covers, watching as though to determine exactly what it was sounding the alarm inside her.

"Mommy?"

"Yes, Nipples Dundee?" But Honey just gazed at her mother from beneath her puckered forehead. And Suzanne waited for her daughter to say something, while Honey swept her mother for undetonated mines. "What's the matter, buddy?" And then that look, that particular storm watch was over. Not gone for good, just for now.

"Nothing," Honey answered simply. "I forgot what I was going to say."

All too soon after her visit south of the border, all the overabundance of joy that had suffused every area of Suzanne's life began to melt away, and in its place something decidedly less airless took root in her and quietly stole her soul. Other than that, everything was fine. Other than that, the road that had so recently opened up to her and continued without limit had now closed back in and crashed down onto her, leaving her anxious and half in shadow. It was a dark and moonless night high up there inside her head. There were noises she couldn't account for, couldn't be certain of having heard, and things around her assumed the shape of frowning, threatening storms crowding in on her, making movement in any direction next to impossible. Which was really okay, as that was where she lived now— adjacent to impossible, on the side with views that never saw the sun.

When they first got back from Tijuana, Craig refused to talk to Suzanne, except to say, "Go to the doctor," in a variety of tones and ways. He would trill, "Go to the doctor" cheerfully, as if greeting her, or sing, "Go to the doctor" as an opera, complete with gestures and musical accompaniment. It then became, "Did you call the doctor? Maybe I better call the doctor for you, moron." "If you don't call the doctor, I'm moving out."

But after a few days of this routine that was no routine at all, a few days of having sex with Angelica—more than sex, really, something of real feeling was developing between them despite the temporary detour through Tijuana—Craig shifted his focus onto the happy specter of infatuation that just might up and disappear if he looked away.

So Suzanne was safer and safer each day from his scrutiny, especially as she'd been downsizing by inhuman degrees. Each day she was half the person she'd been the day before, sliding more and more in spectrum and scope and lower and lower in her own esteem. Each day it was as if she was losing one more interest, one more ability, one more thing to say, and with each of these, a slick of paint would set her limit by degrees, till at last that paint had locked both her lips and painted her into that one last corner, leaving her the silent and stuck painted lady—looking out at where she used to buzz and be.

She became less and less inclined to talk, feeling that she didn't have anything worthy to share, lacking the energy, the words, or the wisdom, but most especially the vitality to say anything anyone might want to hear. She'd been drained of whatever juice was required to move fluidly in a world among others.

Waking on the wrong side of life, of her head, of everything human, she would stay in bed later and later each day, rarely rising till it was time to pick up Honey at camp, her nanny having driven Honey there, standing in for more and more motherly duties: those last hold-out tasks Suzanne still performed so that she could tell herself she was still a normal mom. But lately Kathleen had learned more and more of the mother's lines, performed more and more of the mother's role until she not only played the usual matinee performances, but was doing the evening ones as well, an understudy to a real-life, highly coveted, albeit commonplace, role.

Suzanne had never had the versatility to play much beyond her own borders, but it appeared even *that* now taxed her talents or just taxed her full stop while she watched the world move around her in various speeds and with a variety of impacts. At another time she might have remarked or marveled at this, but just now every other order of business having dropped away, Suzanne merely lay on her side, watching the light change from lighter to darker gray. Light from the window and the television beat down on her until the hour came that she dreaded—two o'clock—when she had to rise, slip into shoes and some sort of clothing, and manage to make her way down the path, past the guesthouse where on occasion, a worried Craig or Hoyt would watch her exertions through their respective windows, worlds away, as she moved deeper and deeper under the stern specter of the mood weather, snaking her poisonous way to the driveway and her never-getaway car.

Driving toward Sunset, then west and out to Honey's campsite in Santa Monica near the beach, barely registering the blaring radio beating down on her, wearing rumpled clothes and a stricken expression, Suzanne would collect her baby girl, doing all she could to banish the worry from her daughter's hopeful face.

"Are you better today, Mommy?" Honey's eyes were edged with the barest hint of an entreaty. Please be better, let everything be all right.

"Yes," Suzanne would always answer, a smile stretching across her lower face, a gussied-up grimace. The best she could do in these deadly circumstances.

But Honey wasn't fooled. Sitting back watchfully, she'd ask, "What did the doctor say?" But Suzanne couldn't answer, emotion clogging her throat. The big sad thing that came when she heard how she'd turned her child into an alert, overgrown nurse. How could she have done such a thing? Of course, the answer was easy: hadn't Suzanne herself been such a little companion? Oh, not with the medical training like Honey had, but she'd had her own specialties . . . known what kind of bag her mother needed to breathe in and what to tell them when she called the doctor. Still, that was a cakewalk, a far cry from turning her six-year-old into "Nurse Honey, Daughter of Psycho Suzanne and Hospital Man." Surely this was a form of child abuse, and right after she got out of this hellhole she'd dug herself into, they'd throw her in jail and subject her to even more bad lighting. Surely she hadn't meant to do this; rain all this bad weather of her insides down onto her child, hastening her growth in some crooked direction. Once more, she sent up a silent prayer that Honey wouldn't inherit a penny of her dimestore DNA.

When her mother didn't answer, Honey tried again, a little alarm sounding in her voice, a bell to rouse her mother into action.

"Did you talk to the doctor, Mommy? You said you were gonna."

Suzanne quickly wiped the new wetness from beneath her eyes, bearing down on the road before her.

"I left him a message," she managed, navigating the great beast of her vehicle between the lines, heading for home, for protective covers.

"You should call him again," Honey prompted her solemnly. Suzanne had stopped breathing in an effort to burst the bubble of emotion rising in her, this bad flood filling her eyes and throat, heating her face. She nodded, stifling a sob. If Honey knew her mother was crying, it would make her soul even sicker than it already was.

In the ensuing silence Suzanne vowed to turn herself into Dr. Mishkin to spare her child further worry and despair.

"Are you sad, Mommy?"

And that was it. Everything under control came out now, flooding over Suzanne's face, onto her sleeve, and into Honey's young life.

Suzanne half-laughed, sobbing. "Remember what I told you, baby? About the broken faucet?"

Honey, round-eyed, replied, "Yes . . ." guardedly, as though everything depended on how she answered the question.

"And how when the faucet in my head is going too fast it goes 'shhhh'—and that's when you want to go 'shhhh' 'cause I'm talking so much, and how when it goes slow—when it's going drip, drip, drip—then what happens?"

There was a moment before Honey realized she was being asked a question, as she was listening with more than her ears—with everything in her, listening for just how badly off her mother really was—whether there was anything in her to pin her tiny, pink and white hopes on.

"Remember?" Suzanne wiped more of her leaking face onto any and all available clothing.

"When it goes drip, drip, drip, you stay in bed."

Suzanne laughed a laugh with a hiccup of a sob in it.

"Yes," she said smiling and nodding. "It's my weather, remember? It has nothing to do with you—you know that, right?"

Honey sighed with a measure of impatience. "Yes, Mommy, but when are you going to fix the faucet?"

Suzanne pulled up to a red light and stopped. When indeed? She pulled her cell phone out of her bag and pushed the power button.

"Now," and punching in Mishkin's number she listened to the

ringing phone. "Now," she repeated, as the light turned green again and, hitting the accelerator, she headed for home once more.

Doctor Mishkin studied her in silence over his rimless glasses, her file on his lap. He held one hand over his mouth, while the other rested on the the arm of his leather chair.

Suzanne sat slumped miserably on the leather couch across from him, wishing fervently that she could leave. Leave his office. Be set free once and for all, a permanent shrink sabbatical. She'd been sitting in front of these people for well over twenty years now, and it showed no sign of slowing anytime soon. No graduation day loomed, springing her from therapy forever.

What if she were just to walk out? Walk through one of these heavy doors and not come back again? It wasn't as though this was court-ordered. She paid the enormous bills that signaled that it was voluntary, didn't she? Like the rent on her face with the collagen, the shrinks were the landlords from whom she rented her sanity.

But the answer was no—she couldn't stop. Obviously she required some sort of a monitor. A Big Brother clean-up crew keeping track of her crazy. It now appeared there was a considerable mess that needed cleaning up.

"What am I going to do with you?" Mishkin asked her, shifting in his chair, recrossing his legs and settling her file in his lap again.

"Have me stuffed and put over the mantelpiece," she considered saying, but settled instead for the more shamefaced, "I don't know." She tore the skin on her hand, hating the sound of his nasal voice and avoiding his eyes by reading, with apparent rapt interest, the titles of the books on the bookshelf: *Mind, Mood, and Madness, Understanding Bipolar Disorder, Women and Madness.* "That's what we're here to determine." She concluded with *On Death and Dying, The Man Who Mistook His Wife for a Hat, The Ego and the Id.*

Mishkin sighed, rose, and crossed to his desk."I'm going to put you on a few new medications." He took out his prescription pad and began scribbling on it. "I need to know how many days you've been off your Depakote and your Paxil, and how many days you took the OxyContin." He wrote and spoke without looking at her, pursing his lips pensively.

"I *told* you," Suzanne said irritably, turning to look out the window. "One day." Doctors and what she assumed were patients were crossing back and forth in the square below. "And the night before, I guess. So . . . I don't know . . . maybe twelve OxyContin? Give or take. 'Cause I threw up a lot of them." She looked at him hopefully and he shook his head, pushing his glasses further up his nose.

"Why should I believe you? You've always said that this is the one thing you lie about."

Suzanne scowled, sighing impatiently, then sat back and looked at the ceiling.

"I lie till I tell the truth," she reminded him, as though this was common knowledge, as if everyone in the world knew this fact but somehow he'd forgotten. "And I hate lying. I'm no good at it, which is why I was such a mediocre actress." She regarded the ravaged nails on her hands as though reading a complicated text from them. Mishkin peered at her intently again, which she hated, and squirming under his well-educated scrutiny, she once again wished this whole far-from-brief encounter would end.

"I really should alert Leland to your relapse, you know." He said this gravely, eyebrows raised slightly from high on his face where he sent them occasionally, either for rest and relaxation or effect.

Suzanne snapped to attention, her back razor-straight, her eyes brimming with hot panicked tears—suppressed emotion springing to the surface at this threat of exposure and the awful consequences commingling with it menacingly. Consequences that could carry Honey away with them. And worse, consequences she deserved ten times over. She knew this and had known it from the beginning and she hated herself for it. And now, for good measure, she hated Mishkin, too.

"I promise to be good," she all but wailed, leaning forward. "Please, if you tell Leland, he'll take Honey away and then—"

"I said that I *should,*" Mishkin returned to his chair and eased himself into it. "I didn't say I *would.*" That depends on you, and what you do from now on. If you stay sober and take all your meds—well then, you don't need to worry, do you?"

So, doing what the doctor ordered was now more than just a command, it would be a religion for her. The Lord, our God, in His regime of medication, would smite the holy host of a party that had held itself so recently deep within her, and rid her of any further incoming havoc, amen. She'd be a New Christy Minstrel Singer—minus the singing.

Summoning what stores of obedience she could from inside herself—untold resources of willingness—she filled her new prescriptions, and returned to order inch by inch, mood by mood, day by day, doing all she could to redeem herself, from her visits to Mishkin to washing her hair to attending AA.

Her plan was to hum on the inside like a well-oiled machine. A machine in perfect working order.

EVIL CHICKENS

She knew something horrible was about to happen. There's no mistaking something like that. It robs everything around you of color, contaminating anything you might come in contact with, sapping you, and it, of any vitality. Perhaps she was simply en route to her well-earned comeuppance. The comeuppance that would finally take her down. Too late to tell anyone that she'd be good now—she was promising too late. The evil chickens were coming home to roost, and all she could do was try to take it like a man. But which one?

When sleep began to slip away from her, hour after hour after hour of it simply disappearing, she panicked. Explaining her fresh distress to Mishkin, he asked her when and if she would interview Sharon Stone.

"She seems like a pretty smart woman," he commented thoughtfully. "For an actress. I think she'd be a really good interview."

"Yes, well, look . . . I'm not really . . . I can't sleep so much lately. And if I can't sleep, I'm less able to deal with how bad I feel. I mean, it makes me feel worse—almost like killing myself. Not that I'd ever do that, of course, 'cause of how awful that would be for . . . But you know, this morning I thought maybe if I got cancer—or was killed in a car accident, I wouldn't have to feel like this anymore. Plus, it wouldn't be my fault."

Mishkin prescribed a new medicine.

"It's harmless and non-habit-forming. I give it to a lot of my bipolar patients when they're cycling low and I've always gotten good results."

The pharmacy sent the medicine by messenger that afternoon. Suzanne signed for it, tearing open the white paper sack hungrily. She took two of the new pills at eight o'clock that evening—which she figured was all right, as she'd only gotten about seven hours of sleep in the last three days. Then she lay in bed and waited for the sweet balm of sleep to take her far, far away from the restless world.

After half an hour, instead of sleep, a strange feeling overcame her. A new sort of awful—a brand so strange that at first she didn't identify it as bad. It was just Other. Otherworldly, and then . . . maybe not a planet she wanted to be on at all. An ambush was organizing around her so subtly that at first she didn't even see the threat. Then it was as if the air itself had taken a sudden dislike to her, and as she lay on her back with the covers pulled up to her chin, her eyes scanning the ceiling for a friendly escape route, a cold hand closed slowly around her heart. That was when Suzanne inhaled sharply. Just for practice. Just to see.

Reaching for the pills by her bedside, she read the label on the bottle, looking for a reason for why she felt like she did. And here it was!

The label said she could take up to four pills before bedtime. Why hadn't they said so to start with? She'd only taken two! That's what the matter was! And spilling two more pills into her palm, she eagerly washed them down with juice.

To be safe—though she already knew it was too late for anything even close to safety—she dialed Mishkin for instructions, lest this latest charm should fail. His service picked up.

"I'm sorry. He's gone out of town for the weekend."

Out of town? Didn't he know she was scheduled to die?

"Well, but, did he leave a number?"

"No, I'm sorry. He might be calling in, though. Is there a message?"

Suzanne sat rocking, rocking, rocking wide awake.

"But how about a backup? Another doctor in the event—"

"I'm sorry, Miss. Dr. Mishkin has no backup. Now if you'll just give me your name and number . . ."

Suzanne hung up. What next? What to do? Who else could be the net to catch her if she fell? *Hoyt!* she suddenly thought. That's why he was here! He would be Mishkin's backup! Between her and Hoyt, they might be able to save her for Honey! Yes, that's what she would do with the last part of herself that could do anything at all.

Hoyt took his new job of guardian angel quite seriously. He would watch over Suzanne in her new state of grace. As in, There but for the grace of her goes a bunch of other people. There but for the grace of me goes you. So here she was, poised to go once more as a warning to others not to follow. But Hoyt wouldn't let Suzanne suffer this imminent fall on his watch; at least not if he could help it. He'd felt miserable for long enough, and now it was her turn. He'd inadvertently passed the baton, or so he feared, and this made him feel overcome with responsibility. If he'd contaminated her with his sick, sad feelings, there was nothing for him to do but roll up his flannel sleeves and save her.

He would never forgive Mishkin for giving her those suspicious new pills and then disappearing. Nope. His mother had raised him to be loyal, kind, and decent, and to make friends with the same sort of people. And if those friends had enemies, they were your enemies. And if they were sick, you stuck by 'em. And taking a shower and brushing his teeth—which he hadn't done for quite a while—he set up a watchful post near her, in case she needed him, like she said she might. She needed him, yup, that's how things were, and he called up everything in him that he could, putting it at the ready. And then he waited. 'Cause she was scared and sad, and anyhow he didn't have a whole lot else to do. But once everything got to where it was all right, he would again. Do things. But right now, she was all that mattered.

Craig was sitting on his bed doing email on his laptop, a cigarette hanging out of the side of his mouth, fingers clicking across the keys. A few small moths circled the light on his bedside table and the air outside was still. In the distance, cars could be heard cruising up and down the hill, making their way through the canyon and the hot, close night.

He was so intent on the task before him he didn't see Hoyt standing just beyond the screen door out on the porch in the darkness.

"You better come quick," Hoyt urged in a low voice and Craig jumped, his cigarette falling onto his keyboard, spilling ashes everywhere.

"Jesus, Hoyt! Don't *do* that, okay? Or do you *want* me to have a stroke?" Picking up the burning butt, he brushed the ashes from where they had scattered. "What? What's happened now?" Looking up, Craig saw Hoyt's frightened face in the half-light. "What?!" he repeated. "Is it bad?"

"She's not breathing," Hoyt said.

There was a point when she was inside all of it. Inside the bad thing, waiting to get out. This bad thing held her, had its wild, wild way with her. And whoever it was that it made her into, she couldn't say exactly. She was just hunched down inside it, part of it, one of its heavily mortgaged properties, about to be absolutely foreclosed. She could feel the inside of it. So smooth and slippery you could never climb out.

The medicine Mishkin had given her had turned the sound down, tried to put it to sleep. But Suzanne simply continued south with it to nowhere, faster and faster.

Craig yanked open the door and Hoyt scrambled out of the way just in time not to have it slam into him.

"What did you do? Did you call nine-one-one? Did you do *anything*?" Craig sprinted toward the house with Hoyt in tow, his meager thunder following Craig's determined streak of lightning.

"What'd she take? Where's that idiot doctor of hers? Doc Starfuck—where's his number?"

"I called but they said. . . ." They arrived in Suzanne's bedroom doorway before Hoyt could finish his sentence.

She lay in her bed, still as a ceramic figurine, an actress who'd forgotten her cue for good this time, if good was really the right word.

"Oh, *fuck!* Fuck. Fuck. Fuck." Craig crossed to her, leaning his ear down to her mouth to confirm that she was most definitely not breathing, then lifted her up by her shoulders and pulled her to him, her head flopping backward.

"Suzanne!!!" he shook her. "Wake the fuck up! It's Craig!"

But if she heard him, she gave no sign of it, making Craig officially frightened. He looked up at Hoyt.

"What did he say? Dr. Asshole?"

"He didn't say anything 'cause he wasn't there."

"What do you mean, 'he wasn't there'? How can you not be there when you treat suicidal people? What about a . . . what do you call it? A backup?"

Hoyt shook his head.

"No, they said he didn't need backup."

Craig tood a deep breath, considering his narrowing options. "Call nine-one-one," he said quietly.

"Yes sir," Hoyt responded and marched to the den to do his duty, grateful someone else was there to take charge.

Craig bent down, opening Suzanne's mouth with his fingers.

"Okay. Here goes." He pinched her nose closed with his fingers, lowering his face onto hers. He covered her mouth with his, breathing deeply into her several times before drawing back to see if she had responded.

"Come on, man," he prayed, and then breathed into her again.

"Breathe . . . ," he whispered, blowing his warm breath once more through her mouth, into her lungs where it suddenly bloomed, a flower. Suzanne made the lowest of moans.

"Yes!" he yelled to all of it. "Thank you!"

Hoyt appeared in the doorway.

"They're coming." he announced.

"Good man," Craig said. "Help me lift her so we can keep her on her feet until they get here."

Hoyt nodded gravely and moved forward to receive his half of their helpless hostess. Draping her arms over their shoulders, they began to pull Suzanne up and down the room.

READY, SET, GO NUTS

She was being wheeled in a wheelchair into the medical ward at Cedars-Sinai Hospital, where she'd be swallowed up along with so many others lying somewhere west of well. There they'd try to bring her back to where she'd been before she got this far afield, doing their best to cure her, beat the thing down that was roaring her away so utterly. Far away, till she no longer knew who or where she was. She knew only that she didn't know what was happening to her, only that it was frightening, unfamiliar, and all-consuming. And that would have to do until she figured out the rest.

Craig had gone in the ambulance with Suzanne; the EMT continued monitoring her vitals while the driver called ahead. Hoyt had gotten Suzanne's keys and followed behind. The sun was coming out when she was checked into the hospital, light shone down on the dark thing that was wrong with her. She was the black mark on that perfect score of a day.

Once in the room, they slipped her out of her nightgown and into a hospital johnny, one of those blue backless numbers, all the rage in ailing couture. The nurses put a plug in her to prevent the sickness from sailing out. You never know when you might need it. It's always wise to set some sick aside for a rainy day. More nurses massed on her borders with their IVs and other instruments of exorcism, waiting for something to explode out of her chest, runes to appear on her skin, a priest to come by.

Batten down anything you had resembling hatches, a storm was coming. Holding onto her pillow for dear, oh dear life, Suzanne waited to do something like die.

Something ripped through her right mind, which was all right, 'cause she wasn't in it. The stern TV stared down at her with its huge unblinking eye. Suzanne stared back at it, this square porthole above her bed, a window with an unobscured view into another world, a world Suzanne spied on till it began spying back.

Nothing happened in order now. Things simply happened, then failed to stop. The events refused to add up, defying the gravity of description and familiarity. The things she once took for granted were now taken away from her. Little things like sleeping, thoughts coming in order, and not talking were lost to her in what seemed like would now be forever.

Even in the foxhole where she cowered, outmatched and barely breathing, Suzanne didn't feel as though anything could keep her safe from this ominous incoming attack. Events had marched her from her house at gunpoint to this bed she now lay in, where, heart pounding, she waited to see how all of this awful and strange would work out.

The doctor arrived, a dark-haired man with an expressionless face, armed with his ideas for wellness and a stethoscope. "She needs a medication vacation."

Understanding that this vacation was one where she wouldn't get tan or send cute postcards, Suzanne grew alarmed, and sat up in her twirl of sheets, her face electrocuted into an anxious expression.

"I won't sleep," she lamented from the top of her lungs, where she'd lived on and off for years. "If you take me off everything . . . well, you can't! I beg you! Please!" She was afraid.

The doctor looked at her, the merest ghost of an expression haunting his dead face.

"What's one night without sleeping?"

They say things like this, the doctors. Her doctor friend Arnie said the definition of minor surgery is someone *else's* surgery, making one night without sleep *fine,* as long as it isn't *your* night, *your* sleep. Then this doctor, this sleep stealer, referred to his notes, patted her leg, and was gone.

These are the types of situations you make deals in. Deals with God, or whomever you sense might be in charge: heads of studios or of sanity, sympathetic nodding heads guaranteeing your place in a future that you'll find yourself safe in.

"If I get through this, I promise to never . . ."

"If I get through this, I'll always . . ."

But Suzanne couldn't think of anything to stop or start that might keep her out of this particular harm's way.

When did she realize that she wasn't going to miss just that one night's sleep? Probably once she started climbing up into the second night. By then her circumstances had shaped into a situation that knew how to do only one thing: how to get worse and worse over time. It was as though gravity lost interest in her; instead of falling, she ascended up and still farther up, climbing into the rafters of her really bad time.

Did anyone come back from this place, and, while we're at it, where was she? Suzanne tried to make her words her way of weighting herself down in this world she was just leaving. Mastering the alphabet enough to construct words, lining them up in sentences and executing them with her understanding. Who knows? Perhaps she would be able to hitchhike on a fast-moving paragraph that would somehow carry her back to a safe place. Words were one of the capitals of the state of sanity, part of the business she'd once been in. The acting, the talk show. The *blah blah blah* of show business. Words were home. Perhaps she thought that, having talked her way into this disaster, she could chat her way out again through this litter of language she'd left, scattered like Hansel and Gretel's breadcrumbs. She would pick her way back through each thought and discarded paragraph, making her way to safety.

But her sound mind had grown silent, her right mind essentially left. The dark birds were circling, squawking, filling the night air. Pollution, distortion, something's wrong with all this.

She felt as though she had been dropped into the center of her personality years ago and had been trying to crawl to the edge of it ever since. This wide flat expanse of her, spreading out in all directions like something leaking. There were some times, though, when she ended and something else began. Something that wasn't her but had her as one of its ingredients. The funny thing was, having spent her whole life thinking she was either crazy or likely to go crazy and when they finally told her she was, she felt, C'mon. That's absurd. Even though she feared it was true, it just didn't make a certain kind of sense. The good kind. The kind that had her in mind rather than out of it. "Too clever for your own good" a little voice was saying. Whose voice was this? What was clever? What was what? Who said that?

The reason she watched CNN during her psychotic break was, well . . . perhaps she preferred any news but her news. But also, it was *real*. With the extra added attraction that there was always a new emergency unfolding, one larger than the one she was living in. Not that she was such a fan of reality. Quite the contrary. But this was an alternate reality, one with nothing to do with her. That was her usual arrangement with it, anyway. *Their* news as opposed to *hers*. Unfortunately, this arrangement proved to be other than airtight.

Every day she optimistically set off in the direction of her new hometown—home away from homicide—running shoes, sweat clothes, the whole bit, but she could never quite get there. It would always prove to be too great a distance, and she'd have to turn on her heels and go back to where all she did was give a good to great goddamn. Not being one of that lucky tribe of people who boast, "I couldn't care less." She could care a lot less the whole fucking day. Hold all calls. Suzanne's too busy giving a fuck with everything she's got.

She couldn't care less than the more that she did.

. . .

Suzanne discovered that losing your mind was a bad thing. Bad like dying. Like she imagined dying, anyway.

But once your mind is completely gone, it's fine. The afterlife of sanity was a kind of heaven after the long march of hell. But when things started to unravel . . . when Suzanne began to lose her reason . . . well, to put it simply, it was awful. And not the good kind of awful, either. She thought if she fell asleep, she would die, and if she stayed awake, she also would die. Not much margin for error in this arrangement. What happened then was this: She stayed awake, dying that way and not the other. Awake without a commercial break gives not-dreaming a deathlike quality. It was as close to being killed as she had come to, if you didn't count her two overdoses, which she tried not to do.

They say what doesn't kill you makes you stronger, so what actually kills you must make you stronger still. You should glow in the dark after something goes ahead and kills you, Suzanne thought, or something approximating thinking. Maybe that's why they bury people. To turn off their lights.

Lucy came to visit. She was almost frantically upbeat, telling Suzanne not to worry; everything was being taken care of and to just concentrate on getting better. But her eyes had brought the world in with her, a world in which Suzanne knew she wasn't much of a success story. And where Suzanne was going, most of the world couldn't go. A place you were banished to, and, having arrived, it was very complex to escape. She tried making some last-minute arrangements with whatever was left in her. Wrap up her affairs; call a lawyer, an agent, clear her calendar. The saddest Hollywood send-off of the nearly departed. But it turned out these were complicated tasks, requiring more presence of a mind than she actually possessed. The main thing to do at this point was ward off danger, which right now seemed to be continuing lack of sleep. So she got very busy begging for sleep medication, the hopeful Sherpas that would bring her down from this bad Everest, this mountain of awake. Begging for sleep medication became Suzanne's full-time job. Her calling. Calling for help.

It was dark outside now. But in Suzanne's head, it was broad daylight. Where was the sleep medication for fuck's sake? It was ordered, apparently. It was taking so long because they had to get it from the pharmacy downstairs.

"Shouldn't you be able to get it faster because we're in the hospital?" Suzanne pleaded. "Isn't there *any* advantage to being in here?"

Norma was there now. Her regular, nonpsychopharmacologist shrink. Seated by her bedside. Keeping vigil until the long-awaited medicine came. She'd put everyone else from Suzanne's world out in the hallway. The teeming world that waited on the other side of the door. Suzanne's brother Thomas, Leland, Craig, Hoyt, Lucy . . . whoever. Suzanne could hear them. She could hear *something,* anyway. She could hear the sleep medicine taking forever to arrive.

When the medication finally came, it was in a small plastic cup. Red liquid. The blood of better times to come. Chloral hydrate. Suzanne drank it eagerly, making a scowling fist of her face as it burned its bright way down. This was the elixir she'd been longing for. It could burn the doze back into her. Send the thick red to coat her, coax her back into dreaming. But the effects of the burning red medicine came and went like quicksilver. Whatever was wrong with her was stronger than this chemical solution. It was a teardrop in her eye of a stormy ocean. Suzanne blinked and brushed it away. Outsmarting and outdistancing it, she crushed it between her I & Q, like so much nothing. This thing in her drank it, and smiled, continued on. There was no stopping it now, she burned right through the night.

Norma waved the vigil-keepers back across her threshhold, but after a while, she burned them off, too. The only one remaining was her nurse, Antha, and the television. Suzanne told Antha that when she was born, she'd been raised by black women. And, since she'd been too short to see herself in the mirror, she'd thought she was black like they were. Still did, she assured Antha. Telling her this well into the night and after. Antha finally countered by telling Suzanne to "hush up" and close her eyes. Suzanne complied, sulking. Did she think she had some choice in this? Thought it was a good idea? After being silent a while, both of them sitting there in the darkness together, breathing in the night, Suzanne's unspoken thoughts began swelling to an unnatural size.

After a while Antha spoke. "I can feel you over there thinking, missy. Don't think I can't."

Suzanne smiled. The Silent Bubble had burst and now she could talk again. Express the endless dictation she was taking from on high. She wanted Antha to listen and hear while she read her endless mind manuscript. So she talked through the night and into the morning with the nurse who sat slumped in her chair, stone-faced behind her glasses, waiting it out patiently. A line of light running under the curtain signalled another day to run the length of. Run like hell and back again.

Her ex and "Y," spelled both ways, Leland now sat poised by her bedside, awaiting his orders. In the wings, watchful and worried: waiting for his cues. When Suzanne had met Leland that first night, hadn't he looked to her like her last and best emergency contact number? Like the guy who'd someday fill out those pages and pages of medical history forms and when he'd finally come to what he hoped wasn't the end, sit at Suzanne's bedside and cry? And here he was.

Leland sitting by her bedside, an act of containment. Only it didn't work; she couldn't stay in one place. Here she was, spilling out all over everything.

Why was Leland here? Had the alarm been sounded? How was it she hadn't heard? So things really *were* as bad as she suspected after all. Someone had dialed and Leland had been summoned from behind the safety of his desk. All those meetings would have to wait until he understood exactly what on earth had happened or if it had happened on earth at all. Suzanne wanted to slip into the smoothness and safety of his Prada suit. Leland was dressed for success, she for circling drains. Just look at them assuming their positions: each in their way outfitted in ways that would ultimately affect the not-so-unsuspecting Honey.

"Where is she?" Suzanne wept to this man seated at her bedside.

"She's fine, she's at your mother's."

Was any of this really said or did she dream it? Her life was so unreal anyway; was it *that* that was crazy, or was it she? Was it her disposition or her environment? Or couldn't you divide them—couldn't you divide anything? Did this sort of math matter in this place? Did numbers? Who was counting all the different threads of those Egyptian cotton sheets? And were they the same ones that came up with the amount? The one you heard on the day of the dead reckoning? Well, one amount would come up—a day of the Grateful Dead reckoning and to know what it was you had to get good and quiet because only then could you hear the awful little voice whisper, *Better get out your checkbook . . . there's gonna be hell to pay.*

Leland hadn't expected her to be like this. He didn't really know what he'd expected.

Oh, yes, he did.

He'd expected her to be stoned. He'd even revved up his angry thing in the car on the way over, rehearsing, "How could you do this again, you asshole!" and other old-time favorites like what-about-Honey and how-could-you-be-so-irresponsible. He was going to confront her about the reports of various Suzanne sightings while he and Honey had been down in Mississippi. This time he wasn't going to back down or be stupid about it. He wasn't going to let her get away with it like before.

But to look at her now—this couldn't be drugs. Or, no drugs he knew. But whatever it was, it had taken Suzanne away. The parts he could recognize, anyway. He'd never seen anything like this, and for the first time, he didn't really know what to do.

What if she stayed like this? What would he tell Honey? She was already frightened. Suzanne had gotten her on the phone once, before he could stop it, and how was he going to do this and, oh, God, his job? Who was going to take care of Suzanne? She looked so scary and scared and so far from her head now, and he was scared shitless that she would never come back. And now she was trying to tell him something.

Raised up on her knees in the center of the bed, Suzanne pointed to an empty chair. "She's over there, and she let me out to tell you something. And she's her and she's me, so you have to listen. She's gonna come and get me any minute, so it's important that I tell you right away. The thing is, I can't take care of Honey by myself anymore, so you have to help me."

"I'll help you with anything, bun, now just try to keep still till the medicine starts working."

But she was past help. Way out there, heading for this new horizon while Leland stood by helplessly. He went out into the hall to call his office and cancel his afternoon meetings, trying to push away the growing certainty that Suzanne was going to die. He could cancel as many meetings as they lined up for him and that still wouldn't change things. That's what he thought and that's what other people were thinking—though no one wanted to say so. Lucy thought it and so did Craig and even optimistic Thomas.

Leland dialed his assistant's number and she answered on the second ring. *How am I going to explain all this Honey?* he thought again. Someone was saying something into the receiver, but the voice was a million miles away. After his assistant said "hello" the second time, he hung up and began to cry.

Leland had reappeared. Were those tears on his cheeks? 'Cause that would really be a bummer. Suzanne wanted to tell him not to worry because she didn't like putting that sad, scared look on the faces of the people she loved. But she couldn't tell him just now because she was so far away past help and far from dreaming. The dreams she couldn't have ran out of her mouth and all over everyone and then continued out the door.

They tried to get her into Shady Lanes mental hospital in Pasadena, but there was no room at the bin. Suzanne had no choice but to remain pinned to her mattress in Cedars-Sinai Hospital, waiting for promotion—or was it a demotion?—to this next waystation for the unwell. (Nobody starts in a mental hospital. And if they do—well, they're crazy.) Gripping the IV pole, she made circles on the floor by her bed, stirring the flat white surface next to her, because she was beside herself now. Getting the lumps out, mixing secret ingredients. Forever getting ahead of herself and into the next girl. Shooting her arrows of words into some strange future that she was burning her hurrying way into.

When her friend Milton had started losing his vision, he'd said, "I wish things would stop changing so I could know what to get used to."

That's how it was for her then. If only things would stop changing, she'd know which version of her future to get used to.

But who and where she'd been before . . . was that such a good place?

It all sure seemed more welcoming once she'd started to leave it.

The business at hand then, was . . .

On your mark . . .

Gun your motors . . .

Check the engine . . .

This is it.

Ready, set, go nuts.

PASSING CRAZY AND ONTO THE COAST

Once her mind was lost, everything became easy. There were cities out the window in the future, and beaches to roam on in the past. And that light emanating from her head, all warm and golden. That was good—really good and what with her season in bad, this was more than welcome, it was cause for celebration. So, reveling in the headlight, she guardedly considered herself en route to a reprieve.

After that came the thing where everything on TV was about her, which normally might be considered avant-garde programing. While watching a report about twin eleven-year-olds who'd drowned down in Alabama, Suzanne slowly realized the two girls were, in fact, her. Wow. She'd never noticed that about herself. Not only was she everyone and everywhere but now she was all over CNN. Later a doctor told her that was when she'd lost the ability to differentiate, to discern the boundaries existing between her and everything else.

"Was that what that was? I knew it was something."

She remembered being a child and her mother walking by on her way to somewhere important and Suzanne, wanting her mother with her, struggling to bring something out of herself, called out her first word—"Hi!"—and that *hi* had drawn her mother to her with its upper-altitude salutation. Now she realized that a secret pocket of time existed between the things people said. This made her so pleased and peaceful. Out of the rubble, she had just discovered a treasure trove of time. A horde of hidden hours to while away the time in, generating a surplus of historic events waiting for her to happen to them. And the truly amazing thing was that there was so much in there. Closing her eyes, she smiled into the vast expanse of extra time spreading out before her. Oh, that was a rich vein. She wanted to reach up and feel the back of the time she'd found with the flat of her hand. Hunker down in all those newfound hours and look up at the cool, timeless blue of the faraway sky.

A lost mind is a peaceful thing then. Perhaps not worth the wrenching misplacing, but there you were. Or there Suzanne was, anyway, there on the other side of the usual order of things. Nothing that wasn't charmed could touch her again. All that was far behind her now. The prehistoric dark ages of her. This was the golden age of the good part. The dawning of everything all about her.

If she had to lose anyone's mind, she figured it might as well be hers. At least then she'd know what was missing. And then, who knows? She might even have a chance of getting some of the better bits back.

She began traveling into the future and the past, discovering they were within easy reach. The present hadn't treated her all that well lately, so she ventured to either side to see what they had to offer. It was as if she went crazy, sent a few postcards, and just continued. Passed crazy and continued on to the coast. Second one-time star to the left and straight on till five mornings from now. Or maybe six, she couldn't be certain, but once you get out there, all you have to do is ask.

So basically she went crazy but it didn't really have what it took to keep her. It was many things, but adhesive wasn't one. What do you do when you find yourself at the end of everything crazy has to offer? You've seen all its sights, shot its rapids, sampled its fine cuisine. What have you got to lose anyway? Certainly not your mind, so you might as well go for it.

Suzanne just wanted to do right by this world. Perhaps she'd betrayed sanity and then been thrown out. Well, then, she'd better get this world right, because there'd be nowhere to go after this. Suzanne was fresh out of incarnations. This was it. There was nothing or no one else to be.

When the worst thing finally overtakes you, it's not so terrible. And even if it was, she had survived and that was something. Weird as it was, it was still her, just *other*. She was now the capital of this state: Suzanne, Other. Population—Me! The important thing was that the waiting was over.

Now she wanted to touch people. Feel the length of their offered hands and arms. The smoothness of those nearby called out to her . . . the need for kinship, for creature comfort. She wanted hand-holding. To reach out to the familiar hands as lifelines to pull her to safety.

There are stories in your life you sail through. But alas, this wasn't one of them. Suzanne was lucky not to have drowned in this tale. But what sort of ship was she adrift in? Were other passengers onboard? To answer any of these questions, she had to get out of bed, but after being awake for six days and brimming with calming chemicals, this was quite a lot to ask.

Doctors came and went, trying to take her sleepless from her, her frantic. But she clutched it like a quilt, keeping it oh so near. If only she could lose her mind now that it wasn't hers anymore. But the amazing thing was, she couldn't. She was inextricably trapped in an airless unfriendly skull once her own. What was she supposed to understand with? How could she see what she was caught in if it was ensnared in what she looked at it with? And would her ability to wonder leave next, taking the last of her with it?

Or perhaps her mind had lost her. That's more like it. Went ahead without her, leaving her behind. The hapless tail of a comet, a twice-told tale of two cities—one she came from and one the thinking turned it into. Her frame of mind held no pictures that were familiar to her.

The only game she could play then was a waiting one. Wait until it was done with her, as she was more done now than doing. She might as well swoon into the worst of it until it had worn itself out. Then maybe she could lose this mind that was once hers, this not so quicksand she must escape from.

In sickness and in hell, then, for as long as you can stand it. And then maybe just maybe for a little while longer. For who wouldn't want to lose what her mind had now become?

NO ROOM AT THE BIN

Her brother Thomas finally got the admissions doctor from Shady Lanes to come up and examine her, making certain she was crazy enough to be admitted into his ward, which was full. So why was he coming to see her, then? Because if she was crazy *and* thin, could they slip her in with the others? No one knew anything except the doctor who ran Shady Lanes needed to see her. So Thomas brought the tall, thin man with receding red hair and no chin to stand at the end of Suzanne's bed where she could beam at him from the middle of her secret time stash.

"Finally, someone who can tell us what it's like to get his cock sucked." Suzanne smiled gaily at where the man's chin should have been.

"Yeah, well, see, she doesn't mean that," Thomas reassured the doctor, who was nodding absently. "See, it's not like she's faking. She hasn't slept or shut up for over five days, and if that—"

"The sitcoms of the future will only be fourteen minutes long and Antha won't like them," Suzanne informed them. Thomas shot the doctor a meaningful look.

"C'mon, Thomas," she said. "Did you tell the guy we're all going to Europe on a boat and Leland's paying for it? You and me—and

Antha's coming, too. Oh, and by the way, I found out how much cars are going to cost in the future—I told you about the things I was coming to understand through the walls, right? Well, there was this, *plus* the thing where all the women from the four different tribes were going to meet in South America for lunch: the Asian woman and the Indian one and the black one and the Caucasian. . . ."

Finally there was wonderful, glorious news. The results were in and praise be to God, she had done it! *Yes,* Suzanne had qualified for the mental hospital! She'd passed the test with flying colors! Not just those regular walking colors but the reds and blues that took wing. All of this would've been wonderful news if she'd been where news could reach her. But, unfortunately, she was in all that new time she'd found, so news would have to wait.

Where does crazy go when it's not busy with you? Does it rest up for another round? Where did it come from? Was it able to hear some end-of-sanity bell? Crazy curled up and poised, ready to pounce on you? Sane had you—some sort of sane, anyway. And now crazy wants a twirl on the floor. It fills your dance card. And you're crazy's girl, keeping crazy company like mad.

It was a bright, hot day, worried by nothing more than the gentlest of breezes. Thomas and Leland were ready to take Suzanne to Shady Lanes, where she'd be not a fish out of water, but a nut among nuts. The latest loony to hit the bin.

"A great day for psychosis!" she shouted to the policeman who'd come to escort her out of the locked ward at Cedars-Sinai to Thomas's waiting car. Her hair lay plastered against her skull in despair of ever being washed again. "A perfect day for banana fish!" she continued joyously, to Thomas's increasing dismay. His sister acting like a cliché crazy person. Oh, well, at least she didn't have a knife.

"Hitler weather!" She leaned against Leland, her spirit wild, her flesh ever weakening. "That's what they called it in Germany when— Hey! When is Gay Pride Day? 'Cause now would be good, wouldn't it? I'm proud you're gay! Do I get to celebrate? Or is that another week? What day are you proud when you have children with gay people? How about if you're bipolar and have children with gay people who work at a studio?"

She shoved Leland's shoulder, throwing him off balance, and Thomas's expression grew alarmed. He reached out for this new version of his sister.

"Suzanne—" But Leland interrupted Thomas, shaking his head.

"That's okay—she's okay. I've got her." Leland shrugged at Thomas and smiled a little. "Look, what're we gonna do, get upset if she acts a little crazy? What the fuck? And look at the bright side—at least she's in a good mood, right?"

"I'm in a *million* moods!" Suzanne announced gaily.

Accompanied by Leland, Thomas, Antha, the policeman, and an IV, Suzanne and her entourage made their way to her next crime scene. New words were having their way with her, words like *faggot* and *nigger*. Words she never used in her actual life. "You're barking up the wrong faggot." "It's as plain as the nigger on your face." So there was some concern as to what she might say en route to the parking lot. When two black attendants entered into the crosshairs of Suzanne's crazy, Thomas stopped breathing and Leland willed her mouth free of insults so they could get to the car without incident.

As the hospital doors swung wide, Suzanne felt cheerful, even optimistic. She was outside! Her old friend Outside! With its cars and attending daylight. She could wake up the scenery with her will. The time was Suzanne O'Clock, half past her smile, or quarter past this-won't-hurt-a-bit. Everything opened around her, drew back, making room for her royal procession. The cheering buildings lit her way, gave her the hero's welcome she so richly deserved. Cars celebrated her by crowning her queen of each and every street and the sky above looked down at her in awe and amazement, spreading above her a sunset choked with its infinite riches gleaming in its celestial canopy. Everything around her was hers for the taking, streetlights winked at her and palms bowed in supplication as the chariot transporting her streaked by.

"Look at me, I'm Sandra Deity." Only this false idol was true as the

perfect pitch of bel canto, as the truest blue in Christendom as Tammy, please Tammy, tell me true.

Surely the worst was behind her. Suzanne had left it back in the hospital, locked up in the past. She'd walked out of that burning building victorious, navigated through that white water, a heroine. She'd survived, and driven through the city—hadn't she? Who else had done all this? The sunlight was too bright, that's who—the who they held papers in front of her to sign. Her. The one squinting at the papers. The one taking the pen in her left hand and writing "Shame" in big loopy child's writing at the bottom of the page. The one who was there for the long haul, with all the trimmings. Recognize her now? How the fuck had she gotten this far afield? And, most important, why didn't she have a camera with her? Because the colors—the colors were so amazing. Some of them so bright they hurt just like a slap.

TOO PALE TO BE
PAINTED HOME

Shady Lanes was a hospital with bars on its windows and shards of glass around the sills, adornments designed to discourage a hasty exit. It was divided into several houses, each dedicated to returning a different sliver of one's sanity. The main house was an enormous Shaker-style white building at the top of a sweeping hillside. A music room and den were in the front to the west and the great hallway led back into a huge dining room. To the east were the offices and the library for both the permanent residents and those just passing through. Suzanne dearly hoped she'd fall in the latter camp. Didn't she?

At least for now it was sleepaway camp. Navigating the thick syrup of chemicals they plied her with was tricky business, requiring all of Suzanne's remaining concentration. It had taken vast stores of the doctors' cunning to triumph over the thing that insisted Suzanne stay awake for all those days, but they'd finally managed it—she had slept and continued to sleep. But in between she fumbled around in a cloudy stupor. So many stupors she stopped counting them. But in a slowed-down, underwater way, she was feeling better.

Not that this was saying an inordinate amount, since there was only better to feel. There was only "back" to come from. Having recently been dragged to her limits and left there for dead and dreamless, this oh so tight coil could only loosen, could only not have snapped. Suzanne waited, cowering, miles past recognition, alert, lest more be required of her. In case there was farther to go.

Then, when she ceased to hear the sound of derangement happening inside her, Suzanne took a look around with eyes undisturbed by visions. It occurred to her that this danger might have continued on in search of another host. Had it taken all it intended to rob her of, or just slipped off to the store for cigarettes, only to return with a vengeance or two?

She thought it best not to hope, but, maybe, just maybe even perhaps she would dare to revel ever so slightly in this new beginning, and so she ventured forth from her bed that had become her swamp and her crossword puzzle—one unfamiliar foot at a time, one slow-motion move into this world which, not able to await her, had continued on attending to business.

And when her way remained clear of obstacles, Suzanne grew bolder, venturing from her room into the hall. Continuing down this long lit tunnel stretching in both bright directions, entombed by night, she made her way toward a cluster of roiling sounds bubbling at the tunnel's end.

A reader of sounds and familiar with their symbols, Suzanne was pulled on, persuaded by the melody-less tune of them, urged toward the life spilling from this open drain splashing her senses one noise at a time.

Arriving at a threshold, she beheld a cave of wonders brimming with couches, stuffed chairs, and end tables. Grinning from the hearth at the center of this plunder, with its bright busy gaze, was the beaming countenance of her long-lost friend: the TV.

Oh, but she smiled a smile then. Old friend, perhaps one of her oldest, who'd she'd grown up both watching and being watched by— how she'd missed him and his steady never-changing reassuring gaze. *You have no idea how much I've been through!*—she didn't need to tell him, sitting down to visit with him. *Don't EVER leave me like that again!*

With his insides brimming with riches for her bankrupt mind to plunder, she filled her pockets, her eye sockets, and settled in for a mighty, long-awaited feed

A man seated in one of the chairs was already feasting on this banquet of busy images. Glancing at her briefly, he returned his eyes to the screen to resume dreaming its glorious storied beam into his hungry eyes. Oh, strange man, oh, no longer strange land—surely the television was a sign electrically signaling good times lay dead ahead where she would move over its path, easing into her easier chair. *Here I am, remember me?*—Suzanne would have said to him if words were necessary—and the TV was so glad to see her, it invited some other friends to join the welcome, bringing Dean Martin and Montgomery Clift. Amazing sights for Suzanne's sore head, she drank in every eye drop.

Nodding in recognition, Suzanne understood she was watching *The Young Lions*—a planet she'd explored before, but revisiting would be more than welcome after where she'd been.

She silently told the soul-renewing television she was ready to go and as it opened its door, she stepped out onto the floor to dance to the familiar tune of this old movie. Swept into its strong arms, the World War II story danced her away from the last dregs of the demons that had sucked all the sanity from her and with the sunshine of a more innocent time beating hot on her grateful face; having stopped to pick up this passenger, the movie moved on, sweeping Suzanne with it.

She was at the concentration camp, having liberated the Jews along with the rest of her outfit (a blouse, some capri pants, leather thongs). Joining the others in the Commandant's office, she found herself part of the request to hold Passover services for survivors wishing to join in their long denied prayer to an urgently needed God—the God that had sent the American actors to save them—Dean Martin, Montgomery Clift, and Suzanne, along with the rest of their division too numerous to mention. The local French mayor, having aligned himself with the Nazis, was getting a well-deserved dressing-down and Suzanne kept oh so still, lest she break the spell that had alphabetized her there. . . .

. . . And it was surrounded by this same stillness that she began receiving the secret message from the writers of the movie to be delivered to Jewish people everywhere by her—Suzanne Vale.

Subtle at first, of course—how else could it have remained a secret?—it had been skillfully slipped between the folds of the film, behind lines of dialogue, after the cutaway reaction shot, under furniture, just over the shoulder of an extra; a colorful message whispering its long-buried black and white scrawl greeting, waking Suzanne into its meaning with its time-released kiss.

And basking there in this slow dawn of delight, she suddenly knew with the holiest burst of certainties, that she, of everyone in all the world, had been chosen, honored with this sacred mission, and closing her glad eyes, Suzanne could feel the quiet hum of this blessing slowly cool her burning brain. And it was while she was surrounded by this same chill of celluloid that the dialogue began gradually to be decoded, certain words whispered to her and her alone.

Suzanne ventured back out into the fragile hush of the empty hallway on tiptoe, on tightrope. With the dim fluorescent fog hanging over her, she clutched her hospital gown around her like an expired invisibility cloak and made her way carefully so as not to break the silence.

Opposite was what appeared to be a nurses' station. *Castaway.* The word slowly swam up through the fog, a word she apparently had been looking for. Maybe that's what she was. That's what she'd been. One of the things anyway. She'd lost so many words lately, and the . . . well, things, that went with them. Were they abstract? Could nouns be abstract then? Or people? She had to stop trying to make jokes of things, shouldn't she? She was so glib and that was very indicative of something. Glib. Glib. Glib. Stay away. Stay away. Maybe. She'd lost the words in the great big glib pit. Even before she got to Shady Lanes she'd lost words, just far fewer than now, when she'd misplaced acres of them, whole pages in dictionaries gone. So many she didn't even have the language to look for them. Once she'd lost the word *gondola* for a few days, and another time *deconstruct* disappeared, and once even *roman à clef.* But who knew how many were lost in the folds of this fucked-up situation, stolen by the pills?

Pools of pill residue collected in her feet, slowing her step as she made her way away from her cave, her crypt away from home.

She floated down the halls of the third-floor lockup, this not-so-fast-asleep-walker, weighed down by the glue that the doctors had reassembled her with. Looking this way and that, recouping her losses, quietly regenerating, Suzanne vaguely wondered if her hands had always been that far down her body, flapping there like fins.

At the other end of the hall, she found what appeared to be an art room for children. An arts-and-crafts class for fourth graders. A long table with plastic chairs lined either side, and drawings and collages, colorful and childlike, were tacked to the wall—cheerful renderings of rainbows with stick-figure people standing near houses with flowers near bridges over streams. Hopeful, innocent, and disproportionate. She had a child, didn't she? Suzanne moved along, combing the hallways for other castaways, others who might be stranded in this silent spotless place.

Down the long hall, she came to an atrium with a skylight and glass doors leading to the outside. Several lounge chairs circled a round table with an umbrella open over it. And everything was stark white: white concrete floor, white chairs, white table. White—the color of surrender, of brides, snow, holy bone, hero hat, ghost, slavery, whitewash, elephant, knight, Betty, Barry, moon, lunar—lunatic. A lunatic white world—too pale to be painted home.

Standing in this outside on the inside was an elderly man in a hospital gown and paper slippers. He was smoking the last of a cigarette, sucking it like a straw buried in something wonderful—a strawberry shake! His red, chapped feet, extending from both ends of his slippers, showed the wear and tear of crossing parched continents to suck cigarette butts in this white place. Fuming feet needing anger management walked toward Suzanne as the man opened the glass door to admit a blast of warm air.

"Have you got a cigarette?" He still held the lifeless butt tightly between his thumb and forefinger, awaiting her all-important answer under the circle of an indifferent, cloudless blue sky above.

"Sorry, I don't," Suzanne's voice, covered in medication, a study of calm, came from her slow-motion hung-out-to-dry head.

" 'Cause I'd pay you for it." Anguished for her answer, he reached for her. "I'm supposed to get some money from my daughter in Arizona any day now and when I do, I'd give you some, I swear."

Suzanne drew back from his alarm, as though it had an infectious rancid smell to it.

"Really, I don't have any cigarettes. I'm sorry." She backed away from him, anxious to escape. She was about to turn when she felt another hand on her shoulder, startling her. A slowed controlled crazy fish underwater, she turned.

"Norman, you need to get your medication now. Julie is looking for you."

A cooling lotion voice; a voice to ease alarm, to wrangle the fretful-footed Norman back to his stable. Norman recoiled fearfully.

"I didn't do anything! I just wanted a cigarette!"

The stocky blond woman with large hazel eyes, flat nose, and thin mouth with crooked teeth now held him in her gaze effortlessly.

"No one said you did anything, Norman. After you get your medication, I'm sure we can find you another cigarette, all right?"

Nodding suspiciously, he began shuffling past them, scuffing his paper soles until he was out of sight.

"We'll see you later, Norman," the nurse's bright voice called after him, urging him along with its vibrato.

Watching his large shape disappear around the corner, Suzanne hoped that whatever was wrong with him wasn't catching. Starting with the feet and moving up.

"I'm Joan, one of the nurses."

As opposed to two or more.

Suzanne took Joan's hand and shook it, watching the two hands together, fascinated. Hers and Joan's, the patient and the nurse greeting.

"I'm Suzanne."

And yet . . .

From behind them came another one of crazy's conquests, a strawberry-blond man in his mid-twenties with a straggly ponytail trailing down his back and a soul patch nestling in the groove above his chin, his head tilted to one side as if listening to a distant weather station. His hazel eyes were soft and sleepy, and seeing the two of them, he wiped his nose on his flannel shirtsleeve and cautiously approached them on bare feet.

"Elliot, say hello to Suzanne, who's come to stay with us for a bit," as though she was visiting from out of state or here on a holiday. She'd heard about the food and the scenery and couldn't stay away. Perhaps Elliot had also been lured by the charms of this tourist attraction—this awkward man looking at her with something like amusement in his eyes and a smirk engaging his lower face.

"Hey, welcome to Shaky Brains, Suzanne," he said, flashing a crooked smile.

Elliot appeared to have a man's weariness but a boy's softness and a boy's work shirt. Though still a man in stature, his eyes were both distant and frightened, like a child's. There was something furtive about him also. Suzanne wanted to ask him about the remembering. If he really was in the midst of recollecting when they'd come upon him. But she couldn't get her mouth to do what her brain wanted it to. But did he look like a child really? Or did Suzanne just prefer to think so? Or was she actually able to think at all? Assess those around her, mix them and match them and trade them with her friends. But that was the bugaboo in the bin, wasn't it? She didn't have any friends to mix and match (and mayhem) with. Maybe this boy/man man/boy would become her confidant, once she was able to make things like jokes and all the askings and tellings that come with being a friend . . . but to do all that, you needed different outfits, and to be on a lot less medicine.

The other possibility was true love. If Suzanne knew anything when she was in the business of knowing things, it was that romantic comedies thrived on the cute meet: the cuter the meet, the more the romance, and you couldn't get any cuter than meeting in lockup: *"Their minds may have been shattered, but their hearts were made whole—*

the two soul mates who chanced to meet over a cup of electroshock therapy . . ." Maybe Elliot was her soul mate—her destiny—after all,
hadn't Natalie Wood met her doctor husband in a nuthouse? Although she didn't end up with Warren Beatty, the man she wound up
marrying was still a physician. And *David and Lisa*—oh, there had to
be others. People met on the Internet all the time, didn't they? Well
then, this could be the web unelectric—unless you count the electroshock treatment—a chat room you went to when your wiring
misfired. And when people asked where she and Elliot had met, she
could say "Shady Lanes, the mental hospital. Mecca for the mentally
misfit but emotionally sound."

Suzanne couldn't think about any of this now—it made her head
hurt to try—but she promised herself to return to it later as an exercise, as a way of determining just how far from the edge she had
come.

But one thing she secretly hoped, underneath all this determining
and head-hurting business was that while she was in this loony bin
there done that, she would surreptitiously look for the love of her life.
For a few strange and top-secret reasons:

A. He couldn't be annoyed by *her* being bipolar, because clearly he
was something himself . . . and if he *was* annoyed, he probably needed
different medication.

B. He'd have a very good chance of being straight because to
Suzanne's way of thinking, you can't be gay and crazy at the same
time—you can be crazy *because* you're gay or—well, her logic in this
area was clearly deeply flawed. Who else would find herself in a nuthouse and immediately go foraging for the love of her life? What is it
they say? "Find lemons, make lemonade—find nuts, date them?"

Suzanne looked back at Elliot. What had he said? Clearly she was
going to have to listen better if they were to be married.

"Shady Lanes, Shaky Brains . . . get it?" Elliot offered. He held
open the palms of his hands as a peace offering. Suzanne closed her
eyes, relieved and smiling.

"Got it." Now she was sure they'd marry, on the lawn of the institution, everyone in white and medicated. *Do you, Elliot, take Suzanne,*

along with your mood stabilizers and a few antidepressants, to love, honor and cherish, as long as you continue to each see your respective psychopharmacologists?"

It turned out Elliot had also had a psychotic break. And one quite similar to Suzanne's, or at least it pleased her to think so. He'd been found on top of the second L in the HOLLYWOOD sign atop Mount Lee completely naked and howling—barking at the moon up above. Having come to the end of everything he had to say about it, he'd discarded the mantle of language to test the warmer, wilder waters of pure sound. Elliot had howled till they'd found him, and giving him a blanket to cover his nakedness, they'd sent him over the road to lockup, where his thirst for sleep would remain unquenched for the not-so-better part of eight days.

Was it because they'd punched the same ticket that they took up with one another? It's difficult to say what motivates people who *aren't* in mental hospitals, much less those who are. Suzanne felt that both having had psychotic breaks gave her and Elliot more in common than most married people she knew.

And so it came to pass that in group therapy whenever anyone started going on and on about their feelings—feelings about their doctor, meds, or displeasure—Suzanne's and Elliot's eyes would somehow find the other's, and their mouths would curl into the smallest of superior smiles, their eyebrows raised ever so slightly in silent irony.

As if they were better than the others, sent here by mistake: a computer glitch.

"Who *are* these people?" was the unspoken question between them. How had they wound up here with them?

But for the moment, they were willing to be philosophical about their current circumstances, determined to make the best of everything while those in charge of their botched itinerary made things right. Until then, moving among these lost souls, they would find solace in one another's eyes and company.

• • •

Suzanne shuffled down the hallway toward the meeting room. All inhabitants of the ward were required to participate; no matter how incapable, their presence was insisted upon. So the patients of the locked ward made their slow, defective way to the meeting room where Helen, a smiling nurse in gray cotton sweater and comfortable shoes, awaited their arrival.

Everyone wore pajamas or hospital attire. Robes and slippers, socks and T-shirts—comfort clothes—were the preferred wear for these sleepwalkers still under the spell of the wicked witch, obediently awaiting the right medications, true love's kiss. Ron, a male nurse, went around knocking on the doors, making certain these in-house unfortunates knew to assemble in the community room for this morning's informal meeting signaling the start of the day.

Taking a seat in the corner near the window, Suzanne watched the proceedings with heavy-lidded eyes. Helen was already seated, her clipboard resting on her pressed-together knees. Every so often she glanced at her watch. Deep lines ran from the sides of her nose south to her bright pink mouth and down toward her jaw, Howdy Doody lines drawing up her mouth to reveal her happy Howdy Doody teeth in greeting. "Good morning, everyone. For those of you who don't know me already, my name is Helen." She paused and surveyed the ragged group.

"Well, and how is everyone this morning?" she asked, putting on her rimless glasses, which hung from a chain around her neck. She referred to her clipboard, reading it silently.

A pale, delicate-looking man, his cheeks steepled with angry red pimples, rolled his eyes. Sitting hunched over in his chair next to Suzanne, he drew his face down into a smirk, "What do you mean, how are we? If we were anywhere near okay, would we be in here?"

Helen crossed her legs neatly and examined the blond man cheerfully.

"Well, you seem to be feeling better today, Mark," she said in a breezy best-mannered voice. "How are your cuts doing? Didn't Dr. Kidd take your stitches out yesterday?"

Mark's face darkened and tugging his sleeves down past his wrists and over his hands, he slid them under his thighs.

"They're fine, but thanks for asking in front of the new people." His sullen eyes looked off and out the window—away from her. "How's your asshole?"

Helen continued to smile at him serenely, but her eyes narrowed and hardened. After a moment, she fluffed her hair and lowered her eyes to her clipboard.

"You may go to your room now."

Mark looked back up at her.

"Me?" he pointed to himself.

Her chin up imperiously, Helen nodded. "I'll have to discuss this incident with Dr. Kidd, you know."

Mark was already scrambling to his feet. "Hey, whatever. Go for it."

He darted from the room without a backward glance. Helen referred again to her clipboard and then looked at Suzanne.

"Ah, yes, we do have some newcomers with us today, don't we? Tell you what—why don't we go around the room and each just say our name and then Suzanne will say hers. Starting with . . . why don't we start with you, Rhonda?"

It occurred to Suzanne that for many years now she had sat in circles such as this in AA or rehab or EST-like things, introducing herself to alcoholics or addicts or other forms of flawed beings, but here was a whole new group of people. Depressives and manic-depressives and, if she was lucky, even some schizophrenics. Schizoaffectives at least. That was the big one. The go-to-the-head-of-the-class mental illness. The one that really rang the bell. Otherwise there were your run-of-the-mill obsessive-compulsives and bulimics and sociopaths. It appeared all manner of ailments could land you in a place like this—some of which Suzanne had never even heard of. Disphasics, sisphasics, autistics—lions and tigers and bears. But the schizophrenics were top of the heap. Cock of the walk, ruler of the game none of them were playing on purpose, and one in which Suzanne didn't mind admitting defeat.

. . .

It was cruel of them to make her go to arts and crafts so soon. Really, it was completely demoralizing. Not to be able to put together a collage. There were probably a whole bunch of other things no longer within the soothing confines of Suzanne's capabilities, but did she really need to be reminded of that?

"And how are we doing here?" crooned Mrs. Howard, the arts-and-crafts teacher, as she leaned over Suzanne's shoulder, examining the progress she had made. Looking up at her teacher's hopeful expression, Suzanne was frightened that she'd been caught at something shameful. She hadn't been able to cut out pictures and put them together in some meaningful way. Somehow the pictures of cars and people made no sense to her, especially when they had writing on them. She couldn't unscramble these pictures or put them in any sort of pattern, so she just tried to glue them together randomly.

"I can't seem to . . . ," she began to Mrs. Howard. Then clearing her voice. "I mean. . . ." Suzanne looked down at the magazine, frowning. Why couldn't she do even the simplest of tasks? Tasks a child could perform without a second thought?

"What about cutting out that boat there?" Mrs. Howard suggested, pointing at a photo in the magazine in front of Suzanne and leaning down closer to her. Suzanne could smell the sharp tang of the teacher's perfume. She nodded dumbly, struggling to focus on the thing Mrs. Howard was pointing at.

"I didn't notice the boat before." She picked up the magazine skeptically, gazing at its glossy pictures suspiciously as Mrs. Howard patted her shoulder and straightened.

"Well, now you see it, so take it from there, okay?" Suzanne nodded again, clutching the blunt children's scissors that she couldn't kill herself with, considering the complicated task ahead.

She looked over at Rhonda, who seemed to have a glorious collage laid out before her. A world-renowned, profound collage, life-changing and innovative, while Suzanne was struggling with the notion of "boat." No. Not "boat." Another word. This didn't . . . aw, fuck it. But

Rhonda was Suzanne's locked-ward hero. Defiant Rhonda—who'd called her psychiatrist and told him matter-of-factly that she was going to kill herself, as though casually letting him know where she would be in case he should need the car. But Rhonda's doctor hadn't reacted well to her letting him know her upcoming nowhereabouts.

"You promised you'd call me when you were going to kill yourself," he'd said, scolding her for forgetting.

"I *am* calling you," Rhonda pointed out, and then putting down the phone, she'd shot herself in the head. Rhonda had short dark hair and dark eyes. Because of her weight, it was difficult to determine her age. She had the appearance of an amateur wrestler, with thick arms and legs and an aura of strength about her, augmented by her recent bid for suicide that had left an impressive scar across her forehead—a scar certain to spark interest at any dinner party for a normal human, but in here, no one would even bother to ask. Rhonda had pale skin and beneath her dark eyes, five black moles—three under her left eye and two under her right—and a wide face that spread her nose flat in the trip out and was fringed by bangs around her pierced ears.

But where Rhonda had failed at killing herself, she now succeeded in collage work. Suzanne looked down sadly at her own attempt and wished she had the defiant girl's gift. Maybe if she'd been more suicidal, she would have had a larger collage talent quotient. Shit.

Rhonda saw Suzanne looking wistfully at her handiwork and leaned into her conspiratorially. "Hey, don't worry so much about all this shit. It's a fucking collage in a mental hospital, for Chrissakes! I mean, they've probably got you dosed on so many meds you can barely get your teeth brushed. Fuck this shit. Whatever. Don't sweat it." She headed out the door, moving her heavy body in something close to a swagger, menace in her face for any doctor or nurse she happened upon.

Suzanne listened hungrily to Rhonda's reminder that she didn't have to give a shit. Perhaps her arts-and-craftslessness wasn't necessarily a failing so much as her inability to broker a deal between her disorder and the medication they gave her to tame it. She didn't have to be, *couldn't* be, as she once was, so what was the point of beating up her already broken-down being? Well, for that matter, what point had there *ever* been in being so hard on herself? She didn't do it because there was a point to it, or because she thought it was a good idea. She had never known why she was so hard on herself—and if she didn't know then, she sure as shit didn't know now. Fuck it. Better forget it for the moment. Let it all go. This was shit to ponder when better days began. She only hoped she had some better days remaining and she hadn't used up her coupon for good times once and for all.

She couldn't determine just how long things stayed like this. In Earth time, it must have been about a week, but in held-to-the-ground-dream-time, there really was no way of knowing. Suzanne was stored in a slow, timeless place, a place not measured in hours or days. She was given her medicine, ate the food set in front of her, and even slept a little. And this went on until one day, she found herself sitting in the atrium on one of the white pieces of furniture, and she noticed that she could feel the heat of the sun on her. Shading her eyes with one hand and squinting up at the blue sky above, she reckoned with something like a mind that it was afternoon. A warm one. And looking around, she finally registered where she was by working back one by one from where she wasn't. Looking down at her slippers on the ground in front of her, she stretched her mouth into a smile and laughed a little.

"What's so funny?" asked Rhonda, her fellow inmate, lying near her on the plastic chaise sunning the only portion of herself the sun could reach through the small opening in the roof above their heads.

"Well, for one thing . . . I'm in a mental hospital." Suzanne announced this with a kind of wonder.

Rhonda laughed a deep, throaty laugh and, clasping her hands behind her dark head, turned her face further to the healing sun.

"This is the first time that's occurred to you?" She took a long drag on her cigarette. "Where did you think you were? The Beverly Center?"

Shifting position to pull a cigarette out of the pack that Rhonda held out to her, Suzanne slowly put it into her mouth. Then she remembered something.

"Do you have a . . ."

"It's over on the wall," Rhoda said, pointing to what appeared to be an electrical outlet. "You lift that thing and put your cigarette up to it and charge her up."

Suzanne rose and made her measured way over to this oddity.

"Why . . . ?"

"So we won't set ourselves on fire. I assume you've seen that the mirror over the sink is made of that weird-ass aluminum instead of glass. To deter the cutters in here. Which is a big joke, 'cause they can't not have lightbulbs—so if you really want to mutilate yourself. . . ." Rhonda shrugged, letting her gesture finish the thought. "They're so stupid in these places, it's unbelievable." She took a last drag on her cigarette and then tossed it to the ground.

"Have you done that?" Suzanne lit her cigarette and padded slowly back to her seat.

"Only to piss them off sometimes. Like that cunt Helen. I mean, I'd rather cut *her*, but you can't have everything. So the next best thing is causing chaos in her precious ward. Which is one of my hobbies. When it gets too annoying or boring here . . ."

She shrugged, trailing off again. They sat in silence. Suzanne smoked thoughtfully. Rhonda studied her for a bit.

"You looked pretty out of it for a while there."

Suzanne nodded absently, watching through the glass door as Norman and his surly feet came padding over to them. His rumpled pajamas were missing all but two middle buttons, perhaps burned in the fire down below.

"Could I bum a cigarette?"

"Fuck off, Norman," Rhonda told him abruptly. "I've given you, like, three already just today, so eat me."

He looked alarmed.

"My daughter's sending a care package. . . ."

"Yeah, I know. At the end of the week. You said that last week and it's all bullshit. So go mooch someone else's smokes. You've hit your limit with me. Now shoo, Grandpa. Go away."

Standing there sadly, Norman watched Suzanne take a pull on her cigarette, his great sad eyes following it from her mouth to her side where she flicked an ash and back again.

"Oh, just give him one, will ya? Otherwise, he'll just stand there watching us."

Rhonda sighed, shaking her head in annoyance.

"No way. This is what he does, don't you see? He tortures you until you can't stand it and give him one just to get rid of him." Rhonda glared at him murderously while he shrank under her stare, piteous but unmoving. Finally, her mouth tightened and she sighed and held out a cigarette out to him. Norman clutched his prize, running to the wall to fire it up. Sucking on the cigarette, he released the smoke with a rasping great cough.

"What's he in here for, anyway?" whispered Suzanne.

Rhonda snorted derisively.

"You mean, other than to annoy me? He's been recalled, most likely. You know, defective. Dumpster fodder."

Suzanne leaned forward, concerned. "Shhhh—he could hear you," she reminded her new friend quietly.

"Oh, please. Look at him! He can't hear anything but that fucking cigarette."

Norman did seem lost in a trance of nicotine—oblivious to the world around him, a thirsty slave to his oasis of smoke in this crazy desert.

"But that's sad, isn't it?"

"See how sad you think it is after he's pestered you hundreds of times a day. We call him 'the Mooching Cocksucking Annoying Creepy Motherfucker'—or I do, anyway. 'Fuck Off' for short. He's a pill."

Sure enough, by week's end, Suzanne couldn't stand the sight of Norman.

"I'd like to say he's driving me crazy, but that would be giving him too much credit. What do you call it when a crazy person is driven crazy?" Suzanne walked with Rhonda and Elliot on their way to another interminable group therapy with the dreaded Helen.

"Not much of a drive," drawled Rhonda. They passed the empty cafeteria, rounding the corner, and Helen appeared on cue, exiting the nurses station, locking the door behind her. She regarded the three of them imperiously, a member of the royal family attending her crazier subjects—direct descendents of mad King George—and she was not amused.

"Group starts now in Room B—hurry up, people." She advanced on them. "I hope you're keeping in mind our rule of patients not touching." She strode by briskly, her keys jingling all the way. Elliot shook his head in disgust and Rhonda rolled her eyes, scowling.

"What is *with* her?" Suzanne wondered aloud.

"Like I told you," Rhonda said, "She's a cunt! Other than that, she's great. You know, for an annoying bull dyke. Oh, fuck her. She's just a big fish in a little nuthouse, and two things smell like her. And the other one is her girlfriend."

Suzanne trailed after her toward Room B. "You know, if it wasn't me speaking, I'd say you shouldn't keep so much bottled up; you could get cancer—not that *that* makes much sense, 'cause if it wasn't me speaking, who just said all that?"

DOWNWIND
OF THE PRESIDENT

So what was the deal here? They were putting her back together, sure—but Suzanne didn't remember being this big before she came apart. Was this her plus the glue that it took to put the Humpty back into her Dumpty again? She was discovering that the cost of returning to sane back from crazy was paying the rather steep fat tax. In other words, to get back from breakdown, you had to go through fatten-up. That seemed to be the cardinal rule of the mental hospital and its annoying medications, which reminded Suzanne of when people shrugged, saying "Hey, you *wanted* to be in show business."

Only this was: "Hey—you *wanted* to be 'sane' again." But on some level, Suzanne wanted to shout: "Wait a second, not so fast on the 'sane' thing—I'm still thinking about it? Okay? It's a big decision!"

Oh, sure, the medicine had given an ordered world back to her, a world without secret messages in old Brando movies, a world she walked through unencumbered by golden light emanating from her finally wide-awake and no-longer-whirling head. But the catch was that in exchange for all that, the medicine had made her fat. Really fat. The medicine had made good on its most highly touted side effect according to the *Physicians' Desk Reference:* "extreme weight gain." Was it an effort to weigh her down in this world and keep her from soaring far above it at altitudes usually reserved for lost souls?

Suzanne had finally gotten breasts like her mother's. The tit ship had safely docked in the harbor just under her far-from-trembling chin, bulbous piñatas of psychiatric medicine stuffed within an inch of their life with every confection she'd eaten since she was four-teen—plus a few candy apples she'd simply considered. She could swear she was retaining fluid for Whitney Houston, Lara Flynn Boyle, Calista Flockhart, Nancy Reagan, and a few other clothespins who clearly hadn't retained their fluid for decades.

Who would be able to tell *what* she was now other than slowed down with the tits of a locked-up porn star?

After being in lockup for a few weeks, successfully turning out bad collages, Suzanne was deemed sane enough to join the general popu-lation of Shaky Brains. There she was free to survey the residents who eked out their something-like-life in luxury here. Wealthy schizo-phrenics and depressed heirs and heiresses floated through the hall-ways with numbed familiarity. Patients who had failed life school and were being held back a grade.

A few white-haired women strolled the property in loose-fitting dresses, holding the arms of nurses, taking slow turns around the grounds. Noting the trees and flowers that grew plentifully there, liv-ing within the limit of the Shady Lanes grounds, watching the sea-sons change and the inmates come and go. The serious cases lived upstairs where it was also rumored brilliant authors had convalesced. Some said there were the padded rooms; rooms with cold packs and electroshock therapy—now back in vogue.

Mr. Cassidy was a distinguished-looking gray-haired man in spot-less tennis whites. Perfectly groomed, trim, and alert-looking, he would circle round and round the grounds with a spring in his step. But his congenial affect was all there was left to him, because one night, his brain bulb had just burnt out, his mind nowhere to be found one morning. The body snatchers had left his body and taken the rest of him off to play somewhere.

Mr. Cassidy's daughter visited daily. He would sit with her, staring off into the distance, holding her hands, while she combed his hair and kissed him and he would look at her, waiting for some cue to call him into action, but none came, so his daughter would take her leave, saying, "I'll see you tomorrow, Daddy. Roger and the kids send their love." And after watching her disappear down the drive, Mr. Cassidy would resume his ground patrol just as he always did, with his faraway smiling eyes.

Everyone ate in rotation. The anorexics and bulimics were seated at a table nicknamed "I'm Just Picking," "No More for Me, Thanks," or "One Chef's Torment," joining the main population once their weight broke eighty. The group's eating was necessarily monitored. The nurses or therapists watched each fork or spoon go to each reluctant mouth and then back again. Chewing and swallowing were supervised, and all visits to the bathroom were policed to prevent vomiting or use of a stolen laxative. It was a complicated process—something like marshal law was imposed around food ingestion and digestion. Everything on the plate went into the mouth, and once there it stayed there until it was too late for any other food fate.

Of course, to Suzanne bulimia was something of a successful—albeit controversial—diet plan, and it was a possible distant solution for her pesky cumbersome chest. If only she liked to vomit; it was that high hurdle she had always had trouble clearing.

The thing Suzanne couldn't get over was that a president of a small country was in there with her. With all of them. A small stocky man with a dusty complexion and large sad eyes magnified by his square gold-rimmed bifocals. But what she found most distinctive of all about him was his breath. It was horrible—so bad that when she first came into contact with it, she drew back, startled, doing everything in her power to give it a wide berth. It radiated out of everything he said, as if the words had grown ill, finally expiring inside him, escaping as sour, radioactive air glowing with poisonous sighs, the subtext underlying everything he managed to hold back.

"Man, be careful not to get downwind of the President," she warned Rhonda the morning he arrived, once he'd left their little self-serve kitchen where they ate their early-morning quota of coffee and toasted bagels.

"Jesus Christ! What *is* that? You think something died in him?"

"Only the hope for a good, stable economy in his country—that's all," said Suzanne. "And you know, once hopes like those kick the bucket—"

"Are you going to finish that, 'cause if you're not . . ." Rhonda pointed to Suzanne's half-eaten bagel, smeared with bright red jelly.

"Take it." She pushed it across the linoleum counter toward Rhonda. "God knows I don't need it. Three weeks on this medicine and I'm officially fat."

Rhonda shrugged. "I was fat to begin with, so fuck it."

Suzanne was discharged from the third floor lockup a day after Elliot and Rhonda, free to look as she pretended to please. Making her way across the lawn, walking behind her imposing barricade of newly tender bosom, she gazed across the great expanse of who she'd grown to be with the help of modern medicine and sighed. At least she wasn't in Hollywood; a mental hospital was probably the one place it was okay to look like shit. But rounding the corner to the front porch of Bipolar House, she saw one of the most beautiful men she had ever seen in her life. He was leaning against the railing, smoking and looking off into the distance. A man more beautiful than Thor and Craig put together and then pulled playfully apart like Turkish taffy. His shock of black hair falling across his high forehead, his chiseled cheekbones and azure eyes reminded her of some 40s matinee idol—Errol Flynn or Tyrone Power. Looks like his were once described as dashing, and actors with faces like these—all five of them—had played swashbucklers or spies or forlorn kings who wore their crowns at a jaunty angle. Actors who threw wild parties and had closets full of paternity suits of the finest Italian silk. Men with faces like these didn't come to rehab—unless it was on a dare or to pursue a damsel in distress or distemper. But perhaps this was such a case, Suzanne thought, catching sight of the beautiful blonde standing beside him. Perfect people. A matched set sent to remind her of everything she both was and wasn't. She was defective, fat, not only past her prime but the primes of others too numerous to name, end-of-the-roadkill stuck to the bottom of your shoe.

Or maybe Barbie-and-Ken had been put among those who were genuinely crazy by their agents, in order to study them in preparation for parts they'd soon be playing. Ken would depict the manic-depressed. Barbie could make a *Girl, Interrupted* variant. Placed in a mental hospital, losing herself in a sea of other unstable good-looking people, crazy girls in picture-perfect makeup, confronting one another in the secret subterranean catacombs under the mental hospital proper. A place where patients met unsupervised, shouting and sobbing at one another to their broken hearts' discontent. Rifling through their hospital records as though they ran the joint, wearing skimpy sleeping garments, and sporting flattering hairstyles while dry-humping orderlies who appeared out of nowhere, pushing brooms. Where were those guys at Shady Lanes? Where were the subterranean confrontation catacombs?

Suzanne would have to content herself with playing a character part of the friendly fat sidekick who killed herself to show that the urgency and dark side of the institution filled with slim, good-looking, well-groomed people really did exist.

Suzanne had seen any number of films that took place in mental hospitals. Films were her reference, a guide to all manner of exotic worlds she would otherwise have had no access to. Even though she herself had acted in some of these depictions and knew how they were altered to service dramatic requirements, she still looked to them for wisdom and guidance.

But when it came to capturing the world of the mental hospital, she now saw that films had frequently been brought to the knees of known clichés. In a movie, you would enter the hospital and be assigned an older, wiser doctor with an accent, or a large nose, or big wavy hair. This kindly professional would lead you through the wilderness of your towering illness, help you to confront any demons in your past, and escort you to a calm, clear-eyed understanding of everything. And though this kindly doctor wasn't supposed to personally involve himself with you, ultimately he would reward you with his hard-won friendship and even a feeling that, damn it, things weren't going to be perfect but they were going to be okay.

But not in the far-off world of Shady Lanes. There you would be housed until such time as your insurance ran out, your room was required, or someone sold your story to one of the tabloids. In each case, you were discharged without instructions or ceremony. You entered the hospital broken, found some other like broken patient people, and once in their company, looked down on the other more pathetic inhabitants of the bin you shared, those flying even lower than you and your low-flung coconspirators, and that was it. No cute little sassy fat roommate would kill herself, bringing home to you the real seriousness of your tragic plight. Nope. Never happened. Not here anyway, though it had clichés all its own. Nowadays everything did if you gave it enough or as little a chance.

Maybe this other sort of thing happened on one of those I-never-promised-you-a-beautifully-minded ordinary-people-interrupted planet. Maybe there. But not here. Hanging her moon face in shame, Suzanne stole one more glance at Ken and Barbie, then made her way up to her room in Bipolar Palace, residence for Royal Pains in the Ass. Moodswing Manor. Her new alma mater, her insane sorority, her digs until some future date when she might be dug out.

A meeting was called for nine o'clock that night to review the day, introduce newcomers, air any difficulties, and go over possible house infractions. Suzanne was officially introduced to Ken, whose name was actually Nicholas St. John, a pilot for American Airlines and bipolar heroin addict. But he only snorted it, he assured them elegantly, so it wasn't as though he was hooked or anything, but he was glad to meet them all anyway.

Barbie's name was Dylan and she was seventeen years old and she was only there because her parents made her come. Insisting that they were the ones who should be here, not her, allowing that yes, maybe she *had* done drugs, but that was no reason to be sent to a *mental hospital*. Ken/Nicholas watched Barbie/Dylan's pouty mouth as she spoke, revealing even white teeth. Suzanne decided the two of them were the perfect Gap ad—just as soon as Gap started using models from mental institutions. Or they could be off-centerfolds for adult magazines. Play*boy* is she crazy. Play*girl* Interrupted.

The President's name was Carlos, and though he liked the place very much for those with "such issues" and could see where it could "give much great assistance," for him, it was "tiresome. So much repetition. Meetings, meetings, meetings. All we ever do is go to meetings. And this is what I have usually done in my professional life at home!" Some people nodded sympathetically, while others studied the trees outside the window.

The next person who spoke was Martha Shuttleworth, an overweight woman with gray, wispy hair and a pleasantly shiny red face. She insisted everyone refer to her as the "Slut Nun." Unfortunately, just why she gave herself this title would remain something of a mystery, as her insurance only covered a stay of a little over half a day and before morning she was gone.

"What good is half a day supposed to do? I mean, that can't help anybody," Suzanne leaned her breasts forward for additional emphasis.

"It's so fucked up," agreed Rhonda, shaking her head. "Assholes," she added, apropos of no one and everyone—at this facility, and that she'd ever met.

Joan, the therapist presiding over this gathering, explained she was helpless in this matter. "Shady Lanes has to run on money, just like any other business. Who's going to pay the staff if patients are taken in for free?" By the close of the meeting, a gloom had settled over the assemblage. Most were slumped in their seats, arms or legs crossed, staring off into space. Another uneventful evening stretched before them. Sleeping in unadorned dorm rooms, not allowed to smoke inside, or to touch.

But word soon got out that Barbie and Ken had broken this rule not only with a venegeance but with regularity. And they'd set a new land-speed record doing it, since they'd been there less than forty-eight hours. Joan didn't know where or how they were managing it, but this absolutely could not go on. She addressed them all sternly at the next group meeting.

The electric light above buzzed in the brief silence while Joan glared at the two rule-breakers, her mouth tight and her eyebrows slightly arched.

"Once you get out of here, we want you to stay out. That is why we discourage any behavior that we can't oversee. Such as sexual relations, which can be very disruptive to your treatment, as it can be quite unpredictable and destructive when experienced by the wrong person in the wrong environment."

"So what do we do if we find them humping like rabbits or whatever? Throw water on them?" Rhonda asked, jiggling one leg repeatedly.

The President considered her with controlled impatience. "If you would stop making statements such as these, perhaps we can finish this and enjoy some lunch."

"Look, Your Excellency—"

"All right! That's enough from everybody," Joan announced. "I'm simply suggesting that if you happen to see Nicholas and Dylan alone together, you report them to me or one of our other staff members. If no staff is around, we ask that you join them, possibly preventing them from having what might be considered an inappropriate or potentially—"

"Okay, we got it, Joan," interjected Rhonda in exasperation. "There's no need to beat the thing to death, you know? We're crazy, not stupid—I mean, for the most part. Sorry. Except for Lisa, who's an insult to the human race. Otherwise—"

A shapeless woman of about thirty stood and started toward

Rhonda menacingly. "You wanna shut your fat face, or do you want me to do it for you?"

"Lisa, sit down. Rhonda, I'll thank you to not antagonize the others. Now, please—"

But Lisa would not sit down. Rhonda crossed her arms and gazed up at her impassively. "You want some of this, bitch? Then come and get it. *C'mon.*"

As Lisa advanced on Rhonda, the energy in the room turned electric. This was the most interesting thing that had happened in several days, and it was welcome relief from their daily routine of brief checkups, appointments with psychopharmacologists, and the interminable meetings following meetings following meetings.

Lisa lunged at Rhonda. "You arrogant spick, why don't you—"

But sadly for those hoping for a nuthouse rumble—which included Elliot and Suzanne, whose money was naturally on Rhonda— Joan stepped in and separated the two women. By dinnertime, Lisa had been sent to lockup "to regroup and reflect."

Lisa was the goat—the one they all hated. There was one in every grade at school, on every trip of more than two, and in Suzanne's experience, on every movie set. A self-diagnosed opera singer and bigot, Lisa had the dubious distinction of managing to get in almost everyone's face and set fire to their nerves. Like many people when they were manic, she imagined that everything she said was both riveting and worthy of note, and endlessly served up large pieces of her distorted mind. She possessed all the intensity and energy that generally came with intellect, only in her case, those characteristics came hopelessly alone.

"Tell me I'm not like *that*," Suzanne begged Elliot and Rhonda later that day.

Rhonda rolled her eyes. "Oh, *please,* you can't have *all* the bad characteristics. This is Lisa's fuckin' problem; go get your own!"

"But I'm self-obsessed and sometimes I feel sorry—"

Rhonda reached over and put her hand over her friend's mouth. "Give me Librium or give me meth . . . and after you do, shut the fuck up."

Suzanne nodded, and Rhonda continued, "All right. Now that I got Lisa back in lockup, who else can we hate?"

Suzanne thought that the "three's a crowd" method of policing Barbie and Ken was ridiculous. Besides which, it made her feel like an over-the-hill schoolmarm, a spinster chaperone enlisted to prevent the young people from getting up to their naughty shenanigans at the school prom, monitoring the distance between the students groping each other on the dance floor, making certain the punch wasn't spiked.

Of course, it turned out that Ken wasn't actually a commercial airline pilot. He sidled up to Suzanne and explained himself to her as though she'd been waiting all this time for him to reveal his real job so she could finally sleep at night.

"I don't really work for American Airlines," he whispered conspiratorially, smelling of make-out parties Suzanne had been to lifetimes ago. The warm smoky breath of boys who pressed into you, stinking of possibility. "I smuggle heroin from South America to Florida."

Suzanne nodded thoughtfully, inhaling him.

"Well, that's very different," she said. "For one thing, I would think the health insurance isn't as good."

Ken laughed, throwing his head back, his elegant profile standing out against the institutional white of the hallway walls, his Adam's apple the ripe stuff of forbidden fruit.

"Who the fuck needs insurance?" he said. "I get paid enough transporting a few keys to buy the wing of a hospital if I want."

Suzanne smiled, picturing a hospital with its wings spread, bought, paid for, and ready for Ken to take flight into wellness.

People came and went quickly, depending on the strength of their insurance or credit rating. An inconspicuous man seemed to appear out of nowhere in place of the slut nun. Elliot told Suzanne that his name was Bob and that he had been diagnosed as being "situationally depressed."

"What does that mean?" she asked, incredulous. "That the situation he was in got him bummed out, or . . ."

"It means he's depressed because his wife left him and he tried to overdose."

Suzanne was still confused.

"They actually call that 'situational'?"

Elliot nodded. "You know, as opposed to chemical. What you call the mood weather inside. Making what we have 'nonsituational sadness with fluctuations.' "

"Get out!" she said laughing. "It is not!"

He shrugged.

"No, but it could be. We should rename our thing. 'Mood disorder' is so boring. We should rename it like people name stars and flora and fauna and stuff."

"Only this is like naming a lipstick that doesn't really look good on anyone," said Suzanne. She leaned against him, her head on his shoulder, inhaling his dark scent of fractious thinking. "At least on their mouths, anyway."

"Who's your pearl?" Elliot reprised his favorite role from the current movie of their lives.

"My pearl of girl?" Suzanne supplied her line readily.

"The same."

"That would be you, Lisa."

"Oh, David . . . really?"

Elliot raised his hand to her face. She lifted her smiling eyes up at his, her head falling gently into the warmth of his hand.

And from down the hall came Helen's imperious voice, cautioning them.

"No touching!"

Suzanne pulled away from Elliot and rolled her widened eyes at him. He sighed, smiling.

"I don't know about you, but she's pushing *me* into a major situational depression."

"Hey, some people get it and some are carriers."

They left Bipolar Palace and started across the lawn toward the dining room. It was getting dark and the illuminated windows shone invitingly. An inn for travelers who had been waylaid.

"Did I tell you my theory that I caught my mental illness from a toilet seat? Or maybe from a low self-e-steam room?" Suzanne asked. "I mean, obviously I've always known it was highly infectious, but now I plan to give it to a lot of people. You know, for Christmas. As a stocking stuffer."

Elliot nodded absently, inhaling the twilight air. "Mmmm. I think it's pasta night. Want to go find Rhonda and eat near the bulimics and sneer?"

The doctors at Shady Lanes told her she'd been on the wrong medication all her life.

"How could that be true?" she'd asked, incredulous. "What was everyone *not* thinking? I mean, what was all that shit I was taking all this time?"

"You should never have been put on antidepressants," they told her. "Those are bad for manic people—it simply exacerbates the mania, destabilizing them."

But there was a silver lining inside the misprescribed chemical cloud: Being told she'd been given the wrong medicine gave Suzanne an excuse, a Get Out of Jail Free card. It wasn't her fault, then: She'd been driven to it by her demon chemistry! She was guiltless, crazy, and absolved. Or was she?

She didn't believe it. Not really. Maybe she was just a weak, bad person with no principles or backbone who wasn't really manic-depressive at all. A garden-variety fuckup, selfish and undesirable. Maybe the diagnosis was just a lie they told her so she wouldn't hate herself. Well, she'd show them. She'd hate herself *more!*

Her father, Tony, had phoned unexpectedly one day. Any day was unexpected. "Hey, Baby, how's my girl?" Suzanne was stunned to hear from him. And secretly, the little-girl part of her was, as ever, a little thrilled, though she would've been loath, as ever, to admit it.

"Hey, Dad, I'm okay I guess—for a person in a nuthouse."

Tony laughed his big-band, ladies'-man laugh. "Well, but you're getting out soon, right? And don't tell me they're not treating you okay in there."

Suzanne laughed girlishly and grimaced. "Compared to what? The other mental hospitals I haven't been to? While not going to the college I meant to go to but forgot?"

Tony began to sing, *"Crazy, I'm crazy for being so lonely . . . I'm crazy, crazy for feeling so blue*—hey, Suzie, I'm 'sposed to be down there next weekend on a little business . . . you think they'd let your old man stop by for a visit?"

"Sure they would," she told him. "What day?" And then she did something she didn't do when he'd said he was coming to visit when she was two years old—or whenever it was they'd told her that her glamorous daddy would be coming by to pick her up soon—the littler but wiser, better-defended Suzanne would shrug and say, "Maybe," and bounce away with a toss of her head.

But this time, what did the grown-up crazy Suzanne do?

(That's right.) She believed him.

She waited *all* day the day he said he'd be there to visit her at Shady Lanes like he said he would, and like a schmuck, she'd dressed and groomed and waited and checked her watch and called the hotel where he said he'd be staying, not once but twice and then three times, or four. She did that and all the rest of that god-awful daddy/daughter shit until she realized she was actually doing it and had been the live-long-*long* day. With all her hard-won awareness and cavalier understanding that she shrugged off about her weird father/daughter relationship, his emotional ADD, and, because he was unavailable, that "I can't wait to not get what I want" thing she had about men.

After all that, when he didn't come, her whole clever defended head couldn't defend her from another body blow, another heartache.

That night she called Thomas from the pay phone, hunched down on the hard seat, staring up, unseeing, at the harsh light. "Guess who didn't show up today . . . and I want you to take as long as you'd like." Her brother laughed.

"Oh, he didn't, did he? Now there's a big surprise. Normally, he's so darling."

• • •

There was yet another excruciatingly tedious group therapy, where Lisa droned on and on about her moods and her medication, sparing the other inmates no detail of every feeling she'd had since she arrived at Shady Lanes several weeks ago: how the meds they gave her weren't working and she was being passed over in favor of other, saner patients. And how her mother was cold and her father was weak. And how she missed her dog.

"That was brutal," groaned Rhonda afterward. "Someone should just shoot her and put her out of my misery."

Suzanne patted Rhonda on her back. "Down, girl."

"How much further down can you get than a mental hospital?"

"No touching, girls!" Helen's ringing voice firmly reminded them as she breezed past toward her office, a ring of keys at her waist clinking as she went. "Remember, in here we keep a respectful distance." She unlocked her office and pushed it open with her shoulder as she clutched a batch of files to her chest.

"What's with the no-touching thing?" marveled Suzanne. "I just don't get it. Forgive me."

"Hey, don't look at me," said Elliot, shrugging.

"Why, is that against hospital policy, too?" asked Suzanne.

Elliot grinned. "You're crazy."

Suzanne grinned back. "You think?"

Helen stuck her dark head out of her door. "Lower your voices, people. This is a hospital environment and needs to be treated as such." With a cryptic nod, she was gone again.

"Bitch," said Rhonda bitterly, under her breath.

"You know what's great about this place?" Suzanne said in a low voice. "I mean, other than nothing."

They looked at her expectantly.

"Well, are you going to tell us or what?" Rhonda asked in exasperation.

An ambulance wailed by somewhere in the distance.

"I'm going to have to tell you later, 'cause there's my ride."

HOME AWAY FROM HAVOC

It seemed as though practically everyone she knew put in an appearance that Sunday at Shady Lanes. Doris was going to "pop by later" after Craig left, as she was still quite annoyed with him, never mind how furious she was with that horrible Dr. Mishkin. He hadn't heard the last of her, no sir. She was just hashing out this and that with her lawyer as to how best to handle the case before filing or serving or whatever it was.

"You don't give someone strange new medicine and then leave town with no way to find you! It's shocking! Shocking! Well, I'm not going to talk about it anymore 'cause it'll only get me more upset."

Suzanne liked the ". . . No way to find you" part; like if he'd left a little map as to his whereabouts, much of this could be forgiven. But Craig's transgression was another matter, running afoul as it did of Doris's secret glow-in-the-dark charter regarding loyalty and points of order. It seemed Craig had violated Code 9, paragraph 3, line 7: he had ordered Hoyt to call 911 in Suzanne's medical crisis, and this was a mistake that could only be made by someone with water on the brain and no celebrities in their family.

When confronting Craig about his flawed decision—yes, she was grateful that he'd been there—"We all have to thank the good Lord that everyone is okay, and if I had one small complaint, it would be that in the future—not that this, God forbid, would ever happen again—but medical emergencies happen to all of us, I had two last week, ask Donald. The whole thing with my broken heel flared up again—anyway, what I'm trying to convey is that we *don't call nine-one-one* . . . we call *family*. You call me. And I call Jerry, who's virtually a doctor, I mean . . . he's literally an RN, and he takes care of it." Doris's eyes narrowed as she pondered the enormity of what Craig had done, the potential public relations debacle of it all. And she was going to do the magnanimous thing and let it go, this time . . . for her daughter's sake, but *don't* let it happen again.

Lucy had said she was going to visit, but called at the last minute because she'd decided to go into labor instead.

"You'll do anything to get out of visiting me in a mental hospital in the valley. I suppose if I was a patient at some ritzy eastern nut-house, you'd be over here like a shot and carry those kids to term while you were at it."

Lucy sighed. "Listen, I'm gonna go enjoy my last motherless moments while on an epidural—but I want you to know that I love you and I want you to do whatever those jerk-offs in there tell you to do so they'll let you out while you're still on that tit-making medicine, and we can do a night club act whose fan base is—oh, look, I have to go, the doctor's here. I'll call you after they rescue the twins from the rubble in the middle of what used to be my waist. Bye!"

Suzanne watched Craig arrive, trailing Angelica and Hoyt, from her window upstairs. She took a deep breath and pushed her un-washed hair off her face. She didn't exactly feel up to seeing people from her other life—the one that had, in some ways, driven her crazy, albeit with her behind the wheel. But she had to see them sooner or later—or more accurately, both sooner *and* later—and even at intervals in between. So she headed down the stairs toward her friendly firing squad, ready as she would ever, never be, to act as though nothing was amiss. Arriving on the front porch, she greeted them as they approached her from the parking lot.

"Hi." She smiled sheepishly, unable to think of a hello joke, which was probably good, right? She didn't always have to jest and jibe, but the thing was she felt as though she did. And then others, they did—oh, God, now she'd *have* to joke 'cause she was fat. Fat people *have* to try to be funny. Now she couldn't be a funny and cute girl. She'd be a desperate, roly-poly nut who made jokes 'cause that's what the roly-polys did.

Hoyt brightened upon seeing her and, taking the stairs two at a time to get to her, he enclosed her in a big ole boy bear hug.

"Well, aren't you a sight for sore eyes!" He swung her off her feet and around and down again.

Suzanne exhaled the breath she'd been holding and smiled anxiously, smoothing her hair shyly and backing away.

"Watch out," she warned. "If the nurses see us touching, I could get in big trouble." Or was it okay for sane people to touch her? "Actually, the crazy people aren't allowed to touch each other—I think it's bad luck or—"

"Quick! Get inside me! Someone's coming!" Craig shouted for all the world to hear, making his big-strided way over and up the stairs to her. Grabbing her head, he proceeded to squeeze it between his flat hands. *"Heal!"* he prayed, with eyes lifted to the heavens for assistance but coming to rest on Helen, whose head had appeared in the window above their heads, "Heal this poor child, oh Lord, I beseech thee," and closing his eyes, he suddenly released her as though struck by lightening and raised his trembling hands to the skies. "Praise, Jesus, she's fine—let's get in the car and get out of here. There's nothing wrong with this girl that a poorboy sandwich can't fix."

For the life of her, Suzanne couldn't think of a reply. She stood there frozen, watching Craig while he wriggled his devout hands about her head.

"Has anyone seen Lisa?" Helen called down to them, temporarily relieving Suzanne of her vain attempts to craft an easy-going reply.

"No, thank God," said Suzanne, shaking her head, grateful the focus was off of her. "Is she missing, I hope?"

"Just send her up to me if you see her," Helen commanded briskly before disappearing from the window, leaving Suzanne with her friends, to whom she could still think of nothing to say.

"Just ignore him," suggested Angelica, moving to Suzanne and kissing her. "That's what I do." Angelica put her arm around her and moved some limp hair from Suzanne's forehead. "You look great."

Suzanne glanced at her skeptically. "I do *not*. I look awful. Some spa *this* is."

"Stop it now," Angelica said softly. "Just take the compliment, okay? Anyway, it's great to see life in your eyes."

"That's not *her* life in there, countess," Craig interjected, lighting a cigarette between clenched teeth. "That's mine. What you see in her eyes is the result of looking at my womanly ass and feeling the excitement, I mean—"

"Shut up for *once,* will you?" Angelica snapped at Craig, seeing a look of anxiety stealing over Suzanne's face. "I mean, *can* you? Is it ever *possible*?"

Craig opened his mouth and then closed it, having thought better of speaking the moment he saw Suzanne's face. He held out his pack of cigarettes to her as a peace offering. "Are they treating you okay?" he asked her evenly, as she extracted a cigarette hungrily and placed it between her lips.

Suzanne shrugged.

"Compared to all the other mental hospitals I haven't been to, everything's great."

Craig lit her cigarette with his lighter, closing it with a snap.

"Just so you know, Hoyt and I were married early in the week," he said, pausing to look at Hoyt adoringly, his new bride who stood beside him. Hands thrust deep into his jeans pockets, Craig rocked back and forth on the soles of his worn boots. "It was a simple ceremony, nothing fancy. Right, darling? By the way, in case you want to get us anything, we're registered at the House of Pain and Dunkin' Donuts."

Hoyt's eyes narrowed briefly with disapproval. "Hey, come on, man, shut up and let Suzanne say something," he scolded. "We came here to see her, not to listen to you talk a blue streak."

"Nag, nag, nag, all the live long day. See what you've done? You've created a monster. I think I liked him better when he was depressed. I'm even starting to miss all those hugs he used to ask me for."

. . .

The afternoon was hot and sticky, the humidity so thick that "you could hang a painting on it," Craig observed to no one in particular. The heat even seemed to permeate the shade—feeding off it and growing stronger as the hours lengthened. The shadows, such that there were, seemed to lie down, giving up without so much as a sigh. The heat froze everything stock-still in its tracks, holding it held-breath still, lest anything disturb the surrounding landscape and its mad occupants.

The patients of Shady Lanes moved through this motionless background as if leading their visitors astray. They sat on stairs or chairs, heads together, commiserating, reflecting on some not too distant future when they would leave this place and resume their lives back in the world. A fire had been contained, a certain disaster averted—with plans and explicit instructions pocketed, ensuring everyone's safety from here on out.

Doris stepped up to the front desk at Shady Lanes.

"Hello, I'm Doris Mann, Suzanne Vale's mother. She's a patient here."

The nurse at the front desk looked at her. "I'm sorry, Mrs. Mann, the next visiting hours are from six to seven. You'll have to wait in reception."

Doris put her large patchwork quilt purse on the counter. "Well, yes, but I've just flown in from being away on an extended engagement and this is the first chance I've had to see my daughter."

The nurse shook her head sadly. "I didn't make the rules, Mrs. Mann—"

Doris interrupted her, her smile now hardened.

"It's *Miss* Mann, and I realize you don't make the rules, so may I now please see someone who does?"

Doris had wanted to cancel her engagements when she heard of her daughter's trouble, but Thomas told her he had everything under control once Atlantic City was through. So, now, armed with provisions, she'd come to nurture her little girl. It might not be visiting hour now, but it soon would be, or she would meet with one of the doctors in charge and things would change. After all, she'd been doing charity work for thirty years for mental-illness places, and she wasn't asking so much, was she? All she wanted to do was give her only daughter a bacon sandwich and some applesauce and some sliced cheese. Was that too much to ask for after being on the road for six-and-a-half weeks at her age, with her foot killing her like it did after she broke it last year falling off the stage, and the arthritis in her hands, and her hips—even her back. It got so bad sometimes she had to take something, but when she did that, the burning started in her stomach.

At that thought, her eyes started to tear and by the time the doctor in charge arrived, Doris was weeping in earnest. He turned out to be something of a fan. "My mother took me to see you in *Magical Time of Day* four times when I was a kid."

"Did she?" asked Doris graciously.

"Well, you weren't much more than a kid then yourself." He escorted her to Suzanne's room, where she lay sleeping. Doris gazed lovingly and piteously at her daughter.

"I should've stayed home more," she sobbed quietly. The doctor patted her shoulder.

"Now, now."

Suzanne had fallen into a deep sleep after Craig and his cohorts had left. She was secretly relieved when the visit was over. As funny as Craig was, sometimes funny just wasn't that funny. Sometimes funny was just like any other obligation—exhausting, something you can't wait to be over with. When Suzanne woke, she found Doris and all her childhood favorite treats next to her bed.

"Party in my room!" she called weakly.

Doris kissed her tenderly on the cheek and stroked her flattened hair. Then she straightened up in her chair and cleared her throat, a preamble to a well-rehearsed speech. The old Suzanne would have winced away, but now she lay in bed, smiling expectantly. It's not what you're given, it's how you take it, and Suzanne planned to take whatever bruisings and blessing she was given from now on just right.

"You know, dear, I don't want you to go around telling people you're mentally ill. That gives them the wrong impression. You're manic-depressive. That's what you say and that's quite enough. It's from being very creative. And when you see the baby, you do *not* bring it up. If she asks, fine, but don't you do it. And I know you—you get nervous and you joke about things and that's fine; but I urge you to not do this with the baby. She's too young."

While they were on the subject, wasn't Suzanne too young for all this, too? Probably not, but she hoped so. Cut off her head and count the age rings, and she was actually, truth be told, long overdue.

And at the very end of the long day Leland brought Honey—the best having been saved for last after all.

Suzanne saw her daughter's little head just clearing the window as they drove up. Leland swung the car into a nearby parking place and Suzanne's heart began to pound as she started down the stairs.

Leland opened the door for Honey and she stepped down onto the graveled drive hesitantly, the stones crunching under her bright blue tennis shoes. Seeing her mother, she checked her father first to make sure it was all right for her to go to Suzanne, not sure what the new rules were. Leland gave her the slightest of nods. Honey approached Suzanne shyly, chin down, dark eyes up and then down again, shining.

"Hi, Mommy."

Suzanne crossed quickly to her, holding Honey tightly to her, inhaling her familiar powdery fragrance. What had her daughter ever smelled like but holiday feeling?

"Hi, buzzy butt."

Honey squirmed a little in her mother's embrace.

"Mommy, I can't breathe."

Suzanne reluctantly released her and looked into her daughter's pretty face.

"I'm sorry, baby, I just missed you so much."

Leland approached them, passing his signature one hand over his blond, fuzzy head. Looking straight and offhandedly elegant—as ever a magnet for everything fine—he lightly kissed the cool of her cheek, and she squeezed his arm gratefully.

"Thanks for coming, and bringing her and for being so—"

"Shut up, okay?"

As they looked at each other, a warm breeze broke the spell of the still day and blew between them.

"Didn't we have a child together at some point?" she asked. Unsure of what to say, she had no idea how to express her gratitude to him or contrition about the events that had brought her here.

Leland laughed and squinted off into the distance, as if looking for the cavalry he expected any time now.

"That's crazy. With my busy schedule? When would we have done that?"

Honey had spotted a boy of no more than nineteen sitting under a tree in a wheelchair reading a book, and was staring at him with great interest.

"Mommy, is he staying at the hotel with you?"

Suzanne looked up at Leland, perplexed.

He leaned into her, saying quietly, "She's always referred to it as a hotel." He shrugged. "She's more comfortable thinking you're at a resting hotel I think is what she calls it."

Suzanne nodded thoughtfully.

"Yes, buddy. He's a regular guest here."

Honey started back toward them. She wore blue shorts and a paler blue T-shirt that said MARTHA'S VINEYARD, a place Leland frequented on those rented yachts of his, sipping chilled drinks.

"She's so pretty," Suzanne marveled, watching her approach them.

Leland smiled.

"Just so long as she doesn't become an actress."

"Where's the pool?" Honey inquired hopefully, eyes wide and blinking, and scratching her ear with a chubby little hand.

Suzanne frowned as though remembering. "I know I put it somewhere. . . ." Lifting Honey's arm, she said, "Is it here?"

Honey drew away, giggling. "Stop it, Mommy!"

Suzanne followed her, apparently perplexed. "No, seriously, just let me check your pants, because . . ."

Honey was doubled over, trying to escape from her mother's urgent pool search. "Don't Mommy. Stop! Seriously!"

Suzanne stopped abruptly. "Oh, *seriously*. That's different. You didn't say *seriously* first, so . . ."

Honey leaned nonchalantly into her daddy, holding onto his large hand with her smaller one.

"Can I change camps next year to one with a cafeteria, Daddy? 'Cause I hate cold lunches. All I ever have is dry carrot sticks and some stinky sandwich and chips. Which is crazy, don't you think, Mom?"

Suzanne smiled at her daughter, and shook her head sadly. "It's insane, baby," she said simply. "Totally nuts, and believe me, I oughta know."

Honey looked at her dad with satisfaction.

"Told you."

For a moment, Suzanne didn't know what to say next and then that moment grew legs and ran to awkwardness. What was she supposed to talk about with her child and her ex-husband in the mental hospital? Perhaps she was the one who was supposed to be asking them all these questions. Yes! Maybe that was it.

"So, what have you been doing all this week?

Honey thought for a minute to make certain she got the answer right, then brightened suddenly. "It was my birthday, right, Daddy? You missed it!"

Suzanne received this information like a body blow. Her daughter's seventh birthday! How could she not have remembered? Of all the many things she'd missed—those six nights' sleep, making sense, the ability to assemble a collage—this was perhaps the most brutal. No, not perhaps, this was absolutely the worst of all. She knelt down in front of Honey and took her hand. "Oh, baby, I am just so sorry."

Honey looked up at her father for a clue as to what to do in this particular situation. Should she do anything at all?

Suzanne just stared at Honey and Leland, this perfectly matched set, like figure skaters, graceful in their affection for one another, with Suzanne stomping like some tongueless oaf in and around their shining outskirts. It was mesmerizing and wrenching for Suzanne to look at—to be necessarily shut out of, like a carrier of a coming plague.

"Aren't you going to tell Mommy about your party?" Leland prompted his daughter gently.

Honey's eyes were wide with remembering as she disengaged from her father and landed as though jumping from a balance beam.

"Oh, yeah, so guess what! I had a sleepover party and we slept outside in a tent in Daddy's backyard. Bennett was too scared to do it, probably 'cause she's not gonna be seven for four and a half more months, but I wasn't scared at all, was I, Daddy?"

Suzanne looked up at Leland with stricken eyes—with her big, bad, guilty, medicated parent eyes—

". . . And we had a piñata and these party favor purse things that I helped Kathleen fill with stuff I got from the ninety-nine-cent store—"

Suzanne felt as if she were about to free fall over the bad mother cliff where she'd land on the pile populated by such luminaries as Joan and Lana—well, Judy couldn't have been that good but at least she was funny . . . and she'd heard Anne Sexton was pretty weird . . . and it couldn't have been great having Sylvia Plath die in the kitchen downstairs—hey, she was starting to look better . . . Still, they were allowed to be worse as a prize for being so talented, the great artist get-out-of-jail card for this low, low price, while those less blessed paid the full tax for their irresponsible doings.

Either way, it was still way too soon to feel better or worse about things at this point. To even *feel,* period. She was going to need a lot of practice. She had spent too many years being stoned, or way up and then way down, and then being hard on herself for both good and no reasons to just throw in the towel now. It was second nature when her first nature had proven itself to be such a bust. Maybe she'd have to make something third nature to her. Being good to herself in order to be good to Honey—fuck all the other stuff. Well, some of it. She couldn't fuck her chemistry. Her chemistry was too busy fucking her. Maybe they could fuck each other; a double Dutch cluster fuck! And to the degree she could tame the wild beast by bombing herself with those damn-fool pills—theirs, not hers—oh, fuck all this. She just knew she needed to get out from between that rock and hard place. Shady Lanes was the hard place and her real life was the rock. She'd see to it—soon she'd jump onto that rock like it was the most welcoming place in the world—she'd act "as if" she'd depict someone who was sane till she was—that's the stock she came from, right? She'd do it for Honey. Whatever she couldn't do for herself—which was most things—she'd do for Honey.

Suzanne saw Honey and Leland off, waving as the black Mercedes SUV headed down the gravel road. Once they'd gone, she was glad not to have to be on her best behavior—whatever that was, it was tiring just trying to determine it. As she headed down to the dining room, she saw an elegantly dressed man get out of a limousine and walk toward the admissions office to check in, a hanging bag flung over his shoulder like an animal pelt. Helen and Joan appeared on the porch to greet him; Joan took his two Louis Vuitton trunks and led him off unsteadily to the Bipolar Bed & Breakfast, Suzanne's home away from havoc.

So many people came and went that it was impossible to keep track. But even more baffling to fathom was what good their brief sojourn at Shady Lanes could have possibly done them. It was as if they'd been spirited away—plucked from their other-than-ordinary lives, having grown useless or dangerous—certainly undesirable. Some to themselves, some to others. And there they'd remain till they were ready to return to normal or at least within normal's borders. Not good as new, just better than before.

What else was there to do with someone going going gone awry? Off the rails—which was where Shady Lanes was located, and there these casualties would remain, till deemed fit to return to the world to try another round. They were the inhabitants of the "funny farm," crazy crops waiting for their heads to be harvested by the experts in their field hands on staff until they could be put out to pasture, later to enter the land of remission—surrounded on all sides by held breath.

• • •

Ken went back to his old job, leaving Barbie distraught and worried. The day he called her from jail, she sneaked up to the music room during the night, broke a lightbulb, and made cuts up and down her arms.

When rumor of this circulated the following morning, Rhonda smirked.

"What did they expect? They're so stupid. I told you, everyone knows about the lightbulb out."

"Yeah, but what can they do? Light the place with candles? Go for the early Spanish Inquisition look? People would just set fire to themselves." Suzanne shook her head.

The only constant seemed to be patients coming and going. Blurry people. Gina, who had abused her insulin to kill herself, the one who knitted pink scarves in front of the television, got released. Then Stuart, the guy who'd put his fist through his kitchen window to prove a point to his wife. And Rachel, always on the verge of hysterics, whose doctor had encouraged her after her sixth suicide attempt to take life "with a tincture of time" ("And what the fuck does *that* mean," sneered Rhonda.). And that chick who tried to buy crack from a flamboyant gay guy who turned out to be straight and raped her. They all got out before Suzanne. Even Lisa was deemed fit to enter a residential program, and this was a mere two weeks after her discharge from the third-floor lockup.

"Fuckin' Lisa got out before me! Lisa!" she all but wailed to Rhonda and Elliot. "I'll never get out!"

Perhaps it was because she'd agreed to let the doctors experiment with different medications on her.

"We're waiting for you to stabilize," the nurses told her.

Well, what was taking so long? Couldn't they get this thing straight?

Then one morning she awoke. And she just kept waking and waking, as if alert had no apparent end.

"I feel absolutely illegal," she beamed exuberantly at Joan.

Once again high on her brain chemistry, Suzanne was snorting herself—and in a word, it was good.

So they sent the prim lady doctor down from the main house to burst each and every last little bubble in her and temper her carbonated thrill. She sat listening to Suzanne with her blank face—a face Suzanne felt like scribbling on a tattoo!—then finally gave her something to take the up up and away away. The doctor snapped her black bag shut and returned to her post up at the main house. "Don't be a stranger," Suzanne shouted after her cheerfully, "be two if you can!" Taking the yellow pills like the good girl she was going to be from now on, she paced the halls, waiting to see what effect their charm would have on her. About twenty minutes later, a cloud of syrup surrounded and filled her, slowing her eyeballs and slurring her speech. But she still chattered like a magpie—whatever they were—so the blank doctor was sent for once again.

She told the doctor at great length—miles and kilometers of telling—how she had medicated a city when all Suzanne had requested was a pill to temper a village—didn't she see? And not only a city but a suburb and an outskirt. Didn't she see? How difficult was that to understand? What the good doc had done was too ambitious—too much—too awful. Better to just subdue her village and be on her way. Was that asking too much?

In the midst of Suzanne's tirade, she could see the doctor's mind wander and wondered where it went to. Probably somewhere waiting for this top to wind down. Trouble was, Suzanne rarely ended. There was no longer any official finish line to cross.

Ultimately the mental hospital merely provided storage for Suzanne, keeping her in the wings until she was able to rejoin the play that was still in progress, the play that had gone merrily along in her absence. What finally sprung her from the trap was the outside world insinuating itself into her little corner of Haldol Heaven.

She could never figure out who sold her story to the *Globe* no matter how many angles she approached it from. It wasn't Rhonda or Elliot, she knew that much. And obviously the aphasic man was completely out of the question. After that it was anybody's guess.

Of course the President was an unlikely candidate, having matters of national importance in his own country to attend to. Norman could've done it to bankroll a supply of cigarettes, that is if he were able to overcome his agitation and inability to focus to do so—which was also a highly unlikely bet.

So who else could gain from her loss of face? Could it have been Barbie or Ken or Lisa? Was it the man who had situational depression or the slut nun or even Helen or Joan?

Sure. Why not? And in the end, what did it matter? The important thing now was that she had a great excuse to leave Shady Lanes. She no longer had to wait till she fit anyone's criteria of sane but her own.

It was now or never—never being what it would feel like to Suzanne to remain. She was ready to try the world again.

The story in the *Globe* had been entitled "Suzanne Vale's Tragic Life," which Suzanne had thought was a hearty mix of hilarious and humiliating—like so much of her existence. A mix of accuracy and embellishment for all the food-buying world to see, it was located on the first page at the very bottom—complete with unflattering photos and quotes from "friends" and "close sources." A tale destined to follow her like that vague exotic smell of celebrity, a smell she'd have to account for to strangers and friends alike. ("I so admire your courage." "Are you *sure* there's nothing the matter?" "You're better now though, aren't you?" "Well, you seem all right to me!")

So there it was, Suzanne's shameful interlude on display at supermarkets and airports everywhere, signaling it was time for her to go. Her story had been retailed, her medication reconsidered, her ability to make a mean collage restored—what more could be required for her reentry?

If there were a real answer to that question, Suzanne would never know it. So, packing her things and taking a parting glance at her room, she turned her back on it with relief and shut the door.

She'd taken her leave of almost everyone that morning in the kitchen at breakfast. Everyone that was still there anyway—as most had either been transferred to a residential program or halfway house, one of the various launchpads-cum-restricted finishing schools that paved the way to an unsupervised life. A life without nets or checkpoints.

Elliot and Rhonda waited for her outside, smoking on the steps. Seeing her in the doorway with her suitcase, Elliot sprang to his feet, dropping the last of his smoke and crushing it under his boot heel.

"Here—let me get that for you. It's heavy."

Suzanne released her suitcase into his hand, smiling. She loved it when guys did guy things. She found it so appealing and compelling that it was a wonder to her when again and again she kept returning to those males who were sexually ambiguous. Why did she take so much pleasure in identifying and admiring these decidedly male men, only to set them free back into the world, pursuing instead all those boy/men with a vengeance—again and again. Was it because the boy/men could be chased down and bent to her androgynous will and those manly men . . . well, those guys usually wanted things their way or not at all. Maybe that was all it boiled down to: control—or the illusion of it.

Yet here was Elliot, a male male—he watched the sports, did the belching, and carried the bags. Of course the psychotic break would most likely keep him out of the finals of "Who's the hot guy on the motorcycle?" contest. But he'd been a great daydream during her recent nightmare stay here. A sympathetic someone off-limits but well within reach. A fantasy all the more delicious because it was inappropriate. Having been one of the few things she enjoyed—her secret campus crush at Sanity School—Elliot would be one of the few people she would miss—him and Rhonda. They could keep the rest.

Oh, she'd have stories to tell. At dinners and meetings for years and years—that was for sure. Once she could find the through line and the funny, her place in anecdote heaven was assured. But she'd happily leave the rest behind—taking Elliot and Rhonda with her. As unrealistic as that might prove to be. What had realistic ever really done for her anyway, when you got right down to it? And she planned to get right down to it real soon.

Doris was due to pick her up in front of the main house after signing some paperwork in the business office. Then she'd bring the car from around the side.

"My mommy's coming! Like I'm a kid!" Suzanne looked at Rhonda in exasperation, who shrugged without comment. "That should be your biggest problem," she told Suzanne with a raised eyebrow, still sucking her toothpick from lunch.

After walking in silence, listening to the gravel on the path crunch under their feet, Rhonda put a heavy hand on Suzanne's stooped shoulder.

"I swear to fuck, if I ever find out who sold that fucked-up story, I'll beat the living shit out of them." Her dark eyes were alive with menace, her face tight with the excitement of violence. Suzanne smiled gratefully at her friend, giving her a playful shove.

"Why? It's because of them I can finally escape this horrible place! You should *thank* them. Save the killing for Helen."

Elliot put Suzanne's suitcase down and turned toward them. "We've got five minutes till afternoon group and her leaving, so why don't we do something more . . . I don't know . . . *useful* with our time other than murder, like smoke or . . ."

Suzanne saw Helen's face appear at an upstairs window. But Helen wasn't the only reason that she did what she was about to do. She did it for many reasons. Because she'd wanted to for a long time now, because she was starved for human contact and affection and because of how male Elliot was being at the moment, and because if she didn't do it now, she probably never would. She moved toward Elliot, leaning into him as far as she could with her head at a slight angle, she gently but firmly kissed him. And like any good stain the kiss spread, first into the flush of a smile then a deeper, darker feast, going from the tall of them to the small of them only the right places kisses reach. And all the while behind them Rhonda was bellowing.

"*Look,* you better get out here, Helen! Oh, my God, they're *touching!* Hurry! This looks fuckin' daaangerous!"

And with the siren thus wailing, in front of God and some of his everyones, these two nuts cracked, finally kissing that last forbidden crazy kiss.

SANE OLD SANE OLD

Getting out of the mental hospital wasn't all Suzanne hoped it would be. There was no waiting throng of well-wishers, no ticker tape parade. She'd imagined she would go running through the gates of Shady Lanes with a spring in her step and a sparkle of certainty in her eye. As she passed by, a nurse would turn to a newly admitted patient and say proudly, "That's Suzanne Vale. We learned more from her during her stay with us than I think she ever could've gotten from us. Why, in the end, I don't think she's mentally ill so much as a kind of misunderstood eccentric, more unique than mad, really."

In reality, she crept timid and frightened out of her recent place of incarceration, peering back over her shoulder at the friends she'd left there, groping tentatively for whatever it was that would keep her what others called "sane."

Sane old . . . sane old . . . you know what I mean?

But no such thing happened at all. Doris picked her up and drove her home in virtual silence, piloting her green Lincoln Town Car with the tan seats and the emergency brake on.

What had begun as an overcast day showed no sign of clearing, enabling Suzanne to return home under a cloak of cloud cover. Walking around her house, she examined the rooms carefully like a potential buyer, scouting locations for the saner human she hoped now to become. As the one bird who got to fly out of the cuckoo's nest, she would live within the margins, putting one foot in front of the other, taking the pills, going to the meetings and the psychopharmacologists' office, mouthing the words. And over time, she would return to being someone. Who, just for the moment, remained to be seen.

Though Doris had wanted to kick everyone out so that Suzanne could "spend some quiet time with herself, healing," that was the *last* thing she wanted, preferring company to her constant self-diagnosing and monitoring—what Craig came to call her "Closely Watched Brains Syndrome." She wanted to be with other people. All-right people whose stability was neither questioned nor threatened. There was always an outside chance that these people could act on her insides. And if they didn't help fix her, well, at least in the meantime she would have had some company.

Suzanne found that once your mind goes to a place as far as hers had gone to, it tends to take a while for it to come back. And if by some miracle it did come back, it wouldn't be, could never be, the same brain. But would you want the same one anyway, now that it had turned on you and in you so completely?

Sure. Who are we kidding? Suzanne would have liked nothing better than to have everything return to the way it was. Fat arms and all. Even without being certain which way everything had been to begin with.

But the doctors had told her she might never get back all the equipment she'd once had to play with. The familiar toy behind her eyes. The one that gave the world back to her with its own peculiar spin on things, the mind that had purchased her the funny slant she'd always had to look at life with. The mind that had protected her from that mountain of feeling by keeping her well-supplied with all that endless explaining of things or glib playing on words. There was no telling what her mind might do now that it wasn't all hers.

So with Hoyt still staying in the guesthouse, and Craig dividing his time between his room there and Angelica's condominium,

Suzanne was back to living, if not actually *in* a fraternity, then happily around one.

Suzanne's mother had gotten her a beach house in Santa Barbara so she and Honey could spend the last few weeks of summer together. Situated halfway between the ocean and the train tracks, it was large and white, with several decks overlooking the sand. The steady sound of the breaking of waves was occasionally punctuated by the lonely whistle of trains passing; trains whose destinations ranged from San Luis Obispo to Los Angeles. And twice a day the train with the name Suzanne liked the best passed through: the Starlight Express, like the name of a musical, traveling up and down the coastline, from Seattle to San Diego and back again, with unobstructed views of the ocean almost all the way, blowing its lonely whistle while it rolled along. Suzanne thought it the most wonderful sound in the world. A sound to fasten your mind to, to see where it might take you while you slept.

Not that she was interested in fastening her mind to anything right now, sound or otherwise, and have it traipse off into the night. Seeing as how it had already been off on an extended jaunt to the third or fourth ring of hell. The best thing was to let the thing rest for a while. It had been through enough, and Lord knew, so had she.

"Now's the time to get away, and let things settle down a bit," Suzanne's mother Doris announced on one of her daily visits to her daughter's house, by way of informing her she'd gotten the house. "You go off and figure out just what it is your next move is going to be. After your father left me, I just collapsed. If it hadn't been for my mother and daddy, I might not have been here. I only wish *my* mother could've afforded to get *me* a beach house so that I could have stood back and assessed just exactly where was the best groove for me to pursue once my wounds had healed as I was ready to fly."

Suzanne frowned at her with concern. "But we can't afford one, can we? I mean, you can't and I can't, so . . ."

Her mother waved her small hand dismissively. "Please, dear, it won't cost us anything. I borrowed it from Melanie Bowers, you remember her?"

Still frowning, Suzanne shook her head and Doris looked at her with exasperation. "Oh, yes, you do." She retied her colorful chiffon scarf expertly around her pale neck. "She was in . . . oh, what was she in? . . . Well, you would know her immediately if you saw her. Not *now*, of course, she looks as bad as I do. And I haven't had as many lifts as she has. But she did a lot of films in the fifties. Not successful ones, but she worked steadily, which is more than a lot of people did. But she was smart; she hooked Richard Eddington. I know you remember him, dear." It wasn't spoken as a question, but Doris paused, expecting a response of some kind from her daughter.

But Suzanne had been arranging and rearranging her medicine on the bed with great absorption, the yellows with the yellows, the pinks with the pinks, and the blues with the blues. "Never mind, you're not listening to me. I'll come back another time and we can—"

Suzanne was vaulted out of her daze by the newly stoic lilt her mother's voice had assumed. "No! I *am* listening. I was just arranging my medicine." She indicated the neat little piles of pills in front of her. "See? It arranges me in the night, and I arrange it in the day. It's kind of a 'you medicate my back, I medicate yours' kind of thing."

Doris looked perplexedly at her daughter for a moment. Then her face suddenly seemed to pucker with effort. She shrugged helplessly and her pale eyes filled with tears.

Struck by her mother's upset, Suzanne winced as though in danger of violence. "I *swear!* I was *listening!* You were talking about how she married a guy named—"

"It's not that," Doris managed, her face struggling with emotion, "When I think of you having this manic depression thing, I just get . . ." Her eyes looked to the heavens for assistance as she fanned her reddening face with one hand.

Watching her nervously from her perch in bed, Suzanne barricaded herself safely behind her pile of tablets. "Mom . . . ," she began miserably, "Please, we've talked about this. I'm *all right* now. *Really.*"

Doris had sunk her hand into her big patchwork bag and was rifling through its contents busily. "I know you hate it when I get emotional, but I can't help it. When I think you got this from that ridiculous *father* of yours, I get so angry. . . ." Finding some tissue, she brought it to her nose and blew.

Suzanne watched, rigid with tension, picking the skin on her toe.

Doris was right. Suzanne *did* hate it when her mother got emotional. But not just her. *Everyone.* Figuring once one person sprang a leak it was only a matter of time before everybody blew until finally it would be her turn again. She couldn't let that happen. Not ever, but especially not now. Now she was practicing being in control. Her version of practicing law. *Her* law. The law of Suzanne Vale, Esquire, governing herself into right action. Not that she ever expected to manage it, but she couldn't very well practice control *or* law with someone sobbing at her bedside.

"I should've married Nick Manning," her mother continued despondently, "The one man who loved me just for me and was impotent, which would have been a relief, believe me! And who would've left me a *fortune,* I might add." Wiping her eyes, she crossed to a wastebasket, disposing of the damp tissue. "But I was young and—"

Suzanne sat up on her haunches. "Mom! I thought you were telling me about some house in Santa Barbara!"

Looking at her daughter blankly, Doris blinked, brightening. "Oh, the *house!*" Beaming, she brought her hands together enthusiastically. "Did I tell you it has a *pool!* And *four bedrooms!* Three guests and a master!"

Suzanne found herself caring for all manner of people and things so easily now. Almost as though you could add water and stir up love— as long as the water wasn't tears. But now that she'd swum to the other side of her unpleasantness, she found that all she wanted was to go along with the best in everything, cast herself in calmer currents, drift along.

Not that she didn't have responsibilities as a recovering alien. She was going to a new psychopharmacologist, one who had promised not to prescribe medicines that she would be allergic to or that would keep her awake for six days. This was her new nonnegotiable criteria for psychopharmacologists. Not being certain of anything—least of all her instincts—she'd asked Leland to pick out the doctor, just to be safe. For her end of the bargain, she'd take every pill as prescribed. A psychoactive nip here, a tuck there, taking herself down a peg, down to size—from super-sized to bite-size, long-playing album to single, unending text to Cliffs Notes, everywhere to somewhere, someone more manageable, more managed—someone whose less was more than she or anyone ever expected it to be.

And after she and Leland met with the doctor a few times and went over what they would and wouldn't tell Honey, it was decided that she would stay with her mother initially for a whole day. If that went well, the time would increase to overnight. And one night would become two and grow to three again, until finally Honey stayed with each parent half the week, living three days with Suzanne and four with Leland, then the other way round. Not returning to normal, but keeping normal in mind. A destination where Honey could eventually feel safe, a good place to begin. A place where her daughter could finally stop checking Suzanne out of the sides of her eyes or sweeping her for those pesky mind mines.

One day as they left the doctor's office together, Suzanne reached out and touched Leland on the shoulder. "Thank you for being so unbelievably—"

Leland grabbed Suzanne in his arms so she couldn't move and put one ringless hand over her mouth. "Stop. You'd do the same for me." Her startled eyes held his for a moment before she began to laugh and he looked down and thought for a moment. What did he say that was so funny?

"All I meant was—," he amended.

"You are totally right. Anytime you have an overdose or a psychotic break, I'm your man . . . or girl—whatever—I'll be right there for you. I'm your man/girl."

But she was so grateful to him for not blaming her for being the way she was or having the thing that she had. He let her be in the blaming-her business—he already had a job, he said. Was he really this good of a guy? Was anyone? Well, who could last long as a creature of her invention with so many other things to threaten it? The Leland in

Suzanne's mind—Honey's Leland—had that smooth, shaved head—that bright idea balanced neatly on two shoulders. This Leland was like the feel of cool cotton on warm skin, food when you're hungry, sleep when you need rest, and that well-ironed shoulder to cry on. After all, he was still her emergency contact number, wasn't he? And she? Why, she was his little emergency . . . remember? How could she not love this man? And if there was an answer to that question, it was in the wrong language or she didn't want to know it.

Suzanne and Honey would stay in Santa Barbara for the month of August—just until Honey started school again. In exchange for the house, her mother had agreed to host a charity benefit for the owner, Melanie Bowers, an event it appeared Suzanne would also be attending. The charity happened to be amfAR, an organization Suzanne had written speeches for in the past, with the proceeds of the event going to AIDS research. Since the benefit was scheduled for deep in the fall, Suzanne didn't have to organize herself around going yet, so she did what she normally did about such things, and tried to forget it would ever happen. Who knows? Perhaps she wouldn't be alive by then, or, worse still, she might even be back in the hospital, hiding her cigarettes from Norman.

But it turned out that she was a survivor, like her mother. Her one-of-a-kind, next-of-kin, head-held-high, knock-'em-dead-kid parent. The trooper whose show would go on, come hell or high daughter.

"You know the bad thing about being a survivor, Mom?"

Doris was helping her pack for her stay at the beach. "I don't see anything wrong with it, dear." She tucked a bathing suit into the suitcase's side pocket. "I mean, considering the alternatives, what do you suggest? *Not* surviving?" She let go of the elastic on the pocket with a dramatic snap.

"No. But you know what's wrong with it?" Suzanne gazed at her mother, triumphant. "You keep having to get into difficult situations in order to show off your gift." Throwing her hands up in the air in exaggerated exasperation, she watched as Doris thought about this.

"You complicate things too much, dear." Doris headed out of the room toward her daughter's closet purposefully. "Now, why don't you think about what you're going to wear in the evenings in case it gets chilly?"

The most important thing, and the thing Suzanne looked forward to most, was spending all that time with Honey. And she would forever be grateful to Leland for overriding his low-level alert with regard to her stability and allowing Honey go away with her this soon, and for this long. She scrutinized her reflection with measured distaste. Still overweight, but not as Michelin-like. The other secret reason she liked the idea of the trip was because she thought she might be able to use the time away to get herself together, lose weight, and look fantastic by summer's end. Then no one would ask her if she was okay. They would automatically know she was fine. And they would know because she looked better than she'd ever had. So perhaps losing her mind had been a *good* thing in the end. Perhaps she'd only lost bits she didn't need. Like the part that liked food and smoked and wanted to take drugs and . . .

"Are you listening to me, dear?" Her mother called from the next room. "Suzanne?"

"I was listening! Just say the last part again."

Sighing, Doris repeated, "I said that I didn't think that you should have any of those *people* around you. I don't care *how* many guest rooms there are. And I'm still a little mad at that Craig fellow, although he is *darling*—so handsome—I don't know why you don't date *him*—but of course, I know, an actor is tricky."

"Mom—"

"Anyway, I just think that it'll be heaven—just you and Honey and the beach. *Just* what you need."

Sitting on the deck overlooking the beach in Santa Barbara, her face turned up into the sun, Suzanne listened to Honey singing along as she practiced the piano, "Alive, alive-oho, alive, alive oho, crying cockles and mussels alive, alive oh." Suzanne smiled.

Now that they were here, what exactly were they supposed to do? Suzanne hadn't ever fully understood the concept of "relax." Maybe if she were the type of person who knew her way around a lounge chair, she wouldn't have stayed awake for six days to begin with. But having outlasted all her sleepless hallucinations, she found herself facing the daunting challenge of seaside relaxation. Daunting in that it didn't need her. Her surroundings were weird without being urgent—urgent being all she'd ever understood.

Honey stole up behind her and gripped the back of Suzanne's chair. *"Mom,"* she pleaded, "I'm *bored!* Can I have a playdate?"

"But we don't know anyone up here, nibbler."

Honey frowned in exasperation. "Then let's *send* for somebody. What about Katie? *Please?"*

Suzanne closed her eyes. "Like a mail-order playdate?"

Honey learned into the back of her mother's chair. "I'm *serious!"* she all but yelled in a bright keen of frustration.

Ugh, thought Suzanne. This relaxation shit is a *nightmare.*

It was true what they said about kids being resilient. Soon after they'd arrived at the beach house, Honey had ceased her watchful ministrations. But no wonder, Suzanne now patrolled enough for two. Watching both her poles, making sure they stayed in their proper places, and managing the simplest of tasks were enough for her.

She knew she still owed Honey—just how much she'd have to figure out as she went along. But she knew one thing for certain. She had to keep making to Honey what she'd heard called "living amends." Show her that she was trustworthy by doing what she said she'd do and showing up and doing all that regular, real, reliable stuff good people do for their children.

Like cooking. Blindsided by recipes one day, the next thing she knew she was walking down supermarket aisles once more like a bride. Her bouquet was a bag of groceries, brimming with ingredients intended for her new altar, the oven. The wonderful thing about recipes was, they whispered their suggestions without inflection or blame, an edible I Ching. You could measure and mix at your leisure, a slow, solemn march to mealtime. You might bake, baste, or even sauté. Or not. Mr. Recipe didn't care too much either way.

"Hey, maybe go get some flour if you feel like it, but whatever. I'm just saying," crooned the cookbook, and humming, Suzanne would comply. Then she'd do the next step, even the one after that one. And before you knew it—*food!* Suzanne was amazed what egg whites did to the soufflé. And who knew risotto was made with so much soup? Soup that went by the nickname broth.

"So maybe you can't teach an old dog new tricks," she said to her Cuisinart as she fed an onion into it. "I wouldn't know about that. But you can teach older people." She nodded with satisfaction as the food processor sprang to life and ground the onion to bits. She turned it off and began to scoop the contents into an aluminum measuring cup. A silver chalice receiving its sacrament. Honey appeared in the doorway.

"Mom, are you talking to the soup again?" she asked her sternly, hands on hips.

Suzanne looked at her daughter, mildly defiant.

"No, as it happens, Ms. Smarty Pants, I'm talking to the Cuisinart."

Honey rolled her eyes and walked back out.

Suzanne turned back to the food processor.

"Now do you see what I have to put up with?" she said, shaking her head and then crossing to the stove and throwing the minced onion into a large frying pan. "And how are *you* this evening, my beloved?" she asked its flat surface, already slick with butter and olive oil. "Ready to kick a little risotto ass, baby?" She turned on the flame, grabbed a wooden spoon, and raised it over the crackling contents of the pan. "Go ahead," she commanded it, Chef Eastwood. *"Make my meal!"*

But on the heels of this cooking came grumpy old exercise. Something she'd avoided assiduously for most of her life. "I know it's hard, dear," Doris told her sympathetically. "But it has to be done. When a woman gets older, she tends to get a little . . . toady." Now it was Suzanne against the exercise machines—and she wasn't going to let them get the better of her. Whatever better was at this point.

"Okay, you motherfucker," she would say to the treadmill, when Honey and her swearing tax were out of earshot. "It's you or me—and I think you know who's going down . . . *punk!*"

But she figured if she could do the six days without sleep, what was exercise? If she could outlast that unpleasantness, what was this but a teeny bit of fog for her practiced sun to burn off in a snap, just so much *nothing*.

She had to stick with it, because next month she would start interviewing celebrities again. The cable people actually liked the idea of having a mentally ill celebrity talk-show host. Suzanne thought this was redundant, but she did what she did about everything—pretended she didn't care and made a joke about it—then privately she worried what people would say about her. Oh, fuck it. Let's go on with the show. The talk show.

BOO RADLEY'S TREE

The phone out on the deck beside her rang, and Suzanne looked at it as though waiting for an encore, perhaps for it to do the dishes. But unlike the Mecca clicker, it could merely continue to ring, so she answered it. "Hello?" she drawled into the receiver. "Speak, memory."

There was a pause on the other end before a voice cautiously asked, "Suzanne? Is that you? This is Dorothy. Dorothy Jacobsen?"

Suzanne thought for a moment. Who? Then it all came flooding back in a quiet rush.

Suzanne had recently gotten an email from Louise Madigan, whom she knew only vaguely. An older wife of a famous producer, Louise had suffered an unthinkable tragedy. Her daughter had been run over by a drunk driver and Louise had seen it all happen from an upstairs window in their Maryland house. By the time she'd gotten to her child, she was gone. As a result, Louise moved with a quiet dignity the brave sometimes have. So when Suzanne got her email, though she felt disinclined to involve herself in a fresh tragedy, coming from this noble, older woman, Suzanne found herself unable to say no. Thing of it was this—Louise Madigan wanted her to talk to a woman whose husband had recently left her for what turned out to be a boyfriend. He'd made a lifestyle choice that didn't include her.

Suzanne had heard of this thing and kept a respectful distance, preferring anything to a predicament that smacked of déjà vu all over again. *Déjà voulez-vous coucher avec moi?* as it were. No. It seemed a better idea to keep these familiar fires far from her doorstep.

But it sneaked in on mincing little cat's feet, through the open door of her email. The thing she referred to as Boo Radley's Tree because she found all manner of things stuffed in it when she looked inside the Internet hole every morning. Who knew what the electronic cat would drag in next?

So when Mrs. Madigan had suggested in her email that Suzanne get in touch with Dorothy, Suzanne put her hand over her eyes and moaned out loud.

"What's the matter, Mommy?" Honey stood in the doorway. Her hair, wet from her recent bath, fell down past her shoulders, leaving wet spots on her blue-flowered nightgown. The sunlight seemed to Suzanne to be drawn into her daughter, radiating out of her once again only reluctantly.

"Nothing, creature. I just remembered that I am mortal and what an annoyance that's gonna one day be."

Looking suspiciously at her, Honey rolled her eyes.

"Are you gonna read to me?" She started back toward her bedroom, rubbing her nose with the flat of her hand.

"Just let me answer this email and I'll be in."

Honey stopped and turned back toward her. "Not a long one," she cautioned her mother sternly.

Suzanne shook her head. "You have no idea how short."

This answer satisfied her daughter, who wandered down the hall, taking her funny walk with her.

Suzanne quickly typed, "Dear Mrs. M.: Do I have to?" She paused, considering what she might say next, then wrote, "Loud love of the long-lasting variety—Suzanne." Sending the email, she signed off, and went to her desk to get the P. G. Wodehouse book she was in the middle of reading to Honey, who had a mad passion for Bertie Wooster and Jeeves, largely due to the fact that Suzanne acted them out complete with accents and expressions. Besides which, Honey liked most first-person narratives in grown-up books. "As long as they don't have teeny-weeny little print all clumped up together and everything," which meant *To Kill a Mockingbird* and anything by Kerouac were out.

Never sure where in the story they were when Honey fell asleep each night, Suzanne often read the same bits over and over again. But Honey didn't mind; she loved the clipped singsong British accent that animated each character. Clicking off the light after she determined Honey's sleep was sure and steady, Suzanne tiptoed from the room.

The next morning, she received an email from Louise Madigan:

"When we have experience and strength to share with someone who's gone through a similar difficulty, then the right thing to do is share that experience and give comfort and hope when we can. I know you'll do the right thing.

Bless you,
Louise Madigan
p.s. It's good to have you back among us. Dorothy's number in case you don't have it is . . ."

Of course Suzanne had no choice but to call this woman. Especially once Leland suggested she stay away.

"Excuse me? You had lunch with the husband, didn't you? Welcoming him to the fold? Gave him a coming-in party?"

See, that was the bummer of getting into this thing. To go there was to bring the finally buried business back, feelings and all.

The service picked up when she called.

"Hi, is Dorothy there, please?"

"May I ask who's calling?"

Suzanne sighed and jiggled her knee up and down.

"Suzanne," she said impatiently then added, "Vale" in a more pleasant tone.

Why punish the service for this exasperating errand?

"Just one moment."

The service clicked off the line, leaving Suzanne in telephonic limbo with annoying hold music. Suzanne tightened her mouth in irritation. Gone were the good old days when being put on hold meant being left in a respectful silence. Now you were serenaded until someone returned with news. But in the meantime, you wouldn't be able to entertain any thoughts unless they were hummable.

"I'm sorry, she doesn't seem to be picking up. Would you like to leave your number and . . . ? "

So Suzanne had left her number, hung up the phone, and returned to her life.

This, then, was Dorothy calling her back.

"Oh yeah, hey, how ya doing, Dorothy? How's your horrible thing doing? Are you okay?"

From inside the house, Honey faltered on the piano keys. "Darn it! Man!" she exclaimed, banging on the keyboard before continuing.

"Can you believe it?" Dorothy said sorrowfully. "Well, of course you can, because of Leland, but I mean I've been with this man for sixteen years. And hey, never mind that, are you okay since your breakdown thing?"

Suzanne nodded and picked at her toenail. "Psychotic break-dancing is the medical term for what happened to me, and I'm fine. Now, what's the deal with *you*?"

Dorothy took a deep breath. "Well, he meets a guy on a plane and—well, I don't know it's a guy, right? All I'm told is he met a person and wouldn't have been attracted to 'this person' if I had paid attention to him or hadn't gained so much weight."

Suzanne shook her head. "Female fat is a known fag-making substance. It's been well documented by scientists."

There was an abrupt silence on the other end of the line. When Dorothy spoke again, there was fear in her voice "That's a joke, right?"

"Yes, it's a joke. It's a joke that someone tells you that you turned him gay. But I figure he tells you that because he's upset and he feels like a victim himself, you know? 'Cause it can't be because of the guy that's giving him the great blow jobs—it's the fat chick that neglected him all the way up to that point. That's just something we do, right? Hey, now that you've practiced turning him gay, and I practiced on Leland, we could get together, go out and make some more new gay guys. Maybe even improve our aim a little. I'm telling you, a few weeks with me and you'll realize you have a superpower on your hands. If you play your cards right—and I'm not promising anything, mind you, but who knows?—I might even be able arrange the cape and the decoder ring."

Dorothy laughed a little breathless laugh, punctuated by squeaks and hiccups. While she composed herself, Suzanne gazed out at the ocean, craving a cigarette. But smoking was off-limits when Honey was around. That was her *rule*. Ironclad and without loopholes. Turning Suzanne into a furtive criminal smoker, puffing away just outside doorways and in out-of-the-way bathrooms. The one time Honey had caught her, she hadn't spoken to her mother for the rest of the afternoon. And when she finally did say something, it was "Your lungs are gonna be real black, you know. Plus it's *nasty.*" Great. One more thing to give up and get fatter after. Fan-fucking-tastic. Safer now to wait until the next virtuous phase. In the meantime she'd remain the sneaky smoker, puffing quietly, her back tense with anxiety and guilt.

"So," Suzanne asked, "Have you already had the privilege of meeting the boyfriend?" She smiled wistfully, wishing she'd had someone like herself to talk to when Leland had left her for Nick. Nick, the oh so pleasant theatrical manager. Carefree hairstyle Nick with nice clothes. With an agenda a mile wide and a six-pack a few inches deep. It would have been funny sooner if the present Suzanne could have chatted with the past one. Oh, well. That's what you get for getting in on the ground floor of one of these off-center sociosexual groundswells. Someone has to spearhead the movement, and that was the person who usually got speared.

Dorothy groaned. "Yeah, but like *now* all he wants to do is confess to me. You know, about all the times he told me he was going to buy a book when really he was going to meet Rudolfo in the back of—"

Suzanne interrupted her firmly. "Okay, *look,* I'm laying down the law here. You're not allowed to talk to this guy for a while, do you understand me? I mean, you know he's trying to get you to absolve him, so he can forgive himself or deal with his guilt or whatever. Anyway, it doesn't matter, because the end result is that he's taking a shit in your head. I mean, in exchange for absolution, you'll get a head full of pictures you will never be able to get rid of. So for the next few months, your head is closed for business. He has to go be gay now. No more final farewells in Straight Town. He can't have his Rudolfo cake and . . . You get my drift, no? I'm sorry, but you're not here to make this easier for him at this point. Your gig is to make it easier for your kids. Your son's older, right? I mean, a walking, talking creature?"

"He's thirteen, and I have to tell you, Suzanne, he's very upset about the whole thing. I mean, he doesn't even want to see him. The baby's three. She barely knows it's happening."

Suzanne drummed her fingers impatiently. "Well, you need to hire a child psychologist to be your son's advocate, and not get yourself in the position where you become the target messenger who your husband can say is poisoning his son against him, blah, blah, blah."

Dorothy gasped. "He already *said* that! You're brilliant! You know, you should write a book! Really! It would help people a lot. I can't tell you how much this is helping me."

"Yeah," said Suzanne ruefully, *"Chicken Soup for the Fag Widow."*

So she told the breathless, scattered Dorothy what she could. She even cried a little in the telling, which was annoying, and one of the reasons she didn't like revisiting this crime scene. She welcomed

Dorothy into the exclusive club whose membership she could never revoke.

Long ago, at one of her New Age workshops, Suzanne had heard a phrase that had stayed with her over the years and certainly applied to her current situation: "We are addicted to chaos and excitement in all our affairs, preferring constant upset to . . . *blah blah blah.*" She could never remember what the blah blah blah was that she was meant to prefer the constant upset to, so obviously she preferred the upset to that thing a *lot.* But the rest of it, the addicted-to-excitement-and-chaos thing—even the constant upset—*that* all rang true with a disturbing clang of resonance. Now that she was the cock of crazy walk, she could laugh in the face of danger. Or at least snicker—a start toward giggling, a door in her life quietly pried open so she could stealthily wander in. And behind her through that door walked crazy. Now that she was no longer crazy—or *as* crazy, anyway— her life was. Chaos and excitement accumulated around her, the master of ceremonies at the crazy convention. Things simply refused to faze her; whoever or whatever came, she'd remain imperturbable. Imperturbability filled the air, emitted a faint welcoming sound—a come-hither noise you could only hear if you were broken down: "If you build it, they will come" became "If you break down, even more will."

Her new motto was apparently "Anyone's Crisis but Mine." First so quiet, it seemed to whisper its way out of her, barely audible. But if they couldn't hear it, all anyone had to do was look up, because there she was, materializing on the horizon, giving off a shine, the gleam of the newly reconstructed, so recently back from the grave—with gifts! A sunspot fixed in their swirling solar winds, she glowed in their dark. The dark of people who had been sucked into their own shadowed experience. Suzanne spoke their language, knew their secret handshake. And one mess to another, they'd chew the fat of the fucked, the shit-out-of-lucked and in the mood to talk.

First came the addicts, which had always happened. Nothing

new about that. She'd been a viable, visible addict for quite a stretch of time now. But now there were other brands of derangement—people whose brain chemistry ebbed and flowed began to appear at her erstwhile window and trickle over her borders—or the place where her borders should have been. They could smell her somehow, smell her over-developed sense of responsibility, that thing in themselves that just *had* to be like her. They came, heads in hands, seeking fraternity.

Addicts and bipolars and schizophrenics, even some troubled celebrities. Suzanne housed them and gave them the shelter they hankered for, protecting them from evil. And it wasn't so bad. It was all right actually. What could be bad after all that, anyway? As long as Honey was happy and healthy, not much. And she was—so fine, bring on the limping people, fill her ark with them.

Now that she was sane and sober, Suzanne began to feel as if she was haunting her own life. "This was where I once . . ." and "Oh, God, that's the guy that . . ." or "Jesus, I haven't been here since . . ." Oh, she was still her, but in another sense, not her. She would surely never be as she'd been. And that was a good thing, wasn't it? It had to be. She'd never again take things for granted the way she had. No, she'd take them for granted in another, better way.

Improbably, she started speaking at various functions on subjects ranging from mental illness to gay pride. The new poster girl for the journey to substance abuse and back again.

Suzanne stood up at the amfAR event and pulled the mike down toward her. "I'm Suzanne, and I'm an alcoholic . . . ," then, as if waking from a daydream, she added, "Oops! Wrong room!"

Most of the men laughed. Even Leland smiled.

"You'd be an alcoholic, too, if you had my life—and a few of you *did* have my life! I can prove it! I have the receipts and the Polaroids. You'd be an addict, too, if you'd discovered that you'd had a child with a man who'd forgotten to tell you that he was gay and you forgot to notice!" Suzanne looked at them straight-faced. "I was distracted, what can I tell you? Pathologically distracted. My mind was

on other things—it was on acid, on Dasher, on Donder, on Blitzen. I
was about to go insane, so I was on a bit of a time crunch: I was going
to need to stay awake for six days, be everyone on TV, see a yellow
light glowing out of my head, receive a secret message from the Jews
in an old movie—wait . . . I'm getting ahead of myself—and how
many manics have you heard say *that*?! Anyway, where was I? Oh,
that's what we're here to determine, isn't it? Or is the question really,
was I? Or just where?

"But here's the thing I'm here to complain about. We have no
Bipolar Pride Day! Now why is that? Because I think it's a major oversight. I mean, can you imagine the parades? With the bummer floats:
depressives lying on beds staring off at nothing? And what about the
manic marching bands? With nobody carrying instruments but
everyone talking and shopping and making bad judgment calls? I
mean, can't you just see it? Or is it just me? Never mind—don't answer that. But I mean, why not? Why don't we have bipolar pride?
We have discrimination and shame and all, just like the best oppressed
minorities. But other than that, what do we have? I ask you: Do we
have bipolar bars? *No!* And why is that? 'Cause I've got the names for
them. There's the Lithium & Lockup. And the Thorazine Shuffle
Club. And the Depa Coat & Tie Bar. I mean, look, obviously, all this is
still in its early planning stages—and knowing bipolars, it always will
be—oh, and if you were getting in the mood to be offended about all
this? Be my guest, 'cause yes, I know, it's very serious stuff, this mental illness business. I've been serious ever since I caught this particular
strain I have from Anna Nicole Smith's toilet seat, so you should be
serious, too. Please. And responsible. If you've hugged me or had some
other sort of humiliating contact with me in the last six weeks, I urge
you to contact your doctor and your horse whisperer—and your hair
stylist."

They all laughed and clapped at her then, and she found Leland's
face among all the others and looked at him with an expression both
pleased and helpless.

"Hey, it's not funny!" she said mainly just to him. "Actually, it *is*
funny. It fucking better be. Always remember what Miro said 'cause I

told him to: "If my life wasn't funny, then it'd just be true, and that would be totally unacceptable.' "

And smiling, she lifted her ubiquitous glass of Diet Coke to Leland and nodded. And sipping her drink, she bowed and walked off the stage.

WE WEREN'T LOVERS
LIKE THAT

Suzanne and Leland sat on a wicker couch on the patio of the house the two of them had once shared. The house where only she and Honey now lived. The house that still bore his brand, still bore the marks of him. The red room, the Biedermeier furniture, the daughter sleeping soundly in the back room just beyond Suzanne's—these were a few of the indicators that he'd once resided here. Indicators that sometime ago changed from painful reminders into nice additions. She'd made it so. Putting out the fires, taming the wild to manageable, and singing the subversive to sleep. This was her busy-making job right now. Smoothing, cajoling, coaxing—keeping on the right side of the magnifying glass, where you made big things small. She knew you met a better class of people there, and it was something she'd become good at by the doing of it.

And the man sitting so serenely next to her? The one who put the "co" in co-parenting? This was a Leland who radiated confidence, who was oh so much more confident than when they'd been an item. With an easy smile and laugh—but still with that watchful way about him. Only now it came with less worry. And it came without her.

There were still remains all around them from Honey's makeup seventh birthday party. Of course, Suzanne had missed the real party on the real day—a crime punishable by something close to death by the Bad Mother Patrol in her head that kept a close watch on her every maternal deed. So now it was time for—maybe not second chances, but an encore party! The first one had been so good they were just going to have to have it again! A reunion party where everyone got together and reminisced about how great the original party had been and how its like would never be seen again. And yet even though it couldn't be duplicated—like a reunion Stones concert— how bad could anything truly be with the same magic elements?

Suzanne had bashfully asked her daughter if she might give her a better-late-than-never birthday party—not to make up for being away the first time but "to give you an extra party for being so good about Mommy being sick for the real one. So think of this as your pretend party with real presents in it!"

Honey looked up at her mother with guarded hope from the orange beanbag chair on her bedroom floor. "Can I invite real friends?"

Suzanne pretended to consider this carefully. "Well, all right, you can invite four real friends and two imaginary ones."

Now Honey sighed in exasperation. "So then you're kidding, right?"

And Suzanne fell to her knees beside her daughter, terrified lest she'd been any kind of misunderstood by this now-more-than-ever cautious little girl. It had been so painful when she realized, really realized she'd missed such a major milestone in Honey's life while she'd been incarcerated in the locked ward. Had she dealt Honey a blow from which she'd never recover? How could Honey learn to trust her again? She *shouldn't* trust her. She'd abused that trust by—oh, everything.

" I'm completely not kidding, pinky. You can invite whoever you want. Real people, real cake, real time."

So Honey had asked five of her best girlfriends. And Craig and Angelica and Doris and Hoyt (who Doris had taken a shine to because she said he reminded her of her uncle Wally, "so charming, a real Southern gentleman, like so many in our family"—but Suzanne suspected it was also because he sat up with her and listened raptly to her tales of Hollywood, fixing her with his adoring sad eyes). Lucy would come, too, with Gloria the nanny and the twins in tow. (Lucy had let Honey, their godmother, give the twins their middle names, so the babies were called Charlotte Reese—for Honey's favorite actress—and Michael Skip—for her favorite beagle.) Then Leland had gotten in the act with a guest list of his own, not quite a ratfuck but certainly extended rat foreplay, with the keepers of those magic clickers, jet mongers, fellow yachtaholics turning out to partake of his crown jewel, pièce de résistance luxury item—his coveted, beloved daughter, the birthday girl herself.

And after the list, the arrangements and the invitations and the party favors and—well, they didn't have to order a cake because Suzanne *insisted* she be allowed to make that. "But no weird stuff in it, Mommy," Honey ordered. "Just vanilla cake with vanilla icing maybe dyed blue."

Suzanne saluted her daughter. "Aye-aye, Captain January."

Honey eyed her mother suspiciously. "I *mean* it."

Honey and her friends had played and swum in the pool for hours, their grown-up handlers ringed around them sipping drinks with melted ice, watching the light in waving lines across the aqua water, until the girls were too wrinkled and sunbeaten not to admit defeat. Then they'd all shuffled back as the shadows lengthened to change into dry clothes and blow out candles and have that blue cake and melting ice cream and open gifts and let Honey thank her family and friends and whoever those other people were.

Then, after the girls had donned their pj's and turned their worshipful eyes up toward the magic glow of the TV back in Honey's room, the remaining grown-up revelers sat or stood in stunned clusters here and there all over Suzanne's spacious patio. The night was warm and a gentle balmy breeze occasionally tussled the leaves in the trees ringing her property—stern, silent oak trees, chaperones to the life that went on idly beneath them. With the moon beyond, unblinking, overlooking everything yet unobserved.

Leland wore his crisp white shirt open at the collar, well dressed in his usual effortless way from the top of his well-shaped head to the scuffed soles of his feet, feet that took him where he wanted to go, for he was a man who had come far and was going places. He again ran his hand over what remained of his thinning blond hair, which he kept shaved close to his head—"the comb-over of the new millennium," Suzanne had heard it called. Nature had taken its course by taking Leland's hair prematurely, so Leland had trumped nature and shaved the rest. He seemed even better-looking than when he'd lived with her, and Suzanne had concluded it was that extra confidence as much as anything. In the years since the two of them had separated, Leland's career had soared. He'd gone from being one of many that toiled in the lower order of the studio to being the head of it. Now people kowtowed to him and he greeted those who came to pay their eager respects with the calm patience of a good king. A popular president who knows his approval rating is higher than ever.

A casting agent had just finished paying homage like a good subject. When she'd gone, Leland turned to Suzanne, looking worn-out and world-weary.

"Jesus, just shoot me, will you?" He took a drag of his cigarette and reached for the drink resting on the couch between them. Suzanne regarded him with smiling eyes.

"But this is what you wanted. You're an important guy now," she reminded him, as if he were suffering from amnesia and she'd been sent to fill him in on himself, bring him up to speed on how fast he was going and what his chances were for winning the race he'd forgotten he was in.

Leland smiled ruefully and sipped his drink. "Hey, I'm not complaining." He sat back, smoothing his pant legs.

"Yes, you are."

He laughed easily, looking up into the night sky. "Okay, maybe I am, but don't get me wrong, I like a lot of it. But, Jesus, some of the people. . . ." He let the sentence hang in the noose of the night air, the same noose she assumed he would put around the necks of a lot of his subjects as the head of his studio.

"You mean they're not all principled, generous, good, salt-of-the-earth types?" Suzanne said with mock astonishment. "Shit, I'm gonna have to see someone about getting my money back."

Leland laughed again. "Fuck the money," he said. "I want my time." Suzanne nodded thoughtfully. She wanted to say, "I want your time, too." She wanted to offer to run him down to the Time Mart to see if they had any specials. Instead, she simply said, "Let me see what I can do."

She sipped her Diet Coke and listened to a few people laughing just beyond them. "Hey, what are you doing for Christmas?" she asked him suddenly. "I mean, about Honey? What's the plan? Do you want to take her before New Year's or—"

"I don't know who I'll be talking to by Christmas, much less going away with, which means that Jack Frost will *really* be nipping *my* nose to shit this year, if you know what I mean," he said bitterly, hunched over, elbows on knees, looking without seeing into the space before him. "And what does *that* say about me?"

Suzanne stroked her chin, as though considering in caricature. With eyes squinted, she surveyed him, apparently giving his face some real thought.

"After careful consideration," she began after a meaningful beat, "I've decided—"

"You know what *I've* decided?" Leland sat back, crossing his legs and looking at her steadily.

"What?" she raised her chin, almost defiant.

"That I'm as bad a homosexual as you are a heterosexual."

Suzanne's slow smile started at her mouth, spread to her eyes, and then went everywhere else. "That's the nicest birthday gift on behalf of Honey I've gotten all night." She glowed with pleasure.

"It's true." He looked at her sadly, his big, recently lasered eyes blinking in their unaccustomed nakedness.

"That's what makes it so nice." She leaned back, putting her head on his shoulder. Leland reached up to stroke her hair. "Let's get back together," she said, taking his hand in both of hers. Leland leaned in and gently kissed her forehead.

"Okay," he said simply. And they sat together in the aftermath of what they'd once been and now had oh so slowly turned into.

There was a way about him that she'd wandered into—wandered into one day and just never quite managed to get out of though she knew there were reasons—reasons as long as Hollywood Boulevard and back again. How could she move on from Leland when she found moving so complicated? How do you move on in the fast-moving to motionless motion-picture industry? It took all her energy just to stay where she was and see that that was good—that more was not always better so much as just more. So in much the same way that she ran in place to keep her figure, she lived and lived in the same place she'd been living and would apparently always live—one block down and two streets over from Leland—to keep her head.

So here's the thing—would they really, could they get back together? Would they reside in the same elegant home with a wild underside and the initials on towels and the horse porn magazines in the guesthouse? Would they get back together for all the world to see—attending screenings and christenings and trips to Euro-Disney?

Well, no, they would Hollywood get back together—meaning they'd *appear* to get back together but don't look too close or those appearances could get a little less personal—perhaps sometimes deceptive. Yes, that was them at the screening with Honey and her friend—and yes, Leland's arm was around Suzanne, wasn't it, and yes, she was whispering to him and he was laughing and holding her close to his side. And you did hear him tell her, "I was just telling Josh—you know he and Christine are having some trouble—and I said, 'You know, the happiest couple I really know are Suzanne and me.'" And Leland was laughing and leaning his head next to hers when she said softly, "If they want to be as happy as us, they should live like we do."

So, yes, they were back together in that they weren't so far apart.

Suzanne had learned that nothing is just one thing, and that there was a difference between a problem and an inconvenience—and given that, she'd only had one problem in her whole damn life, and that was the hell that had just happened. If she could live through that, from now on, she could live through anything—even love. But maybe instead of happily ever after—or maybe in addition to it—this time it would be everything. Everything ever after. And when they asked her if she was happy, this time she'd answer, "Among other things."

The way Suzanne saw it was that most things were ultimately manageable if you went at them the right way, even if they started out all wrong and hopeless and wrapped so tight around you that you just can't breathe. Even the things you never thought you could get over or get through, those hurts you knew would never heal, those visions that troubled your sleep. . . . All that eventually quieted and ceased to pull at you, if you wanted it to badly enough, if you were willing to outlast your difficulties. And you could rest in the easy, pleasing way someone feels about you, breathing in what's best in each other, breathing out what's not.

Leonard Cohen sang out of the speakers, and Suzanne closed her eyes and nestled closer to Leland.

Don't turn on the lights, you can read their address by the moon.
And it won't make me jealous to learn they've sweetened your night.
We weren't lovers like that and besides, it would still be all right.
We weren't lovers like that and besides, it would still be all right.

ACKNOWLEDGMENTS (PART II)

For: Bruce Wagner (Special Needs); Doc Podell and his magic beans; Beatriz Foster and her unwavering heart and eye; Dr. Arnie Klein; the good Mother D'Angelo; Ms. Ebay; Teresa Crites; Bruce Cohen; Melissa Mathison; Melissa North; "Thoroughly Modern" Mirkin; George (likeness wrangler) and Ewan (trick-talking meat 7.0); Geffen; Nina; Ruby; Matthew; Greg Stevens; Buck; Salman; Bill Lavallee; Blob; Charlie; Griffin; Marianne; Gavin; Brassel; Meg; Graham; Mr. Begley; Edgar and Rachel; Cyndi Sayre; Gloria Crayton; Mary French; Dion Jackson; Alfredo "Freddy" Reynaldi; Mr. Gurko; Mr. Kitrinos; Milton Wexler; the Yeos; the Tolkins; Sarah Paulson; Kerri Kolen; Sydny Miner; and Michael Gendler.

And for my unclear nuclear family: Uncle Bill Reynolds; Harper Simon; Joely and Chris; Trisha, Blaine, and Crystal; Stephen; Christi . . . and all of their kids.

About the Author

Carrie Fisher is the author of the bestsellers *Postcards from the Edge, Surrender the Pink,* and *Delusions of Grandma.*

She has a daughter, Billie. They want to see the aurora borealis.